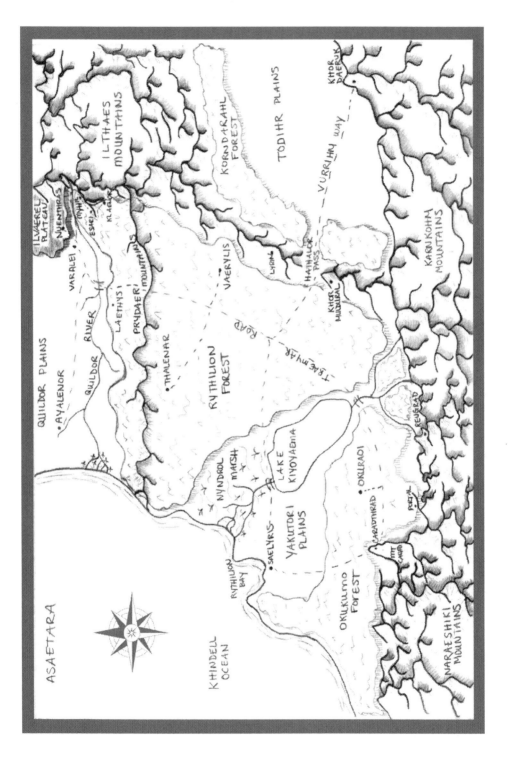

Chronicles of Asaetara

Book 1

Whispers of Time

Gwendolyn Ilimaris

Saehyvn Publishing

Library of Congress Control Number: 2019902711

ISBN: 978-0-692-10697-6

Printed in the United States of America

Saehyvn Publishing: PO Box 64 Clayton, Ohio 45315

For all my friends and family,

without whose encouragement this might still be unfinished.

Whispers of
Time

A young elven woman stood staring at herself in a large ornate mirror in the middle of a large room. Intricate bands of silver and gold formed into the shape of delicate leaves, which created the frame around the glass. She frowned the longer she took in her appearance. The deep forest green velvet gown she wore fell to the floor and was lined with silver fabric that matched the knotwork running along the hems of the sleeves and neckline. A belt, also silver, wrapped around her slender waist and clasped in the front. The loose end trailed almost to the floor. Her long silver hair, which was usually tied back, was free and flowing with curls that extended down to her waist. The smattering of black and red curls made the rest of her hair seem to shine. Her brilliant green eyes narrowed in discomfort, "Mother, must I wear this?"

A beautiful, timeless face looked up from the hem of the gown. "Yes darling, it is your coming of age ceremony today. The daughter of the king must always be prepared to set the example." She stood up and took a step back. "Let me look at you."

With an exasperated sigh, the young woman turned in place so that her mother could look at her. She scanned the room as she turned. Her mother's bedroom was quite large, and the lavish décor complimented the mirror. Long red and brown pieces of silk hung from the high vaulted ceiling and provided a privacy wrap around the bed, which was in the back corner of the room. Plush dark brown rugs covered the brilliant white stone floors.

"I believe there is still something missing," her mother said, pulling the young woman from her thoughts. She glanced over and watched as her mother walked over to her dressers. Pulling open the top middle drawer of a dark maple dresser, her mother took out a small wooden box. The elder woman smiled when she opened the box and lifted a small delicate tiara from it. It was crafted from slender bands of silver that were braided together into the shape of crescent-shaped leaves.

"Rilaeya[1], you look beautiful," her mother said after she pinned the tiara into her daughter's hair.

Rilaeya grimaced at her mother's enthusiasm. She knew her mother would not be so pleased if she knew about the dagger strapped to her thigh. "Mother, you know I dislike it when you call me by my full name. Can you not just call me Rin like everyone else?"

"No," her mother replied. "That is not the name that I chose for you. Now come, I have something for you to see before your ceremony." She took hold of her daughter's hand and led her across the room to a thick black wooden door, which she pulled open to reveal a hallway. The two walked together across the white stone floors of the passageway. Rin slowed when they passed the floor to ceiling windows that lined this section of the hall. She gazed with longing at the views of the forest and majestic mountains in the distance. Every part of her wished to be outside and not stuck in the palace.

With a loud sigh, Rin quickened her pace to keep up with her mother. They made their way down multiple hallways before Rin's mother stopped in front of a wrought iron door. Rin glanced around with curiosity. She had never been in this section of the palace and the difference between the rest of the light and airy palace and this place was profound. The stone floors here were made of coal black stones, and there were no windows found along the dark, gray stone walls. A handful of torches lining the walls provided dim light.

Rin's mother took the nearest torch and placed it in the holder closest to the door before she pulled a chain out of her shirt. It had a small golden key hanging from it, which she used to unlock the door, but she did not open it. She turned to face her daughter.

"You should be aware of the part of the coming of age that proceeds the ceremony; however, since I know you do not often pay close attention to your studies, I shall remind you." She paused with a knowing look and Rin just shrugged. "Beyond this door lies the Well of Sages, it is an ancient well that was built prior to our reckoning. When the palace was built, they discovered it." She paused again and looked toward the door. "Every member of the royal family upon coming of age is permitted to look into the well. It shall show you one event that may be past, present, or future. The well

---

[1] Pronunciation Guide - Appendix

determines what is most important for you to see. This could affect the course of your li--."

"What did father see?" Rin asked.

Her mother smiled and placed a hand on her daughter's cheek. "He was shown your birth."

Rin's eyes widened in surprise before she appeared confused. "Why would it show him that? How is that important enough for the well to--?"

"Now is not the time for these questions," her mother said, her voice firm. "There is not long before your ceremony, and you must decide if you wish to look. Only if you go willingly will the well show you anything."

Rin stared at the door beside her and shivered when a sudden sense of dread washed over her. She swallowed hard before she nodded.

"Very well," her mother said. "I shall wait for you here. I am not permitted to enter." She put her hand on Rin's shoulder. "Keep an open mind, daughter, and learn from what the well shows you." She took a step back and pulled the iron door open, and Rin took a hesitant step through the doorway into an ancient courtyard. Rin looked around in wonder at a place that appeared to be frozen in time. Thick, green vines covered in beautiful white and yellow bell-shaped flowers blanketed the high dark, gray stone walls. Graceful, cascading willow trees filled the majority of the courtyard and prevented her from seeing more than a few feet ahead. A small black stone path led into the grove of trees before it disappeared around a bend. Everything appeared well kept as if it had recently been pruned, but Rin knew that could not be true. The last elf in this courtyard would have been her brother at his coming of age ceremony eight hundred years ago.

A smile crossed Rin's face as she walked up to the nearest tree. Willow trees were her favorite, and she held a special connection with them. She held her hand out to the tree, and it reached out a thin, ropelike branch to touch her.

'What is this place?' She asked with her thoughts.

The tree's reply came in a disconnected manner, 'Sacred... ancient... sad... dangerous.'

'Why is it dangerous?' Rin's head tilted as confusion clouded her face.

The tree and several others around it shook their long branches as if they were agitated. 'Ahead... well... shows... hurtful.' The tree tapped her hand with its leaves. 'Caution... caution.'

Rin's brow furrowed when the tree did not say anything else and she lowered her hand. She glanced back at the door leading out of the courtyard. Another feeling of dread coursed through her, and she took an involuntary step toward the exit. She stopped and shook her head; it felt like something was beckoning her to continue. Taking a deep breath, she took slow, hesitant steps as she followed the stone path deeper into the grove. After walking for several minutes, an opening in the trees came into view. She stepped into the small clearing and found a small well constructed from grey and red stones. It was quite simple and only stood a couple of feet high. When she drew closer to it, she noticed the surface of the water appeared flat like a black sheet of glass. She knelt next to the well and peered into it.

After waiting a few moments, she frowned when nothing happened. Tilting her head to the side, she hesitated before she reached out and touched the stones with her fingertips.

"Child of royal lineage," a voice boomed from the depths of the well. Shocked, Rin tried to jerk her hand away but found it was stuck to the rocks. "You have come to the Well of Sages. The wisdom of the sages must be heeded. We shall show you one event that affects your future destiny. However, be warned that you shall not be able to change the event, nor will you be able to interact with what is shown. Do you wish to proceed?"

"Yes," Rin whispered in a shaky voice. As soon as the word was out of her mouth, the scenery around her grew hazy and began to change. A few seconds later, she was no longer in the courtyard. She struggled to fight off the wave of dizziness caused by the sudden change when she noticed, much to her relief, she was no longer stuck to the well.

She stood and took in her surroundings. A look of awe crossed her face when she found that she was in an ancient forest. The trees around her had dark brown bark with leaves of red and gold. They towered above her and appeared strong and proud. These were makae trees, an ancient breed rarely seen in her time. Her brows furrowed when she realized this must be a long time ago. She reached out to touch one of the trees, but her hand went right through it. Staring at her hand, she breathed a disappointed sigh before she turned away from the tree.

Looking to the left and right, Rin wondered where she needed to go. She was about to pick a direction and start walking when a sudden movement from above pulled her from her thoughts. An enormous silver dragon passed overhead, and without thinking, she started to follow it. She paused and took off her heels when she had to jog to keep up with it. The dragon flew over a clearing in the trees before circling back and dropping to the ground.

Rin peered around the trunk of a large tree so that she could see the dragon. He was such a deep color of silver that he appeared to have a bluish sheen in the sun. Looking at the way he stood, Rin could tell that the dragon was a member of the royal family or nobility at the least. She edged closer but remained hidden in the shadows of the trees as the event started to unfold.

The dragon scanned the clearing as if he was checking to see if he was followed. His gaze landed on the spot where Rin was hiding and lingered there. He made a soft growling sound that almost sounded like a sigh and seemed to give Rin a sad smile before he looked away. Rin could not help the confusion that crept across her face. The well said that she could not interact with anything, but it seemed like the dragon could see her. She shook her head and turned her attention back to the dragon.

He stood in the center of the clearing, and it appeared as if he believed he had not been followed. Closing his eyes, his body began to glow, and a few seconds later he polymorphed to his elven form. He opened his eyes and pushed back the edges of his cloak while he kept a wary eye on the clearing. Rin tilted her head as she observed him. She had the strangest feeling that she should know him. He was tall and lean and wore no armor, just the brown traveling cloak over his clothes. The clothing was crafted from fine cloth of black and gold, and there were silver runes along the hems. His long silver hair was tied back with a bright blue ribbon that matched the streaks of color mixed into the silver. He slid his sword belt to move his katana more to the side before he looked up at the sky with brilliant green eyes.

"You may land," he called.

Two small silver dragons dropped toward the ground from behind a large cloud where they were hiding. Once their claws touched the ground, they both changed into elven form. They were both small boys about the size of a ten and twelve-year-old human. Both boys had silver hair like the older dragon, but the older of the two had red streaks while his brother had blue.

"Can we go to the river? Please?" The older of the two asked while both boys were trembling with excitement.

"Yes, you may go ahead," the older dragon laughed. "I shall be along shortly. Be certain to keep an eye on your brother."

The older boy rolled his eyes, "Yes, father I know; I always do."

Smiling, the old dragon waved the two boys off and watched them run into the forest. Once they were gone, the smile slipped from his face, and he turned his attention back to the clearing. After standing in silence for several minutes, he shrugged with impatience.

"You should come out if you wish to speak, Kilvari," he called, his voice deep and clear.

On the far side of the clearing, a tall slender figure walked out from the shadow of the trees. The hood of his cloak was pulled up to conceal his identity. He moved closer to the dragon but did not say anything.

"Do we hide from each other now, old friend?" The dragon's voice grew wary as his friend approached.

"Old friend?" Kilvari sneered as he pulled back the hood of his cloak. "I know about you and Luaera." His golden hair gleamed in the sun while his bright blue eyes blazed with fury.

Rin gasped, and her hands flew to her mouth when she realized that she was looking at her father. Her mind started racing while she tried to piece together what was happening. Why did he mention her mother?

"What do you mean?" The dragon asked as he held up both hands in front of him in a defensive pose.

Kilvari was quivering with anger. "My ayen just gave birth to a child that is not of my blood. She is yours." He yelled at the dragon who was supposed to be his closest friend. The dragon appeared dumbfounded for a moment before a look of profound dread crossed his features.

"We have been used," he said, his voice filled with apprehension. "Allow me to explain, or we shall begin something that cannot be undone." He took a hesitant step toward Kilvari.

"I did not come here to talk," Kilvari hissed as he jerked out a dagger that was concealed in the sleeve of his cloak. With one quick motion, he stabbed the knife into the dragon's heart before he could think to reach for his katana. The dragon gasped and stared at the dagger in shock. "This secret will die today. No one shall ever know she is yours, Kanamae."

Kanamae sank to the ground when Kilvari jerked the dagger out of his chest. His face was still frozen in shock. He never imagined that his best friend would betray him.

"H..er n..name?" He somehow managed to stammer between gasps for breath. The dagger had injured his lung and heart and he knew he was not going to survive. His breathing was too labored for him to get enough breath to cast a healing spell.

Hatred burned on the elf's face as he glared at him. "*My* ayen named her Rilaeya."

Kanamae's eyes started to glaze over after he heard the name of his daughter. He struggled to see the spot where Rin was hidden in the trees. "Ri... laeya," he whispered as he lost consciousness.

Kilvari watched with no remorse while the dragon at his feet bled out and passed. He wiped the dagger off on the grass before he concealed it back inside his cloak.

"No, no, no," Rin muttered over and over. She started shaking her head as her mind became lost in turmoil. All she wanted was to look away, but she remained glued to the scene still unfolding.

Having heard a movement in the trees, Kilvari disappeared back into the shadows before the two young boys came running back into the clearing. They both stopped for a split second before they sprinted to the body on the ground.

"Father!" The older of the two cried as he dropped to his knees beside the body.

Rin started to shake when all the pieces fell into place. The children were her best friends, Ronin and Riku. They were the sons of the silver dragon king. She now understood why the murder of their father was never solved. Her father had killed him and made certain to hide it.

Her heart began to ache as she watched Ronin and Riku cry next to their father. Riku sobbed in desperation as he frantically tried to wake him. Ronin grabbed hold of his little brother around the waist and pulled him away from their father's body. He forced him to look away. Riku clung to his brother as he held him and continued to sob.

Rin wrapped both arms around herself and fought to keep from trying to reach out to the boys. The pain they were in was almost too much for her to witness. She could not understand how her father could do what she saw. The elf who raised her would not do something like this. She struggled to reconcile what she knew with what she just learned. Her father was Lord Kanamae, and the elf who raised her murdered him.

Unable to continue watching Ronin and Riku, Rin grabbed the side of her head and clamped her eyes closed. "No more," she cried. Everything started to spin. When it stopped, and she opened her eyes, she found herself lying on the ground next to the well. She scrambled to her feet and dashed through the grove of trees. Every part of her wanted out of this courtyard. Tears streamed down her face as she pushed branches of the willow trees away when they sought to comfort her. When she reached the door, she jerked it open causing her mother to jump in surprise.

Her mother's eyes widened with worry when she saw her daughter's appearance. She hurried over to her and grabbed her by the shoulder. "Rilaeya, what in the worl--?"

"Luaera, impatient as always, I asked you to wait for me, my dear. I wished to be here when Rilaeya entered the well," a well-dressed elven man said with a strained smile as he stopped beside Rin's mother.

"Fath…" Rin could not bring herself to say the word father as she backed away from him and moved to stand beside Ronin. He and Riku had walked up with Kilvari, their smiles slipped when they noticed how shaken Rin appeared.

"Ril…" Her father trailed off when he watched her flinch at the sound of his voice. Ronin also noticed, and he placed a gentle hand on her shoulder. She peeked up at him and a shiver ran down her back.

"Ronin," she whispered.

"Do you plan to ignore your father?" Kilvari asked before she could say anything else. His voice was filled with impatience.

Rin's head snapped up and even though she was trembling she forced herself to make eye contact. "You are not my father." Her voice started to shake when she said the word father.

"What did you just say?" Concern flashed across Kilvari's face as he took a step in her direction.

"You are not my father," Rin said, her voice getting louder. "You murdered him." She struggled to remain in control of all the emotions

7

threatening to overwhelm her.

Kilvari made a quick lunge at her and tried to grab her by the arm, but Ronin shifted forward enough that he stood between the two. His face was confused, but he could tell something was very wrong. Kilvari glared at him before he looked back at Rin, "You must be unwell. Come with me; I shall return you to your rooms." He again tried to grab his daughter, so he could take her down the hallway away from everyone, but Ronin stayed in his path.

"I am not unwell," Rin cried, her voice taking on a hysterical edge. "The well showed me everything. You murdered him. You killed Lord Kanamae." She once again grabbed the sides of her head as she struggled to accept the truth. A grimace crossed her face when she got a sharp pain in her head, and a strange power started to build inside of her.

Kilvari's face went ashen as he listened to her. "Rin, you must calm down. You cannot…" He tried to reach for her again.

"No! Do not touch me!" She hastened to back away from him again. Her eyes were wild with panic as she stared at everyone gathered around her before she spun and bolted down the hallway.

"Rin no!" Kilvari yelled. He moved to follow her when Luaera grabbed his arm.

"Kilvari, what does she mean? What did the well show her?" she asked.

He looked down at her and his mouth opened but it took him a moment before he could formulate a reply. "I am uncertain what she could mean. She must be unwell as I said before, I shall go and find her." He slipped his arm out of her grasp, but it was apparent that she did not believe him.

"Is it true?" Ronin's angry voice caused Kilvari to look over at him. "Did you murder my father?" His hand strayed to the katana strapped to his waist.

Kilvari shook his head, "As I said, Rin must be unwell. I shall be happy to discuss things with you later, but right now, I must find her. If we do not stop her powers from awakening not only our world will be at risk."

Ronin's brilliant green eyes burned with anger as he stared back at Kilvari. He could tell that the elf was not being truthful with him, but after a few tense moments, he nodded. Without waiting on Kilvari to say anything further, he spun and grabbed Riku's arm. They headed down the hallway in the direction Rin disappeared.

"We must find her first," Ronin whispered to his brother. "I do not trust him." His brother glanced at him and nodded.

***

Rin raced through the palace frantically looking for an exit. Her home for the last four hundred years now seemed foreign and dangerous. In her frantic state, her thoughts were so scattered that she took a wrong turn and ended up in a dead-end passage. Spinning in place several times, trying to decide where to go, she turned and ran back the way she came.

Without taking any turns, she ended up running into the palace's enormous kitchen. Skidding to a halt, she narrowly managed to keep from crashing into one of the kitchen maids. She turned to the right and pulled up the long skirt enough that she could leap over the large open cooking fire. It was in a huge stone hearth in the middle of the room. Once she was over the fire, she continued to sprint toward the door at the far side.

When she reached the door, a tall lean young man with silver hair appeared beside her. He shrugged out of his embroidered light tan coat and dropped it on one of the counters. The katana strapped at his waist was now visible and he could move freely. His sharp grey eyes were filled with concern when Rin ran past him and jerked the door to the outside open.

"Rin," he called as he ran out the door after her. It only took him a few strides to catch up with her since he was much taller than her. "Rin, what is wrong?" He kept pace at her side and waited for her to speak to him.

She glanced at him a couple times. "Did you know about my father?"

"Know what?"

"That… that Kilvari is not my father? He murdered him." Her voice cracked.

With a sudden quick movement, he grabbed both of her shoulders and brought them to a quick stop. "Tell me what happened."

Rin started shaking her head. "I cannot explain it all now. I must get out of here."

He looked around them, his manner calm and collected. "I am here." His voice was soft when he could sense her panic and fear. Rin took a deep breath when she looked up at him. A sense of calm washed over her as the calmness he exuded started to ease her anxieties. "I shall transform, and we shall go."

"Kaedin," she started but shouts from the palace caught her attention. Glancing back, she saw Kilvari and Ronin racing across the clearing toward them. She stepped away from Kaedin and raised her hand.

"Ksāetras," she said. As soon as the word was out of her mouth, the advancing men ran into an invisible wall.

"Rin, you cannot run," Kilvari yelled as he raised his hands to dispel the wall in his way.

Knowing she was at a disadvantage, she looked up at Kaedin. He moved closer to her and put his hands on her shoulders again. "Go, I shall keep them from following and catch up to you." She hesitated, and he gave her a soft push. "Go."

She started to step away before she half jumped into his arms. He wrapped both arms around her and held onto her for a few brief moments.

9

"Hurry."

"Be careful," she whispered. Once he nodded, she closed her eyes. "Ēlipor ntāera." A split second later, she disappeared.

Rin looked around the clearing she just teleported to as she struggled to get her bearings. She never ported without a destination in mind and had no idea where she ended up. With a shake of her head, she chastised herself for how dangerous and careless that was when she realized she could have appeared in a different realm or ceased to exist.

She sighed before she started to walk around the outside of the clearing. It did not take her long to figure out that she was somewhere in the Okukumo Forest. Adjusting her course, she headed toward the mountains when bright colors caught her attention. She looked over and saw a small well-kept flower garden. Her curiosity piqued, she moved closer and a faint smile crossed her face. Reds, yellows, oranges, blues, purples, almost any color imaginable were present in one species of flower or plant. She continued walking deeper into the garden as she wondered who the garden was for; it had to be someone important to be so well-tended. Her face fell when she came upon a huge headstone in the center of the garden. She slowed and approached with cautious steps. The stone was carved from a large slab of obsidian into the shape of an elaborate obelisk that stood a little more than double her height. Delicate silver lettering carved into the obelisk stood out in stark contrast to the blackness of the stone.

Rin drifted closer to the stone so that she could read what was carved into the surface. It only took her a few minutes to realize it was a poem, but it appeared like it was a letter from the person laid to rest.

Storm clouds gather
blotting out the sun.
Fear rises.

I have fallen.
Never fear. I am here.

Fight the falling tears
do not mourn for me.
You are safe.

I have fallen.
Never fear. I am here.

Blessed child of mine.

10

Grow proud and strong.
Do not give into revenge.

I have fallen.
Never fear. I am here.

Rin felt a strange tightening in her chest after she read the final lines of the poem. A sense of overwhelming fear gripped her heart when she shifted around the stone. Her eyes fell to the various runes of protection that were carved along the bottom. She paused just before she reached the front, and she swallowed hard before she moved enough to see who was buried here.

Kanamae Silvaerin
14.27.959047 – 13.26.964780

Beloved king, father, friend, protector.
Our thoughts are with you always.
Rest well my friend.
-Kilvari Rilavaenu-

The tightening in her chest grew worse when she saw the name on the stone. Unbidden tears filled her eyes as she stared at the beautiful carving of a silver dragon below the writing. It depicted a massive elder dragon, sitting in a dignified manner on the clouds, looking down over the world below him. She tried to stifle a gasping sob when she reached out with a trembling hand and touched the name on the stone.

"Father," she whispered before she sank to the ground in front of the stone. Tears streamed down her face. Why had the spell brought her here? Could everything she saw really be true? What should she do now? These thoughts whirled through her mind while she struggled to make sense of everything.

Rin did not know how much time passed when a loud crack of thunder brought her attention back to her surroundings. She glanced up just in time to see the skies open with a torrential downpour. Her head dropped, and her hand slipped off the wet stone.

"Rabāenhi ravi," she whispered, and a single sunflower appeared in her hand. She laid it at the base of the stone before she stood up. After taking one last look at the name on the grave, she turned and started walking toward the mountains. She hoped that she would be able to find a place to take shelter from the rains. Once she reached the base of the cliffs, it did not take her long to find the entrance to a small cave. She quickened her pace and hurried just inside the entrance. After she was out of the rain, she sat down and watched while the storm passed overhead.

"What do I do?" She muttered and dropped her head onto her knees. Only a couple minutes passed before she raised her head with a deep frown. She was shivering when she looked down at her rain-soaked, muddy dress. Her frown deepened as she wished for her normal rider gear. At least then she would have the flint she needed to start a fire to warm up. Shaking her head, she stood up and looked around. She decided to see if there might be supplies inside the cave she could use. Looking around, her head tilted when she caught sight of strange runes running along the entrance of the cave. She could tell that they were some sort of spell runes but could not make out what they said. Her brows furrowed as she turned and looked closer at the rest of the cave walls. Another carving on the right side of the entrance drew her attention. She walked over to it and studied the lettering.[2]

The language it was written in was unfamiliar to her, and she grew concerned. She studied many forms of magic as well as multiple languages, so it was rare she came across something she did not recognize.

She turned to walk away when she paused and looked back at the letters. A sudden feeling that she should know them washed over her. After staring at them for several long minutes she sighed and forced herself to turn her attention back to trying to find a way to start a fire. Peering deeper into the cave, she moved forward. Once she made it a few steps, she paused and looked up at the ceiling. Her eyes widened in surprise when she saw a strange blue rock that glowed in the dark. She raised an eyebrow as she wondered what kind of stones those were to provide light. Pressing her lips together in irritation, she again turned her attention back to where she was going. It bothered her not to know something.

Following the stones, she walked along the only path in the cave until it ended abruptly in a small room. She hurried over to the stone tables that were carved into the walls. Her frustration only grew when she found all of the tables were empty. There was nothing in the room other than a circle carved into the cave floor. It was lined with the same type of runes she saw around the entrance. She studied them for a while before a sudden shiver caused her to look up. A strange energy was radiating from a large archway etched into the wall. Rin stood and moved a little closer. Beside the archway, there were six stones embedded into the wall: three on each side of the arch, and all six were a different color from the rest.

Feeling an unexplainable pull, she took an involuntary step toward the arch before a sudden noise in the cave broke through the feeling. Her hand reached for where her daggers should have been, and she cursed under her breath. She patted her clothing, and her eyes widened when she remembered

---

[2] Fig. 1 - Appendix

the small dagger concealed under her skirt. Once she removed it from its scabbard, she crept toward the entrance of the small room. She crouched by the wall and waited.

A few minutes passed before a tall elven man walked into the room while shaking water off his traveling cloak. Rin waited until he passed her unnoticed before she sprang at him. She kicked him hard in the back of the leg, dropping him to his knees, while she twisted his arm behind his back.

"Who are you?" She demanded.

The man did not move, but he chuckled. "Lady Rin?"

"Londar?" She asked, her voice surprised as she released him and stepped back. "What are you doing here?" Her eyes were filled with suspicion as she regarded him.

He did not appear to be in a hurry as he got back to his feet and stepped away from her. Rubbing his arm, he turned to face her. "I could ask you the same question, my lady. Are you not supposed to be attending an important ceremony?" His voice was filled with innocence as he avoided the question.

Rin's eyes narrowed when she heard his tone, and her distrust grew more plain on her face. "Plans change."

He shrugged as if he was not interested before he moved closer to her. Using the tips of his fingers, he lifted her chin, so she was looking up at him. His brown eyes studied her face. "Will you not reconsider my marriage proposal? Your father supports our joining."

"I shall not," Rin snapped as she smacked his hand away. "You care nothing for anyone other than yourself. The people deserve better than that."

"And the dragon would be better?" His face filled with disgust at the mention of Kaedin.

"He is more caring and in possession of many favorable qualities that you do not."

Londar's eyes flashed with anger before he smirked, "Yes, yes I know; it really is most unfortunate that you will not reconsider my offer." He paused and pushed his dark brown hair out of his face. "I must now resort to less pleasant methods to achieve my goals." His voice grew icy before he gave her a sudden hard push.

Unable to keep her balance, Rin stumbled and fell into the rune circle on the floor. She leapt back to her feet and tried to move forward, but when she came to the edge of the circle, it was like she ran into a wall. Taking an unsteady step back, she raised a hand and let it rest on the magical wall.

"What is the meaning of this? Release me at once." She started to probe the wall with her magic while she watched Londar stalk around the circle. He inspected each rune to be certain that it was activated. Once he was satisfied they all glowed, he looked up at her.

"I am most pleased that it is holding," he said. "It took months to get that strong enough to hold you."

Rin glared at him before she closed her eyes in concentration. "Entījikatrāes." Her hands began to glow with a faint yellow light. She pushed more magic into the spell and waited until the light was so bright it was almost blinding before she touched the wall. Instant concern flashed across Londar's face when he saw the runes glow diminish, but a moment later, they regained their glow. Rin glared up at him as she breathed heavily from the exertion of the massive spell. She rested her hands on the wall before resignation crossed her features. She was trapped.

"Quite clever to use an anti-magic spell, unfortunately, it is not quite strong enough."

"You did not do this on your own. I know that you are not that strong."

Londar smirked at her again as he started to flip through a small book in his hand. "You are correct; however, that is not something that you need to know."

Rin glanced at the book before it caught her full attention. It appeared to be ancient black leather with a small silver willow tree on the cover. Inside, she saw the book was written in the same strange lettering she found at the cave entrance.

"You do not recognize this, do you?" He asked when he noticed her gaze. When she did not reply he chuckled. "You really should." Her eyes filled with suspicion, causing him to laugh. "I am not lying this time."

"What are you planning to do?" She asked ignoring his last comment. "You cannot keep me here. Kaedin will find me."

"I am counting on it."

The cold smile on his face caused Rin to shiver, and she turned her attention to Kaedin. She could sense that he was on his way to the cave. Glancing back at Londar, another deep shiver ran down her spine, and she tried to will him not to come to her.

"Why? Why do you want him to come here?"

Londar tilted his head; the cold smile was still fixed on his face. "I have been ordered to awaken your powers and fulfill the beginning of the prophecy."

"What are you talking about? What prophecy?"

"So clueless," he scoffed. "To think one as useless as you holds the key." He shook his head before he looked down at the book. "It is time to begin. I hope you are prepared to lose what you care for most."

Rin felt all the warmth drain from her body when she realized he meant Kaedin. Her eyes filled with panic, and she tried probing the wall of her prison again. She had to get free.

14

Londar did not even glance at her before he began to read an incantation from the book. The runes around the archway began to shimmer in response to the words. Rin felt the same power she had felt in the palace return. It continued to grow as Londar continued to recite the incantation.

"Stop," Rin gasped. She sank to her knees inside the circle. Her insides felt like they were on fire, and her mind was bombarded by uncontrollable emotions.

Londar chuckled under his breath as he watched her pain. He did not pause the incantation when he slipped the book back in his pocket. Unsheathing his katana, he moved to stand beside the entrance to the room. He only waited a few moments before Kaedin ran into the room.

"Rin," he exclaimed as he hurried toward her. He was so focused on her that he did not notice Londar by the entrance. Reaching for her, worry flashed across his face when his hand smacked into the invisible wall.

"Look out," she managed to gasp when she tried to warn him, but it was too late. As he turned, Londar stabbed him in the chest before he drug the blade across him. Kaedin crumpled to the floor with a small gasp of shock.

"Kaedin! Londar, stop! I must help him! Kaedin!" Rin cried as she started beating her hands on the invisible wall. "Kaedin!" Her frantic cries caused Londar to laugh as he just continued to recite the incantation. At this cold, uncaring reaction something inside Rin snapped. The power inside her reached a new high, fueled by the strong emotions threatening to consume her. She hit the wall as hard as she could with a scream of frustration, and power exploded out of her. The wave of magic was so strong that the entire mountain and earth around her began to shake. Rin lost all sense of what was going on around her as the magic took over and sent wave after wave into the archway. With each new wave, another stone would light until all but the last one glowed.

"Open the gate," Londar said with a crazed laugh. "You have no idea what you have started."

Another strong, massive burst of magic emanated from Rin, and the whole room began to shimmer and twist around on itself as the sheer strength of the magic fractured the wall between worlds. One final explosion of magic hit the archway and flowed into it. An alternating red and yellow spinning vortex formed underneath, and Rin was gone.

The first weak rays of the rising sun shone down on an old forest deep in the mountains. A thick mist weaved through the tall black pine trees that clung to the steep slope. Dancing among the trees was a young Japanese woman dressed in light blue robes. The melody she played on the light golden violin while she danced was lively and fun.

"Damhsa liomsa. Damhsa liomsa. Taidpeáin dom na bealaí ársa agus múineasdh dom labhairt leat. Damhsa liomsa. Damhsa liomsa," she sang in a beautiful soprano voice. Her eyes were closed as she poured herself into the melody. All around her the trees seemed to sway in time to the song as she passed close to them. It was as if she weaved a magic spell with the music she created.

As she continued deeper into the forest, she came upon a small waterfall that spilled over the top of a jagged ledge on the mountainside. The water plunged into a crystal-clear blue lake that was completely still except for the area directly under the falls. In the early morning light, the towering trees surrounding the lake cast long shadows across the surface of the water.

On the far side of the lake, the young woman stopped beside a massive lone willow tree that grew on the edge of the lake. She opened her bright blue eyes and peered up at the tree. Her face was filled with certainty. She just knew she would make contact this time.

"Damhsa liomsa, dance with me. Show me the ancient ways and teach me to speak with you," she sang as she switched from Irish back to Japanese.

"Dance with me." She started to move again and danced through the cascade of willow branches. The old tree's branches swayed in time to the music she created. When the tree appeared to be trying to reach one of its rope-like branches toward her, she stopped dancing but continued playing the melody. She forced her excitement down when her fingers started to fumble the melody.

The branch drifted closer to her as though it was moving a heavy weight when a sudden ringing from her pocket broke the spell. With a discouraged sigh, when the branch fell back into its normal place, she lowered the violin and pulled a cell phone from her pocket.

"Hello?" She asked in a soft, quiet voice after pressing a button.

"Sara!"

Sara jerked the phone away from her ear when a loud voice shouted her name. "Whoa, Paige, that was really loud."

The voice on the other end of the line laughed, "Come on Sara! Are you ready to go yet? We will be late for our graduation if you don't hurry!"

Sara pulled the sleeve of her robe back and looked at her watch. "Oh, my goodness. I didn't realize it was this late. I'm on my way back now." She snatched a small violin case off the ground and rushed up the well-kept stone trail that led away from the lake.

"Where are you?" The voice on the phone paused before it continued, "Please tell me you weren't trying to talk to the trees again?"

"Uh... well," Sara replied as her face started to redden. There was a loud sigh on the other end of the line.

"You really have to stop doing stuff like that. People already think you are weird enough as it is. I mean, it doesn't bother me, but imagine what people would say if they found out."

Sara grimaced at what her best friend had just said. She did not even want to think about what would be said if anyone found out. She had always been different from all the kids who grew up around her. Being raised at a temple high in the mountains with a strict emphasis on the traditional ways had set her apart. Plus, her dad being an American of Irish descent, which was where she got her crimson hair and blue eyes, and a devout Catholic had caused countless awkward situations. She had been without a real friend until Paige transferred to her school from America when she was in middle school. Since Sara's father was also American, this gave the girls something in common, and they had been inseparable ever since.

"I know, but I was so close this time. The trees were responding to my music. I think just a little longer, and I'll get it."

There was a lengthy pause on the line and then a sigh. "You aren't going to give up, are you?"

Sara bit her lip before she answered, "I can't. I feel like I'm supposed to make contact and I just can't explain why. It's only a feeling." She could practically hear her friend's eyes roll through the phone.

"You've only told me like a hundred times," Paige joked. "Anyway, hurry or we will be late!"

"I know," Sara said as she hung up the phone and shoved it back into her pocket.

When another narrow stone path came into view through the trees, she turned to the right and followed the new path up the mountain. When she approached the top, a large wooden Torii gate appeared. The ornate structure was carved from black pine and had several Japanese characters carved onto a plaque attached to the poles.

She rushed under the gate, careful to remain to one side and not pass through the center, before she headed up the steps to the front of a house. Once inside she hurried to pull off her robe and hang it on a hook on the wall. She was wearing a high school uniform underneath. In a rush, Sara looked over her uniform; her crisp white shirt was tucked into her dark blue plaid skirt that stopped just at her knees. The red and blue striped tie was just peeking out above the top of the dark navy jacket that was held closed with two silver buttons.

"I'm leaving," she yelled as she tugged up one of her stockings that had slid down before she ran back out the front door and dashed down the long gravel drive toward the base of the mountain. When she finally made the half-mile trek and reached the small parking lot tucked among the trees, a light tan, four-door wrangler style jeep came into view. It was immaculate, but its overall appearance was rugged since it was decked out for any off-road terrain.

A girl with short dark brown hair in the same school uniform was pacing nervously back and forth next to the jeep. When she glanced up and saw Sara running up to her, her blue-grey eyes filled with relief.

"It's about time," she called. Sara, who had now joined her, was leaning on her knees trying to catch her breath.

"I'm sorry," she gasped between pants.

"Are we ready, ladies?" A handsome young army officer asked as he held open the passenger door of the jeep for them. His almost black, dark brown hair was cut short on the sides but had been left longer on top. It was a spiked, styled mess, which was a stark contrast to the well-kept fatigues that he wore since he had just come off duty a little while ago.

Paige grabbed Sara's arm and dragged her over to the door where she scrambled into the back of the jeep.

"Hi Sara," the young man said with a friendly smile.

"Hi Jake," Sara muttered in a soft voice. She flushed red as she climbed in the back next to Paige and did her best not to look back at Jake.

Once she was settled, he closed the door and climbed into the driver's seat. He started the jeep and drove down the steep mountain road.

The trip into the city flew by as Paige talked excitedly about the move they were all about to make after finally becoming high school graduates.

"Aren't your parents coming to graduation today?" Paige asked, changing the conversation topic again.

"No, they can't make it. They're too busy getting ready for the festival tonight," Sara replied with a frown. "But it's okay, though. They have a lot of responsibilities with the shrine."

"Well, me and my brother are here for ya, so you aren't alone," Paige said with a grin. "Oh! I almost forgot. We're heading back to the base to change after graduation. Will you be able to get back home okay if your folks aren't coming?"

"Yeah, I'll be fine. I can just take the bus."

Paige frowned and looked at Jake who was watching them in the rear-view mirror.

"I can take you back before we go to the base," Jake offered.

Sara shook her head. "That's okay. You guys are heading up there later to pick me up anyway. It would be silly to spend all that time driving. The bus is okay."

Neither Jake nor Paige seemed pleased by Sara having to take the bus back home, but they let it drop.

"Oh! Oh! Oh! We're here!" Paige interrupted with an excited squeal. She was bouncing up and down in her seat with excitement when Jake pulled up in front of the high school and stopped the jeep.

"The two of you are late, so go, and I'll be there in a minute," he said as he glanced back at them over his shoulder. Both girls hopped out of the jeep and ran toward the school. Once they entered, the girls split up and hurried to find their homeroom classes. They slipped into the lines with the other students standing in the hallway.

Moments after they arrived, the teachers ushered the students into the auditorium. The boys and girls were separated and seated in their own rows. Once all the students were settled, the principal stood up and gave the opening address for the ceremony. When he finished, all the students stood and sang the national anthem. Next came the many speeches from influential members of the community such as the mayor, PTA reps, and several current students. Sara tried her best to focus on the speeches, but in a short time, she found her mind wandering to the festival later. She was worried about her dance as usual.

"Paige Riverwood." Hearing her friend's name called drew her attention back to the graduation. They had moved on to handing out the diplomas.

Sara waited with her class until her name was called, and when it was, she could not keep from fidgeting with her sleeve as she proceeded to the stage. Her anxiety at being the center of attention grew more pronounced when she accepted her diploma with a trembling hand. Once she had hold of it, she fought to keep from running off the stage and back to her seat. She exhaled in relief when she was once again safe in her chair. Her mind started to wander again when the ceremony droned on and on. It seemed like an eternity before the closing address began. Sara was relieved that it was almost over. These formal functions had never been enjoyable for her.

What felt like hours later, the closing address was finished, and all the students were released from the auditorium. Most of the students gathered around the front of the school taking pictures with each other and saying their goodbyes before they started going separate ways.

Sara weaved her way through the crowd looking for Paige. She found her standing near the front gates.

"We did it," Paige squealed when she caught sight of her. Sara smiled and gave her a hug.

"Finally," she said with a chuckle. "I never thought the mayor was going to quit talking."

"I know, right!" Paige's loud laugh drowned out several of the people trying to talk near them. Sara glanced at their unhappy faces before she just shook her head. Paige was completely oblivious.

"I have to get back to the shrine and help with the preparations. See you later, okay?" Sara said when she looked back at her friend.

"I'll see you in a few hours," Paige said with a sigh. Her excited smile slipped a little, but she waved to Sara as she started down the street.

Sara quickened her pace and managed to make it to the stop just in time to catch the current bus. Happy that she did not have to wait for the next one, she climbed aboard and picked a seat by the window.

The trip out to the mountains where she lived took an hour, but she did not mind. It gave her time to enjoy the sights around her since this would be the last time she took this trip home for a while. She was leaving Japan in the morning to go to college in the states with Paige. Jake was being reassigned to a base in Colorado, and Paige would be moving there with him. They offered to take Sara with them, and she jumped at the chance to get away from the shrine.

With a small sigh, she felt sadness course through her at the thought of leaving her home, but she only allowed it to bother her for a moment. This was her choice after all. She turned her attention back to the views out the window, and before she knew it, they arrived at the stop closest to her home. She exited the bus and began an unhurried walk up the gravel road to the shrine. It took her a little over half an hour to reach the stairs in the side of the mountain that led up to the main stone path.

When she reached the top of the stairs, the first of the shrine's Torii gates came into view. She paused beside it and ran her hand along the red poles before passing under on the right side. Continuing along the path, she passed through a magnificent grove of cherry blossom trees, which were almost ready to bloom, before she reached the second Torii gate. She passed through this one in the same way as the first. After she was passed it, she stopped and glanced at her house. Normally, she would have headed straight inside, but today, she was feeling more apprehensive than normal about her dance.

She looked back over her shoulder at the Torii gate that stood more than double her height before she sighed. Unable to shake her nerves, she turned her attention to the shrine in front of her. She needed to pray for her dance; that was the only thing she could think of to help ease her worries. As soon as she made her decision, she headed toward the purification water pavilion off to the left side of the second Torii gate. When she reached it, she took a long slow breath before picking up one of the ladles with her right. She scooped the water into the ladle before pouring the water over her left hand. Her movements as she continued with the purification ritual were sure and steady since she had done this many times in the past. Switching the ladle to her other hand, she poured water over her right hand before pouring the rest of the water into her cupped right hand. She rinsed her mouth with the water from her hand and then put the ladle back in place. With the purification ritual finished, she could approach the shine.

She headed to the altar in front of the main shrine where she rang the bell that was there. After ringing the bell, she bowed twice and then clapped her hands twice. Still holding her hands together with her head bowed, she expressed her gratitude to the deity and her desire to perform well at the festival. With one final bow, she opened her eyes and stared almost blankly at the altar before she walked toward the house. The sun was just starting to sink behind the trees when she climbed up the front steps.

"I'm home," she called as she stepped through the door. She slipped off her shoes and placed them in the holder near the door.

"Welcome home," an older gentleman, who shared her red hair said when he joined her in the small entryway. She could not help but smile at his thick Irish accent.

"Hi dad," Sara said as she gave him a hug. "How are the festival preparations? Do I need to help with anything?"

"They are all finished. All you need to do is get ready for your dance. The festival starts soon, and you took longer to get home than we expected," he paused with a chuckle. "I assume you were enjoying the scenery?"

Sara shrugged with an embarrassed smile, "Yeah, I was."

Her dad reached out and ruffled her hair. "Aye, I suppose that's all right," he said with an amused smile. He had never truly been able to be angry with her.

"Sorry I took so long. I'll go and get ready right now." She hurried down the hallway to her room. Once inside, she changed into her kimono before she went to find her mother, who was waiting on her. The two worked the omamori stand until it was time for her to take the stage.

Sara fidgeted with the sleeve of her ornate kimono she wore as she walked up the stairs of the stage. The kimono she was dressed in was an elegant navy-blue that was adorned with flowers of orange and red. These complimented her brilliant shade of hair, which was stick straight down to her shoulder.

Sara risked a hasty glance at the crowd. There were a lot more people present at the festival today than usual. She was trembling with nerves, as she stood on the stage waiting for the music to begin when she noticed Paige waving at her. A smile started to cross her face until she saw Jake was standing next to her. Flushing red from head to toe, she gave Paige an exasperated stare, to which her friend just shrugged with a grin. Sara swallowed hard as she shook her head, she was going to kill her friend later.

Forcing her attention back on the festival, she looked over at the musician. He was about to start playing and she took a deep breath to steady her nerves. When the beautiful flute music caught the full attention of everyone gathered around the stage Sara raised her left hand. Reaching forward, she rang the bells in her hand before shifting to the right and ringing the bells again. Her arms swung in an arch as she slowly turned around. The sleeves of the kimono appeared to be gracefully fluttering in the wind.

Left, right, forward. Sara gave herself to the music and quit thinking about which directions to move. With another large sweep of her arm, she was facing the audience again. She peeked a quick glance at them and was about to turn again when she saw a young woman who appeared very out of place. Her brows furrowed as she tried to catch glimpses of her as she continued to dance. The young woman wore a deep green gown that was caked with mud along the bottom.

Sara made her final turn and rang the bells once more as the music ceased. The crowd erupted in applause. After giving a formal bow, Sara made her way off the stage while she tried to keep sight of the woman. She could see that the woman appeared to be confused as she pushed silver curls out of her face and headed into the forest. As quickly as she could, Sara weaved her way through the crowd. She had to stop multiple times to accept praise for her dance and bow respectfully to the guests of the shrine.

When she eventually reached the edge of the forest, she headed in the direction she had last seen the woman. After stumbling through the dark for a short while she caught sight of the woman's silver hair ahead of her on the trail. It gleamed in the moonlight which made it easy for Sara to see her in the dark. Sara hesitated before she tried to call out to her, but the woman did not seem to notice and kept walking deeper into the forest. Wringing her hands in indecision, Sara could not keep from following her, a strange pull beckoned her forward. Biting her lip, she hurried along the path so that she would not lose sight of her. She followed her for a while before she noticed that they were nearing the old willow tree by the lake. Sara paused when she saw that the woman stopped walking. She was resting her hand on the trunk of the tree before she slipped under a large black Torii gate and disappeared. Sara gasped in surprise and rushed up to the wooden pole before skidding to a halt.

"This wasn't here this morning," she stammered. After staring at the poles, she reached out and touched one. Sara's breath caught in her throat when her fingers met solid wood. It really was there. She glanced back over her shoulder before she looked back at the gate. It felt like something was beckoning for her to walk under the gate. Taking a deep breath, she closed her eyes and stepped through the gate. Once she did, she opened one eye. A split second later her other eye flew open in a panic when she found that she was surrounded by a different forest. Panicked she spun around to run back through the gate but found that it was gone.

"What do I do?" Her voice cracked with fear as she sank to the ground. She hugged her knees to her chest and put her head down on them. Not even the slightest bit curious about her surrounding, she started to hyperventilate.

"Why did I do that? I never do anything without thinking, that's Paige's job." She stopped suddenly when she said her best friend's name. Her friend would be telling her to calm down. It drove her nuts that Sara panicked when things did not go the way they were supposed to. It had been a miracle Sara did not panic over being late to graduation but her nerves about the festival kept it a bay.

Slowly, Sara managed to calm down and she lifted her head. She looked around and took in her surroundings for the first time. The old willow tree was still there but all the other trees were like nothing she had ever seen. They stood much taller than the old tree with dark brown bark and cascading leaves of bright red and gold. She craned her neck as tried to look up at one. It was so huge it reminded her of pictures she had seen of redwood trees.

Sara got up off the ground and approached the tree with cautious steps so that she could get a closer look at the leaves. When she neared them, she noticed that the gold color wrapped around the red, crescent-shaped leaves in delicate bands.

"This is really weird." She thought aloud when she noticed that even the sounds of the birds were strange, and the reassuring sound of crickets was missing. Tilting her head to get another look at the leaves, she spotted a small altar near the base of the willow tree. Confusion crossed her face, there was no altar by the tree. She walked over to it and noticed an etching with characters she did not recognize. After studying them for a few moments she turned away and something on the ground reflecting the moonlight caught her attention, it was a small delicate tiara.

"Where in the world did this come from?" She could not help but think out loud in an attempt to ward off the unnerving feeling the strange sounds of the forest caused. She started to reach for the tiara but stopped just before her fingers touched it. Another feeling of dread mixed with a strong pull washed over her. Her hand started to tremble before she finally touched it. The moment she was in contact with it, images started appearing in her mind.

A woman dressed in an exquisite white gown. The tiara was woven into her light brown hair while she stood holding hands with a man. The two stood in front of a large crowd of people as they exchanged vows..... then the vision began to change, and she watched the same woman carefully placing the tiara in a box in a drawer..... the image shifted, the young woman she saw in the forest was being given the tiara by the older woman. The young woman looked uncomfortable as the older woman pinned the tiara into her hair.... the image faded. The young woman was panicked as she raced through stone corridors. She ran through a kitchen and then through a door...

The images stop flashing by and stopped on one event.

The young woman was trapped and could not get free. She was in pain and screaming to someone that was not visible in the vision.

Sara gasped when she suddenly realized that she could feel the woman's pain and fear. As the woman continued to scream, Sara could feel her desperation.

"No!" Sara cried when she saw the event through the woman's eyes. Her entire body felt like it was on fire while a strange tingling sensation ran through her. Clamping her eyes closed, she could not hold back the screams of pain as hers mixed with those of the young woman's.

"Sara!... Sara!" Suddenly, a familiar voice calling to her broke through the pain and she tried to focus on the sound. It sounded like he was calling from a great distance, "Sara!" Her brows furrowed as she fought to focus on his voice. A few seconds later her eyes flew open and she found herself laying on the forest floor. Struggling to get her bearings now that the pain had vanished, she jumped in surprise when she noticed Jake kneeling next to her. His hand was on her shoulder while he ran the fingers of his other hand through his rain-soaked hair.

"Are you okay?" He asked when he noticed her looking up at him, his voice was filled with concern.

Sara sat upright causing Jake's hand to slip off her shoulder. Her eyes were filled with a mix of panic and confusion. "Where's the Torii gate? Where's the woman?" She asked, her voice cracking.

Jake put his hand back on her shoulder, his grip firm. "What're you talking about? There is no gate or woman. You're the only one here," he said as the concern on his face grew more pronounced.

Sara shook her head, "Bu--."

"Come on," he said. "It's raining, and we need to get inside. We can talk about this later." He picked her up and stood in one quick motion before he headed toward the path.

"I can walk," Sara muttered. Her face was becoming more red the longer he carried her.

"I've got you." He paused before he looked down at her. "But I don't really know my way around up here. Which direction is it?" A sheepish smile crossed his face. Sara smiled half-heartedly in return before she pointed up the hill. Jake did not hesitate as he headed the direction she indicated.

While he continued to walk, Sara folded her arms over her chest to hide her discomfort at being carried. Her body stiffened when she felt something in the pocket of her kimono. She slipped her hand into the pocket and slowly pulled it out so that only she could see. Staring at it wide-eyed for a moment she realized it was the tiara. Her breathing started to increase as the memories of the strange vision flooded her mind. Before she could shove it back into her pocket, it started to break apart. She jerked her hand away, but the tiara burned its shape into her palm as it disintegrated into nothing. Biting her lip to hold back a yelp of pain, she shoved her hand back into her pocket.

"Everything okay?" Jake asked when he noticed the sudden movement and glanced down at her. She only nodded and refused to look up at him. His eyebrow rose before he continued, "What were you doing out here?"

Sara glanced up and started to answer but paused when her thoughts were derailed by the sight of the moonlight reflecting off his wet hair. She tilted her head to the side as she watched the raindrops run along his strong jawline. Her mind went totally blank as she stared at him.

"Is there something on my face?" He asked, his voice becoming uncomfortable.

Sara's face already red, flushed even brighter, "No.... no." Her voice came out sounding like a strangled squeak. Jake chuckled at her reaction but looked away from her.

"So again, what were you doing out here?" He asked after he had given her a few moments to be less embarrassed.

Sara looked down and started fidgeting with her sleeve while keeping her injured hand hidden. She just shrugged as she peeked up at him out of the corner of her eye.

"Who's this woman you were talking about?"

"You said there wasn't anyone." She carefully avoided eye contact. A few long minutes passed before she risked a peek at him. He appeared to be in deep thought before he noticed her gaze and looked down at her.

"Sara, I know something strange is going on. You were screaming. That's how I was able to find you out here in the dark," he said, his voice taking on a businesslike tone. Sara frowned, she had heard him use that tone with his subordinates on base when she would visit Paige. She pursed her lips together in irritation.

"I really don't know anything," she whispered.

Jake did not respond but his eyebrow raised as they continued along the path to her house. He could tell she was being honest but knew there was more to it than she was admitting to him. The two fell silent until the lights of a house came into view. Sara was again confused. There should have been festival lights everywhere.

"Where are all the festival lights? Is it over already?"

Jake stopped and looked down at her in surprise, "The festival has been over for a while. Why do you think I was searching for you? You've been missing for hours." His voice raised on the word hours letting a little of his frustration show. "We've been worried about you."

"Hours," she asked, her voice shocked. "It only seemed like a few minutes."

Jake exhaled loudly before he set Sara back on her feet, "Let's go in. We have an early flight tomorrow." He gestured to the house. "That is if your parents will still let you go." He gave her a knowing look which caused her eyes to narrow.

"They'll let me," she said. Without waiting on his reply before she marched up the steps and opened the front door.

"Thank goodness!" An older Japanese woman cried as soon as she saw Sara walk into the house. She rushed over to her and grabbed her by the shoulders, "Are you all right?"

"Yes, I'm fine, mom," Sara replied with a heavy sigh.

"Where were you?"

Sara sighed again before she prepared to answer her mother's barrage of questions. While she was busy, her dad approached Jake who had entered silently behind Sara.

"Thanks for finding her for us, Jake," he said as he extended a hand to the younger man. Jake returned the handshake without a moment of hesitation.

26

"It's no trouble, Mr. MacCoinnich. I'm just glad she was all right."

"So am I," Mr. MacCoinnich replied as he glanced over at the two women. He could already see the frustration on Sara's face. "Why don't you get some dry clothes? This could take a minute." He added with a chuckle.

"I think I'll take you up on that," Jake said with a laugh before he headed into another room. While he was gone Sara continued to be interrogated by her mother until her dad spoke up.

"Honey, Sara needs to go and get her things together. I'm sure Jake and Paige would like to get back to the base soon."

Sara looked up at her father, her face filled with relief as she dashed out of the room. She was so relieved when she reached her room that she did not notice Paige sitting on her bed waiting for her.

"It is about time," Paige exclaimed making Sara jump in surprise. "Let's go! I already finished packing your bags. Just change quick and we can get on the road." Paige grabbed her bags and skipped out of the room before Sara even had a chance to respond. Sara shook her head with a small smile before she started to get dry clothes out of her dresser. She stopped with a gasp when a sharp pain ran through her left hand. It felt like her entire body turned to ice when it was difficult to turn her hand over so that she could see it. Her eyes widened when she saw an ugly red burn on the palm of her hand in the shape of leaves and knotwork.

"The tiara... that really did happen," she muttered.

"*Yes, it did.*"

Sara jumped and looked around the room when a voice answered her thoughts. "Is someone there?" She asked, her voice timid. When she did not hear an answer, she got up and started getting ready again. Maybe she was just really tired.

Once she was changed, she wrapped a cloth around her hand before heading back downstairs. When she got to the living room, she found Paige and a changed Jake waiting for her.

"Are you all ready?" Her dad asked when he saw her walk back into the room. She nodded before he came up and gave her a big hug. "Be careful and let us know when you get to the states."

"I will dad," she replied as she tightened her grip before letting go and moving over to her mom. She gave her a hug as well.

"Are we sure about this, George?" Her mom asked suddenly after she released her daughter from the hug. "She should remain here and fulfill her duties as the shrine maiden. She was raised for this."

Her dad shook his head, "No Yoko, we've already discussed this. It's not what she wants."

Yoko looked down at the floor with a scowl on her face, "All right. Have a safe trip."

"Thank you," Sara whispered to her mom before she gave her another hug. Once she stepped back, she headed for the door. "Bye mom, bye dad." She called as she followed Paige out to Jake's jeep. She waved to her parents, who were standing in the doorway, as they drove away from the house.

$\mathfrak{E}$veryone was quiet for the drive to the base. They were all absorbed in their own individual thoughts after the long day. When they reached the base and neared the guard house at the entrance Jake broke the silence.

"The two of you need to get your I.D. ready. The guard will need to see it."

Both girls rummaged in their backpacks while Jake pulled up to the guard house.

"Good evening, Captain Riverwood," the guard said as he approached the vehicle. "I see you have a couple of guests with you."

"You know my sister Paige, and this is her friend Sara. They will be staying on base with me tonight. We will be flying out tomorrow morning," Jake said.

"Yes sir, I just need to look at their I.D.s."

The girls handed the guard their identification. After reviewing them thoroughly he handed them back.

"Young ladies, be sure to remain with the captain tonight and keep yourselves out of trouble." They both nodded to the guard. "Have a nice evening, sir." The guard stepped out of the way so that Jake could pass through the gates. They drove onto the base and in just a couple of minutes pulled up to what looked like a large apartment building.

"These are the barracks we will stay in," Jake said as he got out of the jeep. The girls both climbed out of the back and grabbed their bags.

"I can't wait to get in our room," Paige said, her voice filled with excitement. "This is going to be the start of the best trip ever!"

Jake shook his head at his sister, "Try not to embarrass me please." His tone was serious as he led them into the barracks and up to the third floor. He stopped outside of 309 at the end of the hallway. "This is where the two of you'll be staying. I'll be right across the hall in 310 if you need anything."

"We'll be fine. Let us in!" Paige was quivering with excitement as she pointed at the door several times. While laughing at his sister, Jake unlocked the door, and both girls headed inside. The room they entered was fairly small. It had a modest kitchen area with a dining room table and a small living room area with a TV. There was a door leading to a bathroom and one to a bedroom where there were two twin beds.

"This is perfect," Paige squealed causing Sara to smile. She could not help but agree with her. This was going to be great and being away from the shrine would be a nice break.

"All right ladies lock the door when I leave and have a good night," Jake said as he turned to leave their room. Paige followed him to the door.

"Night big brother," she called after him as she locked the door behind him.

Finally, alone with just Paige, Sara sank exhausted onto the couch. It had been a long night already and her hand was throbbing with pain.

"Tell me what's up," Paige said as she plopped down next to her. Sara grimaced at the thought of revealing everything that had happened to her friend. Even Paige might have trouble swallowing this one. With a heavy sigh, she glanced at her friend.

"If I do you have to promise that you won't think I'm totally crazy," Sara replied causing Paige to laugh.

"I already do so nothing will change," she said with a huge grin. When Sara gave her a dirty look she laughed again, "Okay, Okay I won't think you're crazy, now spill!"

Sara looked down at her hands resting on her lap before she started to relay the events of the night to her friend. She only managed to get through a little bit before Paige was already interrupting.

"But there's no gate anywhere near the willow tree, is there?"

Sara held up her hand to stop her friend from talking and Paige trailed off, "Let me finish all of it please." Paige frowned but remained silent so that Sara could continue. After staring at the floor for a few moments to collect her thoughts Sara started again. When she was finished, she glanced at her friend. Her face fell when she could see the skepticism on Paige's face. Why had she expected her to believe her?

"Do you have the tiara?" Paige asked several minutes after Sara finished talking.

Sara shook her head no but started to unwrap her hand, "It disintegrated, but it left this on my hand." She held out her hand so that Paige could see the burn. Paige's eyes widened in a mix of surprise and excitement.

"Oh Sara," she paused for dramatic effect. "That's so awesome! You have the coolest stuff happen to you. I wish I could have cool things happen to me!"

Sara just stared at her friend in disbelief before she burst out laughing, "Only you would think this is cool."

Paige shrugged with a large grin before she began to bombard Sara with questions. The two discussed what happened in more detail for a while. Once Paige finally exhausted all her questions, she leaned back on the couch and was silent for a minute before she looked at Sara again.

"You know you really should have Jake look at that. It could get infected."

Sara's eyes opened wide, and she shook her head. There was no way she could show Jake.

"He'll ask too many questions. You know that and what am I going to tell him?"

Paige nodded in agreement to Sara's concerns, "You are right but if you wait, then he'll ask the same questions and your hand will be even more painful. It already looks a little infected." Sara dropped her head and sighed in resignation of defeat. "You better go now before he gets in bed. He's grumpy if you wake him up." Paige paused with a giggle. "Good thing my brother is a combat medic and aspiring surgeon, huh?"

"Yeah great," Sara said, her voice laced with nerves. "Are you going to come with me?"

"Nah, I'll get our beds ready," Paige answered as she stood up and walked toward the bedroom. "Besides my brother doesn't bite." She added with a grin.

Sara rolled her eyes as she got up and left the room. She stood staring at the door to Jake's room, but could not get the courage to knock. What was she going to tell him? Her face started to flush the longer she thought about having to talk to him. He was going to think she was nuts. She turned around to walk back to her room when her hand brushed against her pant leg. Reflexively, she reached for her hand when pain ran all through it. She bit her lip and faced the door again. There was no way to get out of this. She needed help to care for her hand.

Without allowing time to talk herself out of it, she raised her hand and knocked softly on the door. She held her breath hoping that he would not hear, but a few seconds later the door opened. Jake appeared as if he had already headed to bed. He stood there with tousled hair, no shirt, and flannel pants.

Sara's face flushed a brilliant red and her eyes dropped to the floor.

"Oh hey, Sara," he said when he saw who was at the door. "Hang on a second." He stepped back into his room and grabbed a shirt before coming back to the door, "Do you need something?" He asked as he pulled the shirt over his head.

Sara swallowed hard trying to hide her nerves before she held out her hand so that he could see it.

"Can you help me with this please?" Her voice shook when she asked the question.

Jake looked down at her hand before he took hold of it with his and angled it, so he could get a better look in the dim light of the hallway. When she peeked up at him, he was looking back at her with a carefully composed expression.

"Yes, I will definitely take care of this. It is a bad burn, but you are going to have to tell me something." He knew this had to have something to do with what happened in the woods.

Sara started to look back down at the floor.

"No, look at me." She raised her head and Jake frowned when he could see the timid look on her face. "You will tell me, yes?" Once she nodded, he released her hand and walked back into his room to grab a key. "I have to go and get some supplies. I don't have them up here. Go wait with Paige and I'll be back in a bit."

Sara nodded again and headed straight back toward the door to her room. She was about to open the door when Jake paused partway down the hall.

"You know you can trust me, right?"

Sara paused with her uninjured hand on the doorknob and looked down the hallway.

"Yes, I know," she whispered before she opened the door and disappeared into the room. As soon as she closed the door she called to Paige in a panic.

"Paige! He wants to know what happened. What in the world am I going to tell him? I can't tell him the truth. He'll think I'm a total nut job."

Paige glanced up from the TV show she was watching with a mischievous grin, "I guess that means we'd better come up with a believable story in about the next fifteen minutes. I figure that is about how long it will take him to get back from the infirmary."

Sara paced around the living room trying to think of the best thing to say. She would not lie but she had no idea what to tell him. The idea of making him think she was as weird as everyone else thought caused a strange ache in her chest.

"I can't think of anything," she said as her whole body started to tremble.

"Calm down," Paige said getting up from the couch. "He'll see right through you if you're freaking out. I know that from experience." She paused and looked around the room. "What about you burned it with fire? Like you were building a campfire or something?"

Sara shrugged, "I don't know how to build a fire."

"There that's perfect. You were trying to learn to build a fire and burned your hand on some wood that you were putting in. That sounds believable."

Sara sank down on the couch and put her head in her uninjured hand. "He'll never believe that. It was raining and why would I be in the woods starting a fire after the festival?"

"I know! You could tell him you burnt it on the stove. That'll totally work."

Sara shook her head, "I doubt he'll believe that either but that's better than the fire idea."

"Well then perk up and make it believable," Paige said in an enthusiastic voice as she sat down beside Sara. "Unless, of course you just want to tell him the truth." A large grin appeared on her face when Sara gave her an exasperated stare, but before she could formulate a reply a loud knock on the door caused her to jump.

"It's me, I'm coming in," Jake called before he pushed the door of the room open. He glanced at the girls as he walked into the room. When he made eye contact with Paige, he raised an eyebrow. She just shrugged in response and grinned at him. He shook his head when he knew immediately that she would be no help. With a slight frown, he crossed the room and headed to the small kitchen area. He flipped on the light and arranged the supplies on the counter. There were packages of gauze, gloves, a bottle of sterile water, tape, and a bottle of ointment.

"Let's get this over with, Sara," he said motioning for her to come over to the sink. She hesitated before she got up and walked toward him. He noticed right away that she was shaking, and he grabbed a chair from the table. After pushing it right next to the sink, he looked back over at her.

"Here, sit," he said as he reached out and absentmindedly patted her on the head like he would do to Paige. "This won't be pleasant, but I'll be as gentle as possible."

She only nodded before she sat down and held her hand, so it was over the sink. Jake watched her for a moment before turning his attention to the supplies. He opened the bottle of sterile water and several packages of gauze, careful to leave them laying on the sterile inside of the packages. Once he was finished, he put on a pair of gloves before he took a gentle but firm hold of her hand. He started to work on cleaning up the wound. Sara jerked when he poured the sterile water on it but tried to remain as still as she could. After a few minutes, she found herself watching him to keep her mind off the pain. His long, lean fingers using the gauze pads to very gently remove the dirt and the concentration on his face as he studied the burn.

It was not long before she found that she was totally mesmerized by his face and wondered what it would be like to touch his cheek. It looked firm and soft at the same time. She was so absorbed in her thoughts that she did not notice when Jake leaned in closer.

"Did I cut myself when I shaved?" He asked with an awkward chuckle.

She was so shocked by the sudden closeness of his face that she tried to jump back and pushed the chair over backwards.

"Whoa, careful." Jake said as he caught the back of the chair in time to keep her from tumbling to the ground. "Where are you trying to go? I'm not finished with your hand."

"No… nowhere," Sara mumbled as she kept her eyes locked on the floor in front of her. Jake tilted his head before he went back to work on the wound. He managed to keep his attention on it for a few minutes before he started glancing back at her out of the corner of his eye.

"What were you thinking about? You looked like you were in your own world," he said as he was drying the burn with more of the gauze.

"N… nothing," she stammered, and a deep blush crept across her face.

"Doesn't look like nothing." His voice dropped so that only she could hear what he was saying. Sara swallowed hard and refused to look up at him. She was red all the way up to her ears.

"Okay, okay you are about to give my best friend a heart attack," Paige called from across the room. She had her arms folded across her chest with an irritated scowl.

"I don't know what you're talking about," Jake joked as he turned his full attention back to covering the burn.

Paige gave him a *yeah right* look, "Aren't you done yet?"

"Yup, just finished," he said as he wrapped the last piece of tape around the gauze. The moment he released her hand, Sara scurried out of the chair and hurried to put distance between her and Jake. Paige was right, she felt like her heart was going to leap out of her chest if she stayed that close to him any longer.

Jake watched her bolt with a conflicted look on his face. He shook his head a second later and turned to clean up the extra supplies. Once he finished and turned back to face the girls, he was his normal all business self.

"We have some things to discuss, don't we?" He asked as he motioned for them to sit on the couch. The girls shared a hasty glance before they sat side by side on the couch. Jake followed them and sat down in a chair he pulled over. "Who's going to tell me what happened?"

Paige just shrugged at her brother before she looked at Sara. She looked back at her with panicked eyes. Paige frowned before she tilted her head to which Sara immediately shook her head no. With a heavy sigh, Paige started to talk.

"It was just the stove, Jake. We were getting ready to make... uh... soup... for a snack and she accidentally touched the burner. She didn't know I had turned it on."

Jake's eyebrows rose as disapproval appeared on his face, "I am going to stop you there. That stove was not even the slightest bit hot nor was there any food making items out in the kitchen. I also know that burn is several hours old and not recent. And before you try saying it was a fire, yes, I know how you think Paige, I know that it was not wood. Whatever made that burn was metal. Now, will one of you please stop insulting my intelligence and tell me the truth?" His tone was stern as he leaned back in the chair and folded his arms across his chest. "I have all night, ladies."

Paige shrank back from her angry brother and gave Sara an apologetic look before she bolted from the room, leaving Sara to fend for herself. Sara stared after her open-mouthed when she realized her best friend had just abandoned her. Her eyes narrowed in irritation, see if she helped her get out of trouble with her brother again.

Jake cleared his throat softly and brought her attention back to the current situation. She looked down at her hands in her lap and bit her lip.

"You wouldn't believe me," she whispered.

Jake slid forward in the chair, "Sara, look at me." He lifted her chin with a couple of fingers. "You don't know what I'll believe unless you tell me, and you have nothing to be afraid of when you're talking to me. Just tell me the truth."

Sara's eyes flicked to his face and she could see the sincerity in his gaze, "It was a small tiara. I found it in the woods after the festival."

"A tiara?" His eyes narrowed as he thought. "That would fit the shape of the burn. What happened to it?"

"It disintegrated after I picked it up."

"Where did you find it?"

"By the large willow tree where you found me."

"Anything else you can tell me?"

Sara shook her head. She could not possibly tell him about any of the rest of it. He regarded her for a moment before he sighed.

"I know you aren't telling me everything, but you at least told me about the burn. I believe you about that part, so I'll leave it at that for tonight. You need to get some sleep before we leave in about three hours." He stood up and put the chair back by the table before heading to the door. "Oh and tell my sister that I'll have a chat with her later." A somewhat cold smile crossed his face as he slipped through the door and closed it behind him.

When he was gone, Sara sagged back on the couch. She could not believe he had believed her. It all sounded so crazy to her and she had experienced it. With a shake of her head, she headed straight to bed and collapsed. She was so exhausted by the day's events that she was asleep as soon as her head hit the pillow.

A couple of hours later, Sara was thrashing in her sleep. She started flailing her arms around like she struggling to break free from something. Her hand connected with the lamp on the bedside table and she sent it flying across the room. It slammed into the wall with a loud crash causing Paige to jump out of bed at the sudden noise.

"No, don't hurt him," Sara cried out in her sleep. Her struggles continued as she fought with the covers.

Paige ran over and grabbed her hands to keep her from hitting anything else, "Sara! Sara wake up!" Her face clouded with concern as she shook her by the shoulders. Sara did not wake up, and she started screaming as her struggling became frantic.

"Sara!" Paige shouted, her voice filled with agitation. When Sara still did not wake up, she smacked her friend on the cheek. Sara woke with a startled gasp and her hand flew to her face in shock. She rubbed the spot where Paige had just smacked her and struggled to get her breathing back under control. She shivered when the cooler air of the room chilled her since she was soaked in sweat.

"What happened?" Paige asked, her normal bubbly personality was gone and replaced with apprehension.

"I saw her again in the cave. She was desperate to save someone. I couldn't see who, but I felt her pain and fear like it was mine," Sara said, her voice shaking. "I'm goin--."

A loud knock on the door caused both girls to jump in surprise. Paige leapt to her feet.

"Oh no, someone must have heard you. I'll be right back." She dashed out of the room and pulled the door open to find her brother standing there. He stepped past her without a word and scanned the room. His sharp blue-grey eyes were assessing for a possible threat.

"What is going on?" He asked when nothing caught his attention right away. "I heard a loud crash and screaming. Are you both alright?"

Paige grabbed his arm when he tried to move further into the room, "We're okay. Sara was having a nightmare and she knocked a lamp off the table."

Jake glanced down at his sister, who was still holding on to his arm as she spoke, he could see that she was anxious and confused.

"What's wrong?"

"I had to smack her to wake her up," Paige admitted with a frown. "I didn't know what else to do." She let go of his arm with an embarrassed chuckle. "But we're all good. You can go back to your room. I can take it from here." She gave him a halfhearted grin. It was obvious to her that she was worrying her brother.

"Paig--."

"Hey, what're you doing up anyway? Shouldn't you have been sleeping too?" Her tone turned indignant as she regained her equilibrium and Jake could not help but smile.

"We have to leave for the plane in half an hour. I was about to come and make sure the two of you were awake."

"What?! It's already that late," Paige exclaimed with wide eyes. "Oh, my goodness we have to get ready. Out! Out!" Without waiting on him to say anything, Paige spun and dashed back into the bedroom. Jake chuckled as he watched her leave.

"I'll be back in about twenty minutes since we need to be at the transportation office by 0500," he called as he let himself out.

The girls gathered their belongings as quickly as they could before they changed for the trip. Sara was just putting away the last of her things when Jake knocked on the door.

"Let's go," he called through the door. The girls grabbed their bags and followed Jake out of the barracks into the still dark early morning. After getting back in the jeep, Jake drove them toward the transportation office. When they got close, he glanced in his mirrors quickly to see if anyone was around before driving the jeep around the back of the hanger. He turned the car off but left the keys in the ignition.

"Let's go, ladies," he said.

Paige glanced at her brother with a look of suspicion. She had caught the slight apprehension in his voice, but before she could ask him about it, he was already walking toward the hanger. The girls scrambled out of the jeep and ran in the direction Jake was walking. Once they caught up with him, they headed to the front of the hanger and into an office off to the right. Jake held the door open for them as they entered.

"Hey, Sam," Jake called as he walked in. The man sitting at a desk behind the counter stood up with a grin.

"What's up, Jake?" He asked as he walked up and shook Jake's hand. "Are you and these lovely ladies taking the MAC flight today?"

"Yes, we are."

Sam grabbed a manifest from his desk and walked back up to the counter, "Man, we're going to miss this guy. We've had all sorts of fun." He flipped through a few pages before he glanced back up with a sly grin. "Do you have all your possessions on board the plane?"

"Everything but us and our bags," Jake replied as he made a small motion like he was steering a car.

"Excellent," Sam said with a grin. "All right then we have a couple of standard questions. Are you still about one eighty, Jake?"

"Give or take."

"Okay and now you lovely ladies. Paige, what are you at these days?"

Giving him a dirty look, Paige folded her arms across her chest before answering, "I'm still one thirty and it's because I'm tall."

"You're still short to me," Jake said with a laugh as he playfully poked his sister in the side. She swatted his hand away.

"That's because you are a six one giant," she said with a pout. "I'm still five nine and that's not bad. Sara over here is the short one." She grinned at her friend when Sara rolled her eyes at her.

"So, you do have a name," Sam said, his tone teasing. "How about it? How much do you weigh? We have to have it for the flight manifest."

"One fifteen and since everyone is sharing, I'm a measly five three," she whispered as she turned a light shade of red. Sam chuckled at her response as he wrote her weight on the manifest. Once he was finished, he handed her the pen, so she could sign, that yes, she was going to be aboard the flight.

"Alright, the plane is still being loaded so if you wouldn't mind waiting over in our lovely waiting area. I'll let you know when you can board." He gestured to a couple of chairs set up by the wall.

Sara walked over with Paige and sat down while Jake and Sam continued to chat. She glanced around the room while she waited. It was another fairly small room with light tan walls. There was not much in it besides a counter and a desk. On the desk was a nameplate that read Capt. Samuel McMillagen. Sara looked back over when she figured out the man Jake was talking to must be him. He was much shorter than Jake but quite a bit stockier. He appeared like he could handle himself in a fight despite his strawberry blond hair. A large scar ran down his forearm, which could be seen due to his rolled-up fatigue sleeves.

"What happens now?" Sara asked. Paige turned to answer her when the door of the office flew open, and an important looking man strode into the room. Jake and Sam immediately snapped to attention.

"As you were boys," the man declared in a short, commanding tone. "Captain, I need to be on this MAC flight."

"Yes sir, I'll get you on today's flight right away," Sam replied as he shared a look of concern with Jake as he moved over to stand beside the girls. "Will it just be you sir or are any of your aids joining you?"

"Do you see anyone else?"

"No sir," Sam replied with a frown. "I need your weight for the manifest please."

"One eighty," came the clip reply.

"Yeah more like two eighty," Paige whispered to Sara as she snickered.

Jake looked down at her, his disapproval clearly visible, as the man marched over to where they were waiting.

"Name and rank soldier," he snapped, his face turning red with anger.

"Captain Jacob Riverwood," Jake replied without skipping a beat. The man narrowed his eyes with a look of disgust.

"And who are you?" He demanded looking at Paige.

"I don't have to tell you that," she snapped back as she stood up to look him in the face. He stood about an inch shorter than her. "I'm not in the military."

"As long as you're a guest on this base, you'll tell a commanding officer who you are, or I'll have you removed," he growled. "Who's responsible for this child?"

Paige bristled at being called a child, but Jake grabbed her arm with a hand behind his back before she could reply.

"I'm responsible, sir," Jake said, without taking his eyes off the wall on the far side of the room.

The man appeared pleased when he realized that Jake replied, and the anger started to fade from his face. "Is this how your guest treats a superior officer?"

Paige glanced back and forth between the man and her brother and it only took her a split second to realize she could get Jake in trouble.

"Paige Riverwood," she snapped causing the man to look back over at her.

His expression darkened as he glared at her, "You're Jeremiah's brats." He paused with a scowl when he turned his attention back at Jake. "His overachieving brat." He added with a sneer as he gave Jake a look of pure disdain.

Jake tightened his grip on Paige's arm to prevent her from responding. Paige pursed her lips in annoyance but managed to stay quiet.

The man appeared to be considering his next course of action when he noticed Sara still sitting in the chair.

"And who are you?" He demanded shifting his attention to her. She flinched at the glare he was giving her.

"That's Sar —."

"I don't believe I asked you," he said, his voice cold as ice. Jake snapped his mouth closed and clenched his jaw in anger when he could only watch. "Well? I don't have all day?" The man snapped, his voice filled with impatience.

Sara stood up and did her best to look him in the eye, "Sara MacCoinnich." Her voice came out a terrified whisper. The man scowled at her for a moment before he spun around and marched back over to the counter. He snatched the pen out of Sam's hand and signed the manifest.

"Best to pick better friends," he sneered at Sara before looking back at Sam. "I require all eight seats in the front of this aircraft. I have a reputation to think about."

"It'll be taken care of sir," Sam said.

"I'm boarding now. I don't care if all the equipment is loaded yet." He snapped these last words before he threw open the door of the office. It closed behind him with a loud slam. As soon as he was gone the tension in the room dropped noticeably and Sara sank back down in the chair with a thud.

"Paige, so help me," Jake started. "I swear you'll be the death of me."

She looked up at her brother with a sheepish grin, "I'm sorry. I couldn't help it. He was being such a jerk."

Jake grimaced and shook his head before glancing over at Sam.

"You have no idea who that man was, do you?"

"That was Colonel Tibus Ravencraft, th--."

"The girls don't need to hear the rest," Jake blurted when Sam chimed in. "All you need to know is that he could make my life miserable, so please watch yourself on this trip."

Paige grinned at her brother again, "I'll try my best."

Jake walked slowly back over to the counter and rested his head in his hands. Sam chuckled and slapped him on the back.

"It's time to board folks," he said motioning toward the door. "Try not to get a court-martial before you make it to Washington."

"I think that will be completely up to my sister," Jake answered without lifting his head. Sam laughed as he glanced at Paige.

"Yeah, I think you're right. Good luck man."

Jake stood up with a heavy sigh and shook Sam's hand before the three of them headed out of the office and toward the plane.

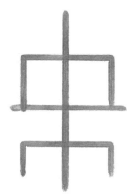

Sara clutched her bag tighter as she followed Jake and Paige out of the transportation office hanger. She was getting more and more nervous about the flight. When they reached the tarmac, she stopped walking and just stared up at the enormous aircraft sitting there. A few seconds later she rushed after Jake and Paige who were both still walking.

"Whoa!" Paige gasped when she noticed the plane. "I've never been on a plane this big. What is this, Jake?" She looked up at the wing on the aircraft as they passed underneath.

"This is a C5 Galaxy," Jake said as he glanced at the plane. "It's one of the largest military cargo planes in the world. They're capable of carrying multiple smaller vehicles as well as large numbers of troops."

"Wow," Paige replied. "I wonder what they put on here." Jake gave her a look of disapproval, which she ignored, as they walked up the open cargo ramp in the tail of the plane. Once inside they were met by a sergeant.

"Welcome aboard, Captain Riverwood," the sergeant said. "I trust that you have everything you need, sir." He subtly tilted his head toward a large item covered with a tarp and Jake tried to keep the grin off his face.

"Yes, Sergeant Fields, I believe we're all set," Jake replied.

Fields nodded as he attempted to keep his own smile hidden, "I hope you all have a pleasant flight."

They walked past him and continued further onto the plane until they found a ladder on the left side of the cargo hold. The three of them climbed up and found several rows of seats.

"Find a seat and get comfortable," Jake said as he dropped his bag onto a seat. "I'll be back in a few minutes." He started to walk away when he stopped and glanced back at them, "Stay here." He added looking right at his sister.

"I will," she said with a roll of her eyes. Once he disappeared down the ladder the girls found a place to sit and put their bags into the overhead compartments along the walls.

"What did that colonel mean by Jake being an overachiever?" Sara asked, her voice filled with curiosity. Paige looked away from the compartment she had just clicked closed.

"Well, you already know Jake is only twenty-five, right?" Paige asked and when Sara nodded, she continued. "He graduated high school early with two years of college finished because of taking college classes in high school. So, he's already graduated with a bachelor's degree and he's finished medical school. He's going to the states now to finish his residency toward becoming a surgeon. He's done one year already."

"Wow," Sara said, her eyes wide with surprise. "I knew Jake was smart, but I didn't know any of that."

"That's really only part of it. He's done everything on his own too. Dad hasn't been any help. He said Jake had to earn it all for himself so Jake having the rank of captain already is all him too. Plus, he was deployed twice in all that." Her voice was filled with pride when she spoke about her brother's accomplishments. Even though she would never admit it to him, she looked up to him.

Sara smiled at her friend before she turned her attention to the cabin. It was much larger than she had expected. There were enough light blue cloth covered seats for about seventy people and the walls were lined with cargo compartments on both sides. A frown crossed her face when she realized there were no windows anywhere along the grey walls.

"Time to get seated," Jake said as he climbed up the ladder and back into the room. "Sergeant Fields said the load is secured, so we should be taking off soon."

Sara sat down next to Paige and fastened her seat belt. Jake joined them a few seconds later.

"What happens now?" She whispered to Paige. The quiver in her voice gave away her nerves. Paige gave her a funny look before her eyes widened.

"You've never flown before, have you?" Paige asked. Sara shook her head as she tried to keep her nervousness off her face. "It's so much fun! Kind of like a rollercoaster but not." Paige paused with a frown. "I guess it is kind of hard to explain." She added with a giggle.

"I like roller coasters but I'm not sure I am going to like this," Sara said with a grimace.

Paige just rolled her eyes. "Oh, you'll be fine."

Sara gave her an exasperated look before she looked away and tried to prepare herself for the plane to take off. She did not have to wait long before the plane started to roll with a sudden jerk and made its way out to the runway. When it stopped moving, she glanced over at Paige in confusion.

"They are probably waiting for permission to take off," Paige said glancing beside her at her brother. He had his seatbelt fastened and was reclined back in his seat.

Swallowing hard, Sara jumped when the engines on the plane started to get much louder as the pilot increased the power in preparation for takeoff. Sara glanced at Paige to ask if the sudden shaking of the plane was normal but before she could, she was pushed back hard in her seat when the plane lurched down the runway. She grabbed both arms on her seat and flinched when she hit the burn on her hand. She let go with the injured hand but clung to the armrest with the other.

A few moments later she felt the strange almost weightless feeling of leaving the ground when they were airborne. Once it gained some altitude the pilot banked the plane hard to the right to make a large turn to the correct heading. Sara was grateful for the seatbelt that was keeping her from sliding out of her seat due to the steep angle. A few minutes later the plane leveled out and continued its climb to cruising altitude. When the plane quit climbing, Jake and Paige both unfastened their seat belts.

"Now we have to occupy ourselves for the next eleven hours," Paige said with a mischievous grin. Sara and Jake both gave her a *please behave* look. "Really? I'm not that bad." Her voice took on an indignant tone.

"Uh huh, sure," Jake said as he moved over to sit along the wall. He pulled out a medical journal to read. Sara kept peeking over at him, but his full attention was already on the journal.

"Paige," she said with a quiet sigh. "Where are the bathrooms on the plane?"

Paige's brows furrowed as she thought for a minute, "They're back downstairs on this side of the plane, I think I saw them on the way in. Do you want me to come with you?"

"No, I'm good," Sara said with an amused smile.

"Then hurry up!" Paige said.

Sara unfastened her seatbelt and headed across the room and down the ladder. When she reached the bottom, she found that she was in an enormous cargo hold, which was crammed full, with a Blackhawk helicopter, a tank, a Humvee, and whatever was under the tarp. After looking around for a few minutes, she turned to the left and walked toward the front of the plane. It did not take long for her to find and use the airplane restroom, but when she exited, she almost ran right into Colonel Ravencraft who was waiting outside.

"Sorry," she mumbled as she tried to walk by him, but he held out a hand in front of her to stop her.

"Come with me," he ordered.

She glanced toward the back of the plane before she peeked up at Ravencraft. The look of loathing on his face caused her to shiver and she started to shake her head no. His expression darkened, and he stabbed a finger toward the front of the plane. She hesitated before she dropped her head and followed the colonel. He led her toward the front of the plane and up a set of steep stairs off to the left side. At the top of the stairs were several rows of rear-facing seats and at the far end a door that led to the cockpit. He walked to the nearest chair and sat down. Sara kept her eyes on the floor and waited for him to speak.

"I want you to tell me about the Riverwood brats," he said, his voice dripping with disgust. "I want to know any deep dark secrets they have, their drug use, anything."

"They don't have any secrets," Sara whispered after she raised her head just enough that she could look up at him.

Ravencraft was already tapping his foot on the floor. His impatience showed on his face, "Everyone has their secrets. You will tell me what you know. You have to be close to them or you wouldn't be on this plane." Sara was shaking her head before he even finished the sentence.

"I don't know anything that they have done wrong," she said as she fought to keep her voice from giving away her fear. The colonel slammed his fist down on the arm of his chair making her jump.

"They can't be perfect," he snarled as his face began to turn red with anger. He paused and fell silent for a few moments. "I suppose something will have to be done to tarnish that good reputation. I will have that general promotion." He stood up from his chair. "That boy has a temper, right?"

Sara looked at the colonel as confusion clouded her face when he stalked toward her. Before she had a chance to back away, he pulled his hand back and slapped her hard across the face. With a yelp of surprise, Sara stumbled and fell into the arm of one of the metal chairs. Her head exploded with pain and she saw stars when it connected with the chair. The colonel scanned the room to be certain no one had heard her.

"Damn, you have no balance," he snapped, his tone indifferent. "But no matter, it'll help support the story that the Riverwood boy is dangerous. Ruin the son, ruin the father." He marched over to Sara and reached down to grab her. As soon as he touched her, he jerked his hand back as if he had been shocked. Sara looked down at her hands and saw that they had what looked like small electrical charges running up her fingers.

"Get out of here before someone sees you. We'll finish this conversation later," he snarled while he rubbed his fingers. She pushed off the floor and got back to her feet before making her way for the stairs. She stumbled a couple times since she was still disoriented from hitting the chair.

"Hurry up!" Sara flinched at the tone of his voice and scurried out of the room. Once she made her way down the stairs, she started to cry. She had no idea what to do. He was going to lie and say that Jake hurt her. The more she thought about it the more panicked she was becoming. Nearing the point of hyperventilation, she ran into the cargo hold of the plane. She was frantic as she searched for a place to hide. When she noticed that the Blackhawk helicopter had been left open, she headed for it. She moved to climb inside but as soon as her hand touched the side the gauges and lights on it began to power up. Jerking her hands back she stared at them with wild eyes, as she scrambled backwards and bumped into the tank that was secured behind the helicopter. As soon as she made contact with it, it also began to power up. It tried to roll forward and broke one of the chains securing it. Sara barely had time to jump to the side as it lurched to the right and caused a massive shift in the weight of the plane. The sudden change caused the plane to lean to the right, and Sara, already off balance from the jump, fell and slid into the wall. She slammed into the side of the plane and touched it with both hands.

"No! No," she cried.

"*Calm down.*" Sara heard the voice in her head again when the lights in the plane started to flicker like it was losing power.

"What do I do?" Her voice was frantic as she cried out to the voice that was speaking to her.

"*Calm down, nothing can be fixed if you are not calm.*" Sara tried her best to calm down but was even more panicked after hearing the voice again. She looked up and suddenly realized the pilot had been able to quickly correct the pitch of the plane, it was once again level. Sara jumped to her feet and ran, careful not to touch anything else, until she found a small alcove. She darted inside and just sat down where she was and focused on her breathing. When she was almost breathing normally again, she looked down at her hands and noticed that the electricity she had seen appeared to be gone. She put her head in her hand. What was happening to her?

Seconds later she heard a loud commotion, and she peaked out of the alcove. There were several soldiers running around trying to secure the tank so that the plane would once again be stable. The loadmaster was yelling commands as they worked.

"Fields! What in the hell is going on down here?" A man asked as he rapidly approached the loadmaster from somewhere in the front of the plane.

"I'm not sure, Captain Anders. It's the strangest thing. It appears the tank turned on somehow and snapped one of the cables securing it. We're doubling them right now and should have the load secured momentarily."

"Turned on? That shouldn't be possible if all procedures were followed to the letter sergeant," Captain Anders snapped.

Sergeant Fields nodded his head in acknowledgment. "Yes sir, I know, and I've already verified the check off sheets. Everything looks like it was done according to procedure." He handed the paperwork to the captain.

"Major Vollen will want to speak about this after we land. That was a huge shift in load and threatened the safety of this entire aircraft. This can't happen again."

"Yes sir," Fields answered with a grimace as he watched the captain head back toward the front of the plane. Shaking his head, he turned his attention back to the tank. When he saw the men were finished, he made his way around the tank to inspect all the lines before dismissing them. He followed them back toward their seats.

Sara sat back into the alcove again after she watched them all walk away. She sighed when she realized Sergeant Fields was going to get in trouble because of her. She went to rest her head back on her hand when a sharp pain caused her to pull it back. Now that the adrenaline was leaving her system, she was becoming aware of the pain in her face, head, and hand. After sitting for a few minutes more she shook her head and stood to head back. She knew Paige and Jake would be wondering where she was after all this time. When she reached the base of the ladder, she pulled her long bangs forward to cover her face and adjusted the gauze over her burn. It had torn in a couple places when she fell. Once she pulled the hood of her sweatshirt up, she took a deep breath and started to climb. Upon reaching the top, she was careful to keep her head down as she walked toward her seat.

"Oh, my goodness Sara," Paige exclaimed. "Where have you been? I thought you got lost."

"Sorry," she mumbled with a shrug. After she sat down, she carefully glanced at Paige through her bangs. She also noticed that Jake was nowhere to be seen.

"What's wrong?" Paige demanded.

"Nothing."

Paige stomped over until she was right in front of her, "You know better than to hide something from me. Now tell me what's up." She put her hands on her hips which caused Sara to sigh before she pulled her bangs back and lifted her head. "What happened to you? That looks terrible." Paige's voice filled with concern when she saw her friend's face.

"Colonel Ravencraf--."

"He did this?" Paige asked as her eyebrows shot up with an incredulous look. Sara only nodded, and she started to fume. "Oh, he is going to rue the day he messed with you. I'm going to take care of that jerk!" Sara grabbed Paige's arm before she could walk away.

"No, you can't," she said, her voice urgent. "He's trying to get Jake into trouble. He wants me to say that Jake did this."

Paige's mouth dropped open as she gaped at her, "He is threatening to mess with my brother? What could that possibly gain him?" Her tone became more and more angry as she spoke.

"He said something about ruin the son, ruin the father. I think he wants your dad's rank and job."

"You've got to be kidding me," Paige snapped, she trembled with rage. "There is no way that jerk would ever be smart enough to take on my brother. He had to stoop so low as to attack you."

"Who's not smart enough?" A voice interjected cutting off Paige's rant. Both girls looked over to see that Jake had returned. Paige pointed at Sara as soon as she saw her brother.

"Come and look at what that jerk did to Sara," she spat. "And, he's going to try and blame it on you."

Jake walked over to them with cautious steps. He knew he was still missing part of the information in the conversation.

"Who did what?"

"That jerk colonel. Look at her face, Jake." Paige pointed at Sara again. This time he saw what she was pointing at. He knelt in front of Sara's chair and reached up to move her hair out of the way. She had a large bruise over the temple and cheekbone on the left side, and on the other side, there was a large red handprint that was starting to bruise on her cheek. Jake exhaled hard as he clenched the hand he had resting on his knee into a fist.

"How did this happen?" He asked, his voice taking on a flat almost hollow tone. He was falling back on his training to maintain a calm facade. Sara shifted in her seat. Her head was bothering her, and she did not want to relive anything right now. Jake noticed her hesitation, "You need to tell us what happened. This involves more than just you now." His tone did not change, and Sara was a bit taken aback. It seemed like he did not care and only wanted information. Her eyes narrowed in irritation before she started to speak. She relayed the events that had taken place with the colonel but was careful to leave out everything about the electrical anomaly. When she was finished, she noticed that Jake was pacing back and forth across the room, and Paige was just watching him.

"Jak—." He raised his hand to keep Paige from talking. He appeared to be struggling to keep his frustration in check. After a few moments, he turned to face Sara.

"I just want to make sure I have all of this straight," he said, his voice cold. "Ravencraft wants my dad's job so bad he's willing to try and ruin my career by claiming that I assaulted you. And, this is all to damage my dad's reputation?" By the time he was finished his voice was beginning to rise and Sara only nodded. She had never seen Jake angry and it was making her uncomfortable.

Without another word, he turned and headed for the ladder, but Paige rushed forward and grabbed his arm.

"What're you doing?" she asked. "You can't go do anything to the colonel as much as he deserves it."

Jake pulled his arm out of her grasp. "If he's going to try to court-martial me over something, then it sure as hell is going to be over something I actually did," he snapped.

"No," she yelled. "You're better than this. You can't let that colonel ruin everything you've worked so hard for." She paused, and a look of determination flashed across her face. "I'll take care of a little revenge."

"What?!?" Jake exclaimed, completely losing what calm facade he had left. "You don't think for a second that I'm going to let you anywhere near that man? That I'd let there be a chance he'd hurt you?"

"I won't be anywhere near him. I have a plan in mind." She looked up at him with a look of complete confidence.

Jake appeared to momentarily be at a loss for words as he opened and closed his mouth several times before he responded.

"Are you out of your mind?" He snapped. "Do you know what could happen if you were caught? I forbid you to do anything!"

Paige glared at her brother, "You aren't my dad! You can't keep me from doing anything!"

A momentary look of pain flashed across Jake's face before it was quickly replaced by a blank stare.

"No, I'm not," he said in a short-controlled voice. "But I have to look after you and I take that job seriously."

The anger fled from Paige as soon as she heard her brother's response, "I'm sorry. That wasn't fair of me to say."

Jake raised an eyebrow before he nodded. He seemed a little suspicious of the sudden change. Paige gave her brother a quick hug before she walked over to sit back down. She glanced over at Sara and noticed she was sitting in the chair holding her head.

"Don't you think you should check on Sara? She could have a concussion or something, right?" Paige asked in an innocent voice while she rummaged through her bag. "I think I have some pain killers in here if she can have it."

Jake's full attention shifted to Sara and his face fell when he saw her holding her head. He walked over and sat down in the seat beside her.

"I'm sorry," he said, his voice quiet. "I don't know what I was thinking. Are you all right?"

"I have a headache," Sara replied when she could hear the concern in his voice.

"That is to be expected," he said, his medical training taking over. "Do you feel nauseous or have any vision changes?" When Sara shook her head no to both questions, he pulled a penlight from one of his pockets. "I'm going to check for pupil reactivity just as a precaution." He held the light up and quickly flashed the light into each of her eyes. Satisfied with what he saw he put the light away.

"You'll probably have a headache for the next couple of days but otherwise everything looks okay. Let me know if you feel nauseous or have any vision changes?" After Sara nodded again, he continued. "Paige said she had some pain reliever if you want some. I think you should take some and try to rest. I'll be checking on you every little bit for a while."

"I think I would like some please," she whispered.

Jake turned around to talk to his sister but found she was not in the room. He leapt from his chair and hurried over to the ladder. When he saw that she was not there either he turned around shaking his head.

"She is going to get herself in so much trouble. She has no clue what she is doing." He moved over to his sister's bag. Once he found the pain reliever, he gave some to Sara before he sat down and waited on his sister to return. He did not have to wait long when he heard noise on the ladder, and he got up out of the chair.

Paige crept back into the room and surprise crossed her face when she saw her brother was no longer helping Sara. She glanced up and found herself facing a very angry older brother. He stood with his arms folded over his chest just watching her.

"Jake, I... uh... just had to use the bathroom," she stammered. "I didn't want to bother you while you were helping Sara." She looked up at him with the most innocent look she could manage. He continued to regard her silently, and she started to shift under his gaze. "Come on Jake --."

"I have nothing to say to you right now," Jake said when he raised his hand to stop her from talking. "I don't want to know so if anyone asks me later, I can truthfully say I have no idea what you were doing. Just go sit down, Paige." She opened her mouth to argue but he pointed at the chair. "Go, Paige!" His voice rose this time and she gave him a dirty look before stomping over to her chair. Jake sighed before returning to his own seat. He hoped this long day was almost over.

Almost half an hour later a loud commotion could be heard coming from the bottom of the ladder. Sara glanced at Paige who shrugged her shoulders. They both turned to watch Colonel Ravencraft hobble off the ladder with a wad of plastic wrap in his hand. Behind him, two other men followed. Sara pulled her knees up to her chest and shook her hair forward to cover her face as she glanced over at Jake. He was already standing and watching the colonel with a stone-faced expression.

"I want this man arrested!" The colonel demanded as he threw the wad of plastic wrap at Jake's feet. "He has assaulted a superior officer. Sergeant Fields, take him into custody."

Sergeant Fields shifted under the colonel's glare but made no move toward Jake.

"Now colonel sir, I think we need to ascertain a few facts before we arrest anyone," the third man said with a thick southern drawl and a light chuckle.

"Major Vollen, I don't see what the issue is. The plastic wrap that caused me to fall down the stairs did not appear by chance," Ravencraft snapped at the major.

Vollen looked down at the colonel. He stood an easy six three with dark bronze skin, brown eyes, and was built like a football linebacker. He could be quite intimidating but most of the time had a refreshingly calm demeanor.

"I'm sure it didn't sir," he replied. "Sergeant Fields, you were present with the colonel when he took his unfortunate tumble, were you not?"

"Yes sir, I was present."

"Did you see anyone else in the vicinity when the colonel fell?" Vollen asked.

"I didn't see anyone else."

"Very good sergeant," Vollen said as he faced the colonel again.

"What difference does that make?" The colonel snapped with a scowl. "Someone had to put it there."

"Well sir, since none of these lovely people appear to have plastic wrap in their hands, I'd say we're missing the needed evidence to make an arrest at this time."

The colonel glared at the major as his face began to turn red, "Fine, I won't pursue the assault on myself, but I won't let the assault of the young lady go unpunished." A triumphant gleam flashed in the colonel's eyes.

Sara pulled her knees tighter to her chest when three sets of eyes shifted to her. She looked down at her hands.

"That's her," the colonel continued with a smug smile.

"It wasn't Jake." Her voice was quiet but firm. She would not allow this man to blame Jake even if she was afraid of him. Her gaze flicked to Jake from behind her bangs. He was watching her and gave her a barely perceptible reassuring nod before she garnered enough courage to look back at the colonel.

Major Vollen noticed the subtle interaction, "What did happen to you, young lady? I can see you've got a nice shiner there." She peeked up at him before taking a deep breath. She was trembling with nerves.

"I fell," she whispered before looking back at her hands. Vollen nodded as a frown crossed his face. He already figured out who really was at fault by watching her reactions to Ravencraft.

"Do you need medical attention?" He asked, his voice gentle.

"No," she whispered before she glanced at Jake again. Once she responded to him, Vollen looked over at Jake.

"It sounds like we have all this figured ou--."

"What?" The colonel exclaimed. "You can't leave it at this! He's getting away with everything."

Vollen spun in place and moved closer to the colonel so he was forced to crane his neck to look up at him.

"Sir, as far as I can tell, without definite confirmation from the young lady, you would be the only one in trouble if we continued with this. The young lady wishes for it to end now and you should thank your lucky stars," the major snapped, his eyes flashing with anger. The colonel just stared up at him in stunned silence. "As of now, with everything that has happened with this flight, from the load shift and the instrumentation failure, no one is going anywhere without an escort."

"You can't confine me," the colonel snapped.

"As long as you are on my plane, sir, yes I can. I don't care if you have to take a leak, it will be accompanied by one of my crew." Vollen looked over at Fields. "Sergeant, escort the colonel back to his seat."

Fields gestured to the ladder, "This way please, sir." The colonel gave Vollen one last furious glare before limping down the ladder. Once the colonel was gone, the major turned to look at Jake with a grin.

"Oh, my my, you sure know how to make some enemies my friend," he said with a laugh as he slapped Jake on the back.

Jake gave a weak smile in return as he let out a huge sigh, "I'm so lucky this happened now, and I had you to help me out."

"Darn right!" The major laughed again. Paige and Sara were both watching the interaction with curiosity and Jake noticed the looks.

"Major Vollen is a buddy of mine," he said. Vollen nodded at Jake's statement.

"Ever since he saved me from getting in huge trouble by sewing up a… well… we'll just say a party injury," the major said with a grin.

Jake shook his head at the memory. "Yeah, a party injury," he said with a chuckle. "That is probably the best thing to say." Vollen let out a hearty laugh.

"You've done plenty more to help me out over the years."

Jake nodded before it appeared like a sudden thought occurred to him, "By the way what did you mean about the instrument failure you mentioned earlier?"

"For about twenty minutes I was flyin' blind. Every instrument we had all died at once."

"All of them?" Jake could not keep the shock out of his voice.

"Yup, every single one," Vollen said, his tone becoming serious. "It's never happened to me in ten years of flyin' and I hope it never does again."

"I wonder what caused that," Jake mused aloud.

"I don't know. We had to replace almost every circuit breaker to get them to power up. It had to be some kind of major power surge."

"That's pretty strange. I mean with all the fail-safes."

Sara got a sudden cold shiver while she listened to them talk when she realized that she could have caused the plane to crash.

"Major Vollen, you're needed back in the cockpit." A call over the intercom system echoed around the room from the multiple speakers in the cabin and the atmosphere in the room changed in an instant.

"I'll send someone up with a radio in case you need anything," Vollen said as he started down the ladder. "Don't go anywhere without an escort."

"Thanks, Stan, I owe you one," Jake called after him. They heard a laugh from the bottom of the ladder.

"I know!"

After the major left and silence fell over the room Jake looked over at the girls. Sara was still curled in a ball in her chair with her head on her knees. She was shaking from head to toe. Paige, having time to start processing, sat with wide eyes from the events that had just taken place. Jake sat down in the seat between them before he put an arm around each of them.

"Come here you two," he said, his voice soft. He could tell that they were both struggling to deal with what had just happened. Sara could not help but lean against him. She was comforted by his warmth. Paige just sat there still staring at the ladder.

"I'm so sorry," she said. "I had no idea he'd try to arrest you." Her eyes were rimmed with tears when she looked at her brother. Jake rubbed her arm with his hand.

"I don't tell you things without a reason," he said. "You have to start thinking about the consequences of your actions." She sniffed and nodded before resting her head on his shoulder. "And you," he continued as he looked down at Sara. "Why did you go with the colonel? Didn't you know that wasn't a good idea?"

Sara raised her head so that her chin was resting on her knees and she could look up at him, "I didn't want to cause you any problems. I thought if I refused it would have been worse. I didn't think he'd actually do something." She paused. "I guess I was wrong." Her voice was quiet, but every word rang of honesty. Jake tightened his arm around her.

"Try to be more careful," he said before he paused. His gaze became gentle and grateful. "And thank you for standing up for me. I'm sure that wasn't easy."

"I couldn't let them do anything bad to you," she whispered without thinking. After a moment, Sara realized what she had just said and flushed red. Glancing up at him, she noticed he was regarding her with a complex expression. She looked away and tried to scoot over in the seat further from him, but he did not loosen his grip.

Moments later he exhaled loudly and pulled both of his arms back from around the girls.

"It has been a long flight so far and we still have about nine hours until we make it to Washington. Why don't you two try and get some sleep?" He made a move to stand up.

"Please don't move, I was comfortable," Paige protested. "And you were keeping me warm, right Sara?"

The flush on Sara's face darkened but she nodded without looking up. Jake appeared conflicted for a moment before he eased back into the chair again. He put his arms back around the girls.

"Okay," he said in a quiet resigned voice. The two girls leaned back against him and were both asleep within minutes. Jakes listened to their slow, rhythmic breathing as he rested his head back against the seat and looked up at the roof of the plane. He remained this way for a little while before he glanced down at his sister. She was such a handful he was not sure what he was going to do with her. These pranks of hers were not going to go over well in the adult world.

She suddenly let out a loud snore in her sleep. Jake grinned and chuckled. He knew she would have been mortified if she knew. Jake watched her for a few moments longer before he glanced down at Sara. His mind went momentarily blank as he looked at her. With a gentle hand, he brushed a section of her bangs out of her face and tucked it behind her ear, and almost involuntarily kissed the top of her head. A split second later he realized what he had just done and jerked back from her. He stared up at the ceiling as he chastised himself.

"What in the world am I doing?" He muttered. "She is way too young, moron." He shook his head when noise on the ladder pulled him out of his thoughts.

"Captain?" A voice said. Jake glanced at the girls before he lifted an arm and pressed a finger against his lips.

"Shhh."

The man grimaced, "Sorry sir. Here is the radio Major Vollen asked me to bring you." He whispered so he did not wake the girls.

"Set it over there," Jake whispered as he indicated his chair. The man walked over and put the radio down on the chair.

"Major Vollen also wants everyone to wear their seat belts. We will be encountering a storm soon." Jake nodded in response and the man headed back down the ladder.

A short time later a loud crack of thunder caused Sara to jump in her sleep. Jake glanced down to see if it had woke her, but it did not. He wondered what she was dreaming about, but he did not dwell on it long before he closed his eyes and tried to take a nap.

Sara was nervous about falling asleep next to Jake, but the events of the day had taken their toll, and she was exhausted. The warmth radiating from him and the smell of his bodywash caused her to relax. She only lasted a few minutes after she closed her eyes. Her mind drifted into a peaceful, dreamless sleep until a loud crack of thunder changed that.

She suddenly found herself looking around a strange forest in the midst of a torrential downpour. Her brows furrowed in thought when she realized this looked just like the forest she had seen before. She started walking along a path that ran through the trees when she spotted a glimpse of a girl running. It only took her a few seconds to realize she was looking at the young woman she had seen before, but this time she looked like she was still a teenager. As the girl ran a young boy appeared at her side. He was also a teenager.

"We have to hurry," he said as he grabbed the girls' hand and pulled her after him. She went with him with no protest. Sara hurried to follow them.

"What are we going to do?" The girl asked, her voice filled with panic.

The boy pushed his silver hair out of his face, "Run. I think if we can get near the cliff and I transform we can get away that way." The girl was already shaking her head.

"We cannot," she said. "You cannot transform that well yet. You might not even be able to."

The boy grimaced at her response.

*"Look ***," he said. "I have to get you out of here and I do not know any other way to do it."*

Sara noticed when the boy tried to say her name it was like the memory cut out. She thought that was strange and wondered what could cause the name to be scrambled.

"But…" The girl started to protest when a large orc leapt out in the path in front of them. The boy turned to the left, pulling her with him, and continued to run as fast as he could. The girl tried to keep up, but she was shorter than he was and could not keep up with his long strides. She stumbled and lost her grip on his hand causing her to fall face first into the muddy ground. Rolling onto her side, she barely managed to get out of the way of the large sword the orc slammed into the ground next to her. She rolled again to try and get back to her feet, but the slope was too steep, and she started sliding down the hill toward the edge of the cliff. She pulled a small dagger out of her boot and stabbed it hard into the ground to try and slow her fall. The ground

was so rain-soaked that the dagger could not bite into anything and slid through the ground like butter. Releasing the dagger, she clawed at the ground frantically trying to stop.

*"****!" She cried as she slipped over the edge. The boy ran toward the edge of the cliff and did not hesitate as he jumped off after her.*

Sara gasped in shock. He just jumped off? She hurried to the edge and saw that it was a fifteen-foot drop to where the teenagers landed. On either side of the small ledge they landed on was a hundred- and fifty-foot drop. The girl was holding her ankle and her face was etched with pain.

"Are you all right?" The boy asked as he hurried to her side.

"I think I broke my ankle," she replied as she tried to stand on it and it would not hold her weight.

A sudden loud laugh brought their attention back to the top of the cliff where the orc was standing.

"Look what we have here. Little birds stuck in a nest. Watch out for that fall little birds," he growled at them from above. The boy stood in front of the girl trying to protect her as the orc started lobbing large stones at them.

"I will try to transform," he said as he closed his eyes. His entire body started to glow while he concentrated but nothing changed. A few moments later he let out a heavy sigh and sat down with a plop.

"I cannot do it," he said breathing heavily. He looked up and saw a small force wall between them and the orc. The orc's rocks were bouncing off it, but the girl was starting to breathe heavy from the exertion of holding the field in place. The two of them looked at each other with a resigned look. They were trapped.

"We will jump," the boy said.

"But we will die," she answered. Fear flashed across her face and he grabbed her hand.

"We die if we stay here," he replied. "At least we have a chance if we jump."

She hesitated before she nodded, and they jumped from the ledge. Sara reached out as if to try and stop them but found herself falling right along with them. The boy wrapped his arms around the girl as they fell, and she held onto him.

A few seconds before they hit the ground an enormous silver claw appeared from above them and plucked them out of the sky. Sara looked up in shock and saw a huge silver dragon fly away. Before she had a chance to look back down, she landed on her back in a flower filled field beside a black obelisk. She looked around in confusion before getting back to her feet. Wondering where she was now, she moved around the black obelisk and found the young woman sitting on the ground in front of it. This time she was an adult again. Sara looked up at the stone and could not read any of it, but a finely carved image of a silver dragon caught her attention. Then there was another loud crash of thunder.

Sara awoke with a sudden gasp and sat up so fast that she fell out of the chair and onto the floor.

"I think that is me." She heard the voice say in her head.

"Who are you?" She cried.

"I do not know."

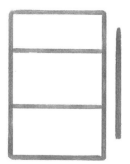

Sara sat in her seat with her head on her knees. She was mortified by what happened after she woke up and wished she could sink into the seat and disappear. Jake, who had been half asleep, was startled awake when she sat up. He tried to grab her, so she did not fall, but was too slow and all he accomplished was causing all three of them to end up on the floor in a tangled heap.

"Who were you talking about?" Jake asked again from where he was sitting on the other side of the cabin.

"It was just a dream," Sara replied without looking up. Since she had cried out when she fell to someone who was not there, Jake was worried she might have hurt her head more than he thought. She already told him several times it was just a dream. Shaking her head, she almost rolled her eyes. There was no way she could tell him she was hearing a voice in her head.

"Okay everyone," Paige said, her voice annoyingly loud as she clapped her hands together. Sara jumped at the sudden noise and looked up at her with a frown. "I think we have established it was just a dream. Let's enjoy the little bit of the flight we have left. I mean we should be arriving anytime now." She grinned at her brother and Sara when she stopped talking. They both just stared at her before returning to their own individual thoughts. Paige glanced back and forth between them before she sighed. They were no fun.

A few minutes later a private appeared at the top of the ladder to inform everyone that they would be landing soon. The three of them moved around the cabin and secured their belongings before returning to their seats. Not long after they finished the plane began its descent into the Seattle, Washington area, and made its landing without incident at Fort Lewis army base.

Once the plane stopped moving Sergeant Fields poked his head above the top of the ladder and motioned for them to follow him. He seemed nervous which caused Paige and Sara to share confused glances. Jake did not appear to be fazed by this and he jumped out of his seat. After grabbing his bag, he went straight to the ladder.

"Let's go," he said as he followed Fields.

"Don't we have to wait for the plane to unload first like usual?" Paige asked as she grabbed her stuff to follow Jake. Her brother smiled.

"Not today." A look of suspicion flashed across Paige's face as she and Sara followed Jake. Something was not right, and she wondered what was going on. Once the three made it off the ladder they headed for the back of the plane. The large cargo doors were open, and the crew was unloading what had been hidden under the tarp. It was Jake's jeep.

"Are you kidding me?" Paige exclaimed with a roll of her eyes. "Did you seriously smuggle your jeep on the plane?"

"I have no idea what you are talking about," Jake said with a smug smile. "According to the manifest there was no vehicle on this flight." He quickened his pace and hurried to his car. After throwing his bag in the back he looked around.

"Let's go, Let's go," he said as he motioned to the jeep. Paige and Sara rushed over and tossed their things in before climbing into the back seat. Jake glanced back at Fields. The sergeant gave him a thumbs up with a large grin. Jake returned the thumbs up before he got into the driver's seat. Once he started the jeep, they headed off the tarmac toward the nearest road. He drove through the base and out the front gate before he headed southwest toward the city of Olympia. When they reached the city, Jake found a gas station and pulled into the parking lot. Sara glanced up from the book she was reading in time to catch Jake attempt to stifle a huge yawn.

"I'm going to get a coffee," Jake said as he opened the door of the jeep. "I'll be right back." Sara frowned when she could see the dark circles under his eyes when he turned to walk away.

"Hey Paige," she said. "Jake looked really tired."

Paige glanced at her brother's back as he entered the building, "You know I don't think he's slept since we left, and he had to work the night shift before graduation." She frowned as she spoke.

"That's almost two days," Sara said, her voice filled with worry.

"Plus, who knows how long he's been up before that. He works the night shift and then studies during the day. Sleep is an afterthought to him." Paige folded her arms over her chest before she looked over at Sara with a mischievous grin. "I will just have to drive then." She climbed into the driver's seat before her brother got back to the jeep.

"He'll let you drive?" Sara could not keep the surprise out of her voice.

Paige nodded, "I just have to give him the proper motivation. Let me drive or spend the rest of the day in this parking lot." She laughed at the disbelieving look on Sara's face. "It will work." Sara just shook her head. She could not imagine that Jake was going to be pleased with this idea.

A few minutes later, Jake walked out of the gas station with a large coffee in hand. About halfway across the parking lot, he stopped when he saw Paige sitting in his seat. He tilted his head to the side with a disapproving look as he walked the rest of the way.

"What're you doing?" He asked as he pulled open the door.

"Can't you tell?" Paige said with a large smile. "I'm driving."

Jake was already shaking his head no before she even finished, "Oh no, you aren't driving my jeep."

Paige's grin slipped into a pleasant smile and Jake narrowed his eyes.

"We aren't going anywhere unless I drive. You look exhausted and need to sleep."

"Paig--."

"Sara even thinks you look tired. She's the one who brought it up."

Sara tried her best to focus on the book in her hand but could not help but glance up when she felt Jake's eyes switch to her. He regarded her for a moment before he looked back at his sister. When he sighed the grin returned to Paige's face and she held out her hand for the keys. He hesitated before he handed them to her.

"If you put a scratch on my jeep you're dead," he grumbled as he walked around the front of the car.

"I know, I know," Paige said with a roll of her eyes. "Wait, what're you doing?" She gave him a funny look when he started removing the front passenger seat from the vehicle.

"If I throw this in the back I can sit in the back and stretch out," he said. "May as well be comfortable while my life is in danger." He grinned when he saw the scowl that appeared on his sister's face.

Once he finished pulling the seat free, he put it in the very back with the bags before climbing into the backseat next to Sara. She glanced at him out of the corner of her eye while she tried to continue pretending to read. He did not notice as he fastened his seatbelt and stretched out his long legs. Paige glanced back at him before she started the car and headed back onto the interstate heading south.

"You do remember how to get to Uncle Steve's, right?" Jake asked through a large yawn.

"Yeah, I got it. North of Denver," Paige replied. After she answered Jake leaned his head against the side of the jeep and was asleep within minutes.

Paige waited a little while before she peeked in the rearview mirror. She watched her brother before another grin crossed her face.

"Okay, I'm sure he's out now," she said. "So spill, what really happened on the plane? Was it a dream or what?"

Sara could not help but glance at Jake before she scooted forward in her seat, until her face was even with Paige. When she did not start talking right away Paige started tapping her thumbs on the steering wheel.

"Come on spill!" Her voice raised, and Sara frowned.

"Shhh," Sara hissed. "You don't want to wake him up."

Paige laughed, "He'll be out for hours so don't worry about it. This always happens when he's been up too long. He will usually sleep for almost a day."

Sara looked over at Jake again just to be sure before she bit her lip. She was not sure she really wanted to tell Paige everything, but she needed to talk to someone.

"It was a dream," she began in a hesitant voice. "But, I think I am seeing someone's memories. That and I keep hearing a voice in my head. It has happened a couple times since the festival."

"What?" Paige gasped, in surprise. "Tell me everything!"

Sara hesitated again before she told Paige about the dream and the times she had heard the voice speak to her. She even told her about the rest of the events that took place on the plane. When she was finished Paige kept glancing between the road and her. Her eyes burned with curiosity, but Sara could also see a hint of fear. It was the same look she got from all the people who thought she was so weird.

When Paige did not say anything right away Sara just shrugged and slid back in her seat. She started to fidget with the coat that was draped across her lap. It took a little while before Paige seemed to sort through everything Sara told her, and her full curiosity returned.

"I wonder who it could be," she mused aloud as she looked in the rearview mirror again and made eye contact with Sara.

"I don't know," Sara said.

Paige frowned before she glanced out the front of the jeep, "Whoa!" She yelped as she jerked the wheel hard to the right to miss the slower moving car in front of them. The force of the sudden swerve caused Jake to slide over in his sleep and his head landed on Sara's leg.

"Guess I should pay more attention," Paige said with a sheepish grin. "He would kill me if he saw how close I just came t--."

"Your brother fell over," Sara exclaimed, her voice filled with panic.

Paige glanced back over her shoulder. "He's still asleep," she said with a giggle. "He really can sleep through anything."

Sara was bright red and refused to look down at Jake, "He can't stay here." Her voice was filled with nerves and she was holding her right arm up to keep from touching him more than necessary.

"Why not? I mean you like him, right?" Paige asked with a grin.

"I don't even know where to put my arm!" Sara squeaked. Her face was so red Paige could not help but start laughing.

"Just rest it on his shoulder or something. He won't care."

"How could he not care?" Sara asked and could not bring herself to put her arm down. Paige was laughing so hard at this point she had tears in her eyes.

"Oh, come on, Sara. He likes you," she said between gasps for breath. "I swear the two of you are so clueless."

Sara just stared at her in disbelief, "There's no way th--."

"He does," Paige interrupted. "I don't think he wants to admit it to himself yet, but he definitely does. He acts so different around you it's pretty funny to watch."

"No way," she said, almost like she was trying to convince herself. "No way."

Paige shook her head as she continued taking deep breaths to try to stop laughing but was not succeeding.

"Believe what you want," she said with a giggle. "But you'll see, just wait."

Sara, at a loss for what else to do, wrapped her arms around herself and leaned as far away from Jake as she could get. She knew she could not move him on her own and Paige was going to be no help. Once she was leaning against the side of the jeep she could not keep from looking back down at Jake. She shook her head. There was no way he would like her. A fleeting look of sadness crossed her face before she tilted her head. He looked so peaceful in his sleep.

A couple hours later, Sara wished that she could fall asleep too. The pain reliever she took on the plane was wearing off and her head and hand were both throbbing. She closed her eyes again and tried to go to sleep, but Paige's singing kept that from being an option. With a heavy sigh, she turned her attention to the scenery streaking by the car and allowed her mind to wander. She managed to deal with the pain until well after sunset but once it became dark, she had nothing else to focus on. The pain in her head was now so bad that the rocking of the car was starting to make her car sick. She fidgeted trying to get comfortable, but her head and the leg Jake was laying on ached.

"Paige, we need to stop soon, please," she whispered.

"Can you hold on just a little longer? We'll be there soon, and we really need to make it before Jake wakes up."

Normally Sara would have wondered what she meant by that, but right now she did not care. She rolled down her window, to get some fresh air on her face, hoping that would help.

"Yikes, Sara, that's cold!" Paige yelped when the sudden inrush of cold air caused her to shiver. Sara laid her head on the door by the open window.

"I'm sorry," she mumbled. "I just feel very sick."

Paige reached back and handed her a bottle of water, "Will this help?" Sara shrugged and took a small sip of the water. It seemed to help for a moment but a second later she knew she was going to be sick. She did not have time to say anything and she put her head out the window.

"Whoa! Are you okay?" Paige called back to her. Sara could not respond as she continued vomiting out the window. She was startled when she felt a gentle hand pull her hair back from her face.

Jake woke up the moment she started being sick and he was watching her with a look of concern, but he did not say anything until she was finished and sat back in her seat.

"Are you okay?" She shook her head no.

"My head and the rocking," she managed to whisper.

Jake nodded in understanding and motioned for her to lay down on the seat, "Laying down might help until we can stop."

At this point, Sara felt so bad that she did not even feel embarrassed when she laid down on the backseat. Jake reached behind them and grabbed his jacket. He folded it and had her lay her head on it before he reached across her and rolled up the window.

"If you feel sick again tell me," he said. She barely nodded and her eyes were closed while she tried to relax. Jake watched her for a moment before he took a moment to glance around them. His brows furrowed, "Where are we? Where are the mountains?"

"Well," Paige began in an innocent voice. "It is kind of a road trip. We needed to go somewhere cool."

"Where are we?" Jake demanded as he glared at her.

Paige grimaced and began tapping the steering wheel but did not answer. Jake was about to ask again when he caught sight of a road sign. Fifty miles to San Francisco.

"San Francisco," he gasped as his mouth dropped open. "Why are we almost in San Francisco?"

"It's Sara's birthday tomorrow and we have to do something to celebrate," Paige stumbled over her words as she talked very fast. "Plus, this is our first real road trip, so we had to do something awesome."

Jake pinched the bridge of his nose as he took a deep breath, "Paige, what is wrong with you? You know that I have to report to the new base soon. We can't be on some extended vacation!"

"Oh, you have plenty of time. You always plan too much time, and besides I only planned for a couple of days anyway," she snapped, raising her voice.

"That's not the point," he said, trying to keep his voice level. "This is completely irresponsible and s--."

"Oh right, I want to have fun once in a while, so of course, that makes it irresponsible," she yelled at him.

"Yes, it does." He frowned when he had to raise his voice to be heard over her.

Sara flinched at the noise from the raised voices and covered her ears with her hands. The yelling was making her head throb worse. Jake noticed her movement out of the corner of his eye, and he glanced down at her.

"Paige," he said, his voice much quieter.

"You're always like this! Why can't we ever…," she continued to rant.

"Paige," he tried again but she continued to ignore him. Jake clenched his jaw in frustration before he reached down and placed his hand over Sara's.

"Paige," he yelled. The suddenness of his shout caused Paige to jump, but she stopped talking. "You need to stop yelling and we'll finish this later." Jake continued in a quieter voice. Paige glanced back and saw Jake's hand covering Sara's hand and ear.

"Oh, Sara I'm sorry," she said. "I forgot you weren't feeling good." Sara only nodded and did not open her eyes.

"How much farther?"

"I think another forty-five minutes," Paige replied but she did not appear like she was sure.

"Stop at the next exit."

Paige crossed all the lanes of traffic to get off the interstate. She headed to the first small convenience store she saw and pulled into the parking lot.

"See if you can get some liquid pain reliever and some instant ice packs," Jake said as he handed her his wallet. "And nothing else." He added when Paige started to walk away from the jeep. She rolled her eyes before she walked into the store. A couple minutes later Paige returned with a small bag. She pulled open the backseat door and was surprised to see Jake still in the back.

"Aren't you driving now that you are awake?"

"No," he said, his voice unpleased. "I have to take care of your friend. Plus, I have no idea where we are going." His face clouded with disapproval as he held out his hand for the bag and his wallet. Paige narrowed her eyes in annoyance but managed to bite her tongue as she handed him the stuff she was holding. After he took them, she climbed back into the driver's seat. Once they were back on the interstate Jake gave Sara some of the pain reliever, and she remained laying on the seat.

"Here this might help too," he said as he handed her an ice pack. She took it and laid it on her forehead. The cold was a welcomed relief to her throbbing head. It was not long before the medicine started to relieve the pain and she began to doze off. She was vaguely aware of Jake picking up the ice pack when she dropped it and putting it back on her forehead. She drifted deeper into sleep.

The cool hand felt good on her forehead. An elven man looked down at his daughter in bed before looking at his wife.

"Will she be all right?" He asked, his voice filled with worry.

His wife smiled and nodded, "She will be fine. It is just a little fever. You worry too much."

The little girl looked up at her father.

"Qinaros, "she said in a whisper. "Please stay."

"Of course, child," he said with a smile. He placed his hand back on her forehead and brushed silver curls out of her face.

"Sara... Sara," Jake called while he shook her by the shoulder to wake her up.

"Qinaros," she mumbled before she woke up all the way. She rubbed her eyes and sat up to find Jake watching her with a raised eyebrow.

"What?" She asked in confusion when she noticed that Paige was also giving her a funny look.

"What does qinaros mean?" Jake asked.

Sara stared at him for a moment, "I have no idea."

Paige and Jake exchanged glances, but Jake decided not to press for any more information.

"Well, we're here at the hotel Paige apparently booked for us," he said giving his sister an unhappy stare. "And since it's midnight already we may as well stay the night."

The three of them gathered their things and headed into the hotel. The girls were in one room with an adjoined room for Jake. Once they were inside, they were so exhausted they all went straight to bed.

The next morning Paige talked to Sara about all the places she had figured out for them to do. She was exuding excitement as she talked. Sara listened while she changed the dressing on her hand.

"So, what do you think?" Sara finished taping the gauze before she looked at her friend.

"I think it sounds like a lot," she said. "Are you sure Jake is even going to let us stay?"

Paige gave her a *come-on* look, "It's your birthday, of course, he will let us stay." Sara shook her head. She was not sure he would be so generous since he was still very unhappy with his sister.

"What about your uncle," Sara asked. "Wasn't he expecting us to arrive today?"

"I already called him and let him know that we wouldn't be there for a few days, "Paige replied with a smile. "See, I think of everything."

"And what were you planning to have happen with your brother?" Paige pouted at the sarcasm in Sara's voice.

"Okay, okay, okay maybe I didn't think of everything. I always underestimate how mad he gets," she said with a giggle.

Sara rolled her eyes. She knew Paige never thought about the consequences. She was shaking her head when a soft knock on the adjoining door drew her attention.

"And speak of the devil," Paige said with a grin as she skipped over and opened the door. "Good morning, big brother." Her voice dripped with sweetness.

"Morning."

"Aww, don't be like that," she said with a frown. "We're going to have tons of fun today!"

"We aren't staying Paige. We have to get to Uncle Steve's," Jake replied, his face blank as stone. He appeared like he prepared to have this conversation ahead of time.

"What?" Paige snapped. "We aren't leaving yet! We have so much to do before we can leave." She started listing all the things she had told Sara earlier in the morning. Sara watched as Jake lost his patience when he tried several times to interject a comment, but Paige would not let him. He finally stood there regarding her in complete silence. It took Paige several minutes to notice that her brother was no longer talking, and she glanced over at him. He was giving her a look of disapproval.

"Oh, come on Jak--."

"No, we're leaving," he said, his voice hard. Paige gave him a calculating look when he turned to walk back to his room.

"Are you really going to make Sara spend her birthday in a car all day?" she asked. Jake paused, and Paige grinned. "I mean especially since she was so sick yesterday." She knew she got to him as soon as he paused, and her grin widened.

Sara narrowed her eyes in irritation as she watched the interaction. She did not like being used so Paige could get what she wanted. After a few moments, Jake turned around and looked over at Sara.

"How are you this morning?" he asked. There was genuine concern in his voice and Sara looked down at the ground as she flushed a light pink.

"I still have a headache but I'm fine. I took the pain reliever already," she said before giving Paige a dirty look. "We don't have to stay if you need to get to Colorado soon." Paige only rolled her eyes in response. Jake watched the interaction and appeared to be debating. He did realize his sister had a point about Sara's headache, but he knew she was just using it as an excuse to get what she wanted. He really hated the idea of letting Paige think she had won.

"It's okay," he replied with a sigh. "I think it would probably be best if we stayed here until tomorrow. It gives you a day to help get over the headache without being stuck in the jeep."

"Yes!" Paige squealed. "Out Jake!! Sara and I have to get ready to see the city!" She shoved her brother toward the door.

"We will go see a few things, but if Sara needs to come back, we will come back," he said, his voice firm.

"I know, I know," she muttered but she was already not really paying attention to him. Jake shook his head.

"Let me know when you two are ready to go," he said before he pulled the door closed behind him.

Paige skipped over to her bag and started pulling out clothes," Let's get ready."

About forty-five minutes later both girls were ready to go. Paige went and knocked on Jake's door, "We're ready." Jake walked through the door and rolled his eyes when he saw his sister. She was dressed in an all black tank top with a lace up back, camouflage pants that had random zippers up and down the legs, combat boots, and her black leather jacket. Her short brown hair was an asymmetrical bob which she had styled to flip out in multiple directions.

"So freaky as usual," Jake said in a goading tone. Paige gave him a dirty look.

"And you look boring as usual," she quipped back with a sweet smile.

Jake opened his mouth to reply with a sarcastic comment but was interrupted when Sara walked back into the room from the bathroom. She was dressed noticeably different than Paige. She wore a navy-blue dress, that was ruched along the sides and ended mid-thigh, with white and navy ruffles along the bottom, white capri length leggings, navy blue flats with small daisies, and a dark green military style jacket. Her shoulder length red hair was pulled back in a ponytail with a side swept bang. Paige did her makeup so the bruises on her face were almost completely hidden.

Jake tilted his head as he watched her cross the room. When Sara noticed his gaze, she flushed a brilliant red.

"All right," Paige said, raising her voice to get their attention. "Let's go."

They left the room and headed out of the hotel. Sara sighed as she followed behind Jake. He looked good in regular clothes too. She was used to always seeing him in his military fatigues, but today he wore a pair of jeans with a button-down navy shirt, brown hiking boots, and his brown leather jacket. His hair was its usual messy look.

"Oh, by the way, happy birthday," Jake said interrupting her thoughts.

"Thank you," she said with a shy smile.

"You're the same age as Paige now, right?"

"No, I'm older than Paige," she almost whispered. "I'm twenty today." She trailed off when she saw the confusion flash across his face.

"But yo--."

"It is a long story," Sara muttered. "My mom didn't want me to go to school. She wanted me to tend the shrine and it took my dad two years to talk her into letting me go."

"Oh," Jake responded. He had no idea that she was older than he thought. He started to ask another question when he noticed that she was looking back down at the floor. With a frown, he turned his attention back to where they were going.

After leaving the hotel, they headed around Fisherman's Warf. Paige found a laser challenge that she insisted they do. Sara was not the most coordinated and came in last on the first several attempts. Jake teamed up with her after that and with his help she managed to beat Paige. Once Sara beat her, she pouted and wanted to move on. After the laser challenge, they spent several hours at the Aquarium of the Bay, which Sara enjoyed. She loved seeing the variety of sea life. Next, much to Paige's displeasure, they made their way to the USS Pampanito, which was a fully restored WWII submarine. Jake insisted they at least stop by one of the two WWII attraction. By the time they were done, it was already evening, and they headed back toward the hotel.

"Did you have fun today?" Jake asked while they were walking. Sara only nodded in response since she was tired and ready to rest. Her head was still bothering her, but she did not want to complain.

"No, "Paige whined. "You guys really are no fun. We should've ridden the Darkride roller coaster or gone to Alcatraz."

"I don't think Sara would have enjoyed those," he said with a knowing look. "And wasn't this supposed to be for her birthday?"

"Yeah, I know," Paige grumbled.

Jake chuckled at her before they fell silent. Once they arrived back at the hotel the girls and Jake went back to their separate rooms. Paige tossed her jacket on the bed and went to her bag again.

"Present time," she said.

Sara sat down on her bed as Paige handed her two boxes. She opened the larger of the two first. It was a book of Irish sheet music for the violin.

"Thanks," she said with a smile. "I needed new music since I've already learned everything I had at home."

"I know," Paige said as Sara reached for the second box. "And just so you know, that one is from Jake. He told me to tell you it was from me too." A sly smile crossed her face.

Sara paused as she stared at the box before she opened it. Inside was a small delicate white gold charm bracelet. There were several different charms on it. A small violin, willow tree, music note, and a single bloomed rose. Sara smiled as she looked at it.

"Aww, that's cute," Paige said as she looked over her shoulder. Sara held the box up, so she could see it better. "See I told you," Paige added when she walked away. This time Sara did not argue she just smiled.

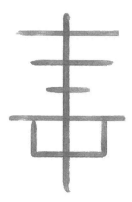

Early the following morning Jake, Paige, and Sara headed out from San Francisco for Colorado. It was an uneventful two-day drive since Jake was back in control of travel plans, and they reached their destination in good time.

Leaving the narrow two-lane road, they drove up a steep mountain gravel driveway and pulled up to a cabin in the late afternoon of the second day. The one and a half story log cabin was nestled among large pine trees. It was constructed from trees on the property, which gave it a rustic feel. There were large windows all along the cabin and a wrap-around front porch with a swing that gave a place to enjoy the beautiful view of the surrounding forest.

When they climbed out of the jeep an older gentleman with blond hair and the same blue-grey eyes as Jake and Paige walked out the front door. He had a large smile on his face.

"Kids," he called. "It's so good to see you. It has been far too long."

Paige ran up the steps and gave him a huge hug. Her uncle chuckled when he had to peel her off him. She frowned until she noticed Sara standing at the bottom of the steps.

"Oh," Paige said with a grin. "Uncle Steve, this is my friend Sara."

"Hi," Sara said, her voice quiet.

"Nice to meet you," Steve said. His mannerisms were warm and welcoming. He turned to Jake and gave him a hug before he beckoned for them to follow him into the house. "The two downstairs bedrooms are set up for the girls and Jake, I set up the office for you. I hope that will be okay."

"Of course," Jake said with a smile. "We'll stay wherever you have room." His uncle patted him on the shoulder.

"I assume all of you'd like to get settled, so I will head upstairs to the living room. Come find me when you are all set."

They all nodded and headed back out to the jeep to get their things. Sara carried hers to the first of the downstairs bedrooms. She walked inside and smiled. The room had two, floor to ceiling, windows that provided an unobstructed view of the mountains. There was a large stone fireplace on the back wall and a large, thick black rug covering the light brown wood floor. Situated on the rug was a large queen-sized bed made from more logs, and a wooden dresser.

She set her bag down next to the dresser and looked out the window. The smile did not leave her face as she stared at the massive trees just on the other side of the window. She was already missing the forest around her home in Japan, so this was a nice distraction. It took her several minutes to be able to pull herself away from the view. Once she did, she left her room and headed down the hallway to go see Paige's room. She stopped when she heard Jake's voice coming from Paige's room.

"I said we would talk about things later," he said. "Let's go up with uncle Steve."

Sara ducked back into her room just as the two left Paige's room and headed upstairs. It was not long before she could hear raised voices through the floor.

"Paige, you have to think about other people and not just yourself," Jake said.

"I do think about other people," Paige snapped back at him.

"That drive to California," he said, struggling to keep his voice level. "Who were you thinking about then? I'm sure it wasn't Sara and me."

"It was for Sara's birthday."

"No, that is just the excuse you came up with to justify your irresponsible actions. I trusted you to drive us where we needed to go."

"Wanting to have fun once in a while is not irresponsible," she yelled. "You might not be so mean if you had fun occasionally. I mean all you do is study and work!"

"I have to work. I have to support both of us."

"You aren't my dad," she continued to yell. "He has to take care of me, not you! Besides I'm eighteen now and I don't need you to take care of me."

"No, Paige," Jake said with a heavy sigh. "I have to take care of you. I have for a long time."

Sara put her hands over her ears. She could not stand listening to the fighting and looked around for a way to get away from it. Her eyes went to the windows and she decided a short walk would be the best. She hurried to her bag and pulled out a notebook. After leaving a note on Paige's bed she slipped out of the cabin.

Once she was outside, she breathed a huge breath of fresh air. She was so relieved to be away from the fighting in the house that she did not mind the light rain. Her smile returned as she gazed at the forest surrounding her. There were enormous pine trees everywhere and a few piles of snow left over from the last major storm. She closed her eyes and allowed the forest sounds to flood her senses. Her eyes opened again when the faint sound of a stream caught her attention. She headed in the direction of the sound and it was not long before a small mountain stream running down the steep slope came into view. It was barely two feet wide, but Sara watched the water flowing over the rocks for a while before she decided to follow it. She ventured deeper into the woods and before she knew it, the sun was starting to slip behind the mountains.

When she glanced up and noticed the orange glow to the sky she stopped and looked back over her shoulder. There was no indication that there was a cabin anywhere near her. With a heavy sigh, she turned around to head back when she caught sight of a cave out of the corner of her eye. Turning to face it, she stared into the blackness and took an involuntary step toward it before she stopped and hesitated. Normally, she would have been too nervous to go inside alone but she felt like something was beckoning her to come inside. Swallowing hard, she took slow steps toward the entrance.

"*Do not!*" Sara flinched when the voice yelled in her head.

"Why?" She asked out loud as she tried to peer inside the cave. When she got no answer from the voice, she started to approach the cave again.

"*No!*" Sara gasped when she was thrown backwards by a hurricane force wind. It was so strong it picked her up off the ground and hurled her toward a dead pine tree near the entrance. She slammed into it and screamed in agony when she was impaled by a large branch. Her breath came in quick gasps as she collapsed, and the branch slid back out of her stomach. She sank to the ground as blood poured from the large wound.

"*What have I done?*" The voice gasped.

Sara tried to focus on the voice as she clutched at her stomach. Darkness was already closing in on her.

"I... I am going to die," she stammered.

"*No! You must hang on. We cannot die yet!*" Sara could hear the voice calling to her but could not make sense of what she was saying. The darkness was encroaching, and she could feel her consciousness slipping away. Suddenly, she felt a strange burning and tingling sensation in her stomach and back, the darkness trying to swallow her was pushed back. She tried to make sense of what was happening but could not form a coherent thought. It took her several moments to realize the voice was speaking to her again.

"*The wound is healed. The bleeding has stopped but you must get up.*"

Sara attempted to roll onto her stomach but cried out in pain the moment she tried to move.

"The pain will fade soon but you must get out of the rain."

She tried again but collapsed back on the ground.

"Get up!"

With tears streaming down her face, Sara managed to get onto her knees, and dragged herself up the small slope to the mouth of the cave. Once she made it over the threshold she collapsed again. She wrapped her arms around herself to try and warm up. The front and back of her clothes were soaked with blood causing her to shiver in the cold. Her face was deathly pale from the blood loss. She tightened her grip and frowned when she realized it felt like she was burning with fever.

"Why?" She gasped. When the voice did not answer right away, she hit her hand on the ground in frustration. She gasped again when the impact with the ground jarred her and caused pain to lance through her body.

"I am so sorry."

"Why?" She demanded again, her voice becoming angry.

"I… I do not know. I cannot remember why, but I fear this cave."

Sara shook her head in frustration before she passed out.

***

Paige stormed down the stairs and slammed the door of her room behind her. Jake watched her leave before he sat down on the couch and rested his head on his hand. His uncle sat down next to him.

"I'm sorry," Steve said as he patted him on the back. "She has always been a handful. I would have taken you both in if I had known."

"I know," Jake said without looking up. "She really has no idea what I've had to do and give up for her. I mean I'd do it all again, but heaven help me she is so frustrating."

"Most kids don't have a clue what the adults, or in this case older brother, in their lives give up for them, but yours is not a normal case. No one should ever hand a three-year-old to a ten-year-old child and say raise them."

"No, they shouldn't," Jake said, unable to contain the bitterness in his voice. "Though, it wasn't until I was fourteen that he just quit coming home. He'd just send me money. I know he blames Paige for mom's death bu--."

"Which is not fair to both of you," his uncle said. "But all we can do now is move forward. Look at all you've accomplished since then."

"I didn't really have much of a choice," Jake replied. He started to say something more when Paige came rushing back up the stairs.

"I can't find Sara," she said as she held out a slip of paper. "She left this and said she was going for a walk. It's already dark outside."

Jake jumped up and grabbed the paper from her hand before he glanced at the clock, "We've been up here for three hours? I had no idea we were up here that long." He started to make his way for the stairs, but Steve grabbed his shoulder.

"Jake wait," he said. "You can't go out there now. It'd be too dangerous to try and look in the dark, especially since it is raining."

"I have to. I can't leave her out there all night."

Steve tightened his grip, "She could come back at any time and then we'd have to search for you instead. We don't need anyone else out there getting lost."

When Jake realized his uncle was not going to budge, he clenched his hand into a fist. He could not stand the idea of just sitting and waiting.

"I'm sure she'll be fine," his uncle continued.

"You don't know Sara," Jake replied with a shake of his head. "She seems to be a bad luck magnet." He sighed and when his uncle let go of his shoulder he headed toward the kitchen. He knew it was going to be another long night and he needed coffee.

***

Several hours passed before Sara woke with a loud groan. She looked around in confusion. She felt terrible and struggled to piece together how she had gotten in this cave. When she tried to move, and severe pain lanced through her stomach and back, the pieces started falling into place. She pushed off the floor and got into a sitting position before she leaned against the cave wall breathing heavily. Glancing down for the first time, she noticed a small fire lit beside her. Her brows furrowed when she had no idea where it came from, but she did not think about it long as she reached out and tried to hold her freezing fingers over it. With a frown, she pulled her hand back when she was shaking too bad to manage it. Her gaze shifted when the jingle of the bracelet on her wrist caught her attention.

"What am I going to tell him this time?" Her voice was laced with uncertainty and fear.

"The truth?"

"What?" Sara squeaked. "I don't know where you come from but, around here people would think I was insane." She frowned when she heard the voice chuckle.

"In my experience, the truth is always the best option."

Sara did not respond and leaned her head back against the wall. Her mind was racing as she tried to figure out what to do next. It was not long before she shook her head. She knew she needed to get back to the cabin as soon as possible. Her shivering was getting worse from the chill in the air, and she could tell she was still feverish. She glanced down at the fire and realized it was only helping a little bit since her clothes were still soaked. After debating for a few minutes more she got onto her knees and tried to stand.

Her whole head began to spin, and she grasped at the wall to keep from falling.

"Careful! You lost a lot of blood." Sara bit back a sharp reply when she heard the worry when the voice spoke this time. She ground her teeth together against the pain and took a weak step out of the cave. After only taking a few steps she knew she was not going to make it back without something to hold onto. She was too weak. Scanning the ground in the dark she spotted a large branch laying on the ground not far from her. It took her several minutes to make it over to it. Once she reached it, she pulled it up off the ground before she leaned on it.

Now that she was not in danger of falling, she took the time to look around as best she could. The rain seemed to have slowed and she could just make out the stream as she made her way toward it. When she reached it, she could barely see the flowing water in the dim moonlight that was struggling to shine through the rain clouds. Taking a deep breath, she started following the stream. She hung onto the branch with every labored step and had to stop multiple times on the way back up the slope when everything would start to spin.

"I thought you said the pain would fade soon," Sara snapped. Her hand was pressed hard to her stomach.

"I said fade, not be gone. It must be better than it was."

Sara frowned before she admitted that, yes, it had faded a little bit, but it was still more pain than she had ever experience in her life.

"Healing takes away the wound, but the pain will remain for a day or two. An injury cannot be taken away in an instant."

Sara's frown deepened before she forced her attention back to moving back up the mountain. It took her almost an hour before the lights of the cabin could be seen around the trees in the distance. She put her head down and kept moving up the slope at a crawl. When she reached the top, she paused to catch her breath. Her face clouded with worry when she realized she was about to have to face Jake. She bit her lip before she decided she would try and slip back inside without being seen. If they were still fighting it gave her a good chance.

She started moving again, but when she got closer to the cabin she noticed figures moving around in the kitchen. Adjusting her course, she headed for the front, maybe she could slip in that way without being seen. The idea of all the attention caused her to try and walk faster. She only made it about halfway when she stumbled and fell. When she landed hard on her stomach, she cried out in pain. Before she could move the door to the kitchen flew open.

"Sara?" Jake asked. He could not quite make out the figure in the dark as he approached her. She struggled to get back to her feet before he reached her.

"Yes," she stammered as she struggled to catch her breath from the exertion of standing. She clung to the branch as the world spun again. When it finally stopped, she took a few leaden steps forward so that she was visible in the lights from the cabin. As soon as Jake saw her all the color drained from his face. He closed the distance between them in an instant.

"I'm fine," she whispered when he reached her side. "Just very cold." She tried to keep walking. Jake watched her struggle for half a second before he scooped her into his arms. She cried out in pain at the sudden movement causing Jake to flinch. He could feel her shaking as he strode back inside the cabin.

"I'm fine," she repeated.

"Wha--?"

"Please just a shower so I can warm up," she said. "I'll explain everything after, I promise."

Jake gave her a long look. He could tell just by looking at her that she was burning with fever, and the sickly pale pallor could only mean all that blood was hers. He clenched his jaw in frustration. As much as he wanted her to tell him what was going on, he could not force her to tell him.

"Can you even stand up?" He asked, sharper than he intended when he stopped inside the bathroom.

"Yes." Her response was almost inaudible. He frowned before he set her back on her feet. Once he was sure she was not going to fall, he stepped out of the room. He started to walk away when he stopped and looked back, "Please tell me the truth."

Sara looked up at him and felt guilt wash over her when she saw the defeated look on his face. "I always do," she whispered.

He just stared at her for a moment before he closed the door. Once it was closed. he stood in the hallway at a loss before he glanced down at his clothes. The front of his shirt was wet with blood. He took a deep breath and disappeared down the hallway.

A little while later, Sara was back in her room. She was staring at the half dollar sized scar she now had to the left of the belly button and a matching one on her back. It was the first time she realized the branch had gone all the way through her. There is no way she should have been able to survive that wound. She should be dead.

Shaking her head to chase those thoughts away, she finished getting dressed. She threw away the blood-soaked clothes and was just sitting down on the edge of the bed when the door flew open. Paige rushed into the room.

"What happened this time?" She asked, her voice filled with worry.

Sara winced while she tried to wrap a thick blanket around her shoulders. Paige hurried over and helped her before sitting down beside her.

"Well?" she demanded. Sara glanced at her before she told her everything that happened. When she was finished Paige was staring at her with wide eyes.

"I think it's time that we tell Jake everything," Paige said after a couple moments. "I mean he was beside himself when you were missing, and I don't think we can handle this on our own."

"I was planning to tell him," Sara said, her voice shaking. "Do you think he'll actually believe me and not think I'm making it up?" She started fidgeting with the blanket.

"I don't know but I think you have to try. I'll go get him." Paige got up and left, and a few minutes later she returned with Jake. He did not say anything as he stood waiting for one of them to talk to him. His gaze shifted to Sara and she looked down at the floor, took a deep breath, and then told him everything. Starting with the events of the festival all the way through what happened that night. When she was finished, she peeked up at him. An incredulous look was frozen on his face.

"Show him," Paige said breaking the silence.

Sara glanced at her before she pulled up the bottom of her shirt just enough that the large scars could be seen. Jake's brows furrowed as he walked closer. His eyes flew back to Sara's face before he knelt to look at the scar on her back. You could almost see his brain working when the doctor in him realized the amount of blood he had seen could have come from these scars, and knowing if it did, she should not be alive. He brushed a finger across the one on her back as if checking it was real. She gasped and winced in pain.

"Sorry," he mumbled before he stood and walked over to the window, where he rested his hand on the sill as he looked outside. He was deep in thought as he remained by the window for a while. Paige took the opportunity to slip from the room.

"You don't believe me, do you?" Sara asked in a shaking voice while she continued to fidget with the blanket. She did not glance up when she heard him leave the window and walk over to her. He sat down beside her and took one of her hands in both of his. His were so much larger than hers they completely enveloped it. They sat for a while in the silence and he started spinning the charm bracelet around her wrist with his thumb before he sighed.

"Yes, I believe you."

Sara could not keep the shock off her face when she looked up at him. She started to relax when she could see that he was serious.

"I do need some time to process all of this," he continued. "It's a lot to take in all at once." She nodded. "For now, I need to focus on getting you well." When Sara did not reply, the two fell silent again. After a few minutes she shifted, she was beginning to get over the shock of him not thinking she was crazy and was becoming hyper-aware that he was holding her hand. He glanced down at her when she moved, and she flushed a light pink.

"I'm not sick," she muttered trying not to look up at him. Jake tilted his head when he noticed her coloration. She normally would have been bright red.

"You are," he said. "I can feel your temperature is up, and you are pale as a ghost, so you need to rest." A half smile crossed his face when she started shaking her head. He was beginning to return to his normal self. "I'll get you some juice and then you need to try and sleep. It has been a long night." He let go of her hand and crossed the room.

"I have never lied to you," Sara whispered so quiet to his back that it could barely be heard.

He paused and looked back at her. "I know, that's why I believe you, even if it doesn't make sense."

Relief flooded through her when she realized he did not think she was crazy. After she watched him leave, she got up carefully and climbed into bed. Moments later she was asleep, the events of the last several days caught up with her.

Jake returned a couple minutes later carrying a glass of orange juice, "Her--." He stopped talking when he saw she was already asleep. After setting the juice on the bedside table, he reached down and covered her with the blankets before he turned to leave. He paused in the doorway and glanced back.

"Please be more careful," he whispered to her sleeping form. "I need you to be more careful." He slipped out of the room and headed toward the kitchen.

Sara woke just before noon the next day. She found, to her delight, that she could almost move without pain. Even her head and the burn on her hand no longer bothered her. The scar from the burn was still there but the pain was gone.

"I wonder if that healing did this?" She thought aloud. It was the only thing she could come up with that made sense. After sitting up, she looked around and noticed the juice on the bedside table. She picked it up and drained the glass. Her throat was so dry. Once she was finished, she set the glass back down and attempted to stand. The room tilted sharply causing her to half fall back on the bed. She winced when she landed, and a frown appeared on her face.

"You aren't ready to get up yet."

She glanced up to see Jake standing in the doorway. When he noticed her look at him a crooked smile crossed his face. "Well, at least not without help." He walked over to stand beside her and offered her his arm.

She flushed and hesitated.

"I won't bite," he said with a chuckle. "Plus, Paige is driving me crazy. You need to come and talk to her. She's been up for hours."

Sara could not help but smile at the mock drama he used in his voice when he talked about his sister. She reached out with a trembling hand and set it on his arm with a feather-light touch. He raised an eyebrow as he looked down at her.

"You are going to need to hold on tighter than that," he said with a smile. She tightened her grip a little bit. Jake shook his head and chuckled again before he put his hand over hers and squeezed it tighter. "You aren't going to hurt me. Just hold onto me."

The shade of red on her face grew brighter when she nodded and tightened her grip without looking at him. Once she did, she tried to stand. This time when the room started spinning, she could stay standing. She closed her eyes until the spinning stopped.

"Ready?"

"Yeah."

Jake readjusted so that her arm was hooked through his before he rested her hand back on his forearm, "Here we go. If you need to, you can lean on me."

She nodded, and they started to make their way to the kitchen. The going was slow, and by the time she made the short walk down the hall, she was already feeling winded.

"You really did lose a lot of blood," he observed.

"Why do you say that?" She asked in confusion as she sat down in one of the kitchen chairs.

"That's what's causing you to be dizzy and winded. You don't have enough red blood cells in your system to carry oxygen, so you need food, liquids, and lots of sleep." He glanced over when Paige came bounding into the room.

"Sara!!" She yelled. "I've been soooo bored without you this morning."

Sara smiled at her friend's enthusiasm, "Sorry."

"It's all good," Paige said with a shrug. "So, what are we going to do today? Are we going to go and find that cave?" She asked with a mischievous grin.

"Paige, I...," Sara trailed off. She could not believe Paige wanted to go there after everything that just happened.

"Absolutely not." Jake's firm voice cut into their conversation. "I can't believe you'd even think about going somewhere so dangerous."

Paige rolled her eyes at her brother, "Oh, come on Jake! Don't we need to get some information?" She glanced over at Sara, who shivered when she remembered the cave.

"No, you can't go there. I will not have one of you almost die again."

Paige gave her brother a long, hard calculating look before she shrugged, "Okay, we won't go." She turned back to Sara and started chatting about the school tour they had soon like she had not even mentioned the cave. Jake narrowed his eyes before turning back to the food he was preparing.

Over the next several days, Jake kept an annoyingly close eye on the girls. By the third day, Paige was getting so annoyed with him that she started locking the door to whatever room she was in. Sara was feeling almost back to normal and was ready not to be under house arrest anymore.

On the morning of the fourth day, the girls finally got their much needed reprieve. Jake walked into the kitchen that morning with his duffle bag and was dressed in his full-dress uniform. His dress blues were a very dark navy-blue jacket with a lighter blue pant. The pants had a yellow strip down the sides and under his jacket he had a crisp white shirt with black tie. He had multiple ribbons and various other awards on his jacket, plus his captain's bars on the shoulder. His hat was sitting on top of his duffle bag. It was time for him to report to the new base and begin his next year of surgical residency.

Sara was eating breakfast with Paige when he entered the room and she did a double take. She watched him for a minute while he was getting his coffee.

"You should probably stop staring," Paige whispered with a giggle. "I mean I know he looks--."

"Shhh," Sara hissed at her as her face flushed bright red. Paige giggled again and rolled her eyes. They needed to get together already.

"It's time for me to go," Jake said as he walked over to the table. Paige jumped up and gave her brother a hug.

"Knock'em dead," she said with a grin.

"Making people dead in my line of work would be bad, Paige," he replied with an amused smile causing her to roll her eyes.

"You know what I mean."

He laughed at her before he turned to look at Sara. It seemed like he was at a loss for what to do. After a few awkward seconds, he reached over and gave her a quick one-armed hug, "See you later."

"Bye Jake," she said while he walked over to grab his things.

"Please stay out of trouble you two," he said, looking at his sister. "And stay away from that cave."

"We know," Paige said with another roll of her eyes. She waved bye when he turned and left.

Paige and Sara returned to their breakfast. Once they were finished, they started clearing the dishes when Paige glanced at the clock for the hundredth time.

"What are you doing?" Sara asked when she could not stand it anymore. Paige grinned at her.

"Just waiting until I think Jake is far enough away that we can go exploring."

The cup Sara was holding slipped from her fingers, "You can't be serious?" She gasped as her face clouded with fear.

"Heck, yes, I am," Paige replied. "I've just been waiting for our chance when Jake wasn't being a mother hen. We have to get more information about all this and that's the only lead we have."

A little while later Paige was half dragging Sara through the woods with her toward the cave. The closer they got the more Sara slowed down.

"Come on," Paige said for the twentieth time. "We don't have all day. Uncle Steve will be back from work in a few hours."

"This is a really bad idea," Sara stammered when the cave came into view. Fear flashed across her face as they approached the entrance. Sara kept waiting for the voice in her head to talk to her, but she did not hear anything.

The two stopped right at the entrance and exchanged glances. Paige even looked apprehensive when she pulled a flashlight out of her pocket. She hooked her arm through Sara's, and they stepped into the cave. They looked around the entrance for a few minutes and when they did not find anything they went deeper inside. The cave only had one passage to follow and it ended in a small room. Sara could not shake the feeling she had seen this before when they stopped in the room.

"Are those letters[3]?" Paige asked as she shined the light on the wall and illuminated some strange carvings."

Sara shrugged and turned to look at the rest of the room. Her attention was drawn to a glowing arch on the far back wall and as she approached it with cautious steps, it started to glow brighter. When she got closer, she noticed that there were six individual stones around the outside of the arch. Five out of the six were glowing and she wondered why the last one was not. She stared at it before she could not help herself and lifted her hand.

"Do not touch that! It is a portal."

Sara jerked her hand back, "How do you know that?"

"Know what?" Paige asked from the other side of the room. Sara did not answer and walked over to where she was standing. A sudden look of realization crossed Paige's face. "Was that voice talking to you?"

"Yeah," Sara admitted. "She told me not to touch that glowing arch. It's a portal."

Paige's eyes burned with curiosity, but she remembered the object she

---

[3] Fig. 2 - Appendix

was holding, "Look what I found." She held out a small ornately carved silver dagger. Sara looked at it and, remembering the tiara, did not touch it. "Aren't you going to take it?"

"Don't you remember what happened with the tiara?" Sara asked holding up her hand so Paige could see the scar again.

"I'm holding it, and nothing happened," Paige said as she held it out to her again.

Sara sighed, but took it from her this time and the moment she touched it, she gasped as images began flooding her mind.

A tall elven man with golden hair and blue eyes was forging the small dagger. He had a smile on his face as he pulled the little weapon out of the water…. The same elven man was giving the dagger to a little girl with silver curls. She was jumping up and down with excitement as she took it…. The little girl was practicing attacks with a silver-haired boy. He was very careful and gentle when he blocked her attacks…. The images stop changing and stayed on one. The young woman was crouched by the wall of a cave as a man entered. Sara could not see his face but the young woman….

The memory suddenly cut off and Sara came back to her senses with a gasp. She was laying flat on her back on the cave floor. Paige stood next to her with a terrified look and the dagger was back in her hand.

"Are you okay?" Paige asked.

"We have to get out of here, now," Sara gasped, she was shivering as she stood up. "Something very bad happened in a cave that looked

just like this. I've seen that portal before."

Paige grabbed her hand and the two started to head toward the cave entrance. They only made it a couple of steps before a loud growling sound caused them to pause and look back. There was something trying to force its way through the arch on the wall. All they could see of the creature was blood red eyes and a black gnarled arm with a large claw.

"*Run!*"

Both girls bolted for the front of the cave. They managed to make it outside before they heard a loud roar from behind them. Sara glanced back over her shoulder as they ran and saw the creature leap out into the forest. The creature was like nothing she had ever seen. It was the size of a large grizzly bear and walked on all four legs. Its skin looked like gnarled black leather with two large wings sticking out of its back. The wings were rimmed with fire, and so were the two curled horns that came out of the top of its head. It appeared confused when it first exited the cave while it looked around, but it quickly zeroed in on the girls.

Sara glanced beside her and realized Paige was not running anymore.

She appeared to be frozen in place after the creature burst out of the cave. Sara sprinted back and shoved Paige out of the way when the creature moved to leap at her. She closed her eyes and raised both arms to cover her face as she braced from the impact from the creature. Instead, she heard the sudden ear-splitting sound of a shotgun going off right above her. Peeking up between her fingers, she found herself looking at Jake's back. He had somehow managed to get between the creature and her just in time.

"Stay behind me!" He did not take his eyes off the creature while it was shaking its head. "Paige!"

When she heard her brother's voice it broke through the terror that was holding her frozen, and she managed to stumble over to him. As soon as she reached him, he started backing them up the slope away from the creature. It was getting back up and acted like it had not been shot in the head several times. Its red eyes bored into them as it made another lunge. Jake shot it again and it stopped momentarily to shake off the blow. He reloaded two more shots while it was stunned and grimaced when he did not have time to load all five shots.

This time the creature stalked them with cautious steps and attempted to lunge at them from the side. Jake fired again but only caught it in the front leg, as it swerved to the side, which did not slow it down but diverted its course. He cursed under his breath when he realized the last round did not eject properly and the gun was jammed. Out of the corner of his eye, he caught sight of a large boulder. He put out his left arm and started pushing the girls that direction and waited for the creature to lunge again. As soon as it did, he shoved both girls down and dropped to a knee, so the creature flew over the top of them. He spun and slammed the buttstock against the rock while he pulled back on the action release causing the jammed cartridge to eject.

Jumping back to his feet, he faced the creature as it struggled to turn around on the slick slope. When it came to a stop it narrowed its eyes as it studied them. Paige and Sara scrambled back to their feet and hurried to duck behind Jake. The creature let out a low growl when Sara caught its attention. It seemed interested in her.

Jake struggled to keep himself between the creature and the girls when it started to circle them waiting for its chance to strike. It crouched low to the ground, poised for the strike and the split-second Jake lost his footing on the wet ground it launched forward. Jake managed to get the shot off, but it only grazed its shoulder. With one swipe, it sent Jake sailing back into Paige and they both landed several feet away. Taking this opportunity, it stopped right in front of Sara.

"How did you open the portal?" It growled at her. Sara looked up at it in terror, her whole-body trembling in response. "How? You are not an elf, but you smell of magic."

"I don't know," she stammered.

The creature glared at her and howled in anger. It raised a claw to swipe at her, but a shotgun shell exploded against its side, knocking it to the ground.

"Move!" Jake yelled at her.

Sara scrambled backward and tried to run toward Jake, but the creature caught her foot and sent her sprawling. She thought she was finished when the creature leapt at her again, but a figure all clothed in black appeared out of nowhere. He stabbed the creature through the head with his katana in one smooth motion killing it before he disappeared.

Sara just sat there stunned, staring at the dead creature in front of her. Her whole body was still trembling when she was pulled to her feet and she found Jake standing beside her. His face was expressionless as he slung the shotgun over his back, grabbed each girl by the hand, and headed off in the direction of the cabin. As they walked, he kept a sharp look out for danger. When they reached the cabin, he pushed them inside in front of him before he took the time to reload the shotgun. He set it down on the table.

"What in the world were you thinking?" He asked, his voice hard and controlled.

Both girls were still so shocked by what just happened that they just stared at him. He took a deep breath and struggled to keep his emotions in check as he waited for them to talk to him.

"How are you here? Where's your uniform?" Paige stammered a few minutes later. She seemed to be coming out of her shock and noticed he was wearing jeans and a sweatshirt. "You left for the base."

"I tricked you, though you knew I had two weeks of leave and not just one," he said. "I knew you would pull something like this and it's a damn good thing I did."

Paige's eyes flashed with anger, "You set us up? How could you do that?"

"How could I?" He asked, his voice starting to rise. "How could I not when I knew you were just waiting for me to leave? Do you have any idea what would have happened if I hadn't been there?" He paused and when neither girl replied he continued, "You would have died! That's what would have happened." He was so amped up on adrenaline and frustration that he started pacing around the kitchen to calm down.

"You don't know that for sure," Paige snapped. "We could have handled it."

"You could have handled it?" he asked, his voice taking an incredulous tone. "How? You were totally frozen in terror. Sara had to save you."

Paige glared at him on the verge of tears.

"I'm so sorry," Sara gasped. "This is all my fault. I'm the cause of all of this and I should have stopped her from going. Please don't yell at each other." She ran from the kitchen and went straight to her room. Jake watched her go with a look of guilt. He did not want her to think it was her fault.

"Nicely done," Paige snapped before she followed Sara out of the room.

Jake held up his hands, still not sure how this had become his fault. He saved his sister from dying but somehow, he was the bad guy.

"That girl is enough to make a man start drinking," he mumbled as he continued pacing around the room to work the adrenaline out of his system.

Jake gave the girls space for the rest of the afternoon. They all ate dinner together with uncle Steve and discussed the plans for the next day. The girls had the tour of their college campus, which neither of them really felt like going to, but they put on happy faces. They did not want Steve to get suspicious and they both retreated to their rooms after dinner.

A couple of hours later Jake passed by Sara's room and noticed she was not inside. He went to Paige's and found the two of them huddled together in the corner of the room beside the fireplace sharing one blanket. Neither one of them glanced at him when he walked into the room and closed the door behind him. He sat down across from the fireplace and leaned against the bed. Not saying a word, he stretched out his legs, folded his hands in his lap, and just waited while he watched the flames of the fire.

It was not long before Sara could not help but look over at Jake. She was trying to support her friend, but every part of her wanted to be over by him. She wanted to feel his warmth and know she was at least safe for now. Sara glanced at Paige and when she did not make any form of response, she looked at Jake again. He noticed her gaze right away and gave her a tentative smile. Biting her lip, she looked back and forth between Jake and Paige several times before she could not stand it anymore. She took the blanket off her shoulders and put her end around Paige before she looked back at Jake. He could see the hesitation on her face, and he nodded right away. She took a deep breath before she got up and walked over to him and sat down beside him. Without looking over at him, she started fidgeting with the bracelet she was wearing. Jake just watched her for a moment, seeming not to know what to do, before he wrapped his arms around her, and pulled her closer to him. Sara could feel her face turning red, but she could not help but lean into him. She rested her head against his chest, and he rested his cheek on the top of her head. The normally conflicted look Jake had when he was close to her was replaced this time with a look of peace.

Paige rolled her eyes at the interaction between her brother and Sara. She had never seen two people who liked each other so much, that had no clue what to do about it. A few seconds later she sighed. She could not really blame Jake. He had always put all his attention into school and had never had a girlfriend. She also knew Sara was far too shy to have dated anyone.

"Thank you," Sara whispered, breaking the silence for the first time.

"For what?" Jake asked.

"For... for saving us." Her voice cracked when she started shaking at the memory of the creature. The stress of the day finally came to a release and she started to cry.

"It's okay," Jake said, his voice soft. "You're both safe now." He looked away from Sara when he noticed Paige getting up. She had tears on her face when she hurried over to her brother. He put an arm around her when she sat down and held both of them until they were cried out.

"The two of you should both try to get some sleep," Jake said, breaking the silence. He looked back and forth between them after he watched them exchange worried glances. "You want me to stay, don't you?" When they both nodded, he sighed and pulled his arms off their shoulders.

"What if there are more of them?" Paige asked.

"It's fine, Paige," Jake said as he stood up. "I will stay in here with the two of you. Just let me go and get something to read first."

While he was gone the girls put blankets and pillows on the floor near the fireplace. They were both laying down when he came back. He returned to where he was sitting on the floor and started reading by the light of the fire.

"I'm sorry," Paige said.

Jake looked up from the medical journal with a raised eyebrow. His sister never apologized, "For what?" He could not help the note of suspicion in his voice.

"I mean it this time," Paige said with a frown. "You were right. We couldn't have handled it and we should have stayed away. And... and don't be mad at Sara. I totally dragged her along. So, I'm sorry."

Jake regarded her for a moment before he sighed, "I forgive you. I can't say it's alright because it isn't, but I do forgive you." He paused. "Please, please try to be more careful. I don't want to lose either one of you." Once Paige nodded, he looked back down at his medical journal. "Go to sleep. Both of you, I'll be right here."

Sara closed her eyes. She was relieved that the two of them had made up and she drifted to sleep with a smile on her face.

The first rays of the morning sun woke Sara up when they shined right in her face. She rolled over so that she was not blinded before sitting up. When her eyes adjusted back to the light of the room, she noticed Paige was still asleep by the fireplace and Jake was asleep leaning against the bed with the medical journal still in his lap.

She smiled at him before getting up and leaving the room. After changing, she started to move away from the dresser when her violin case caught her attention. There had been no time for her to practice since they left Japan and she found she was yearning to play. It only took her a few seconds to decide that this was the perfect time to practice since everyone was still asleep. Her brows furrowed when she tried to figure out where to go so that she would not wake anyone. She glanced out the windows and decided to head outside but stay close to the house.

After pulling on her boots and jacket she headed outside. Around the front of the house, she found a large firepit surrounded by evenly spaced logs. She sat down on one and laid her violin case on another. Once she checked that her violin was in tune, she started to play. The melody she played was beautiful but at the same time almost haunting. She closed her eyes as she poured all her emotions from the last week into the music. Her entire body started to move in time with it, she allowed the music to take over. She was so wrapped up in the music that she did not hear when Jake walked around the end of the cabin. He stood watching in stunned silence before the look on his face faded to a sweet smile. A few minutes passed before she happened to glance in his direction. She jumped at his sudden appearance and stopped playing with a painful screech when her bow dragged across the strings.

"Sorry," he said. "I didn't mean to startle you."

Her gaze flew to the ground and she stood up while her face flushed a brilliant red, "How long?"

"Not very long," Jake said with a frown as he took a couple steps toward her. "The music was very beautiful. I can't believe I've never heard you play."

Sara fiddled with the bow in her hand and still would not look up at him. She did not think he would really want to hear her play. Why would he?

"I don't usually play for anyone," she whispered.

"I would love to hear some more," Jake said, his voice quiet as he continued toward her. He stopped when he was standing next to her. "Will you keep playing?"

She finally garnered the courage to peek up at him and he smiled, "Please?"

Biting her lower lip, she glanced at him again through her bangs before she finally nodded. She sat back down on the log and he sat down on the one next to her while he resisted the urge to look back over at her when she did not start playing right away. He did not want to make her more nervous. Sara noticed what he was doing, and a small smile crossed her face before she took a deep breath and started playing again. It was not long before Jake closed his eyes and just listened to the music. He found it soothing and had not felt so relaxed in a long time.

"What's going on out here?" Paige's sudden shout caused Sara to stop playing as she jumped up from the log. Jake opened his eyes and glanced at his sister in annoyance.

"I was just practicing," Sara mumbled without looking at Jake.
Paige gave her a knowing look. "You never play in front of people," she said with a pout. "I mean, come on, you won't even play for me."

"Sorry," Sara said with a shrug.

"It's all good," Paige said with a laugh. "But it is almost time to head to campus for the tour. We need to get ready." She grabbed Sara by the arm and started pulling her back toward the cabin. Sara glanced back at Jake and made eye contact with him by accident. A crooked half smile appeared on his face and she looked away as her face flushed again.

About an hour later the three of them were in Jake's jeep heading toward the city of Fort Collins. Paige was talking nonstop about how cool going to college was going to be as they drove. Sara listened for a little while before she tuned her out and watched the scenery as they drove. The large mountain peeks in the distance and the thick pine trees made her smile. It made her feel at home even though it was thousands of miles away.

"Oh Sara," Paige said, veering the direction of conversation again. "I've been meaning to ask you. What did that thing say to you?"

Sara appeared confused, "You didn't hear it?"

"Oh, I heard it, but it wasn't speaking a language I've heard before. It sounded like a bunch of growling and stuff."

"It asked how I opened the portal and why I smell like magic," Sara said with a frown. A sudden feeling of dread washed over her. How did they not understand it if she could? The feeling grew worse when she watched Jake and Paige exchange glances.

"Do you know what it was speaking?" Jake asked.

"No." Sara's eyes widened in alarm. "Oh no, did I talk like it?" She looked horrified by the idea and Paige looked out the front of the jeep without answering her.

"Yes you did," Jake answered after several moments before he glanced in the rear-view mirror and watched the panic appear on her face.

"But how?" She asked, more to herself than anyone in the jeep. "I don't even know what that thing was."

"Demon, a small one."

Sara jumped at the sound of the voice in her head, "A small one?" She asked out loud, her voice full of fear. Jake glanced in the rear-view mirror again.

"A small what?" He asked, his face becoming wary.

Sara's face turned a brilliant red. She did not realize she said the question out loud and kept her gaze away from Paige when she noticed her turn around.

"Again?" Paige asked, way too excited in Sara's opinion. It took several minutes before Sara could force her nerves down enough that she could talk without her voice cracking.

"Yes, I heard her again," she whispered. "She said it was a small demon." She cringed when she said the word demon. The thought of what they could encounter terrified her if that was just a small one. What would a big one be like? Her attention turned to Jake when he did not say anything. He was staring out the front of the jeep. His face was devoid of all emotions and it did not appear as if he had even heard her. She glanced at Paige who just shrugged before they both waited for Jake to say something.

"Can that voice tell me how to kill them?" Jake asked, his voice hard and cold, breaking the silence. Sara looked at the back of his seat.

"She only says things once in a while and I can't control when she answers," she said as she fidgeted with the cuff on her sweatshirt. Jake only nodded in response before they all fell silent again.

The rest of the drive to the campus no one talked, even Paige was quiet. When they arrived, they headed for the welcome center and were directed into a large room where the orientation would begin. They chose seats and a few minutes later one of the university advisors started the session.

Sara found it hard to pay attention. She was so worried about what had happened the day before that she sat wringing her hands. Her nerves were palpable to anyone close enough to see. Jake glanced down at her a couple of times before he reached over and grabbed her hands with one of his.

"It's all right. I will figure this out," he whispered into her ear. She turned her head to look at him and found his face inches from hers. Meeting his gaze, she shied away a little bit but did not break eye contact. She could feel her heart accelerating the longer they stayed that way. When she bit her lower lip, she heard Jake take a sudden deep breath and he sat back in his chair putting some distance between them. He held onto her hands a few moments more before, seemly reluctant, he pulled his hand back and interlaced his fingers on his lap. Sara was unsure what had just happened as she glanced at him out of the corner of her eye and tried to gather her scattered thoughts.

After what seemed like an eternity to Sara, the session, including the question and answer session, was over and the families were taken on a tour of the campus. When they reached the music building Sara stayed with the group touring the department while Jake and Paige continued with the other group. Sara looked around in awe when they arrived in the concert hall. The room was huge with seemingly endless rows of seats, a two-level balcony at the back, and a stage in the front. Sara swallowed with nerves when she realized at some point she would have to play in this room.

The tour continued through the rest of the building where she saw the classrooms and practice rooms. Once they were shown the whole building, they were taken out to a large open area where all the students in both groups were mingling.

Sara weaved her way through the large group of people as she looked for Paige and Jake. She paused for a moment and stood up on her toes trying to see over the crowd, when someone ran into her. She tumbled backwards and landed hard on her rear.

"Excuse me," a quiet, gentle voice said from above her. "Are you all right?"

"Yes," she mumbled. She got back to her feet before looking up at the person who had knocked her over, and she almost failed to stifle her gasp of surprise. She felt like she had seen him before, or should at the very least know him. He felt so familiar, but she did not understand why.

"Are you certain?" He asked as he brushed silver hair back from his face. "You seem a little lost."

Sara looked down to try and hide her embarrassment.

"I'm fine, thank you," she mumbled before she backed away and walked into the crowd again. It took her a little while before she finally spotted Paige in the crowd. When Paige saw her, her face broke into a huge grin. She grabbed Sara by the arm and pulled her with her.

"Thank goodness," Paige said, her voice filled with excitement. "We have to talk to these guys before Jake gets back!"

Before Sara could even think about protesting, Paige dragged her over to a small group of three men. Sara's face fell when she noticed one of them was the man who had run into her just moments ago. When they came to a stop, Sara glanced up at the two she had not seen before. They were both tall and lean with bright blue eyes. One had jet black hair while the other silver with light blue streaks.

"Raven," Paige said to the one with black hair. "This is my roommate that I was telling you about."

Sara glanced at Paige in surprise. She did not understand how they could already be on a first name basis. They could have only met a few minutes ago.

"Hi Sara," Raven said, his voice a little too loud. "It's nice to meet you."

Sara smiled, but grimaced on the inside when she realized this guy seemed to be a lot like Paige. He even wore the same dark, gothic clothing as she liked to wear. He gave her a warm, friendly smile before returning his attention to Paige.

"So, your name is Sara?"

She glanced up and saw the man who had run into her earlier was standing beside her. He tilted his head when she did not say anything. She nodded when it felt like his grey eyes were looking through her.

"I am Kaedin," he said.

Her brows furrowed when she caught a strange undercurrent to his voice. It felt like he thought she should know his name. When she glanced up at him, he held his hand out, "It is a pleasure." She stared at his hand but before she could take it, she heard someone else walk up.

Jake stopped between the girls and draped an arm around each of their shoulders. Paige looked up and gave her brother a dirty look but knew better than to say anything. Kaedin raised an eyebrow as he glanced at the arm around Sara.

"The warrior," he muttered under his breath.

"Excuse me?" Jake asked when he did not quite catch what he said.

"Forgive me, it was nothing of importance," Kaedin replied with a forced smile. "I do not believe we have met. I am Kaedin." He held out his hand to Jake for a handshake, which Jake accepted only out of politeness.

"I heard your introduction." Jake's voice took on a sharp edge.

"This is my brother Jake," Paige said trying to break the uncomfortable tension.

"It is nice to meet you, Jacob," Kaedin said, his tone taking on a sarcastic edge.

Jake narrowed his eyes but gave no other emotion away as he regarded him, "Let's go, ladies. It's time to head home." He pulled the girls with him as they headed back to the jeep. Kaedin tilted his head with a frown as he watched them walk away.

Once they reached the jeep, Paige spun around and glared up at her brother.

"What is your problem?" She snapped.

"I don't trust them," he said as he opened the door for the girls. Sara climbed in, but Paige just stared at her brother.

"You don't even know them," she said as she climbed in beside Sara.

"They are boys," Jake said, his expression darkening. "I don't have to know them not to trust them."

"When I die single it will be your fault." Paige glared at him as he got into the driver's seat.

He looked over at her with a smug grin. "I think I can live with that."

Paige rolled her eyes in exasperation but let the subject drop. She knew even she could not win this one. Jake started the jeep and drove off the campus.

When they arrived back at the cabin, they were all surprised to see a military vehicle parked out front. Jake motioned for the girls to go in the house before he walked over to the sergeant getting out of the vehicle.

"Captain Riverwood?" The man asked.

"Yes," Jake replied.

The sergeant held out an envelope which Jake took with a frown, "You have been reassigned, sir. The address of your new post is in the envelope. The base is local, so you will not need to relocate again. You must report at 0900 Saturday."

"Why?" Jake asked, his eyebrows raising. "I was just reassigned to Fort Carson. Where am I going now?"

"I don't know, sir," the sergeant replied. "I was only asked to deliver your paperwork.

Jake gave him a curt nod and the sergeant headed back to his vehicle. He watched until he was gone before looking in the envelope. There was nothing inside that told him anything more than the address of the facility. With a heavy sigh, he headed inside.

A few days later, very early in the morning, the girls and Jake were loading their things into his jeep. He was dressed in his BDUs since he was reporting to his new base. Once he finished loading the last of the girl's boxes that had arrived from Japan, they loaded into the jeep and headed for the university. They arrived in front of a large brick building that looked like a large apartment complex. Before starting to carry anything inside they headed up to their room on the third floor and stepped inside their new home for the next four years. The girls were lucky that Sara's parents were paying for the dorm, so they got one that was a small apartment instead of the one room which was normal for a new freshman. The apartment contained two bedrooms, a kitchen with dining area, a living room, a bathroom, and a small balcony.

"This is great!" Paige squealed.

Sara smiled at her and shook her head. Paige was so easy to get excited. She was grinning from ear to ear as she explored their new home.

"It is a nice place," Jake agreed. "Let's get all your things carried in. I have to get on the road soon." He headed back out the door and the girls followed behind him. It did not take them long to get all their stuff out of the jeep.

"All right," Jake said as he carried in the last box. "It is time for me to head out. Both of you be careful."

Paige rolled her eyes, "Aren't I always?" She asked with a grin. Jake just shook his head and gave her a hug before turning to Sara. He gave her a hug too, and this time neither one of them seemed to be uncomfortable. Paige's grin widened.

"If either of you need me just call me," Jake said as he walked through the door. Both girls waved bye and he shut the door behind him. Once he was gone, they shared excited glances before heading to their own room. They had a lot of stuff to put away.

Jake headed back down to his jeep before heading away from the university. He drove for a little while before he noticed that he was leaving the city. His brows furrowed as he picked up the map laying in his passenger seat again. There was nothing on the map showing any kind of base out this direction. Setting it back down, he drove for just a couple more miles before two black SUVs appeared in the road in front of him. They blocked the road, and he was forced to pull over to keep from hitting them. He slid one hand down beside his seat and gripped the pistol that was concealed when soldiers started getting out of the SUVs.

A soldier with a rifle in hand walked up and tapped on the driver's side window. Jake used his free hand and rolled down the window just enough that he could hear the soldier. He noticed the soldier's safety was not on.

"What are you doing out here?"

"I'm following orders, I'm supposed to report to my new base at 0900," Jake said inclining his head toward the paperwork sitting on his dashboard. The soldier glanced at it.

"Let me see it."

Jake still did not release his grip on the pistol as he leaned over and picked up his orders. He had to roll down the window a little bit more so that he could hand it to the soldier. After looking over the paperwork thoroughly, the soldier looked back at Jake.

"I.D."

Jake shifted enough that he could get his wallet out as he glanced around the jeep. There were three other soldiers standing at the ready around his vehicle. He opened it and pulled out his military I.D. card and handed it to the soldier. He took it and looked between Jake, the I.D., and the paperwork.

"All right, sir," the soldier said. "You are cleared to proceed from here." He handed him back all his things. "Proceed along this road until you reach the main gates." Jake only nodded and did not remove his hand from his firearm until the SUVs disappeared down a side road. Once they were gone, Jake took a deep breath. He had no idea what that was about, but he had the distinct impression that they could have made him disappear. After taking a couple minutes to calm back down, he started driving again. It took him about fifteen minutes before a massive set of gates came into view at the base of an enormous mountain. After getting clearance at the gates, Jake drove onto what looked like a top-secret base. He parked in the lot he was directed to go to before he turned off the jeep. Looking around in confusion, he wondered how in the world he had been assigned here. The only thing he could see from where he was parked was a small two-story brick building that appeared like it was being swallowed by the mountain itself. The sheer rocks of the cliff face ran right up to the building. His expression darkened suddenly.

"I had better not be here because of him," he said as he hit the steering wheel. He got out of the jeep and headed into the building to begin his in processing.

After spending several hours getting various forms signed, he finally had the opportunity to ask about his transfer.

"Do you know who requested this transfer?" Jake asked the sergeant currently helping with his paperwork.

"Let me take a look, sir," he responded as he looked through Jake's information. "It looks like General Riverwood requested this transfer."

Jake closed his eyes as he clenched his jaw and took a sharp breath through his nose. The sergeant did not notice as he continued to look through the paperwork.

"Okay, sir, you need to see if the general is in his office for the next signature. Do you need me to show you where it is?" The sergeant asked as he handed the paperwork back to Jake.

"No, I can manage." Jake stood up and left the office before he headed down another hallway. It did not take him long to find the appropriate office. Without knocking on the door, Jake threw the door open and stormed into the general's office. He walked straight over to the desk and glared at the man sitting behind it.

"Why am I here?" He snapped.

"I don't have time to speak to you right now," the man snapped without glancing up from his paperwork.

Jake slammed his hand down on the desk causing a stack of papers to fall off and scatter all over the floor.

"We need to talk now!" He spit out between clenched teeth.

The general glanced at the aide who was standing beside him and waved him out of the room. The aide scurried from the office before the heavy-set general stood and stormed around the desk. He stopped directly in front of Jake and looked up at him. The family resemblance was slight since Jake was several inches taller than his father and the general did not share his son and daughter's eye color, his was a dark brown. The only thing they had gotten from him was the dark brown hair.

"Who do you think you are talking to captain?" He asked in a hard, disapproving tone while gesturing to his four-star status. Jake ripped off his BDU jacket with his captain's bars and threw it on the floor.

"Dad," he snapped while he stared the general right in the eye. "Why am I here?"

"I am helping you out, son," came the short clip reply.

Jake bristled at the word *son*, "I don't want your help. I made that perfectly clear several years ago. Until you acknowledge, Paige, I want nothing to do with you." He started to shake with anger when he clenched a hand into a fist.

"Do not say that name in from of me," the general growled.

"She's your daughter! How can yo--."

"That is enough! You've been assigned here, and I expect you to make the best of it. Now get out of my office." The general turned his back to Jake and returned to his seat.

"I want a transfer now," Jake demanded. He was beginning to shake worse as he struggled to reign in his emotions.

"Denied," the general snapped without even looking up from his paperwork. "Now get out of my office, captain."

Jake ground his teeth together to keep from retorting. He spun and grabbed his BDU jacket, which was now missing several buttons, and left the office. The aide who was waiting outside looked at him with a mixture of shock and disbelief. He had never heard anyone talk to a general like that before and not get demoted. Jake gave the man a dark look as he continued past him and headed straight out of the building. Once outside he turned and kicked the side of the building several times before he took a few deep breaths. Ignoring a couple of disapproving looks thrown his way, he made his way back toward his jeep. When he started to cool down, he was thankful he was not wearing his captain's bars. He could have gotten chastised for his behavior.

After sitting in his jeep in silence for a little bit, he was back in control and dragged himself back out as he shook his head. This could end up being a complete disaster. He knew he was going to have issues being in such close proximity to his dad. Pulling his duffle bag from the back, he headed into his new residence.

Several weeks later both Jake and the girls had settled into their new routines. Sara sat in her room, early in the morning, working on an assignment for the only math class she was forced to take for her music degree. She sighed as she was beginning to get frustrated. Math was not one of her strong suits. She dropped the pencil on the notebook after getting another problem wrong, when the door to her room suddenly burst open. Paige came bounding into the room. She was radiating excitement and Sara grimaced. She was not in the mood for one of Paige's crazy ideas.

"Sara!" Paige exclaimed with a grin. "Drop all that boring old school work. We're leaving for a whitewater kayaking trip in an hour." She hurried over to Sara's closet and grabbed out a small bag to start packing clothes for her.

"I don't really swim well," Sara said with a frown. "Plus, I need to get this finished."

Paige turned around with a pout on her face, "Oh come on! I got Raven and his buddies to come. We are going to spend the whole weekend at the river."

"I'm not going whitewater anything," Sara said, apprehension beginning to show on her face. "Besides, we don't know those boys very well."

"Oh Sara, you might, not but I've been hanging out with Raven and them almost every day while you're in class. They are so cool and so hot," she said with a huge grin. Sara rolled her eyes before Paige continued, "Okay, what if we avoid the whitewater? I know the river well enough. Jake and I have done it tons of times. Will you go then?" She held up her hands like she was begging. "Please?"

Sara sighed with a shake of her head. She knew she was not going to get out of this, "Okay."

"Thank you," Paige yelled as she grabbed Sara in a bear hug. "Let's get ready!"

About an hour later Paige and Sara were putting their bags and

Paige's small tent into the back of Raven's SUV. Sara could not help but wonder where they got the dark blue car. It seemed too new and clean for an average college student. She pushed the thought out of her mind when it was time to climb in and she realized she had to sit in the back with Kaedin and another man whose name she had not caught yet. When she looked to Paige for help, she just grinned at her and hopped into the front seat with Raven, unfazed by her friend's discomfort. She did not even glance back before she started talking to him. Sara gave her a dirty look before she got into the seat behind Raven by the door. Once she closed the door, she slid over as far as she could get when Kaedin climbed in next to her. She kept her eyes focused out the window as they drove.

"Have you ever been kayaking before?" Kaedin asked trying to make conversation with her. Sara gave him a sideways glance before shaking her head no. "What do you like to do?" She started fidgeting with the hem on her t-shirt as she grew more and more uncomfortable.

"Um..."

"Hey, she's really shy. Don't play twenty questions," Paige said suddenly from the front seat. Kaedin raised an eyebrow before he looked back at Sara.

"My apologies," he said.

Sara nodded and turned her attention out the window. Kaedin watched her out of the corner of his eye before the other man tapped him on the arm.

"What Hikaru?" He asked turning his attention to him. Hikaru glanced at Paige and Sara before whispering something in Kaedin's ear.

"Yes, I'm sure," Kaedin replied as he glanced at Sara again. She did not look at them but noticed the interaction and now felt even more certain they should not be there. A sudden desire for Jake to be there hit her hard. He always knew how to handle any situation.

A little while later they pulled up to a small campground right of the edge of a large river. Paige jumped out of the car and stretched before looking back at everyone.

"Who's up to kayaking right away? She asked with a grin. "We can set up camp when we get back. It won't take long to set up the tents."

"That sounds great to me," Raven agreed, mirroring her grin. They both stared at the group waiting for an answer.

"Sure," Kaedin said after a moment. "That sounds fine."

Raven and Paige headed for the back of the SUV and started pulling the kayaks they rented off the trailer. It did not take them long to get all of them lined up beside the river. Sara drifted away from the group and stood watching Paige. She already wished she had not let Paige talk her into this. Paige finished helping Raven and Hikaru get into their kayaks and out on the river before she looked for Sara.

"Come on," she called once she spotted her. "It's your turn."

Sara grimaced before she drug her feet as she approached the river. She pulled her hair up into a ponytail and put on the life vest that Paige handed her.

"I'll hold it steady so go ahead and climb in," Paige said. Sara took a deep breath and tried to climb in, but it tilted precariously with each move she made. "Slower movements and it won't tip so much." Sara tried what Paige told her and was finally able to get seated in the kayak. Paige handed her a paddle and then gave her a gentle push. Sara glanced at Raven and Hikaru and tried to mirror their movements with the paddle, and she was soon out in the current of the river with them. A couple minutes later Paige and Kaedin were both on the river. They caught up with them and the group followed Paige as she took them down the left fork of the river.

"We should be good for a while," Paige called as she drifted over to talk to Raven again.

Sara frowned and shook her head. Why did she need to come? Paige was going to be focused on him the whole time. Rolling her eyes, she took the time to look around at her surroundings. On either side of the river were steep banks that were covered with pine trees. It was a hot day, but the breeze made it quite comfortable. Sara smiled when she could hear the gentle sounds coming from the river and the cicadas. She sighed when she decided this might not be so bad. After leaning back so her elbows were on the back of the kayak, she watched a couple of clouds dotting the bright blue sky. She was so occupied with her surroundings that she did not notice when she started drifting away from the group.

"Sara!" Paige's sudden shout caught her attention. She looked up and noticed that there was a fork in the river, and she was lined up with the wrong side. Paddling as hard as she could, she tried to get back on the right side of the river, but the current was too strong, and it pulled her down the left side.

"Sara!" Paige yelled again while she paddled her kayak toward the center of the river where it split.

"What is down that side of the river?" Kaedin asked while he followed Paige toward the bank.

"A twelve-foot waterfall," Paige gasped in a panic.

Kaedin paled when he heard her response and in a couple very strong strokes, he made it to the shore. He leapt out of the kayak and took off at a sprint down the bank toward the waterfall. Paige followed behind him, but it took her a couple of minutes to reach the shore. She jumped out and pulled her kayak onto the bank.

"What do I do? What do I do?" She cried in a panic as she paced around the bank. "What do I do?"

"Do not worry," Raven said walking up to her after securing his kayak. "I am certain that Kaedin will catch up to her."

Paige did not act like she had even heard him as she continued to pace along the river's edge. Raven looked away from her long enough to glance at Hikaru, who nodded before he disappeared in the direction of the waterfall.

"I have to call my brother," Paige panicked. "He always knows what to do." She ran back to her kayak and dug through her bag. Pulling out her cell phone that was in a sealed plastic bag, she ripped the bag off and dialed her brother's number. She prayed that he would answer the phone as it rang. By the fourth ring, there was an answer on the other end.

"Paige?" The second she heard her brother's voice she started bawling. "I lost Sara. I don't know what to do…. She is… going to fall off… I don't know where to go to find her…"

"Whoa, slow down," Jake said.

Paige struggled to take deep breaths so that she could talk more clearly, "I lost Sara. She couldn't get… across the river and… missed the folk split before Lilac Falls. I don't know what to do." She managed to get out between gasped breaths.

There was a lengthy pause, "Are you two alone?" Jake asked.

"No."

"Did someone go after her?"

"Yes, Kaedin went after her," Paige grimaced when she said his name. She heard Jake make a disapproving sound.

"Stay where you are until they find Sara. I'll be there as soon as I can. I'm not off duty for an hour. I'll meet you at the campground." Paige grimaced again when she could hear the disapproval and concern in his voice.

"Okay," she said before she hung up the phone. Raven walked up to her and put an arm around her shoulders.

"Are you all right now?" He asked, his voice concerned.

Paige shook her head no and turned to look where Kaedin had run. She prayed that her best friend would be okay.

***

Sara was terrified when she realized she was going to miss the split in the river. The current was so strong it pulled her down the river fast and it was only a matter of seconds before she lost sight of the group. She tried to paddle toward the bank, but the current kept her from making it any closer. Realizing it was not working, she tried turning the kayak around, so she could push against the water instead of pull. This allowed her to make minimal progress but a loud roaring in the background caught her attention. She peered down the river and her eyes widened in shock when she noticed the river just disappeared. Her mind went blank of everything but the word waterfall. After a few seconds, she came back to her senses and tried to paddle again with all her might.

"*Stop!*"

"I can't stop," she yelled in a panic. "I'm going to go over the waterfall!"

"*You must conserve your strength to swim.*"

Sara shook her head no even though she knew the voice was right. She was not strong enough to go against the current. As she watched the edge of the waterfall get closer, she had to fight with herself just to sit and wait. It was terrifying. She shook so bad that she could barely keep a grip on the paddle. At the last second, she clamped her eyes closed and went over the edge. Somehow, she managed not to scream as she fell and took a deep breath before crashing into the water. The force of hitting the water forced most of the air from her lungs. She fought with all her might and got her head above the surface long enough to take a quick breath before being pulled back under by the current. It was like being in a washing machine as it tossed her around with the debris under the surface. She flinched as things slammed into her and she tried to keep track of which direction was up. For a few moments she kept the direction straight, but it was not long before she became disoriented.

In what seemed like an impossibly short time, she could feel her lungs begin to burn with the need for air. She grasped at the life vest and wondered why it was not working. A few moments more and she was completely spent, and her lungs were screaming for air. Her vision started to grow hazy as her body went limp. Just before she lost consciousness a strong arm wrapped around her waist and hauled her to the surface. As soon as her head was above the water, she took a great searing breath and started coughing.

"Let me pull you," a voice said into her ear. She tried to figure out who it was, but her mind was still too hazy. A few minutes later she was laying on the river bank taking great big breaths. She glanced over and finally realized it was Kaedin who had pulled her out of the waterfall. He was on a knee next to her but did not appear to be out of breath from fighting the currents.

"Thank you," she said once she caught her breath.

He looked over at her, "You are welcome." He stood up before he looked at the waterfall and tilted his head. It was a long climb to get back to the top. Sara watched him for a minute before she sat up and pulled off the life vest. It was awkward to wear, and she did not need it anymore. She moved to stand up but felt a sharp pain in her ankle.

"It appears as if you hit that on something," Kaedin observed before he offered her his hand to help her stand. She hesitated but before she could take it a sudden growling sound got her full attention.

"Oh no," she gasped. "Not another one."

A demon stepped into view from around several trees. Kaedin pulled her up in one quick motion and set her behind him. She could not put weight on her ankle and struggled to keep her balance. Kaedin reached into his pocket where his dagger should have been and paled when he realized it must have fallen out in the river. He stood for a split second trying to decide what to do. He glanced back at Sara with a conflicted look before turning back to face the demon. A strange glow started to envelop him as he closed his eyes.

"No! I must protect him!"

Sara gasped when she felt something taking control of her body. She put full weight on her ankle and stepped around Kaedin. His eyes flew open and he made a quick move to grab her arm, but she put a hand against his chest.

"Jhyōta." Sara heard the strange word in her own voice as she raised her other hand. Once the word was out of her mouth the demon burst into flames. Kaedin pulled her backwards, as a look of shock and relief crossed on his face. His eyes widened when he noticed that Sara's normally blue eyes were now a brilliant shade of green.

"You are in there," he said, his voice filled with pain.

"Do you know me?" Sara heard herself ask.

"Of course, I do." Kaedin grabbed her by the shoulders and looked into her eyes.

"Who am I?"

A look of complete shock and panic crossed Kaedin's face but before he could answer Sara's eyes were back to normal. She collapsed, and he caught her before she hit the ground. He picked her up and could feel that she was burning hot. His brows furrowed in thought.

"The magic," he muttered when a look of realization flashed across his face. A sudden movement to his left caused him to turn. Hikaru appeared beside him without a sound.

"Is she really here?" He asked when he saw Kaedin was already holding Sara.

"Yes," Kaedin said. "And there is a serious problem." He started walking back to where they left the kayaks.

It took over an hour for the group to get everyone plus all the kayaks back to the campground. Raven and Hikaru hurried to set up the girl's tent and Paige got Sara's sleeping bag. Once it was set up, Kaedin laid Sara on her sleeping bag, and only after getting a suspicious look from Paige, did he leave to help set up the rest of the camp. Paige remained in the tent with Sara after she went to the river to wet a rag. She laid it on her friend's forehead before she sat down beside her in the tent. She did not move until a familiar voice broke the silence.

"Where are they?" Paige leapt up and ran out of the tent. Jake saw her as soon as she opened the tent and walked over to her. She grabbed his arm and tugged him the rest of the way to the tent.

"Please, help Sara," she begged. Jake frowned at her when he had to crawl to get into the small two-person tent. His brows furrowed in concern as soon as he saw her.

"How long has she been asleep?" He asked as he knelt next to her.

"Since Kaedin brought her back," Paige said.

Jake observed Sara for a few moments and his brows furrowed. Her breathing was rapid and shallow, and he knew without touching her, her heart would be racing. He placed the backs of his fingers on her cheek. She felt like she was on fire and he did not hesitate as he picked her up off the sleeping bag.

"I have to get her to a local hospital," he said, his mannerisms becoming business-like.

"You can't," Paige gasped and she grabbed her brother's arm. "With all the weird stuff happening, they'd ask too many questions." Jake looked down at his sister and regarded her silently for a few moments before he breathed a heavy sigh.

"You're right," Jake admitted reluctantly. "But if this gets any worse or does not respond fast enough, I'm taking her anyway."

Paige nodded and held the tent flap open so Jake could get out with Sara.

"Will she be okay?" Paige asked, her voice filled with fear.

"I don't know for sure," Jake replied. "It'll depend on how high the fever is and if it will break." He headed straight over to the jeep and laid Sara on the backseat before he fastened the middle belt around her waist. When he turned around, he found Kaedin standing behind him. He closed the jeep door before facing him.

"Where are you taking her?" Kaedin asked. He was unable to keep the sharp edge out of his voice and Jake noticed right away.

"Home."

Kaedin's eyes narrowed, "Should she not see a healer?"

Jake tilted his head at the odd word choice. "I assume you mean doctor and she already has," he said, his tone becoming a little bit smug.

"You?" Kaedin asked as his eyebrow flew up.

Jake was about to make a sarcastic remark when he caught movement out of the corner of his eyes. He glanced around and realized he had made a tactical mistake. While his attention was fully on Kaedin, Raven and Hikaru moved closer to the jeep. They stood casually but he knew they were making their presence known, and the jeep was now surrounded on three of four sides.

Jake took a deep breath as he assessed the situation. He had been studying martial arts for years, but he did not want to have to fight his way out of here. Sara needed his attention.

"Paige," he called. "Get your things it's time to go."

Paige gave him a dirty look from where she was standing near Raven, "I can't leave, or it will ruin their trip. They still need a guide. You don't need me to help you with Sara."

Jake pressed his lips into a hard line as he looked at his sister, "Now Paige." His eyes narrowed when Raven stepped over and rested his arm on Paige's shoulder.

"We could bring her home with us," he said, tilting his head. Paige looked up at him with a grin on her face.

"No," Jake said, his voice starting to rise. "Get your things.

Raven glanced at Kaedin who shook his head no. Jake noticed the interaction and realized that Kaedin was the one in charge. Kaedin glanced back at Jake before he backed off and headed over to stand with Raven. He appeared to be dealing with some sort of painful internal struggle.

"You should go with your brother," Kaedin said, a fake smile plastered to his face. "We will be fine, and you would be worried for your friend."

When Raven nodded in agreement with Kaedin, Paige's face fell with disappointment.

"We can try again another time," Raven said with a wink. Paige grinned and nodded before she turned, ran back to the tent, and grabbed her bag. She returned and waved to Raven before climbing in the front passenger seat of the jeep. Jake moved to his door.

"Take good care of her, Jacob," Kaedin said with a forced smile. Jake regarded him for a moment before getting into the jeep. He did not understand Kaedin's interest in Sara and he did not like it. As they drove away, he continued to watch them until they were no longer in sight. After they were safely away Jake sighed.

"Paige," he started in a firm voice. "I don't even know where to start this time." Paige grimaced before she looked at him with sad eyes. "That's not going to work. Do you have any idea what you've done?"

She rolled her eyes and prepared for the inevitable argument, "Yes, I made plans for a weekend of fun with some friends. I know you don't understand fun." Jake ran the fingers of one hand across his forehead several times.

"That was not fun," he said, maintaining his flat tone. "That was extremely dangerous and quite frankly, stupid."

Paige crossed her arms across her chest and glared at her brother. "Why do you alwa--."

"No," Jake snapped. "We aren't doing this again. Just know that one of these days I'm not going to be able to get you out of whatever mess you get yourself into."

"What mess?" She snapped under her breath.

"What mess?" Jake shot back in a sarcastic tone. "Oh, I don't know, maybe almost getting your best friend killed? Or having no idea what to do in an emergency? Or better yet trying to stay out in the woods alone with three men you just met a month ago? Come on, Paige. What would you have done if I was deployed?"

Paige blanched at the onslaught of questions from her brother. She knew what she had done was not the brightest, but she just could not admit it to him.

"I'd have figured it out," she said, her voice filled with defiance.

"Before or after Sara died in that river?"

Paige looked stunned and floundered for an answer before turning and facing the window. She refused to speak to him the rest of the way to the apartment. Once they arrived, Jake lifted Sara out of the backseat and took her up to her room. He laid her on the bed before he disappeared into the bathroom in search of a thermometer. When he found one, he headed back to Sara's room and checked her temperature. His eyes opened wide when he saw that she was 103.3*F. He knew she was hot but did not realize her temperature was that high.

"Paige," he called.

She walked into the room a few moments later with her arms crossed. He glanced at her but ignored her attitude.

"I need you to get a bowl of cool water and a couple of rags. Do you have any apple cider vinegar?" Paige pursed her lips and still did not answer him. "Now is not the time to act like this. We can talk later, but right now this isn't about you."

She gave him a scathing look before turning on her heel and leaving the room. A few minutes later she returned with the supplies he had asked her to gather. She handed them to him before she left the room in a huff. Jake frowned but said nothing. He knew he did not have time to deal with her right now and set the items on the bedside table. He opened the vinegar and poured a quarter of a cup into the bowl of water. It was an old home remedy he knew would help pull some of the heat from her body.

Once he mixed the vinegar and water with his hand, he placed the rags in and let them soak before he rung them out and placed one on Sara's forehead and the back of her neck. He took the third and started wetting the skin that was not covered by her shorts and t-shirt. When he reached her left ankle, he paused and shook his head. It was very swollen and bruised. After placing the rag back in the bowl, he left the room. When he came back, he had a bag of ice and another towel. He folded one of her blankets and elevated her ankle before placing the towel and ice on it.

Jake repeated this process for several hours before he left her room to go refill the water bowl. He rubbed a hand on the back of his neck as waited for it to fill. Glancing out the window to the balcony he noticed it was already evening.

"Jake?" He turned and looked down at Paige but did not say anything. He was already tired, and it looked to be another long night.

"Um... how is she?" She asked without looking at him.

"Not that great," he replied. "She still hasn't woken up and the fever is not responding like I'd like it to."

An apprehensive look crossed her face as she listened to him talk, "You worked last night, didn't you?"

"Yes," Jake said, his voice filling with suspicion when he glanced down at her again. He was not sure where she was going with this.

"Then should I help for a while, so you can get some sleep? You've already been up for more than a day," she said, her concern evident in her voice.

"I've been up for forty-eight hours," he said, his tone sharper than he intended. "But it's fine. I've been awake longer stretches than that. I'll probably nap later tonight."

Paige gave him a dirty look, "So you don't want my help then?"

"Normally yes, I would take your help," he said before hesitating. "I... I just need to handle it myself this time, okay?"

Paige nodded when she realized it was not her. It was because it was Sara. Jake picked up the water bowl and headed back to Sara's room.

He had no idea how many hours he was tending to Sara when he checked his watch at two a.m. She was finally starting to make some progress. Her breathing was deeper and much slower, and her heart rate had slowed. She was still 102*F, but Jake thought as long as she did not go back up she should be out of the woods. He only meant to lay his head down on the bed for a minute, but he was so exhausted he was asleep almost immediately.

Sara felt like she was floating. She tried to look around but all she could see was endless black in every direction. After staring into the nothingness, she picked a direction and started walking. She had no idea if she was getting anywhere until she caught sight of a small spec of light a distance away. When she reached the edge of the light she hesitated before stepping into it. She shielded her eyes from the bright light and had to let her eyes adjust before she could look around. It appeared she was in a small white room where the young woman she kept seeing was sitting on the floor. The young woman looked up when she approached, and Sara stopped. She just stared at her with piercing green eyes.

"Where are we?" Sara asked, her voice timid.

The young woman turned her attention back to a small black box she was holding.

"Your mind I would assume," she said without looking up.

"But that doesn't make sense," Sara said in confusion. "How am I talking to you?

The young woman stopped and looked up at her with an amused smile. "Since I only appear to exist in your mind at the moment this should make perfect sense. You are apparently trapped in your mind right now. I would make the assumption that you are at this moment unconscious."

"How can you be so calm?" Sara asked, her eyes widening in panic. "How do you know all of this?

"As I told you before, nothing can be accomplished if you are not calm, and as to how I know all of this, I do not know."

Sara sat down hard and put her head in her hands, "This is so messed up."

"Yes, it is," the woman said as she started fiddling with the box again. After a little while, Sara looked up and watched her.

"What is that box?"

"I am not sure," the young woman said with a frown. "I just get the feeling I am supposed to open it, perhaps my memories are in here." She paused. "Would you like to look at it?" She held the box out for Sara to take. Sara stared at it before she reached out to take it. The moment she touched it, she gasped when she saw another image of the young woman. She yanked her hand back.

"Interesting, it would seem that my inference about this box was correct, but it seems only you can unlock it. Perhaps because I am trapped here," the young woman mused as she glanced around the room.

"If you are trapped here, how did you take control of me?" Sara asked.

"Again, I am not sure. I just felt I had to protect that man and I did it. I feel like I should know him." A look of longing crossed her face.

Sara grimaced now that she understood why she felt like she should know Kaedin. It was not her, it was this woman.

"How do we fix this?" Sara asked, her voice laced with frustration.

"I do not know. I can do nothing to help until my memories are restored. Perhaps something will trigger them to return," she said with a sigh. "I am sorry. I wish that I could be more useful for both our sakes. All I know is for now I am dependent on you."

Sara sighed and started to say something when she felt a strange pulling sensation.

"It would appear you are waking up," the woman said as she watched Sara float off the floor toward the ceiling.

"But I have more questions," Sara called. She could see that the woman was getting farther away.

"Ask them. I will answer if I am able."

Sara tried to fight what was pulling her away. She had to find out what was going on and how to fix it. The unseen force continued to pull her farther away from the light and within seconds she was once again swallowed by pure blackness.

The faint light of early morning was streaming in the window when Sara opened her eyes. She glanced around, and her brows furrowed when she realized she was back in her room. She remembered nothing after the demon attack by the river. A heavy sigh caused her to look down and she saw Jake was asleep with his head laying on his arms on the edge of the bed. She wondered how long he had been there.

"Jake," she said, her voice hoarse. He was so sound asleep that he could not hear her. She slid her hand across the sheet and laid it on his arm. Instead of waking up right away he pulled her hand closer and rested his cheek on it, "Sara." He mumbled still mostly asleep. She flushed bright red when he stayed that way for about thirty seconds before he snapped awake.

"Sara," he gasped in surprise. The relief was evident on his face when he saw that she was awake. She gave him a weak, shy half smile as he reached up to remove the rag from her forehead. Once he moved the rag, he rested the backs of his fingers on her cheek.

"You still feel warm," he said. "Let's recheck your temperature." He handed her the thermometer and she put it into her mouth. A few minutes later it beeped, and she handed it back to him. "101, I can live with that. Hopefully, it will come down the rest of the way today." He paused and glanced at her. "I'm going to get you something to drink. I'll be right back." He did not wait for her to answer before leaving the room.

Sara tilted her head. She heard a strange nervous quality to his voice and wondered what was wrong. It was not long before he returned and handed her a glass of water. She took it and drank all of it. Her throat was painfully dry.

"Thank you," she said as she set the glass down on the end table and finally looked back over at him. Confusion clouded her face when she noticed he was pacing at the end of the bed. He glanced at her a couple of times before he forced his nerves down enough that he could say anything.

"Uh well, I'm sure this is probably the worst timing in the world. Uh, and, and I'm not really sure how all this works. But, uh, I mean I know there is usually dating involved first. Uh, but, I want you to be my girlfriend. I, mean, totally slow. But with, uh, everything that's been happening, uh it doesn't seem to make sense to wait. And, uh, after finding out that you are older than my sister. I, I, uh, would really like that." His face was red while he continued to pace without looking at her.

Sara smiled and lifted her hand to stifle a giggle. She had never seen Jake not calm and collected, and here he was actually babbling. When he risked a glance at her she gave him a shy smile and nodded yes. He froze in place.

"You will?" He asked in surprise, his face still red.

Sara bit her lip before she nodded again, "Yeah."

"Oh hallelujah! It's about time!" Paige yelled as she bounded into the room. Jake and Sara both turned brilliant shades of red.

"Paige? How long?" He stammered.

"Oh, I saw the whole painful thing," she said with a wide grin. She laughed when she noticed that Jake seemed at a loss for words. That never happened.

"I will be right back," he mumbled before he retreated from the room. Paige giggled as she watched him before she skipped over to the bed and sat down with Sara. They sat in silence before Paige spoke up.

"I'm really sorry about what happened at the river," she said with a frown. "I should have been paying more attention. I knew you didn't know how to kayak, and I was too occupied with Raven."

"It's okay," Sara said with a heavy sigh. "But I'm never going kayaking with you again unless Jake is with us."

Paige laughed and hugged her friend. "I don't blame you a bit. I promise if we do anything else, I will do my best not to be totally occupied with the boys."

"Oh yeah sure," Sara said with a laugh.

"I did say try." Both girls laughed before Paige started talking. Sara listened to her for a while before she decided that she wanted to take a shower. She felt all sticky and uncomfortable in the clothes that were soaked by the river and the fever. Once she got Paige to quit talking, she hopped to the bathroom. It did not take her long to get cleaned up and back in her room. She tried to put clean sheets on the bed but was having a difficult time due to her ankle, and the fact she was spent from the fever. After struggling for a few minutes, she sat down in the chair next to the bed with a sigh.

"Let me help you," Jake said, his voice quiet when he stepped back into her room. He made quick work of the sheets without glancing at her. Sara bit her lip and fought with her own indecision.

"Are you okay?" She asked, her nerves evident in her voice. Jake never talked about himself and she was not sure if she could ask him personal questions.

He looked over at her and tilted his head before he seemed to realize what was wrong.

"Yeah, I'm fine," he said with a half-smile as he put the pillow back on the bed. "I just wasn't expecting Paige to see all that." He paused when he finished putting the blankets on the bed. "You can ask me anything you want."

Sara's eyes widened when he knew what she was thinking without her telling him. She bit her lip before she nodded with a tentative smile. He returned her smile before he laid the last of the bedding back on the bed. When he turned to face her again, he was back to his normal self.

"The last thing on the list for today is getting that ankle checked out," he said as he held his hand out to her. She could not help but flush when she took hold of it and got out of the chair. They started across her room, but Jake only let her take a couple hopping steps before he just picked her up.

"This way will be easier," he said without looking down at her as he headed out of the apartment and to the jeep.

It was evening by the time Jake and Sara returned to the apartment. She only sprained the ankle but would have to be on crutches for a week. Hobbling over to the couch, she sat down next to Paige, who was watching TV. Jake followed and sat down on the only other chair in the room. He stared out the window for a few minutes before he looked back at them.

"It looks like everything is under control now," he said. "I think I am going to head back to the base. I have early duty tomorrow and I could use a full night's sleep."

"Yup we have it under control," Paige said as she nudged Sara with her elbow. She nodded in agreement before they got up to hug Jake before he left.

"Thank you again," Sara said when she hugged Jake.

"Any time," he replied with a half-smile. He let go of her and walked toward the door. Both girls waved at him when he closed the door.

"I sure hope there is no more craziness for a while," Sara said with a sigh.

"I couldn't agree more," Paige laughed before they both turned their attention to the movie.

Much to Sara's delight the rest of the summer semester went by without incident and the girls were now several weeks into their fall semester. It was early evening and Sara was sitting in her room practicing her violin solo for her first graded performance of the semester. She was practicing every spare chance she got.

"Sara," Paige whined when she walked into her room. "Can you, please, practice in one of the practice rooms? I can't stand that song anymore."

Sara frowned as she lowered her violin, "You know I have a test coming up."

"I know but I really need to get an hour or two of sleep," Paige said with a yawn. "I'm going out with Raven again tonight."

"Again?"

"Heck yeah," Paige said with a grin. "I can't believe you've hardly seen Jake this whole time."

"I've talked to him but he's doing his residency," Sara said with a frown. "You know he's very busy."

Paige rolled her eyes, "Yeah, yeah he's always busy. So, since my brother is a stick in the mud, I'm going to have a blast." She gave Sara a mischievous grin.

"Shouldn't you be studying?" Sara countered. "Especially after your first semester grades. If you don't do well, you'll be on probation."

"It will be fine. So, how about it? The practice rooms?"

"Do you really want me to go all the way across campus to practice?"

Sara asked with a sigh. She was unable to hide her irritation and Paige gave her a dirty look.

"Yeah, I really do."

Sara snatched her backpack and violin case off the floor, "Fine." She stomped around Paige and headed out of the apartment. It took her almost twenty minutes to reach the music building. She looked around to find an empty practice room but since it was so close to testing time for all the music students, they were full. After searching for a while, she managed to find one open, but it was tucked all the way in the back corner of the building. She paused and looked over her shoulder before going in. Something was beginning to make her feel uncomfortable. With a sigh, she shook her head and walked into the room, it was just because it was quiet so far from everyone else. After closing the door and setting her things on the floor, she picked up her violin and started to practice.

Several hours passed before she stopped and rubbed her sore fingers. She raised her arm to check her watch when she felt the hair on the back of her neck stand on end. The sudden feeling that someone was watching her was almost overwhelming. She peeked over her shoulder and gasped when she thought she saw someone duck away from the small window in the door. Jumping to her feet she hurried to the door and peered through the window. When she did not see anyone, she backed away from the door, but the feeling of unease did not leave her. Not feeling comfortable staying alone in the practice room anymore she put her violin away, grabbed her things, and left. She hurried out of the music building and grimaced once she was outside. It was much later than she thought, and it was already dark. After checking to make sure no one was around, she walked toward the apartment. When she was halfway back, she stopped and just stared at the path ahead. It disappeared around a bend into a poorly lit forested area. She looked back over her shoulder again when the feeling she was being watched returned. After weighing her options, she almost ran as she forced herself to continue along the path. It would take twice as long if she tried to go around the forested portion.

Her breathing spiked when the uneasy feeling in her continued to strengthen. She came around a blind curve in the path and almost ran into someone standing in the way. Letting out a quiet yelp, she jumped back.

"Hello young lady," a deep voice said as the stranger turned around. He stood in the glow from the one light post that was near. Sara swallowed hard, but she could not look away from his piercing brown eyes that matched his hair. She backed away without answering.

"You do not need to be afraid," he said.

Something about the way he said those words made Sara shiver. She continued backing away from him as he stalked toward her. As he got closer

110

to her, she gulped when she noticed he towered over her.

"The music you play is beautiful," he continued with a sly smile.

Sara's eyes opened wide with fear when she realized someone had been watching her. She tried to move faster causing him to chuckle.

"I am looking for someone, perhaps you could help me." Sara shook her head and the man chuckled again, "I believe that you already have." He quickened his pace and Sara scrambled backwards to keep distance between them. She shoved her hand into her pocket and a look of terror flashed across her face when she realized she left her phone in the apartment. Dropping her things, she turned to run but paused when she heard voices on the path behind her.

"Help!" Her strangled cry caused the man to stop and glare at her.

"I suppose we shall finish this later," he said with a tilt of his head. He slipped into the bushes just before Kaedin, Raven, and a man she did not recognize jogged around the corner. They all stopped when they saw her.

"Are you all right?" Kaedin asked with a frown. "Did you call for help?"

Sara just stared at him before she could get her mouth to move. "A man was following me. He went that way." She stammered while she pointed into the bushes beside the path. Kaedin and Raven shared a quick glance before they disappeared into the bushes. Once they were gone, Sara could not keep the fear off her face when she glanced at the man standing next to her.

"They shall return in a moment," he said, his voice calm and soothing. "My name is Jaeha. I am a friend of theirs."

Only nodding her head, Sara looked back toward the bushes. The adrenaline was beginning to leave her system and she started to shake. Wrapping her arms around herself, she attempted to calm back down while they waited. A few minutes later they returned.

"We were not able to locate him," Kaedin said, with a frown. "We shall accompany you the rest of the way home. Paige is expecting us. Are you agreeable to this?"

Sara again only nodded before she picked up her things and started to walk. She felt as if she walked in slow motion because her body was so stiff. When they reached the apartment, she fumbled with the keys while trying to get them into the lock. Kaedin reached up to help her, but she jerked back.

"I apologize," he said, his voice gentle. "I was only going to assist you with the door."

She stood frozen for a moment before she handed him the keys. He unlocked the door and handed the keys back, careful not to touch her. She took them back and walked into the apartment.

"Hey guys," Paige called when she saw them. She was sitting in the living room waiting on them. "Hi, Raven." The smile on her face widened into a large grin. He returned her smile before he walked over and put his arm around her shoulders. Sara watched them for a few seconds before she disappeared into her room and closed the door.

Kaedin raised an eyebrow and glanced at Raven. He tilted his head before he nodded, "Why don't we invite Sara to go along?"

"Why?" Paige asked, her expression darkening. "She won't want to go to a party. All she would do is stand in a corner and not talk to anybody."

"I just thought you would like to spend time with your friend since I have been taking all of your time of late."

"No way, Sara would be happier here." Paige's voice became irritated and she gave Raven a hard look. He shrugged as if he did not care but when he glanced at Kaedin there was a hint of concern in his eyes.

"Okay, then let us go," Raven said. Paige slipped out from under his arm to grab her purse. While Paige's attention was away from Raven, Kaedin gave him a look of disapproval before he glanced at Sara's door.

"Hikaru will remain close," Jaeha whispered to Kaedin. "It would appear unusual if you deviate from your normal routine." Kaedin frowned when he knew he was right.

"Let's go," Paige said with a grin after she had her bag in hand. She headed to the door without waiting on a response and left the apartment. Kaedin glanced back at Sara's door once more before they followed her.

Sara listened to the conversation from inside her room. She was hurt that Paige did not even want to invite her to go along. Her thoughts turned bitter. Why should this surprise her? She was rather boring after all. After she heard them leave, she flopped down on her bed and stared up at the ceiling. It was not long before the silence in the apartment caused her unease to return. She sat up when she realized she was still terrified. What if that man followed them? The thought sent a shiver down her spine. She picked up her phone from the bedside table. Looking at it she wondered if he would come if she called him. She opened the phone and started to dial Jake's number several times before finally hitting the send button. She held her breath and tried to prepare herself for him to be working. After a couple of rings, his familiar voice answered the phone.

"Hi Sara," he said as he stifled a large yawn.

"Did I wake you?"

"No, I just got off. I'm on my way back to my place now."

"Um... are you planning to sleep or anything?" She asked, her voice starting to quake. Jake did not respond for a moment. He could tell by her tone that something was off.

"I don't know," he said, his voice wary. "Is everything okay?"

"No," she whispered. "Would you, maybe, be able to come over for a while?" Even though she was terrified, she still could not keep her face from flushing when she asked Jake to come over.

"Of course," he said without a moment of hesitation. "What happened?"

"Can I tell you when you get here? I don't want to think about it without someone here."

Jake could hear her voice quiver when she even eluded to what was wrong. "Sure," he replied, his voice taking a worried tone. "I am leaving now so I should be there in half an hour." He paused. "Where is Paige?"

"She went out," Sara said, careful to leave out the fact that she was at another party. She heard Jake sigh.

"I probably don't want to know anymore, do I?"

Before Sara could answer, she heard a sudden knock on the apartment door. She got up and cracked the door to her room. When she did not see anyone, she tiptoed to the front door. She peeked out the peephole and had to stifle a gasp when she saw the man from before standing in the hall. Scrambling backwards, she dashed around and crouched behind the kitchen counter.

"Sara?" Jake asked. He heard the sharp increase in her breathing when she fell silent.

"How close are you?" She asked in a terrified whisper.

"About twenty minutes. What's going on?" Jake's tone took on a business type ring. He knew something was wrong.

Sara jumped when there was another loud knock on the door. "A man was following me. He's at the door now." Her voice shook so bad Jake almost had trouble understanding her.

"Go to your room, shut and lock the door, and put your desk in front of the door," Jake said in an instant. "I'm going to hang up. If that door opens and it's not me call the police. I will announce it's me when I enter." He hung up the phone and Sara hurried to do as he instructed. She crouched in the corner of her room behind the door and strained her ears. There was another loud knock and the man tried the handle this time. He knocked once more and then suddenly there was nothing. She held her breath in the suffocating silence and waited for what seemed like an eternity before she heard Jake's voice.

"It's me," he called as he entered the apartment. He shut and locked the door behind him as he surveyed the room. When he noticed nothing out of the ordinary, he released his grip on the pistol concealed under his shirt.

Sara jerked the desk out from in front of the door and rushed out of her room. She hurried across the living room and ran straight to Jake. He wrapped both arms around her and held her as she trembled.

"It's okay. I'm here," he said, his voice calm and reassuring. He held onto her until she stopped shaking before leading her over to the couch with his arm around her shoulders.

"What happened?" he asked.

She glanced up at him before, in a very quiet voice, she told him everything that happened that night. His face darkened the more she told him.

"I'm surprised he'd be bold enough to come to the apartment," he said. "Have you ever seen him before today?" His brows furrowed in thought when she shook her head no.

The sudden, loud sound of a door slamming shut in another apartment caused Sara to jump and Jake looked back down at her. He could see the fear written on her face.

"It's okay. You don't have anything to worry about now." He put his other arm back around her and pulled her closer to him. She did not resist and leaned against him.

"Will you go back tonight?" she asked in a scared whisper.

"Not a chance, I'll be here tonight." He felt her relax when she realized he was going to stay.

"Thank you." She rested her head on his chest and let out a slow deep breath. Jake rubbed his hand on her back and just allowed her to depend on him. It was not long before Jake shifted trying to get more comfortable. She fell asleep in his arms and he did not want to wake her.

The sudden sound of a key in the lock shifted his attention. Jake pressed his lips together with displeasure when he watched Paige and three guys enter the apartment. He noticed that he did not recognize the third from the campground. This man was an inch taller than the others and he appeared to be older. His silver hair was longer than the rest and was pulled back, with a brown leather strip that matched the streaks of color in his hair, at the base of his neck. He seemed to carry himself with a certain amount of dignity. His blue eyes, that were observing the room, were so dark they were almost navy.

"What are you doing here?" Paige asked in surprise when she noticed her brother sitting on the couch.

"Later," he said with a frown as he glanced at the unwanted guests.

Paige narrowed her eyes in irritation, "Really? They're my friends so why don't you just tell me?" Jake just stared at her for a moment.

"Fine," he said, his voice sharp. "Did you realize when you left that your roommate had been stalked on the way home?"

"N—."

"Or that he would come to the apartment while she was here alone?" He continued like she had said nothing. "She called me, so I came."

Sara stirred and woke up when she heard the voices around her. She was groggy as she glanced around but as soon as noticed all the people she tried to sit up. Jake did not let go of her.

114

"You're fine," he whispered to her before turning his attention back to the room. She relaxed back against him and just listened to the conversation.

"I had no idea," Paige snapped. She looked over at Raven when she noticed him shift and her face grew more angry. "You knew? That's why you asked if we could take her along?"

"We found her on the way here this evening," Kaedin said before Raven had a chance to reply.

"Why didn't you tell me?" Paige asked giving him an annoyed glance. He raised an eyebrow as he regarded her.

"I did not feel it was appropriate for me to interject," he replied. "I believed the two of you were close, so I assumed she would tell you."

Paige glared at him, "We are close, but she won't talk if anyone else is around and I thought she'd tell me when I got back."

"You knew something was wrong, but you left anyway?" Jake interrupted.

Paige pursed her lips before facing her brother, "Yes."

Sara shifted, and Jake looked down at her. She was staring at her hands and was trying to keep her discomfort from showing. It was apparent that she believed this was her fault. Jake looked back up with a frown and noticed Kaedin watching them. He tilted his head with a look of disapproval and Kaedin shifted his gaze.

"I believe it is time for us to take our leave," Kaedin said. He again had a conflicted undercurrent to his voice.

"I thought we were just coming back for a minute for me to grab something?" Paige protested.

"Yes, that was the original plan," Kaedin continued. "However, it would appear that you are needed here and there shall always be another time to enjoy a party."

Jake raised his eyebrows at the word party and looked over at Paige. She was careful to avoid his gaze.

"We shall let ourselves out," Kaedin said as he glanced at Raven and Jaeha. Raven headed for the door at once but Jaeha seemed amused for a moment. Kaedin tilted his head before Jaeha bowed his head a little bit then headed for the door.

"I shall see you later Paige," Raven called with a smile as he headed into the hallway. The other two followed and closed the door behind them. Paige locked it before spinning to face her brother.

"I swear the two of you are trying to ruin my life," she snapped at them. Sara flinched at her friend's harsh words, but Jake did not react. "Why can't you be nice? And why can't you get over being so shy and talk to people? And why do I have to get involved in all this crap?" Paige started pacing as she continued to rant. "I just want a normal school experience but with the two of you around that isn't going to happen."

"Are you finished?" Jake asked, his voice hard.

"No, I'm not," she slurred as she turned too quickly and almost stumbled.

Jake narrowed his eyes as a look of realization crossed his face, "Are you drunk?"

Sara sat up and looked at her friend. She was acting a little stranger than normal.

"And what if I am?" Paige sneered at her brother.

"I'll quit paying your school tuition and you can come live with me on the base." He paused. "Are those boys giving you alcohol?"

"You wouldn't do that," Paige taunted. "And no, I'm getting it myself. They tried to get me to stop." Paige laughed and rolled her eyes. Jake just stared at his sister with a look of disbelief.

"Why don't we go talk?" Sara asked.

"Are you sure you can handle it with my brother around?"

"That was rude," Sara said, her face flushing but she stood her ground.

"Uh, huh," Paige grunted at her and rolled her eyes. Sara got up from the couch and pulled Paige into her room. She was not gone long before she reappeared with a worried look on her face.

"She just passed out."

"What is going on with her?" Jake asked with a sigh. "She's always acted out but never this bad." When Jake noticed Sara fidgeting with her hands, he looked over at her. "What?"

"I may know what the problem is," she said. Jake just looked at her and waited for her to continue. "A couple weeks ago she was curious about what base you were stationed at since you wouldn't tell her. She started making phone calls and found out that your dad was here. She tried to go and see him."

"She did what?" Jake asked.

"I tried to tell her not to go. I don't really know the whole story, but I figured that if you didn't tell her he was here…" Sara trailed off when she saw the mix of pain and anger on Jake's face.

"That certainly does explain everything," he said. "I'll talk to her tomorrow after I get off."

"When do you have to go back?" Her voice started to shake again. Now that her friend was taken care of the events of the night were coming back to her.

"I will have to leave in a few hours. I have to be at the hospital at seven." He felt her shiver next to him and he put an arm around her again. "It will be okay. Stay where there are other people during the day. I will check first thing about staying on days for a couple of weeks, so I can spend the nights here until this is sorted out." She nodded and leaned into him again. "Why don't you try and get some sleep?" He watched her glance at her room before she looked back up at him. A gentle half smile appeared on his face as he patted the couch beside him. "Sleep here."

She appeared to consider his offer for a moment before she shook her head. "You need the couch so that you can sleep too. I'll just leave the door open and light on out here. If that's okay?"

"Whatever you need."

She flushed red again and looked down at her hands, "Thank you."

"Any time," he said as he tightened his arms around her. He held her for a few minutes more before he let go and she went into her room.

Sara woke up in the morning to hear Paige talking to herself in the kitchen. She got out of bed and walked into the kitchen.

"Everything okay?" she asked.

Paige jumped at her sudden appearance. She looked very tired and had large bags under her eyes.

"Was my brother really here last night?" She asked while holding up a piece of paper she found on the counter.

"Yes, don't you remember?"

Paige groaned before she dramatically put her head on the counter, "No, I don't remember anything after you left to go practice."

"You were drinking before I left?" Sara asked, her eyes wide.

"How do you know that?"

Sara sighed, and it took her a few moments to work up the courage to tell her. Paige had been so unpredictable lately that she avoided her at times.

"I think we need to talk," she said finally. "Jake is the one who figured out that you were drinking. He'll be back tonight when he gets off duty."

"Oh joy," Paige groaned. "He's just coming to give me a hard time again."

"He's not just coming to give you a hard time," Sara said, her voice becoming annoyed.

"And what would you know about it?" Paige snapped.

"A lot more than you," Sara said, her voice rising. "Since I can remember what happened yesterday. I think you should be worried since you don't have a clue."

Paige stood frozen in place and just stared at her friend. She had never heard Sara raise her voice... ever.

"So, what did happen yesterday?" Paige's attitude changed in an instant and she appeared to be worried. Sara sighed again before she told her roommate everything that took place the previous day. When she was finished, Paige was again just staring at her. Her eyes were wide, and her discomfort was apparent on her face.

"Wow, that's scary and I screwed up royally." Paige fell quiet for a minute before she continued in a whine, "Oh my goodness, my head hurts so much I can't even think. We'll talk later."

"I have to get to class anyway," Sara said glancing at the clock on the wall. "I'll talk to you later."

Paige waved a hand at her with her head sitting on the counter.

"Bye," Sara called as she left the apartment.

"Don't yell," Paige groaned but Sara was already gone.

Sara was on edge for most of the day, but she did what Jake suggested and stayed in the crowded areas of the campus. Her day went by without issue as she headed into the music building for her last class. She took her usual seat near the back and waited for the professor to arrive. When the door opened, she glanced up and froze in terror. The man from the night before waltzed into the room. He was clothed from head to toe in black.

"Good afternoon," His deep voice reverberated around the room. "Your normal professor is on leave for a few weeks and I will be taking her place. I am Lon Hildar." He glanced around the room and his eyes stopped when he found Sara. A sly smile flashed across his face before he turned his attention back to the rest of the room. "Who can tell me where you left off on your music theory?"

A few students raised their hands to answer the question while Sara took the opportunity to snatch her things off the floor and bolt out of the classroom. She did not stop running until she was more than halfway back to the apartment. When she stopped, she bent over and rested her hands on her knees as she tried to catch her breath.

"Is something wrong?" A familiar voice asked. She looked up and found Kaedin standing next to her. His expression darkened when he noticed she was trembling from head to toe and her phone was clutched in her hand. "Sara?"

She jumped when he said her name and started backing away from him. Her hand tightened on the phone.

"I'm fine," she mumbled.

"Are you certain?" He asked as he took an unconscious step toward her. She flinched away from him and he stopped moving while he struggled to keep his conflicted feelings hidden. She stared up at him for a moment before she turned and ran in the direction of the apartment. Kaedin watched her for a minute before he trailed her home at a distance. Once he saw her go inside the building he stopped and Raven and Hikaru appeared beside him.

"We need to find out who is trying to get to her and why," Kaedin said without taking his eyes off the building. Raven and Hikaru started toward the campus but paused when Kaedin did not follow right away.

"Jaeha is near," Raven said causing Kaedin to look back at him. He glanced back at the building once more before he sighed and followed them back to the campus.

Sara dashed into the apartment and locked the door behind her. She looked around and did not see Paige. Fear coursed through her when she realized she was alone, and she hurried into her room. She locked that door also before she sat huddled in the corner of her room. She pulled her knees to her chest and tried to figure out what to do. Her first instinct was to call Jake, but she knew he would not be off yet. She tightened her arms around her legs and rested her head on her knees. Struggling to remain calm she wracked her mind trying to come up with a plan, but nothing came to her.

A sudden, soft knock on the door to her room caused her jump. Her eyes flew to the door, but she remained quiet.

"Sara?" Paige's voice asked from the other side of the door. "Are you in there?"

Sara stood up but did not approach the door right away. She could not figure out why, but Paige's voice sounded a little off. It took her a couple minutes before she decided she was being paranoid. She unlocked the door and went to open it, but it was flung open and hit her. Staggering backwards, she struggled to remain on her feet when a look of terror became fixed on her face. It was not Paige at the door.

"Hello Sara," Lon said, his voice sounded just like Paige.

Sara scrambled backwards to put more space between them when he stalked into the room.

"Where are you going?" He asked his voice back to normal. An amused smile crossed his face when he saw she was already shaking. Sara's eyes did not leave him as he continued toward the back of the room. When he was only a couple of feet away from her, she tried to sprint for the door.

"Pevanas," He said with a small wave of his hand. A sudden wind slammed into her and sent her sailing across the living room. She hit the wall with a loud thud and fell to the floor. Getting up on her knees she struggled to take a deep breath, the force of the impact knocked the wind out of her.

"No, no," Lon mocked. "We do not want to run." He crossed the room with unhurried steps while he acted like a cat playing with its prey. Sara managed to get back to her feet before he reached her.

"What do you want?" She stammered.

"I told you before I am looking for someone." He leapt toward her. She jerked away and opened her mouth to scream. Moving so fast it was impossible for her to react, he grabbed her and had his right hand over her mouth in an instant.

"Now, now," he chastised. "We do not need any unwanted guests." He tightened his grip as she fought to get away from him. "Let us see if my inference is correct."

"Kāepkara," he said, his voice becoming icy as he held up his left hand above her.

Sara's eyes widened with fear when his hand started to glow a strange pale green and as the glow grew brighter, she felt a strange burning sensation. It was like something was being torn inside of her. She started to scream when the pain intensified, but his hand muffled the sound.

"Fight him!"

She almost did not hear the voice speaking to her.

'How?' She thought just before she screamed again. The pain was becoming unbearable.

"Elbow, kick, hit, anything!" The voice sounded like she was also in pain.

"Interesting," he muttered. "But it is not enough proof yet." The glow started to dim as his attention turned from the spell. Sara took the chance when the pain lessened to slam her elbow into his stomach as hard as she could. He grunted more in shock than from pain, but his grip slipped enough that she could pull away. She fought to remain on her feet and scrambled toward the door of the apartment when it suddenly opened. Paige started to walk in but stopped when she saw Sara. She took about half a second to observe before she grabbed Sara's hand and the two of them ran down the hall of the apartment building. They made it outside before Lon appeared on the path in front of them.

"Going somewhere?" he asked.

They skidded to a halt. Sara glanced around and shivered when she realized he had stopped them in a section of the path that was hidden from view of the building by large bushes. She looked down when she felt something hit her hand. Paige tried to hand her the phone she had behind her back. Sara took it and stepped to the left to keep the phone hidden from view.

"That is not going to assist you," Lon said with a dark chuckle. "Pevanas!" He waved his hand and another strong wind hit them. It knocked the phone out of Sara's hand and with another wave of his hand it flew toward him. He snatched it out of the air, and before either girl could react, he crushed it and dropped the pieces on the ground. When his full attention returned to them, they started backing away. He raised his hand again as he stalked toward them but before he could say anything, Jaeha appeared in front of the girls. Lon stopped and his eyes widened for a split second.

"Here babysitting? That leaves someone important alone, does it not?" Lon asked, his normal smug demeanor returning.

"What are you doing here?" Jaeha asked, ignoring his question.

Lon chuckled with a cold smile but did not answer the question, "Cūdāe." He disappeared a split second after saying the strange word but Jaeha did not lower his hand right away. After nothing happened for a few moments, he faced the girls. They were clinging to each other eyes wide with fear.

"Come," Jaeha said, his voice calm. When they exchanged wary glances, he sighed. "I will not harm you. We need to go back inside. It is safer than out here."

They hesitated, but after a few moments decided to follow him back inside. He led them back into the building and up to their apartment. When they were about to open the door, Jake walked around the corner and down the hall toward them. He was not paying attention until he was almost to their apartment. Once he saw them, he stopped and looked back and forth between them and Jaeha. His expression darkened as he took in their appearance.

"I believe this is where I take my leave," Jaeha said with a small head bow to the girls. He gave Jake a small head nod as he passed him. Jake was confused but followed them into the apartment.

"What is going on?" he asked.

Neither of them answered right away. Paige just sat down on the floor where she was, and Sara walked over to Jake. He pulled her into a hug and waited.

"I don't know what happened," Paige said, breaking the silence. "I got here, and some man was in here and Sara was running for the door. I grabbed her hand and we ran. The man caught us outside but Jaeha showed up and he left."

Jake stiffened as soon as he heard there had been a man in the apartment. He looked down at Sara, "The same one?" She nodded but did not look up at him. "Tell me everything."

Without letting go of him, Sara told them everything that had happened. When she was finished and glanced up at him, his face was blank. She knew now that meant he was suppressing his emotions. It took him a few moments before he made any kind of response.

"He touched you," He asked, his voice taking a dangerous edge. When Sara nodded, she felt him clench and unclench the hand that was against her back several times. Paige watched him. She was a little unnerved by his tone since she had never heard him use it before. Sara looked up at him and he gave her a strained smile.

"I am going to need a minute," he said in a controlled voice. "I think we should watch some TV for a little while and then we can discuss this further." The girls did not make any comment as they all headed over to the couch and chair.

A short time later, Sara could tell that Jake had relaxed. He was absentmindedly brushing his fingertips across her back while they watched an outdoor survival show.

"So," Paige said over the TV. Jake looked over at her and waited for her to continue. "What are we going to do?"

"I'll go to class with Sara in the morning," he said without even pausing to think. "I'd like to meet this man."

"Don't you have to work?" Paige asked.

"Nope, I have the day off tomorrow."

The next day the girls went to their various classes for the day much to Paige's displeasure. This was the first day since she started college that she attended all her classes. She found having her brother around to be annoying.

When it was time for Sara's last class, she dragged her feet as they approached the music building.

"It'll be fine," Jake said. "I'm with you this time."

She nodded before they entered the classroom and sat down. A few minutes passed and a kind looking older woman walked into the room.

"That's my normal professor," Sara said confused. She looked around the room and no one else seemed to notice. Turning to one of the other students she asked, "When did our usual professor come back?"

"What do you mean?" The student asked.

"We had a substitute last class."

"I don't know what class you were in, but we've never had a substitute," the student replied before she turned back to her notebook.

"He was her--."

"I'm sure he was," Jake said cutting her off. "He made himself sound like Paige. Who knows what else he can do."

She started tapping her thumb on the desk in agitation and Jake reached down and grabbed her hand.

"Do you want to leave?" He asked in a whisper. She nodded and the two left the room.

The next week passed without Lon showing up again much to Sara's relief. Jake spent all the nights he had off at the girl's apartment. He was unable to get off the night shift rotation, so when he could not be there, much to his displeasure, Raven would stay with them.

On Saturday afternoon, Sara stood looking at a couple of outfits laid out on her bed. She bit her lip when she just could not decide what to wear.

"Sara," Paige said as she walked into her room. "Aren't you ready to go yet? We're going to be late for the homecoming game."

"No," Sara said with a nervous sigh. "I can't pick what to wear."

Paige rolled her eyes, "He'll like anything! Just come on."

"It's our first real date," Sara whispered, her face turning crimson.

"Oh, alright," Paige said with a giggle. After looking over what Sara had laid out, she grabbed a layered blue and white tank top, a pair of brown jeans, a green military style jackets, and her normal navy shoes with daisies. "Hurry and put this on so I can help you with your hair."

Sara took the clothes and changed as soon as Paige left the room. When she was finished, she left her room and found Paige waiting in the bathroom. She pulled up the sides of her hair and put it in a barrette. After leaving her bangs down she curled the rest of her hair.

"There," she said with a grin when she was finished.

"Thanks," Sara said with a smile. "You're in a better mood."

"Yeah, I know I was a real pain." Paige frowned. "Jake and I talked the other day and he explained everything about dad. I never had any idea what really happened. I feel a lot better about it now."

"I'm glad."

"Yeah I'm sure you are," she said with a laugh. "Let's go!" She grabbed Sara and pulled her with her toward the door. They left the apartment and made their way to the stadium via the campus shuttle. When they arrived, Paige met up with Raven and they all headed into the stadium. Sara could not help but fidget with the sleeve of her jacket while she waited on Jake to arrive. It was only a couple of minutes before she spotted him making his way through the crowd of students. She smiled when she saw him. He was wearing his civilian clothes again.

"You look very nice," he said with a smile when he reached her side.

"Thank you," she whispered as she flushed bright red. "You look good to--."

"Aww," Paige's voice interrupted. "How cute." She laughed when her brother gave her a dirty look and turned her attention back to Raven.

The four of them watched the game before the students headed to a nearby field for a large bonfire. When they reached the field Paige and Raven drifted away from Jake and Sara. As they walked toward the fire Jake reached over and took hold of Sara's hand. He interlaced their fingers and she glanced up at him with a shy smile. They stood watching the fire together while groups of students milled around.

"Are you enjoying yourself?" Jake asked.

"Yes, are you?"

"Yup, I wish we could do this more often."

Sara nodded in agreement before she rested her head on his arm. Jake squeezed her hand in response. They continued to watch the flames as they extended higher into the sky as the students added more fuel. It was not long before Jake sighed, and Sara leaned away from him.

"We need to head back?"

"Yeah," Jake said, his voice unhappy. "I have to work the early shift tomorrow."

"It's okay," she said. "I understand."

He squeezed her hand again, "I'm so lucky that you do."

She gave him another shy smile before they headed toward the jeep hand in hand. They were almost back when Sara suddenly stopped dead in her tracks. Jake glanced down at her in confusion before he saw that she was not looking at him. He followed her gaze and found a figure standing in front of them. Pulling her back, he stepped forward to stand in front of her.

"Hello again, Sara," Lon said.

Jake felt her start trembling the moment the man spoke, and he tightened his grip on her hand, "What do you want?"

"I would believe that would be obvious by this point," Lon replied with a smirk. "I shall be taking the young lady."

"You'll have to get through me first."

Lon laughed, "That shall not be a problem." He moved so fast that it was almost impossible to see and appeared behind Sara as he reached out to grab her. Jake pulled her out of the way and blocked Lon's hand with an open palm causing Lon's eyes to narrow.

"You are quick," he said, his tone unimpressed. "But let us see how good you are." He stalked around the two of them. Jake analyzed the situation in an instant. He knew if he let Sara get too far from him that Lon would use that to his advantage. Wrapping his arm around Sara's waist, he pulled her against his chest. Her feet were up off the ground so that he could still move around. It would be harder to fight but he would not have to try and keep track of her this way.

Lon launched at him with a flurry of blows. Jake countered or dodged them as he waited for an opening. He twisted to the left and blocked a blow with his shoulder before he spun back and landed a solid blow to the center of Lon's chest. Lon gasped and took a surprised step backwards. His eyes narrowed as he regarded him, and Jake took the opportunity to adjust his grip on Sara.

"I do not have time to play with you," Lon snarled as he took a step forward and then disappeared. Jake glanced around before he lowered his head and closed his eyes. Sara felt his strong muscles tense a few seconds before he took a quick step to the left as Lon became visible again. He raised his right arm in front of his face and blocked Lon's blow. A momentary look of shock crossed Lon' face before he took a step back.

"It would appear as if I have underestimated you," he said, his voice ice cold. "But it is time to end this game." He pulled out a katana from its scabbard that was laced tight to his back. Jake did not hesitate to pull out the pistol he had concealed at his side. The two leveled their weapons at each other.

"Jake!" Paige's voice carried from around the bushes behind them.

"Hey, Jake!" The sound of Raven's voice joined hers.

Jake did not take his eyes off Lon as he shifted enough that he would be between Lon and Paige when she came around the bushes. Lon's irritation at being interrupted again was palpable.

"Cūdāe," he snapped before he disappeared. Paige and Raven came around the corner just after Lon was gone. Paige froze when she saw her brother and looked around in confusion when she did not see anyone else around them.

"What's going on?" she asked.

Jake holstered his weapon while Raven eased closer to Paige. He had his hand resting on the hilt of a dagger he had hidden under his shirt.

"Not now, get to the jeep," Jake said. He started moving in that direction taking Sara with him. Paige hurried to follow him, and Raven fell in behind her. He tried to appear like nothing was out of the ordinary, but he kept a wary eye on their surroundings. When they reached the jeep, Jake pulled open the passenger door behind the driver's seat and finally set Sara back down.

"Get in," he ordered as he glanced at Paige. She was getting into the jeep on the other side while Raven was standing behind her. He noticed Jake's glance.

"I shall remain here." Jake nodded in acknowledgment before climbing in the driver's seat. He started the jeep and headed in the direction of the apartment.

"Now what is going on?" Paige asked.

"That man tried to take Sara again," Jake said. His eyes did not leave the road as he kept a close on eye on their surroundings.

"What?" Paige gasped. "I can't believe he tried with you right there."

Jake's hands tightened on the steering wheel as his eyes narrowed in thought. There was something strange about that man. He felt like he had been toying with him and he did not like it.

"How did you avoid him when you couldn't see him?" Sara asked, her quiet voice shaking. Jake glanced in the rear-view mirror so that he could see her.

"My martial arts instructor used to make me fight blindfolded sometimes," he said as he looked back out the front. "He always said that you need to know if someone is there whether you can see them or not. When you fight multiple people, you can't only rely on your eyes." He glanced back at Sara again. "It's a good thing he did."

Sara could not repress the shudder that ran through her. She did not even want to think about what could have happened if Jake had not been able to protect them. They all fell silent for the rest of the trip back to the apartment.

Several hours later, Sara woke with a startled gasp. It took her a few seconds to get her bearings and once she realized she was in her room she laid back on the bed and took several deep breaths. She was dreaming about the attack and was panting. When she calmed down, she noticed the light in the living room was still on. She got out of bed and put on a flannel shirt over her tank top before leaving her room. After her eyes adjusted to the light, she saw Jake was standing in the bathroom. He had no shirt on and was looking at a large nasty bruise on his shoulder in the mirror. It covered the whole back of his left shoulder down to the shoulder blade, part way down the tricep, and up onto the top of the shoulder. He grimaced as he tried to rotate the shoulder. With a heavy sigh, he picked up a wrap and started to attempt to wrap it on his own.

"Are you okay?" Sara asked, her voice filled with concern.

Jake startled at her sudden appearance, but he covered well, "Yeah, I'm fine." He shrugged with his uninjured shoulder.

"Do you need any help? Ice?"

"I suppose I could use some help and ice would be great," he said with a sheepish smile. She nodded and went to get an ice pack and towel from the kitchen while he headed over to the couch. He sat down and waited for her. After she grabbed the supplies, she sat down on the couch facing him. He handed her the wrap and she peeked up at him. She had no idea what to do. He took the end of the wrap and put it on top of his shoulder.

"Start here," he began. "It will go back over the shoulder then under the arm twice."

Sara did what he said being careful not to pull it too tight. When she was finished, she looked up at him again.

"Across the back and under the other arm, then it will come back across the chest to the shoulder. That gets done twice too."

She got it wrapped around once before she started to blush. He was so close to her that her fingers started to tremble and on the second time around, she fumbled the wrap. She tried to keep from dropping it and her fingertips brushed across his chest. He took a sharp breath and shivered at her touch. Keeping her eyes away from his face, she pulled the wrap tight before bringing it back to his shoulder.

"Okay," he muttered, his voice low and husky. "The end goes around the bicep before being clipped."

Keeping her eyes glued to the wrap she did what he instructed before dropping her hands onto her lap. "Finished," she whispered.

"Thank you."

She peeked up at him through her bangs and found him watching her. He hesitated before he reached out and brushed her bangs out of her face. He tucked them behind her ear so that he could see her look at him. When he pulled his hand back his fingertips brushed along her cheekbone. She flushed again and bit her lip when she heard him take another sharp breath. He leaned forward and brought their faces inches apart.

A sudden movement on the other side of the room caused both of them to look up and see Paige dash into the bathroom.

"I'm sorry! I didn't see anything. Please continue!" She yelled from behind the closed door. Sara was so embarrassed even her ears were red. She handed Jake the ice pack and without looking at him ran for her room. Jake watched her go before he leaned back on the couch with a frown.

"Sisters are the incarnation of pure evil," he muttered under his breath as he put the ice pack on his shoulder.

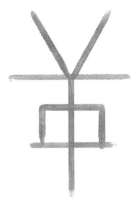

Sara sat on her bed rubbing her sore fingers. Her last performance test for the semester was a couple hours ago. As much as she loved playing, she was relieved to have a break from all the practicing. She chuckled when she remembered Paige's demand earlier. Her violin was off limits until winter break was over.

"Sara!" Paige's sudden yell as she ran into her room made Sara jump. "I'm finished with my last final. It's time to get out of here!"

"How did you do?" Sara asked but made no move to get up off her bed.

Paige rolled her eyes, "I don't care. Let's go!"

"Are you sure it's okay for us to go to your uncle's cabin?" Sara asked with a shiver. "I mean it's really close to the cave and your uncle won't be there."

"It'll be fine like I said before we won't go anywhere near it. We'll stay in the cabin the whole time, and that crazy guy won't know because we haven't told anyone where we're going for break." She paused with a frown. "I didn't even tell Raven."

"What about Jake?"

Paige held up a piece of paper with a grin, "I left him a message on his phone already and I'm leaving this note just in case he doesn't listen to the message, so worst case he will know by tonight." Her grin widened. "See, I already thought of everything."

Sara grimaced and shook her head. She was sure that Paige had not thought of everything. She never did.

128

"Come on! Come on!" Paige whined as she was beginning to quiver with anticipation. "We need to get going. There is supposed to be a snowstorm later and we need to beat it. I can't stand the idea of being stuck here for break."

"Alright," Sara replied with a louder sigh. "I'm coming." She stood up from her bed and picked up her small travel bag. Even though she was opposed to going, she knew Paige was going to insist that they make the trip. After Paige gathered the rest of her things the two left the apartment and headed down the parking lot. When they walked up to an old, beat up red Volkswagen bug Sara stopped.

"Who's is this?" she asked.

"A girl in one of my classes said we could borrow it for break," Paige said as she pulled open the driver's door. "It's her brother's but they aren't leaving for break."

Sara eyed the car with a deep frown. There were multiple rust spots all over the outside and when she opened the door, she could see the plywood and two by fours holding up the floor.

"Are you sure it will make it up there?"

"Oh come on, where is your sense of adventure," Paige asked with a laugh. "I'm sure it will be fine."

Sara rolled her eyes when she showed Paige her seatbelt. It was tied in a knot because the strap was broken.

Paige laughed again, "It just gives it a little character." She put the key in the ignition and started the car. The whole thing vibrated but it somehow stayed running. Sara just shook her head and climbed into the passenger seat. Once she was situated, Paige grinned and pulled out of the parking lot.

About an hour later, the girls stood next to the car pulled off on the side of the road while Paige was staring at the engine. The hood was open, and smoke was pouring out of the rear end. She looked up and shrugged. "I guess it won't make it. We better start walking. I think we're still a couple miles from the cabin."

Sara glanced at her watch. It was still early afternoon, so they should have enough time to make it to the cabin before dark. Looking around she sighed when she realized there was already a foot of snow on the ground from the last snowstorm, and more snow was starting to fall.

"I thought the snow storm wasn't supposed to get here until tonight?" She asked, and Paige just shrugged.

"How often are the weather folks actually right?" She giggled and threw Sara her bag before grabbing her own. The two started wading through the snow. They only walked for a little while before the sky began to darken.

"Wow, it's really starting to come down now," Paige said. Her demeanor lost its excitement and became worried as she looked at the sky.

"We need to hurry."

The girls picked up the pace as they trudged through the snow. In a matter of about twenty minutes, almost six more inches of fresh snow blanketed what was already on the ground. Sara stopped to catch her breath.

"How much farther?" She asked with a shiver. The temperature was steadily dropping as more snow fell.

"I'm not sure," Paige said as she glanced around. "I figured we would have been there by now."

"What're we going to do?" Sara asked, her voice taking an edge of panic. "We're going to freeze with no shelter." Her eyes scanned the area around them and found nothing but trees and snow.

"We keep walking. There's still a little daylight left. If we don't find it soon, we'll have to look for a place to make a camp."

Paige did not wait for Sara to reply before she turned and started walking again. The snow was now nearing two feet deep and Sara was tired from the hour they had spent walking. She folded her arms over her chest to keep warm and followed Paige. She had no idea what to do other than listen to her friend.

"There!" Paige yelled after another half an hour. Sara looked up and breathed a sigh of relief when she saw the cabin up ahead. She started to walk faster when she stopped dead. There was a figure standing in the road in front of them. She reached out to grab Paige's arm, but the man raised his hand.

"Pevanas," Lon growled, and a strong wind sent both girls sailing through the air. Sara lost sight of Paige when she slammed into a pine tree. She tried to get up, but Lon was already there pinning her down, his knee on the middle of her chest.

"Finally," He growled. "You left your protectors."

Sara's eyes widened with fear when she realized who it was holding her down. She struggled to get free, but he held her firm.

"No more playing nice. I have to verify that you are in there." He wrapped both hands around her throat and started to squeeze.

Sara struggled to pull his hands away, but he was far too strong.

"Come on," he snarled at her. "Fight me! Come on! I know you are in there. He would not be here otherwise."

"Fight him!"

Sara could barely hear the voice above the ringing in her ears.

"I should know him. Why can I not remember?"

Sara reached out and hit Lon to get him to release his grip, but it was like hitting a stone. It made no difference.

"Fight me!" He yelled again before he started reciting some kind of incantation.

Sara could not make sense of what he was saying as she started to lose consciousness.

"No! Fight him!" The voice yelled. She sounded like she was in pain while Lon continued reciting.

"No! Do not give in!"

The darkness started to close in on Sara and she tried one last time to get him to loosen his grip. When it did not work her hands dropped limp into the snow. Everything was fading when a multitude of images flashed through her mind.

"Londar! I remember!" Sara was barely aware of the voice when the weight on her was suddenly lifted. She gasped for air and it took a moment before she was able to see her surroundings again. When she could, she found Paige standing over Lon with a large log in her hand. He was now lying unconscious on the ground.

"Get up," Paige yelled. "We have to get to the cabin." She reached down and helped her to her feet. Sara struggled to get her bearing and had to lean on Paige as they hurried to get inside. Once they made it, Paige locked the door before they both headed upstairs. Sara collapsed on the couch and Paige pulled her new phone out of her pocket. She ignored the several missed calls and dialed a number. It only rang once before Jake answered.

"Where are you?" he asked. "This snow is crazy. I can't believe you would go anywhere with that ma--."

"He's here," Paige interrupted. "That Lon guy." She heard Jake curse on the other end of the line.

"Where?" He snapped, his voice laced with concern.

"We're already at the cabin," Paige said before she noticed movement out of the corner of her eye. She spun and gasped when she saw Lon standing in the room with them. Sara was backing toward Paige while Lon glared at them. He had blood running down the side of his head.

"I believe I have a favor to return," he growled. "Pevanas." He threw his hand up and sent Paige sailing into the wall of the cabin. Her head connected with the wood beam with a sickening crack. She collapsed to the floor and did not move. Lon stalked over and picked up her phone.

"Greetings Jacob," he said with a smug smile.

"Where's my sister?" Jake demanded, causing Lon to chuckle.

"She is unable to speak to you at this time." He did not wait for Jake to reply before he snapped the phone in half and dropped the pieces to the floor. Turning his attention to Sara, he paused in surprise. She was not in the same spot. He found her crouched over Paige. Her hands glowed as she held them over Paige's head.

"Oh no, you do not," he snarled as he made a leap at her. To his surprise she deftly avoided him, and he stopped moving. "Rin, nice to see you again." His tone became sarcastic when he saw Sara's eyes were now a brilliant green.

"I cannot say it is nice to see you, Londar," she snapped back at him. He laughed before he launched at her. She dodged to the side before she met him blow for blow. It almost appeared like a choreographed dance, until she ducked to the side and grabbed his arm. She pulled it back hard and dropped him to his knees with a kick to the back of his leg.

"Āega bulāe," he said. He brought up his other hand and a fireball shot from his hand.

"Ksāetras," she gasped as she flinched back and got a force wall up quick enough to block the fire spell. They continued like this for a while before she started to breath heavy and her movements started to slow.

"What is wrong, Rin?" He sneered at her. "The little girl cannot take it, can she?" Before she had a chance to reply to him, he threw his hand into the air, "Vēijal." A lightning bolt shot from his hand. She could not get a force wall up in time and was thrown into the wall behind her. Before she could fall, Londar was there pinning her to the wall. His forearm was across her throat holding her in place. Rin was no longer in control and it was Sara who looked back at him with fear filled eyes. He jerked a yellow crystal out of his pocket and held it up next to her.

"You are mine now," he said, his voice hard and cruel. He tightened his grip on the crystal before he began to recite a different incantation. The crystal began to glow. Sara struggled to get free, but she began to scream in pain. Rin's soul was being ripped from her and forced into the crystal. Her entire body felt like it was burning.

"Do not worry, it will be over soon child," Londar mocked. His eyes were filled with burning hatred when he started to speak the last words of the incantation. He only had a handful of words left when he was suddenly jerked backwards. The crystal flew out of his hand and landed beside where Sara collapsed to the floor. It shattered when it hit the floor and Rin's soul flowed back into Sara's body.

"No!" Londar howled as he spun and came face to face with Kaedin. They were both frozen in surprise before Jaeha, Raven, and Hikaru appeared in the room seconds later. Kaedin made a move to grab Londar when Jake burst into the room. He was armed with a shotgun and everyone in the room froze.

"Cūdāe!" Kaedin's attention shifted to Londar when he heard the spell word. His expression became furious when he turned just in time to see him disappear. He spun back to face Jake and jerked the shotgun out of his hands before he threw it across the room. It slammed into the wall with a loud crash.

"We are here to assist," Kaedin snapped. "And, now you have allowed Londar to get away!"

Jake gave no ground as he regarded Kaedin. He had no idea what was going on but was furious.

Jaeha stepped in between the two. "Now is not the time," he said, his voice taking a commanding tone. "The girls must be assisted."

Kaedin glanced at Jaeha before he moved toward Paige, but Jake grabbed his arm to stop him.

"What are you doing?" he demanded.

Kaedin jerked his arm free. "I can heal her. It is not my strong suit, but I am capable."

Jake tried to keep him from touching his sister, but Jaeha and Raven got hold of his arms and pulled him backwards.

"Be still," Jaeha said.

Jake tried to break free, but he could not budge Jaeha, so he had no choice but to wait. Kaedin walked over to Paige and knelt beside her before he closed his eyes in concentration.

"Rujhāe," he said and a second later his hands were glowing with a pale blue light. He held them over Paige's head and pushed his healing magic into her. Once he stopped the flow of magic it was a few minutes before she began to come around. When Kaedin saw she was waking up he moved over to Sara. Raven let go of Jake's arm and hurried to help Paige sit up.

"I can do nothing for Sara," Kaedin said, his voice frustrated as he stood back up.

As soon as Jaeha released his arm, Jake rushed over to check on Paige and then Sara. When he reached Sara, his brows furrowed when he could feel she was burning before even laying a hand on her. Her hair was plastered to her face with sweat and her breathing was rapid and shallow. He scooped her up off the floor before turning to face Kaedin.

"What is going on?"

Kaedin just stared at him before he glanced at Jaeha.

"It is time," Jaeha said with a nod. "He has proven himself."

Kaedin did not appear convinced as he looked back at Jake. "I believe that he has proven nothing. He caused us to lose Londar and possibly valuable information." Jake opened his mouth to retort.

"Enough," Jaeha said, his voice raising. "Kaedin act according to your station and Jacob if you wish to save Sara then listen."

Both Jake and Kaedin looked away from the other. They both felt like they had been chastised by an elder and it was several minutes before Kaedin broke the silence.

"What do you wish to know?" He asked without making eye contact with Jake.

"Everything," Jake replied before he sat down on the couch still holding Sara. Kaedin glanced over at him and his eyes narrowed as he fought to keep his emotions under control. It was difficult for him to watch Jake holding Sara when he could sense Rin in the same place. He exhaled heavily as he closed his eyes and tried to collect his thoughts. When he still said nothing after several minutes, Jaeha tilted his head with a frown. He knew Kaedin was unaccustomed to taking the lead. It was usually Rin.

"I shall begin," Jaeha said taking over. "The first thing that you must be made aware of is that we are from a different world. We are from a place called Asaetara. There was, for now I shall call it an accident but it appears as if it may have been done on purpose, an accident a little over twenty years ago that caused all of this. Our princess, Lady Rilaeya, or Rin as you have heard Kaedin refer to her, was used to tear open a portal between our world and yours. We are uncertain of the over-all goal and have only recently discovered that it appears to be linked to the demon realm as well, but that is a topic for another time." He paused for a moment and glanced at Kaedin. He was staring out one of the cabin windows. "Over the years we have searched for Lady Rin but were unable to locate her until recently. She began to wake up in Sara and since Kaedin is her bonded, he was able to sense her again."

"Bonded?" Jake interrupted. "What do you mean?"

Jaeha frowned, "Bonding is a complicated process. For now, a simple explanation will have to do. Lady Rin and Kaedin share blood and it allows them to sense each other. They can feel the other's emotions, pain, and it allows them to know where the other is at all times." Jake opened his mouth to ask another question but Jaeha shook his head. "Now is not the time for these questions, there are more pressing matters at hand. As I was saying, Lady Rin started to wake up and Kaedin was able to sense her in Sara. This presents a rather large problem. We have not located Lady Rin's body, and if we do not find it soon, they will both die. Sara's body is not capable of dealing with the amount of magical power that Lady Rin possesses. The magic is burning her which is what is causing the fevers."

"Wait," Jake said, unable to remain silent anymore. "Are you trying to tell me that there is another person inside of Sara?"

"That is correct."

"No," Jake said shaking his head. "No, there is no way, this is all crazy." He glanced over when Paige sat down on the couch next to him and rested her head on his shoulder.

"With all the other crazy stuff going on," she whispered. "I think something like this is the only thing that makes sense." She paused. "I mean Sara said someone was talking to her."

Jake's eyes filled with worry when he could see the pain all over her face. "Are you okay?" She nodded even though she had a massive headache. Jake frowned as he watched her for a moment before he turned his attention out the nearest window. He was deep in thought before a look of realization and apprehension crossed his face.

"What does she look like?" he asked. Kaedin glanced over at him with a look of disapproval but did not reply. "What does she look like?" Jake repeated when no one said anything.

A pained look crossed Kaedin's face, "She has long curly silver hair with red and black streaks, bright green eyes." He paused and swallowed hard. His voice filled with longing as he continued, "She is about the same height as Sara, perhaps an inch taller. The last time I saw her, she was wearing a green velvet dress cake--."

"Caked with mud along the bottom," Jake finished for him as he shook his head. "I know where she is, but I have no idea how you are going to get to her."

Kaedin's eyes opened wide with surprise and a faint glimmer of hope. "Where?"

"She's being kept on my base," Jake replied. "I was just recently shown that she was there. She's in a high-security area. They know she's not human, but she has some kind of energy around her, so they haven't been able to do anything with her."

"Do what?" Kaedin's voice filled with suspicion causing Jake to clear his throat and obviously look away from him.

"Well," Jake began, his voice hesitant. "They probably would have done experiments on her and maybe dissected her if they could."

Kaedin's eyebrow rose as he listened to him. "They would have harmed her?" His voice betrayed a hint of his anger at the thought of anyone harming his bonded.

"Possibly," Jake muttered.

"Let us focus on getting her out of there before I do something I may come to regret," Kaedin growled. Jake glanced up at him before he nodded.

Several hours later, everyone was gathered in the living room. Jake was sitting on the floor beside the couch where he laid Sara. He was changing the rags on her neck and forehead. His expression darkened again with anger when he looked at the bruises on her neck.

On the other side of the room, Paige was asleep laying on the floor on top of several blankets. She refused to go to another room. Raven sat beside her and was running his fingers lightly through her hair. Kaedin, Jaeha, and Hikaru sat on the floor in the middle of the room and all appeared to be deep in thought.

"I wish to verify that I understand the facts," Jaeha said breaking the silence. "This military installation is built into the side of a large mountain and the section that we need is six stories below the surface. There are multiple doors controlled by key cards, which I am still not certain that I understand, and doors with fingerprint scan, painting things." He paused with a frown when he stumbled over the unfamiliar words. "Not to mention painting makers everywhere that shall paint us if they see us."

Jake nodded with a shrug. He was not sure how else to explain fingerprint scanners and cameras to them. It had become apparent to him very quickly that they did not know much about the technology on Earth.

"Do you have one of these keycard, things?" Kaedin asked.

"Yes, I do," Jake replied, his voice hesitant. "Though I would appreciate not having to spend the rest of my life in prison for helping you."

"We shall not require anything from you that would jeopardize your standing," Jaeha said. "We must be more clever."

Raven looked up from Paige. "We could easily slip inside with invisibility and short teleportation spells for the doors. Jake would only have to give us directions."

"We cannot cast that many spells," Kaedin said. "There is no way to know for certain how many doors there will be."

"I can," Raven said with a disapproving look. "I am an elf, not a dr--." Kaedin cut him off with a sharp glance.

Jake noticed, and his brows furrowed when he wondered what Kaedin was trying to keep him from finding out.

"I believe Raven has presented a viable option," Jaeha said. "We do not wish to cause more problems for Jacob."

"But we need a small group to avoid detection," Kaedin said, his voice unhappy. "If Jacob must go then it should be you and me."

"Raven shall go in my place. It is his duty to see to Lady Rin."

"You are going to ignore Lord Wren's wishes?" Kaedin asked, his eyebrow raising.

Jaeha's expression hardened in an instant. "Do not presume to know what my bonded brother wishes of me," he said, his voice rising. "I shall fulfill my duty as I see fit and in this instance, Raven is needed more than me."

Kaedin shrank back from Jaeha before he bowed his head and looked down at the floor. "Apologies," he muttered under his breath.

"When are we going to go?" Jake asked, his full attention on Sara. "Her temperature is way too high and her body can't take much more of this fever."

"We can go now," Raven said standing up and walking over to join them. He looked over at Kaedin.

"Do you need anything before we leave?" Kaedin asked Jake. When Jake shook his head no, he got up and walked to the center of the room. "Both of you come over here."

Jake picked Sara up off the couch and moved so that he was next to Kaedin. Raven joined them with a smile. He was a little too excited for Jake and Kaedin's liking.

Kaedin looked between them before he put a hand on Jake and

Raven's shoulders. "I shall cast the invisibility spell before I port us using the description Jacob gave to us. Once we are there, Raven, you are in charge of all the ports and I shall keep the invisibility active. If we run into any serious trouble, Raven, you are to get Rin, Jacob, and Sara safely back here. I will do whatever is necessary to cover your escape." Once they both nodded, he closed his eyes in concentration.

"Araesya," he said, and they disappeared from view. Once he finished the invisibility spell, he pictured in his mind the description of the outside of the main base building. It would be too dangerous to teleport inside because they might run into someone.

"Elipor ntaera," he said, his voice becoming strained. The room started to become hazy and appeared to blur before it began to change. A few moments later they stood in front of the main building. Kaedin was breathing heavily when he opened his eyes and looked around. He was not used to having to teleport three other people.

"Where now?" He asked Jake in a whisper.

"Follow me," Jake said, his voice low and quiet as he headed for the door into the building. He paused when they reached the door and two soldiers walked out. They walked right by them without a second glance. Jake exhaled the breath he did not realize he was holding. They really were invisible. Now that he was certain, he hurried forward and slipped through the door before it closed. Kaedin and Raven were right behind him. Without any hesitation, Jake made his way through the maze of hallways.

When they reached the end of one hall, he paused by a door and listened before he opened it. There was a staircase leading down. They began to descend deeper into the mountain with each floor they passed. Reaching the sixth floor, Jake paused again by the door. He just managed to leap out of the way when it suddenly flew open. His eyes narrowed when he saw his father walk through the door followed by his aide.

"I want to know what's going on with these creature sightings," the general snapped. "And where is my son?"

"I'm not sure, sir," the aide replied. "His supervisor said he left the base after his duty was concluded for the day."

Jake looked confused as he watched them walk past where they were hiding. Why was his dad asking about him? He could not shake the feeling he was missing something.

"Jacob," Kaedin hissed and Jake was just able to slip through the door before it closed.

"Stay close. This floor is always very busy," Jake whispered as they watched three people walk past before they jumped into the flow of traffic. Being careful not to run into anyone, Jake turned down a side hall that led to a massive steel door. When Jake stopped in front of it Raven stepped forward.

He put a hand on Jake and Kaedin's shoulder and closed his eyes.

"Ēlipor tūinkāe," he whispered. A few seconds later they were on the other side of the door. Jake shook off the momentary wave of dizziness that came with the jump and continued forward. They made several more twists and turns before coming to another massive steel door. Raven repeated the process and they appeared on the other side of the door. They continued like this through three more doors before Raven exhaled a little too loud and caused both Kaedin and Jake look at him in alarm. He shrugged with a grimace as he wiped sweat off his forehead.

Jake started walking again and they finally came to a steel door that was thicker and twice the width of the others. It had several other visible security features besides the key card. Raven once again ported them through the door but sagged against the wall after the jump as more sweat beaded on his forehead. Porting four people so many times was beginning to take its toll. Raven pushed off the wall with a shrug when he saw Kaedin's concern.

Jake hurried across the room to a small door off to the left side of the large room. He glanced around to be certain that no one was within earshot.

"She's in here," he whispered.

Taking a deep breath, Raven ported them one more time and they appeared in the room. Kaedin started to move toward the bed as soon as he saw that it really was Rin, but Jake grabbed his arm to stop him. He was looking around the room and appeared to be concerned. One entire wall that usually had coverings over the windows was open, and it looked like there was a group of scientists observing the room.

"That's not good," he whispered. "I have no idea what they are doing." As soon as the words were out of his mouth, ice cold air poured into the room.

"What good is this going to do?" One of the scientists asked. "We have tried numerous times to wake the alien. How will freezing it help?"

Jake's face paled and he looked up at the vents. He was at a complete loss for what to do. Kaedin jerked his arm free and moved to Rin, but he could not get through her force wall.

"We believe by freezing the body and then warming it slowly after a time, may be enough to shock it awake." Jake shook his head. That made no sense, but he did not have time to dwell on it when Sara suddenly started to shake. Her breathing was coming in ragged gasps. Her body was almost to its limit. He just stared at her when she started to glow with a golden light that came off her in wisps.

"Get her to Rin," Kaedin whispered. "Hurry!"

Jake glanced at the scientists through the windows before he approached the bed. When Sara was right beside to her the force wall vanished. Kaedin took a quick step forward and grabbed Sara's hand. He put her hand against Rin's. As soon as they were brought into contact Rin's body also began to glow. The golden wisps coming off Sara began to flow into her.

"What's going on in there? The strange energy field is gone. Turn off the cooling fans and get someone in there." A scientist called from where he was sitting in front of several monitors.

Kaedin and Raven exchanged glances before Raven nodded and raised his hands.

"Humasa, Ksäetras," he said. A thick fog spread through the room and a force wall appeared on the outside of the door.

Sara's body shuddered violently when the last of the golden light flowed out of her, but her breathing eased. It took several moments before Rin's body lost the glow as it accepted the return of her magic and soul. When the glow was completely gone, Rin suddenly took a deep breath and her eyes fluttered open.

"Rin." Kaedin's voice was laced with strong emotions when he grabbed her hand.

"Kaedin?" Her voice was hoarse and rough when she whispered his name. She was disoriented as she searched for him in the fog.

"We can't get in the door. Something is blocking it!" Kaedin glanced at the door before he reached down and pulled Rin off the bed. Alarms started going off all around them as soon as he moved her.

"We have to get out of here!" Jake said. He could just make out the soldiers moving around the other side of the window. "They'll break out the window to get in here."

Something large crashed into the window. Kaedin hurried over to Jake and Raven appeared beside them a second later.

"Get us out of here," Kaedin said, his full attention on the window behind them. Raven put his hands on their shoulders again and closed his eyes in concentration before he took multiple deep breaths.

"Hurry Raven!"

"Élipor ntäera," he said with a heavy sigh. They heard the sound of the window shattering as they vanished. Moments later they arrived back in the living room of the cabin.

Early the next morning, Rin woke long before anyone else. She stretched and smiled when she found that her body was responding again. When they first returned from the base, she could not move. A quiet sigh caused her to look beside her and she found Kaedin asleep next to her. Her hand started to tremble as she reached out and brushed several strands of hair out of his face. She just watched him sleep for a little while before she kissed his cheek and moved to get up. Before she could do more than turn around, a strong arm wrapped around her waist and pulled her backwards.

"Do not leave my side," he whispered, his voice taking a hollow tone. She moved so that she could look up at him.

"Forgive me, I did not mean to make you suffer so." She rested her hand on his cheek. He leaned into it and fought to keep his emotions under control while Rin ran her thumb along his cheekbone.

"There is much you need to tell me," he said. Rin froze before she shivered.

"No, not yet," she stammered. "I am not ready to relive all of that." Kaedin pulled her against him and wrapped both arms around her when he saw the hint of fear on her face.

"Please forgive me," he said in a whisper, his voice filled with remorse.

Rin rested her head on his chest. "There is nothing to forgive. What happened was not your fault, it was beyond either of our control." He did not reply, and she frowned. She could sense that he still felt guilt over what happened to her.

"Shall we take a walk?" She asked trying to change the subject. "I do not seem to have any effects of being asleep for twenty years other than I am intolerably stiff."

A gentle smile crossed his face before he nodded, "As you wish."

The two got up and dressed alone before Kaedin took hold of her hand. They headed out of the cabin to wander the woods together.

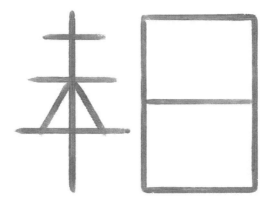

Rin and Kaedin arrived back at the cabin when everyone else was beginning to wake up. When they walked inside, they saw Paige dash across the hallway in front of them as she ran into the room with her brother and Sara.

"Sara," she said as she plopped down on her bed. Sara glanced at her before a small smile appeared on her face. "Are you feeling better?" Paige gave an exaggerated sigh when Sara only nodded and still did not say anything. Jake shook his head with a smile as he looked away from them. He was relieved that they were both all right. He glanced across the room and his smile slipped when he noticed Rin watching them from the doorway.

"Why does she still have a fever?" He asked, his voice taking a sharp edge. "Wasn't that supposed to be gone now that you aren't freeloading."

Rin raised her eyebrow with an amused smile, "Interesting choice of words Jacob." She crossed the room and held a hand out to Sara.

Sara hesitated as she just stared at her hand. Even though she knew this is the woman she had been hearing in her head, she did not feel like she really knew her. It took her a few moments before she reached out and put her hand in Rin's. With piercing green eyes, Rin observed her for several minutes causing Sara to shift as she got more uncomfortable when it felt like Rin was looking through her.

"It appears that Sara has retained a small piece of my magic," Rin said, letting go of her hand. "The fever shall go once her body accepts it."

"You were supposed to get out of her," Jake snapped, his voice started to rise, and he could not conceal all of his frustration.

"Yes, that would have been ideal," Rin said with a tilt of her head. "However, things never go quite according to plan when magic is involved. It seems to have its own will at times."

Jake stood up and moved around the bed so that he was right in front of her. "I want you out of Sara now." He glowered at her, but she seemed unfazed.

"I am out of her, Jacob," she said. "The magic that remains is hers. If I tried to remove it from her it would harm her."

His expression did not change as he folded his arms across his chest.

"Okay, well now that that is settled, let's figure out something to do!" Paige said, her voice filled with excitement. "We are on break!"

Jake glanced up to look at his sister but noticed Kaedin in the doorway. He was leaning casually against the door frame with his arms crossed. When he noticed Jake look at him, his eyebrow rose with disapproval. Jake frowned once he realized he had not noticed he was there.

"He has been there since you raised your voice," Rin answered his unspoken question and Jake narrowed his eyes.

"I didn't realize I raised my voice."

"Hey! I wasn't talking to myself," Paige yelled.

Rin looked over at Paige with a smile, "Forgive me, Paige. I do not know what there is to do here. However, I do have a request for you and Sara." Paige and Sara exchanged a quick glance. "Please do not worry. I only wish to, perhaps, borrow some of your clothes." She paused and pulled the skirt of her dress forward. "You see I have been in this gown for twenty years and would love to get out of it."

Paige's eyes opened wide as more excitement washed over her face.

"You mean I can pick out clothes for you?" She asked, and Sara rolled her eyes at her friend's enthusiasm.

"I suppose that would be all right, within reason," Rin replied, her voice becoming wary. She knew Paige was prone to taking things way too far. "They must be functional." Paige was not even listening to her as she bounded up next to her.

"Let's see," she said with a grin. "You look like you are about Sara's height, but you look a little smaller than her. Oh! Do I get to do your hair too?"

"Uh, --." Rin started to reply but Paige was already starting to shoo the men from the room.

"Out! Out!" Paige yelled. "We girls have things to do!" She pushed Jake toward the door and Kaedin was forced to step back. He was not impressed, and Jake could not keep from chuckling. It was nice to see his sister irritating someone other than him for a change. Kaedin expression darkened when he looked over at Jake. The two frowned at each other before they headed in different directions to wait for the girls.

A little while later, Jake was sitting in a chair in the living room tapping his thumb on the chair in impatience. He did not like leaving Paige and Sara alone with Rin. Sighing for the fifth time, he pulled his phone out of his pocket and noticed he had a missed call. He opened the menu to look and realized there were ten missed calls from the base. His eyes opened wide in shock and he immediately dialed the number.

"This is Captain Riverwood...," he started but the operator cut him off.

"One moment, sir, while I transfer you." Jake tapped on the arm of the chair while he waited several minutes before the phone started ringing again. It was picked up after one ring.

"Where have you been?" A firm voice asked on the other end of the line. Jake's eyes narrowed with anger when he realized it was his father.

"I left the base after completing my duty, sir," he snapped back. He heard a frustrated sigh on the other end of the line.

"Jak--."

"What's this about?" Jake asked. "You've never cared what has gone on with me until now." There was another sigh.

"There have been multiple sightings of creatures that are immune to our weaponry. I'm still your father and want to know where you are."

Jake bristled, and his face became unnaturally calm. "You gave up being my father the day you walked out on us. I will return in time for my scheduled shift tomorrow." He snapped the phone closed, cutting off the call before the general could respond. Jake shook his head in confusion. He did not understand what was going on. Why in the world of all times did his dad want to try and be a dad now? He shook his head again. It made no sense. He glanced at the time on his phone again and hoped the girls would be finished soon.

Rin stood looking at the clothes Paige had picked out for her. She tilted her head with a frown when most of it was unfamiliar to her. Picking up the dark brown cargo pants, she put them on and the sports bra before Paige turned back around.

"I am not finished," Rin said in surprise.

Paige shrugged, "I couldn't wait to see how it looked! Hurry up!"

Rin raised an eyebrow in disapproval before she picked up the black tank top and pulled it over her head.

"Whoa, you have a ton of scars," Paige said, her curiosity piqued. "How did you get all of those?"

Rin paused and looked down at the countless small and medium scars plus one or two big ones on her torso.

"Training and battles," she replied before turning her attention to a black sweatshirt. Her brows furrowed when she had no idea what to do with the zipper. "I do have to say this sports bra is very nice. We do not have these in my world." She continued fiddling with the zipper without looking back at Paige.

Paige tilted her head when she picked up on the fact that she was changing the subject and for once did not push the point. "All right ladies it's time to do hair!" She said clapping her hands together with excitement.

Once Rin figured out the zipper and closed the sweatshirt, she and Sara sat down, side by side on the edge of the bed. Paige gathered all the supplies she needed before heading back over to them. She stopped when she got a closer look at Sara's hair.

"When did you get silver highlights?" She asked in confusion. "And it's curly." Sara looked back over her shoulder and Paige handed her a mirror.

"Whoa," Sara gasped. "That's all new."

Rin glanced at her out of the corner of her eye. She wondered if the changes could have been caused by the magic.

"Well, I think it looks great, so I won't touch your hair but Rin, goodness girl, have you ever cut your hair?" Paige asked.

"No," she said, her voice sharp. "And do not..." She trailed off when she realized Paige had just cut a large section of her hair. "What are you doing?" Her voice raised in agitation.

"It'll look great, trust me," Paige said as she continued to cut her hair. When she was finished Rin's waist-length hair was now just above her shoulder blades.

"Your hair is straight now," Sara said staring at Rin.

"What?" Rin gasped as she snatched the mirror out of Sara's hand. Her mouth dropped open when she saw that her normally curly, frizzy hair was now completely straight and smooth. "It would appear that we are taking on a few characteristics of each other." Rin paused as she looked back at Sara. "It looks as if your eyes have also changed Sara. They are now turquoise instead of blue." Rin turned the mirror so that Sara could see. Her eyes widened in shock.

'Great, I didn't look like enough of a freak before,' she thought, her shoulders dropping.

"You do not look like a freak. I believe that eye color on you is quite lovely," Rin said.

Sara looked at her in panic, "I didn't say that out loud."

"Think something else," Rin said as her eyes narrowed.

Sara looked at her like she was crazy before she started fidgeting with her sweatshirt sleeve.

'Like what?' She thought.

'Anything,' Rin thought.

"Well I don't know what else to think about," Sara said with an uncomfortable sigh. Rin raised an eyebrow.

"You heard me think anything?"

"No, I heard you say anything."

"I said nothing."

Sara looked up at Paige in a panic and noticed she was already on the other side of the room. She pulled the door open and stuck her head into the hallway.

"Jake!" She yelled.

Rin and Sara both stood up from the bed. Sara dropped her brush back into her bag that was sitting on the edge of the bed. A few seconds later Jake appeared in the doorway.

"Are you ladies finally finished?" he asked. His brows furrowed when he noticed Paige glance back and forth between him and Rin. "What?"

"It appears that Sara and I have maintained a bit of a connection, and we have shared some of our physical traits," Rin said, her voice calm and level.

Jake's mouth dropped open before he snapped it shut, "What do you mean a connection?"

"I can hear her thoughts and she can hear mine," Sara whispered while she kept her eyes locked on the floor in front of her.

"Are you serious?" Jake spat at Rin. "This is your fault. Why can't you just leave her alone?"

"Do you think for a moment that this is what I wished to have happen?" Rin's voice raised as she looked up at Jake. "That I wished to disappear and be trapped for twenty years?"

Jake walked closer but kept the bed in between them. "I don't care what you want or wanted. The only thing I care about is Sara and how you're going to fix this for her."

Rin took a step forward so that she and Jake could have been face to face if he did not tower over her.

"I cannot do anything. The magic is hers as I told you before."

Jake clenched his jaw and glared at her. Sara took a hesitant step forward and moved to put her hand on Jake's arm. When she did, she brushed against her bag and sent it tumbling to the floor. The three of them glanced down at the floor and Rin's entire body went rigid. There was a small black book with a silver willow tree on the cover amongst the contents of the bag. Rin leapt back away from it before rounding on Sara.

"Where did you get that book?" She gasped, her voice laced with fear. Sara looked down in confusion before Rin pushed her into the wall beside them by the shoulder. "Where? I do not remember you getting that book."

Jake made a move to get around the bed, but Rin threw her hand into the air, "Pevanas." A strong wind slammed into Jake with a quick wave of her hand and in seconds he was pinned to the wall on the other side of the room.

"Leave her alone," Jake yelled. He cursed when Rin ignored him. Her full attention was on Sara.

"I don't know," Sara stammered. "I've never seen it before."

Rin took a quick step backwards and grabbed the book off the floor. She opened it and found an elven inscription in the front. *This part of history cannot change.* As soon as she finished reading that line a vision of her older self, writing in the book flashed through her mind. She gasped and dropped the book. Her entire body was trembling as she dashed out of the room. She made it outside the cabin before Kaedin caught up with her. He could sense her sudden panic and fear.

"What is wrong?" He asked as he grabbed her by the shoulder to stop her.

"What do you remember of that day?" She asked looking up at him, her face clouded with fear. Kaedin paled at the mention of the day she disappeared.

"Not much," he admitted with a sudden shiver. "I remember coming to the cave to get you, but before I could help you, I was attacked."

"You did not see who did it?"

"No, it was too dark."

Rin's look of fear shifted to one of shock, "It was Londar. He used that book. It contained the incantation." She paused and started to tremble worse at the memory. "Now, the book shows me that I am the one who created it. How is that possible?"

Kaedin pulled her to him and wrapped both arms around her. His grip was firm as he held onto her, "I do not know but we shall figure it out." He did not loosen his grip on her until she quit shaking. Once she did, he let go and stepped back.

"Spar with me," he said. "It shall help you relax as always."

Rin peeked up at him before she nodded and rocked back on her heels and waited. He made the first move and threw a controlled punch in her direction. She blocked it and returned with one of her own. They continued like this and just started to get into a rhythm when Jake burst out of the cabin. He stormed toward the two while Paige and Sara trailed behind him.

"You!" He spit out at Rin. She and Kaedin both stopped moving and watched him approach. She could tell he was furious and was not surprised. He had dealt with a lot of strange occurrences and had nearly lost both of the people he cared most for in the world. Her head tilted when she realized he could probably use a good sparing session as well.

"What?" She asked, her tone goading. She knew he would not agree to fight with her unless she provoked him. "Do you wish to go a round?"

"Hell yes, I do," Jake snapped.

"Then come on," she taunted. "I do not have all day."

He glared at her as he fell into an easy fighting stance. Rin just stood with her hands at her sides, waiting for him to make the first move. He threw a punch with his right hand, which she easily avoided before she came up under his arm with a quick jab. Jumping back, he managed to avoid the blow. They continued in this manner for a while and it became apparent quickly that while Jake had the advantage of a much longer reach, Rin was much faster than him.

After a couple more minutes, Rin appeared to be getting bored. Jake threw another punch which she blocked, but instead of letting go, she jerked his arm backwards. Before he had a chance to react, she swept his feet and a second later she had him laying on his stomach, with his arm twisted behind his back. She was sitting on him with her knee in the small of his back.

"Have you had enough?" She taunted.

Jake ground his teeth in frustration. She was insanely fast, and he was not quite sure how to keep up without hurting her. Ignoring the pain in his shoulder he pushed up off the ground even with her on his back. She leapt off and landed on her feet. He paused long enough to rub his shoulder for a few seconds as he attempted to keep the grimace off his face. She had gotten a hold of the one he bruised in the fight with Londar. He started to circle her again waiting for an opening. She mirrored his movements until she gasped and glanced at her hand. He took the momentary distraction to throw a punch her direction. A look of shock crossed his face when he connected with her shoulder, but before he had time to process, he found himself sitting on the ground a foot away. Kaedin stood between him and Rin.

"What is wrong?" Kaedin asked, not paying any attention to Jake.

Jake scrambled back to his feet and walked back over to the two just as Rin held out her hand to show an ugly burn that had appeared. Kaedin raised an eyebrow as he watched bruises slowly start showing on her face.

"Rin?" He asked, his concern spilling into his voice. "What is happening?"

She glanced up at him and it took her a moment to answer.

"I believe that my body is having to catch up with what my soul experienced inside of Sara," she said before she sank to one knee with a quiet groan. Blood began soaking the back and front of her clothes. Kaedin's eyes opened wide in shock.

"I have got it," she gasped as she held her hands over the large wound in her stomach and back. "Rujhāe." Her hands began to glow with a pale blue light. The wounds healed and quit bleeding.

"You allowed Sara to get this badly injured?" Kaedin snapped at Jake.

"This injury was my fault," Rin interjected before Jake could reply.

"What?" Jake and Kaedin both exclaimed at the same time. They gave each other a dirty look when they realized they had said the same thing.

"I shall explain later," Rin said with a grimace. Her hand was pressed against her stomach.

Jake stared at her for a few moments. "Looks like you're getting what you deserve," he said, his tone sarcastic, before he could stop himself. Kaedin spun in place and decked Jake right in the face. He staggered backwards and ended up sitting down hard on the ground again, his jaw and cheek starting to bruise. Paige and Sara hurried over to him before he could get up and Paige grabbed his arm.

Rin stumbled sideways and sat down on the ground causing Kaedin to look over at her. He moved to her side when he saw her on the ground. His gaze darkened when more bruises began to appear on her, and her face flushed with fever.

"It is all right," she said in response to his worry, that she could sense. "I am just going to need rest. It is a lot all at once."

He picked her up, "Then we shall go somewhere quiet." Without saying anything to Jake, Paige, or Sara he headed into the forest and the two disappeared from view a few minutes later.

Paige watched Kaedin walk away before she looked at her brother in exasperation. "What were you thinking?" she snapped. "Who says something like that? That was just rude!"

Jake gave her a dirty look but did not say anything as he got back to his feet and rubbed his jaw. He had taken many punches in his martial arts training before but that one really hurt. Kaedin was much stronger than he expected. As they walked back into the cabin, he felt Sara touch his arm. He glanced down at her and saw the worry on her face.

"I'm okay."

"Are you going to the living room?" She asked, and he nodded. "I'll get you some ice."

Jake sighed as he watched her walk down the hall. Paige ignored him while she walked by him to go and find Raven. Jake glanced at her before he sighed again and headed to the living room. He sank onto the couch while waiting on Sara. She came up a couple of minutes later with a baggie of ice and a washcloth. Jake took it from her and winced when he put it on his jaw.

"I guess I really screwed that one up," he said, embarrassment creeping into his voice.

Sara looked up at him, "Everyone makes mistakes." She reached out to touch his hand but hesitated before she did, causing him to glance down.

"You can touch me," he said, his voice soft.

Sara flushed and bit her lip as she reached over and interlaced her fingers with his. He watched her for a moment, and she peeked up at him.

"I think the new hair and eye color look good," he said.

"Thank you," she mumbled as she looked down at the couch. Jake set the ice pack down and turned toward her. He lifted her chin with his fingertips.

"Don't look down," he said. "Look at me."

She bit her lip before she glanced back up at him and met his gaze. He held her gaze for a few moments before he leaned forward and kissed her.

"Jake and Sara are joined?" Raven's disbelieving voice broke the silence in the room when he and Paige walked up the steps.

Sara was a brilliant shade of red and she tried to get up, but Jake tightened his grip on her hand and did not let go.

"Please don't leave," he whispered to her. She had a conflicted look on her face before she made herself stay. Hiding her face on the arm of the couch, she tried to pretend they had not just seen Jake kiss her.

"What?" Paige asked. "Why would they be married?"

Raven looked over at Paige with a frown, "We do not kiss until we are joined."

Paige was shocked, but it was only a few moments before a look of realization crossed her face and she put her hands on her hips.

"Is that why you won't kiss me?" she asked.

Jake glanced over at Raven and he shifted under his gaze.

"Yes," Raven replied. "It is our custom and I hold to the rules of propriety that are expected of my people."

"We'll talk about this later," Paige said with a frown before she spun around and headed over to sit with her brother and Sara.

***

Kaedin walked for a while through the woods until he found an old pine tree. He climbed up several branches while holding Rin and stopped on a branch that was wide enough for two large adults to sit side by side. He sat with his back against the tree trunk and another branch that formed a V-shaped hollow. Once he was situated, he put his knee up and rested Rin back against his leg. They sat like that in silence for a while.

"It is cold," Rin whispered breaking the silence.

Kaedin shrugged out of the jacket he was wearing and helped her put it on before he pulled her closer to him. She sighed and pulled the jacket tighter around her. He rested the backs of his fingers against her forehead.

"You are burning," he said, his voice filled with worry.

"Sara had several bad fevers from the magic. They should pass soon. I am a bit stronger than her." She gave him a half-hearted smile but Kaedin tilted his head when he could sense how much the fever was taking out of her. He did not say anything and the two fell silent again.

"What do you need to ask?" Rin asked as she looked up at him.

"Are you certain that you are up for it?"

"I do not wish to relive what happened, but I do not believe there shall ever be a time that I will. There does not seem to be a good reason to postpone just because it will be difficult."

He tightened his grip on her before he sighed, "Hikaru."

A second later Hikaru appeared on the branch beside them. He did not say anything as he stood there waiting for one of them to speak.

"Please give us some time alone," Kaedin said without looking up at him.

Hikaru frowned and shook his head, "You are aware that I cannot do that. It is my duty to keep an eye on Lady Rin."

"Hikaru, go back to the cabin," Rin said, her voice sharp. "We need some time. I understand your duty, but I am asking you to please leave us."

"But my lady, Jaeha and your brother would be most unple--."

"I take responsibility," she said as she raised her hand.

"As you wish, my lady," Hikaru said with a resigned sigh before he disappeared from view a second later. Once he was gone Kaedin absentmindedly started running his fingers through the ends of Rin's hair. He seemed to be having some trouble adjusting to the sudden change in her appearance.

"It looks so different with no curls," he said. Rin frowned and looked up at him. "I think it looks good as well. I believe it shall just take some time to adjust."

Rin relaxed with a relieved smile when he did not hate the change in her appearance. Kaedin let go of her hair before he glanced back down at her. He hesitated and took a deep breath.

"I must know what you needed to tell me about your father," he said. "Lord Ronin told me what you said, but your father denies there is any truth to the accusations."

A dark, sorrowful look crossed Rin's face, "Kilvari is not my father. He killed him to keep my lineage a secret. I am the daughter of Lord Kanamae and my mother, the elven queen." She glanced up when she heard Kaedin take a sharp breath.

"Forgive me."

"For what?" she asked. His expression changed from one of guilt to one filled with pain.

"For everything," he whispered. "For not being able to find the truth myself, for losing you, for being too weak t--."

"Stop," she said, her voice firm. "I have already told you there is nothing to forgive." She reached up and put a hand on his cheek. He closed his eyes and leaned into her hand. After a few moments, Rin's face became clouded with ill-concealed emotions as she brushed her fingertips across his cheek.

"I must know," she whispered as her voice cracked. "How did I not lose you?"

Kaedin opened his eyes and appeared to collect his thoughts, "Lord Wren found me. He was on his way back from a battle when they noticed something strange going on in the mountain. Lord Wren and Jaeha entered the mountain cave and were just barely able to heal me in time."

Rin slid her fingers down his face and neck causing him to shiver. She stopped when her hand was resting on his chest where the large scar could be felt through his shirt.

"I must thank my brother," she said, her voice cracking. "I was certain that I had lost you."

"I promised I would never leave you," he said as he put his hand on her cheek. "I meant it."

She lifted her hand off his chest and place it over his, "I shall hold you to that promise." Her hand quivered when she shivered from the cold. Kaedin took her hand and put it inside the jacket she was wearing before he wrapped both arms around her again. He pulled her all the way onto his lap to help keep her warmer. They sat quietly for a while until Kaedin seemed to remember something and reached into his pocket.

"I have something for you if you will accept it," he began with a nervous edge to his voice. "I had this made for you and was going to give it to you after your ceremony. You had consented to be my ayen before all of this happened. Do you still hold to that?" He held up a delicate braided silver ring. It was three small threads of silver braided together to make one.

Rin looked up at him with a gentle smile, "Of course, I do."

Kaedin smiled, relief evident on his features. He slipped the ring on the middle finger of her right hand before he leaned down and kissed her on the cheek. The two rested their foreheads together and sat in silence, each relishing the presence of the other.

It was nearing evening when Rin and Kaedin returned to the cabin. She was still a little flushed with fever but did not appear to be bothered by any of the bruises or other injuries. They walked into the cabin without a sound and when they reached the stairs Rin paused.

"I must go speak with them," she said. "Please wait for me." Kaedin raised an eyebrow with a look of disapproval and she chuckled. "It shall be fine." She let go of his hand and headed up the stairs. When she entered the living room, she found Raven and Paige sitting together on the floor and Jake and Sara on the couch. Paige was talking about something until she saw Rin. She quit talking and looked over at her brother. Jake lowered the ice pack from his face when he noticed Rin.

"My lady," Raven said when he looked up and noticed Rin. He jumped up and hurried over to her. Without stopping to think, he grabbed her in a tight hug. "Please do not ever disappear on us again."

Rin patted his back before she shrugged out of the hug. She noticed that Paige was on her feet, glaring at Raven.

"My lady?" She snapped at him. Raven tilted his head and did not appear as if he understood what was wrong.

"Paige, it is a title only," Rin said. "Raven and Hikaru are my personal guards and close friends."

Paige pursed her lips together but did not say anything to Rin. Raven walked back over to her, but he appeared wary as they sat back down, and Paige started whispering at him as soon as they were seated. Rin turned to face Jake and Sara with a sigh and noticed Sara fidgeting with her sleeve.

"Sara, I apologize for my actions earlier," Rin began. "I did not mean to frighten you. Seeing that book was quite a shock for me, I believe you may understand. You have seen some of that memory."

Sara nodded and tried to keep from looking at Jake when she could feel his gaze on her, "I understand."

"Thank you," Rin said with a relieved smile. "And Jake, I--."

"I'm the one who should be apologizing," Jake said with a deep frown. "What I said was completely out of line and I'm sorry."

"You are forgiven. I understand that much has been thrown at all you quite suddenly. It must be difficult to handle." Jake nodded as he glanced at Sara. "If you will allow me, I can heal your face. I am sure that must be painful. I am certain that Kaedin was not gentle with you."

Jake hesitated for a minute and looked at Sara again. He seemed to be checking to see if she would be okay with Rin healing him. Rin smiled at the obvious young love between the two.

"Sara can help me heal you," Rin said when Jake still did not respond to her. Jake and Sara both looked up at her in surprise.

"How?" Sara asked.

Rin walked over and sat down beside her. She put a gentle hand on her shoulder.

"Close your eyes, "she instructed. "Can you feel the small spark of magic?" Sara shook her head no. "I shall nudge it with my magic." Rin closed her eyes and focused on pushing a tiny amount of magic into Sara. "Did you feel that?"

"Yes," Sara gasped in surprise.

Jake was not pleased as he watched the two of them, "Won't the magic hurt her?"

"This magic is hers," Rin said. "I am only acting as a catalyst to push it out, so she can learn how to use it. Now allow her to concentrate."

Sara gave Jake a tentative smile. He tilted his head before he sighed and nodded. She closed her eyes again and concentrated on the tiny spark of magic hidden deep inside of her. Her entire focus was on it until Rin picked up her hand and placed it on Jake's cheek. She lost her focus as her face flushed and she bit her lip.

"Concentrate," Rin chided.

She clamped her eyes closed tighter and forced her attention back on the magic. Once Rin was certain that she was again focused, she pushed her magic into Sara until her hand started to glow. When Rin noticed it was glowing, she stopped the flow of magic and Sara's hand continued to glow with her own magic.

"You must first visualize the wound healing in your mind," Rin instructed. "Once you have it you will use the word Rujhāe, it allows the healing magic to flow."

Sara struggled to maintain her magic and picture the wound healing in her mind. It took her several moments to juggle it all.

"Rujhāe," she said. As soon as the word was out of her mouth the bruise on Jake's face started to fade. She managed to hold the flow of healing magic for a few minutes before she exhaled hard and lost control of the magic. Her hand quit glowing. She frowned when she opened her eyes and saw she had not healed him all the way. Most of the bruise on his face faded but it was not completely gone.

"That is quite good for a first attempt," Rin said when she saw the look on her face. "You shall become better at it if you practice." She paused and looked at Jake. "Would you like me to finish the healing?"

"No," Jake said without taking his eyes off Sara. "She did more than enough for me." He could tell without looking at his face that most of the bruise was gone, and a little of the pain vanished.

"Very well," Rin said as she stood up. "I shall take my leave but when you have a moment, I would like to speak to you in private. I need your assistance with a military matter. Come and find me when you are prepared."

"All right," Jake said, his voice confused. "I'll find you later." He had no idea what she could possibly need from him.

Rin nodded and left the room.

An hour later, Jake made his way down to the room where Rin and Kaedin were staying. He found her sitting in a chair staring at the black book they found in Sara's bag. She seemed to be deep in thought and did not notice him right away. He stood in the doorway and looked around the room. His eyes widened in surprise when he found no one with her. A frown crossed his face when he realized Kaedin would be somewhere close by even if he did not see him. After waiting a couple moments for her to see him, he cleared his throat and Rin looked up immediately.

"Please come in," she said as she motioned for him to sit in the chair next to her. Jake was wary when he crossed the room and sat down beside her. "I need to speak with your father before I must return home to attempt to obtain help for your world." She paused and observed him for a moment. Jake's eyes narrowed when it felt like she was appraising him. "I would like for you to represent your people and I believe that you must have permission from your commander, am I correct?"

Jake just stared at her before collecting himself, "Yes, I would have to have permission, but why me?"

"I trust you. I believe that you would keep your people's best interest at heart and would not be moved by personal gain."

He appeared dumbfounded for a moment and struggled to believe what she just said. It was difficult for him to process that she had seen him through Sara and did not just meet him yesterday. The thought was still almost unbelievable.

"It won't be easy to meet with the general," Jake frowned and refused to say the word father. "You won't be able to just walk into the base."

"I have no intention of walking into the base," Rin said with a chuckle. "I shall teleport the two of us directly to your father's office. I believe that would be the best course to prove to him I am not from your world."

Jake paled when his stomach churned at the unpleasant memory of teleporting. He had felt sick for several hours after they got back last time.

"When do you want to do it?"

"I am prepared to go now," she said standing up. "If I am going to get away without anyone else then I must go at once."

Jake could not help but grimace as he unconsciously rubbed his face. He had made Kaedin angry and did not want to get into another altercation with him. Taking Rin somewhere without him was not going to make him happy.

"I shall not allow them to put blame on you," Rin said. "This is my choice, so it is my responsibility if anything goes wrong."

He shrugged but his expression did not change. He was certain that Kaedin was not likely to stop long enough to find out who was to blame if something happened to her.

"All right, let's go," he said, his voice reluctant.

Rin held out her hand as soon as he agreed. He swallowed hard in preparation of the nausea he knew was about to follow before he took hold of her hand. She closed her eyes in concentration as soon as he was touching her. It took her a few moments to visualize the general's office from Jake's description.

"Ēlipor ntāera," she said. A second later they appeared near the door of General Riverwood's office. The general startled at their sudden appearance in his office and his hand reached for the firearm at his side.

"Jake?" He asked, his voice uncertain.

Jake let go of Rin's hand and his face went blank as he crossed his arms over his chest, "Yes, it's me. She wants to speak with you." He gestured to Rin standing next to him.

"General Riverwood," she said as she extended her hand. "I am General Rilavaenu."

Riverwood took her hand but laughed out loud when she said her status. She raised an eyebrow as disapproval flashed across her face. Jake grimaced at his father's reaction.

"Oh, you can't be serious, little girl," he scoffed. "Though, it was a nice trick getting into my office unseen."

Rin narrowed her eyes before she closed them. She still had a firm grip on the general's hand, "Ēlipor ntāera." The second the words were out of her mouth they disappeared and reappeared at the cabin. The general gasped in shock when he recognized their location, but before he could react, she brought them back to the office. Riverwood took a staggered step backwards and yanked his hand out of hers.

"Shall we begin again?" She asked, her voice serious. "I am Rilaeya Rilavaenu, commander of the elven armies, and general of the riders. I am here to offer my assistance with the creatures that have begun appearing." She paused as her expression hardened. "Your weapons are useless, correct?"

Riverwood stared at her for a few moments before he cleared his throat and stood up fully. "Where are you getting your information?" He snapped as he regained his equilibrium. His gaze flew to Jake with a disapproving look. Jake opened his mouth to protest but Rin raised her hand and he snapped it closed.

"I have witnessed your son fight one of these creatures," she said. "His weapon was useless for anything other than slowing it down."

"You've fought one?" Riverwood asked as he looked back at Jake. He appeared to be concerned but Jake only nodded in response. "Where are they coming from?"

Rin moved over to a small table and laid out a map. She pointed to one spot on it.

"There is a cave here. That is the point in your world where they are coming through. This point is apparently the connection between your world, Asaetara, and the demon realm. These creatures you are experiencing are demons."

The general gave her an incredulous look before he glanced away from her and tried to gather his scattered thoughts. A few moments passed before realization crossed his face and his gaze flew back to her.

"You are the Jane Doe," he said.

Rin raised an eyebrow and glanced back at Jake.

"It's what they call someone when they don't know their identity," Jake answered her unspoken question. "He knows you were here."

"I see," Rin said looking back at the general. "I was apparently here for about twenty years, however, that is not the topic at hand."

"How did you escape?" Riverwood asked, his voice becoming sharp and his eyes narrowed when he looked at Jake. Rin noticed, and she shook her head.

"Again, that is not the topic at hand," she said. "All you need to know is that my bonded came for me and I shall be returning home. There is nothing that you can do to keep me here."

Riverwood stared at her and appeared as if he was contemplating whether what she said was true. Jake shifted and held his breath. It could get ugly very fast if his father tried to force Rin to remain because she was not human.

"How does this help me at all?" The general snapped after a few moments. He could sense that the little girl in front of him radiated a certain amount of danger. "I need to know how to kill them."

"I shall come to that," Rin said as her eyebrow rose again. She found this man to be nothing like his children and his arrogance annoying. "However, I would like to make my request of you before I tell you how to make your weapons effective."

"What could you possibly want from me?" He asked, his voice wary.

"I would like for your son to accompany me," she said. "He has proven himself to be trustworthy and capable. I believe that he shall make a fine ambassador for your people."

The general was stunned before he looked over at Jake, "Well, captain, what do you wish to do?"

"I request to accompany her," Jake replied.

A quick look of pride flashed across the general's face. It was gone so fast that Jake thought he must have imagined it.

"You have what you want and my son will act as our ambassador, now how do we kill these things?"

Rin took out a small silver dagger and laid it on the table. "You need to infuse your projectiles with silver. This dagger is silver from Asaetara and needs to be used sparingly. The silver here is not the exact same chemical compound so it will be far less effective. I shall bring more of our silver when I return. I would recommend making daggers and swords with the silver, but I do not believe your men are accustom to such weapons."

The general picked up the dagger and turned it over in his fingers. The carvings on it were beautiful and intricate.

"This looks valuable," he said, suspicion slipped into his voice.

"I do not appreciate what you are insinuating, general. That dagger is mine, it was a gift from someone very important to me." Her voice hardened.

"No offense," Riverwood snapped with a dirty look. Rin only frowned before she walked back to stand beside Jake.

"It is time for us to leave," she said. "Allow us two days to prepare for our journey before you move into the area I indicated on your map."

"Two days," the general agreed. "And the captain is assigned to you until you have no further use of him."

Rin nodded in agreement and put her hand on Jake's shoulder, "Ēlipor ntāera." The two of them disappeared from the office and reappeared back in Rin and Kaedin's room. Jake put his hand on his stomach and sat down in the nearest chair. He felt just as sick as the first time he ported.

"I hate porting," he muttered under his breath. He glanced up with a dirty look when he heard Rin chuckle.

"It does get easier," she said as she turned to face the door. A second later Kaedin and Jaeha both appeared in the room.

"Where did you go?" Jaeha asked as soon as he saw her. "You know that you cannot disappear like that without an escort, my lady."

Rin sighed, "I needed to speak with his father. I could not do this effectively if you were all around. He would have felt threatened and I would not have been able to accomplish my goal." She glanced at Kaedin when he started pacing while he listened.

"What goal was that?"

"I requested that Jacob be the ambassador for this world and his father agreed. I also gave them at least a fighting chance to protect themselves until we can return with assistance."

"Are you certain that was wise, my lady?" Jaeha asked with a frown. "An ambassador should be one with more life experience, should they not?"

Rin's eyes narrowed, and Jake shifted in the chair. He was unhappy being a source of conflict and it irritated him that they did not believe he could do the job. His shoulder dropped with a sigh, he was not sure he could do the job, but he would give it his best effort.

"Jacob has proven himself to be quite capable with experiences far beyond his control," Rin said, her voice unpleased. "He handled them in a calm and collected manner. I believe he shall do a good job, and that should be enough for you. Or must I remind you who I am?"

Jaeha bowed his head, "I meant no disrespect, my lady."

"I consider this matter closed. Tomorrow we must work on some training for Jacob. He must learn to use an effective weapon for our world." She paused and looked over at him. "I plan to create a weapon designed for him." She paused again and took a deep breath. "We leave for home in two days."

Early the next morning Rin already had Jake outside behind the cabin. He shivered in the cold.

"Have you ever used a weapon that is not a...," she trailed off with a frown.

"A firearm," Jake finished for her.

"Yes, that is the word. Have you ever used a weapon that is not a firearm?"

"I've trained a little with a staff but that's it."

Rin appeared to be deep in thought for a moment before she looked back up at him," I think that could work. I will add a blade to it and some other features. Do you have a staff? It would be easier for me to modify one rather than create it."

"I have a wooden one," he said with a frown. He could not imagine how a wooden staff was going to help him fight anything.

"Good," Rin replied. "Please, go and fetch it."

Jake shrugged and disappeared back into the cabin for a few minutes. When he reappeared, he had a wooden staff in his hand. He handed it to Rin. She took it from him and balanced it out in front of her with one hand. Then she spun it and performed a series of simple attacks.

"This should do nicely," she said. "It is sturdy and well crafted. It shall make an excellent base." She handed it back to Jake. "Hold it out in front of you. I shall now begin to manipulate it." She paused. "You must not let go of it. It is being created specifically for you, so you must stay in contact with it or it will not be a perfect match." She waited for Jake to nod in understanding. Once he did, she closed her eyes in concentration and held her hands over the staff.

"Lāekikaravi," she said as she pushed magic into the staff. Her hands started to glow with a red color, and Jake fought his instincts to move. It was unnerving being so close to so much power. He could feel it coming off her in waves.

Her hands were now glowing a bright red as she increased the magic and the staff started to change. It lengthened, became black metal, and on the top, a massive silver blade appeared. As Rin continued, a thin band of silver slowly wrapped its way around the staff from top to bottom, and in the center, a tiny rendering of a dragon appeared.

Rin breathed a long, slow breath and stopped the flow of magic. She opened her eyes and looked up at Jake.

"See how it feels," she said. "It should be completely in balance."

Jake stared at the staff as he moved away from her. Once he was far enough away he would not hit her, he moved through a basic staff form. He was amazed at how balanced the staff was even with the massive blade on the end.

"It feels great," he said with a smile.

"Very good," she said. "However, before you can begin to train there is a feature that I must test. It is imperative that it works." She walked several feet away from him. "Hold it out in front of yourself with both hands. Plant your feet and whatever happens, do not move." She waited on him to nod and once he was in a stable stance, she raised her hand. "Vēijal."

A bolt of lightning flew from her hand in his direction. Before he even had a second to react the bolt slammed into his staff. He was surprised by the force of the blow. It slid him back a couple feet, but he was able to maintain his stance. The silver band and dragon on the staff were both glowing as the electricity arched along the blade.

"Excellent," Rin said with satisfaction. "That worked just as it was meant to."

"What was that?" Jake asked. His eyes still glued to the staff in his hands. Rin tilted her head with an amused smile.

"You do not understand what happened?" When Jake did not respond she continued, "The staff is capable of absorbing magic. You shall need that in order to survive in my world since you lack the ability to use magic."

Jake looked away from the staff and it took him a moment to process what she just said. When he did, he mumbled, "Thank you."

"You are most welcome," she replied with another smile. "I hope this weapon shall serve you well, but now it is time to train with it."

With a sigh, Jake tried to prepare to spar with Jaeha and Kaedin. He almost shivered when he thought about having to fight with Kaedin. He knew Kaedin was not fond of him.

"Come at me." Jake's head snapped up when Rin spoke again. His brows furrowed when she had no weapon that he could see. Rin raised an eyebrow when she noticed his hesitation, "Even if I appear unarmed, it does not mean that I am." A dagger appeared in her hand and then disappeared again. "But I have no need of weapons to train you."

He frowned and still hesitated, "What if I hurt you?"

"If you harm me then it is my own fault," she said, her voice amused. She paused and tilted her head, her face becoming serious. "Wounds are a part of training, Jacob. We heal them, of course, but it teaches you how to handle the pain and keep fighting. The ability to fight through a wound could be the deciding factor between life and death."

Jake took a deep breath and tightened his grip on the staff before he fell into a ready stance. As usual, Rin just stood there with her hands down, waiting for him to make the first move.

"Wait!" Kaedin said. He hurried up to Rin with a small bundle in his hands. When he handed it to her, her eyes opened wide and a large smile spread across her face.

"You have my gear," she said as she looked up at him.

"Of course," he replied with a small half smile. "I have kept them with me. I knew when I found you that you would need it."

"Thank you," she said before she turned toward the cabin. "I shall return in a moment, Jacob, and we will continue." She disappeared into the cabin and a few minutes later reemerged. Jake watched her approach and was surprised by her change in appearance. She used leather strips and the cargo pants were now laced tight to her legs. A well-worn pair of dark brown riding boots came up to her knees over the pants. She still wore the simple black tank top but now had black, worn leather bracers on her arms up to her elbows. They had straps that hooked on the middle two fingers and thumb to help secure the piece that rested on the back of her hand. There was also a strap that crossed her palm. They fit her like a glove. The last thing she added looked to Jake like a tactical vest. It was a dark brown leather vest that was pulled tight with laces in the front. There were pockets on the front and sides.

As she walked over to where Jake stood, she was twirling two daggers in her hands. They had ornate black hilts and silver blades that were as long as her forearms. She flipped one and it rested against her arm before they disappeared. Jake wondered where she hid them.

"Are you prepared?" She asked when she stopped next to him.

He nodded and again fell into a ready stance. He knew she was waiting on him, so he leapt forward and brought the staff straight down. She brought up both hands in a v-block and with a quick twist of her wrists, she pulled the staff right out of his hands. She spun and had the blade against his throat in a second. He took a sharp breath and stepped back.

"Never attack straight down unless it is a killing blow," she said, handing the staff back. "Anyone with any experience shall be able to block that. Use side attacks to keep an opponent off balance. Try again."

He tried again and brought the blade up from the right side. She frowned and leapt backwards to get out of the way.

"Blunt side of the blade for training," she chided. "We can heal most wounds but not if you cut me in half."

Jake sighed in frustration and tried again. His movements were slow as he struggled to try and keep her instructions in mind. She caught the staff again and pushed him back. After a couple more times, Jake finally started to fall back on his martial arts training. He quit thinking so much and just reacted. Rin noticed the change immediately. His movements became less hesitant and quicker.

"Good," she said as she dodged a blow. "Stay grounded, in control, calm." She gradually sped up her movements pushing him to keep up. They continued until Jake was breathing heavy. Rin jumped back to signal she was finished.

"Take a short breather then continue with Raven."

Raven gave Jake an enthusiastic smile as he stood up from where he, Paige, and Sara were watching. Jake frowned when he realized he had not noticed them. He always knew who was around.

"How long have you been here?" He asked as he sat down next to Sara.

"Not long," she said with a shy smile. "You were doing good." She flushed and looked down after she gave him the compliment. He smiled.

"Thank you," he said as he leaned over so she had to look at him. She turned a darker shade of red but could not keep from giggling at his expression.

"Come on," Raven called. "You may spend time with your match later. It is time to train." Jake sighed and walked over to Raven. "Let us go. I believe after I am finished with you, Kaedin gets the next round."

"Great," Jake replied, his voice sarcastic before he fell into a ready stance and waited.

Over the next two days, Rin had Jake training every spare moment he had. By the morning they were ready to leave for Asaetara he was so sore he almost could not move. He ran his hand over his stomach. The training with Kaedin and Jaeha was the worst and he had to be healed several times with them. With a frown, he shook his head. He did realize that Kaedin and Jaeha were teaching him how to deal with brute strength, while Rin and Raven were all about speed, but it still did not make the wounds any less painful, and he got the distinct impression that Kaedin was not sympathetic about the ones he inflicted.

He sighed with a wince when he picked up the bag he was taking with him and his staff. The blade was now covered with a leather wrap. He headed outside and found everyone already present. His eyebrows rose when he noticed the overall change in their appearance. They were no longer dressed in the casual clothing of his world. Jaeha, Kaedin, and Hikaru were wearing various forms of leather armor, black pants, boots, and their katanas were hanging from their waists. Rin was dressed the same as the previous days, except today she even had visible weapons strapped to her back. Raven was dressed the same as Rin. The only real difference was his clothes were black and his katana was strapped to his back.

Jake tilted his head and wondered what the difference in attire meant. There had to be something to the way they were dressed. He shook his head the longer he observed them. These clothes suited them, and he realized now how awkward they appeared in the clothes from his world. After a couple more minutes, he pushed these thoughts out of his mind and walked over to stand with Paige and Sara. When he got close, he could hear Rin talking to Jaeha.

"We shall not port when we arrive," she said. "I wish to get a feel for what may have changed since I have been home."

Jeaha frowned, "We have enough bedding for the nights, but we shall have to hunt."

Rin nodded as if she expected that before she looked over at the group, "Is everyone prepared?"

"Yeah, we're ready," Jake said as he reached over and took hold of Sara's hand. She gripped it tightly and he could feel her nerves.

"Very well," Rin said. "Then we shall go." She walked away from the cabin at a brisk pace. Kaedin walked just behind her while the others fell in behind them. It only took them a few minutes to reach the cave and Rin hesitated before she walked inside. She only made it a handful of steps before she started to tremble. This cave was so similar to the other that every step forward felt like she was trying to push through deep water. She reached back and Kaedin grabbed her hand.

"I am here," he whispered. She tightened her grip and took a deep breath before heading deeper into the cave. When they reached the dead end, she noticed the arch on the wall and looked at the floor before approaching it. The closer she got to it the brighter it began to glow.

"Join hands," she said. "I do not wish for any of you to get sent somewhere else."

Everyone joined hands and waited on her. She looked over each of them before facing the portal. It took her a few moments before she took another deep breath and a strong, determined step forward into the portal. The others followed one by one until they all disappeared through the glowing arch.

They all landed in a tangled heap on the floor of a cave whose walls were lined with torches. Jake sat up as his stomach churned, that was far worse than porting and he willed himself not to vomit. He glanced around, and his eyebrow shot up when he noticed Rin frozen in place. She stood staring at a place where the rocks were stained red, next to a strange looking circle. Kaedin came up to her and pushed her away from the circle. He stopped when her back was against the nearest wall before he turned around. His back was to her, but he was still touching her when he shifted enough to hide her from view.

Jake tilted his head as he watched them. It only took him a matter of moments to realize what he was doing. He was allowing her privacy while letting her know he was there at the same time. Kaedin glanced over at him and his eyebrow rose. Jake looked away as soon as he saw the disapproval on his face. With a sigh, he scanned the rest of the cave and he grimaced when he noticed Paige on the other side of the room vomiting. Raven was crouched beside her rubbing her back while he told her going through the portal would get easier.

"You suck, Jake," she gasped when she saw him looking at her. "We could have stayed at the cabin."

"No," Jake replied. "Not with demons, Londar, and who knows what else, I'm not letting you out of my sight." Paige gave him a dirty look. Jake did not respond as he looked around for Sara. He found her on her hands and knees almost inside of the circle on the floor. She was also being sick. He got to his feet and walked over to her. After kneeling in front of her, he shifted her

163

backwards and she ended up sitting outside the circle.

"Are you okay?" He asked as he slid forward to sit next to her. When he reached the edge of the circle, he ran into something. He glanced down, and his eyes widened when he noticed that the strange carvings in the stone around the circle were glowing.

"Jake?" Sara said, her eyes glued to the carvings. She remembered this circle from Rin's memories. Her gaze flew back to him when he tried again to leave the circle and smacked into the invisible wall. Raising his hand, he reached out and rested it on what was blocking his path. His face became blank when he realized he was trapped.

"I seem to have a little problem here," he said as he looked around the room. He grew more concerned when he watched the color drain from Kaedin's face.

"Rin," Kaedin said, his voice serious. "We need you." He felt her hand, that was clinging to the back of his shirt, release. She took a deep breath before she stepped out from behind him. Her entire body went rigid and she tried to back up but ran into the wall behind her when she saw the glowing circle.

"It is still active?" She asked, her voice quivering.

"You can get him out without it hurting him, right?" Sara asked. Her face was etched with fear when she tore her eyes away from Jake. It took Rin several moments before she looked away from the circle. When she did, she appeared to once again be in complete control.

"I do not know," she replied, her voice quiet and unsure. "I shall do my best to get him out unharmed. The circle as a whole is too strong for me to dispel, I shall have to try and do one of the individual runes. Perhaps, that will be enough." She swallowed hard before she took slow steps toward the circle. Sara could not tell by the look on her face whether she was afraid of the circle, only the slight tremor of her hand gave it away.

"My lady," Jaeha said as he stepped forward to block her path. "I cannot allow you to attempt this spell. Your brother would be most unpleased if I allowed you to be injured. There is no way of knowing what kind of traps may be set upon those runes."

"Who else is there but me who can cast the spell?" Rin's voice became sharp as she looked up at him.

Jaeha frowned, "Raven should attempt the spell, not you." He looked over at where Raven was standing beside Paige. Raven glanced at him before he looked over at the circle. He started shaking his head after only a few seconds.

"I am more than willing to attempt it, but I do not believe my magic is strong enough," he said with a grimace. "I fear I would only cause Jake to be harmed." He started to move away from Paige but a sharp look from Rin caused him to stop.

"Your magic is not strong enough," she said. "I shall do what I can, do not interrupt once I begin." She did not look back at Jaeha before moving over to the circle and kneeling beside one of the runes.

"My lad--."

"No," she said as she cut Jaeha off. "Not another word. There is no other way, now let me concentrate." Jaeha clamped his mouth closed but everyone could see that he was not happy. When he did not say anything else, Rin looked up at Jake. "Move to the far side of the circle and do not touch the sides." Once he nodded, she took a deep nervous breath before holding her hands above one of the runes, "Dūkāerav."

As soon as the word was out of her mouth the rune sparked causing her to gasp. Her hands tingled from the small jolt of electricity. She managed to keep from jerking her hands away from it and focused on pouring more magic into the rune. It continued to send strong jolts of electricity into her at random intervals. She jerked in response to every one but did not relent in attempting to break it. After several minutes the strain began to show on her face. She was beginning to sweat, and a single tear rolled down her cheek when she clamped her eyes closed.

Jake shifted again inside the circle and folded his arms across his chest to keep from touching the walls. He could see the pain on her face and felt guilty about being the cause of it. He started to tell her to stop, but a sharp look from Kaedin caused him to close his mouth.

"Do not interrupt," he growled in a hushed whisper. "If she loses concentration it could kill both of you." His attention turned back to Rin when he heard a sharp increase in her breathing. She ground her teeth together and the rune started to flicker. It shocked her again and she was just able to bite back the yelp of pain before she focused on holding the large flow of magic into the rune. A split second later it flickered and shot a massive bolt of electricity into her when it went out. Rin gasped when the force of the jolt sent her flying backwards toward the wall. She grimaced in anticipation of hitting it but Kaedin was quick enough to get between her and the wall. His back slammed into the wall when she ran into him. He exhaled hard but was able to get a firm grip on her. Holding her with one arm, he slid down the wall and rested on a knee. He ignored the pain running through his back and turned his full attention to her.

"Rin?" He asked, his voice full of concern. Her whole body was jerking from the electricity flowing through her. His expression grew more worried when she could not answer him, and her breathing was coming in short, ragged gasps.

"O...okay," she gasped after a few minutes more. "C...cannot m...move."

Kaedin's face darkened but he said nothing as he continued to hold her. It took several long minutes before the spasms stopped and her breathing returned to normal. Once they did, she sat up with Kaedin's support.

"Are you all right?" He asked while he kept his arm behind her back in case she needed to lean back on him.

"Yes," she said. "However, I never wish to attempt that again, it was almost more than I could handle." She paused and looked around until she found Jake. "Are you uninjured, Jacob?"

"I'm fine," he said with a look of respect. She was a lot stronger than he gave her credit for, "Thank you." He tightened the arm he had around Sara when he felt her shiver. She glanced up at him and he frowned when he saw all the worry had not faded from her face.

Rin sat for a few more minutes before trying to stand. She shook her head in frustration when her legs still did not want to respond. Only Kaedin's arm around her waist kept her from falling.

"Shall we carry you, my lady?" Hikaru asked as he moved to stand closer to Rin and Kaedin.

"No," Rin said with a shake of her head. "I wish for my first steps back home to be under my own power." She glanced up at Kaedin and he only nodded with an understanding smile. He already knew that is what she would want.

It took almost a quarter of an hour before Rin could stand on her own again. She looked around them, "Let us get out of this cave." Without waiting on a response, she headed toward the exit with brisk steps. When they reached the mouth of the cave she paused. A sense of relief coursed through her when she peered into the familiar forest in front of her. She stepped out into the thick mass of trees. It was much warmer than on the other side of the portal. She only made it a few steps into the forest before she stopped again. Her gaze went to the canopy dozens of feet above their heads. Shifting to the side, a ray of the bright sun illuminated her face when it broke through the canopy of crimson and gold leaves. The light breeze that made it through the trees made the shadows on her face dance.

A grin was plastered to her face as she closed her eyes and allowed the sun to soak into her. When she opened them again, she sighed, but a look of excitement was hidden just below her calm surface. With one small hand motion, they all headed deeper into the forest. After a short time, a break in the trees was just visible in the distance. Rin adjusted their course so that they were heading that direction, but a few seconds later she stopped with a raised hand. The group came to an immediate stop. A split second later a sharp, shrill whistle broke through the normal sounds of the forest. Rin spun her hand once and they formed a circle around Jake and the girls. After checking to make sure everyone was in position, she returned the whistle with the same sound.

Before any of them had a chance to move they found themselves surrounded by elven warriors.

Jake tightened his grip on the handle of his staff when he realized they were surrounded. His grip loosened a little when he noticed that Raven, Hikaru, Jaeha, and Kaedin did not appear to be concerned. He glanced at the elves around them. They all wore the same brown leather armor that was similar to what Kaedin and Jaeha wore. Jake frowned when he saw they were armed with bows, that were all trained on them. He shifted to make sure that Paige and Sara were behind him when an important-looking young elf strode up to them.

"What are you doing here?" He demanded, his eyes wary. "This area is off limits."

Rin glanced back at Kaedin. He met her gaze before he shrugged. He did not know who the elf was either.

"Whom am I addressing?" She asked taking a small step forward. The young elf regarded her with a look of disapproval.

"Miss, I am Lieutenant Jyldar Hildvae," he replied. Rin's eyebrow shot up at the condescending tone. "Why are you addressing me? Lord Wren's bonded is the only one present who is in a position to speak to me."

Rin laughed out loud and could not keep from glancing at Kaedin again. She laughed harder when she saw his mouth hanging open. He appeared completely dumbfounded that the lieutenant had just said that to her. With another chuckle, she looked away from him and glanced up at the other elves around them. Several of them bowed their heads to her when they noticed her gaze. She nodded in approval when she realized all of them had lowered their weapons.

"No lieutenant," she said turning back to face Jyldar. "I handle my own affairs." She paused and tilted her head. "Hildvae, that would make you Londar's brother, correct?" Her eyes narrowed when she realized he looked just like his brother. They shared the same dark brown hair and brown eyes.

Jyldar frowned, "I am, though I cannot imagine one of your status would be acquainted with my brother."

"And what status might that be?" Rin's voice grew sharp as she took another step toward the lieutenant. He held his ground but drew his katana in one quick motion. Rin only tilted her head and did not back away.

"Come no closer," he snapped. "You are one of lowly status. I can tell by your abhorring behavior." He paused and pointed the tip of his katana toward the clearing. "You are in a restricted area and will come with me."

Rin regarded him with a raised eyebrow before a movement behind the lieutenant caught her attention. A tall, commanding figure made his way through the elves at a brisk pace. His golden hair gleamed in the sunlight that glinted through the trees. He wore armor similar to the others except his was far more ornate and looked more worn. Rin's hands flew to her mouth before she froze in place. When his bright blue eyes connected with hers, he came to a dead stop. He only remained in place for a second before he ran toward her.

"Wren," Rin choked out before she leapt toward him without thinking.

"Stop right now!" Jyldar bellowed as he swung his katana in her direction. Rin gasped when she caught the movement out of the corner of her eye. She tried to twist out of the way but before it could connect with her Wren grabbed her. He jerked her toward him and brought his arm up in front of them. The sword connected with the bracer on his arm. With a quick twist of his wrist, he grabbed the hilt of the katana and yanked it out of Jyldar's hands before he threw it several feet away. Jyldar staggered back a step, his surprise and shock were visible on his face.

Wren pushed Rin behind him as he shifted so that he was face to face with the lieutenant. Jyldar shrank away from him.

"What is the meaning of this?" Wren asked, his voice hard but controlled.

"M... my lord," he stammered. "They are in a restricted area. I was only doing my duty and was bringing th--."

"Do you mean to tell me that you do not recognize her?" He waved his hand toward Rin with a look of disbelief. Jyldar floundered and tried to figure out who the elven woman was. He felt like he should know her. "I find it most difficult to believe that you do not know my sister. How does one forget their princess?"

Jyldar's eyes widened in surprise, "Lord Wren, please forgive me. I had no idea. I am most sorry for my poor actions."

Wren regarded him with a frown. It felt like the lieutenant was hiding something. There was no one under his command that would not recognize Rin.

"Saeldre," Wren called. An older looking elf stepped forward. "As of now, you are in charge of this unit."

"Yes, my lord." Saeldre made a quick motion with his hand and the elves all disappeared into the trees.

"Hildvae, you and I shall have a long chat tomorrow," Wren said, his voice dropping. "Until that time, I do not wish to see your face."

Jyldar bowed, glared at Rin, and then disappeared into the forest. Wren's eyes narrowed before the suspicion was replaced with a completely different emotion. He spun in place and grabbed Rin in a tight hug. She jumped at the sudden movement but as soon as he picked her up she wrapped both arms around his neck.

"Where have you been?" He whispered to her. "Never again. Do not ever do this to us again." He tightened his grip on her so much it was difficult to breathe.

"I am sorry," she gasped through her tears. "I did not wish to disappear."

Neither one of them moved until Wren glanced up when he noticed movement near them. He set her back on her feet before he grasped forearms with Jaeha in greeting.

"Who has accompanied you?" He asked looking back down at his sister. "I recognize that they are human, but they are quite different from the humans who reside here."

Rin motioned for Paige, Jake, and Sara to come forward, "I shall explain more later. For now, this is Ambassador Jacob Riverwood, his match, Sara, and his sister, Paige." She paused and looked over at Jake. "This is my brother, Thallawren. He is next in line to rule Nuenthras and the general of the elven armies." Her voice rang with pride when she introduced her brother.

Wren stepped forward and extended his hand, "Welcome."

Jake accepted the handshake but frowned when he had a little difficulty following what Wren said. The English he used had strange intonations to it that made it sound different. Wren noticed the look and glanced at Rin.

"Their form of common is a little different from ours," she said. "I believe they are having a little trouble following what you are saying."

"Forgive me," Wren said as he slowed his rate of speech. "I shall endeavor to speak more clearly until you have had the time to adjust."

"Thank you," Jake said as he released his hand.

"It is no trouble," Wren said as he glanced around them. "I am certain that we shall have some things to discuss but for now you will all come with me. The trees have ears and my tent would be a more suitable place to continue." He paused and looked over at his sister. "Plus, I must be filled in on some details."

When she nodded, he turned and headed toward the clearing while the group trailed behind him.

***

Jyldar watched them from where he was hidden on a tree branch. He was seething with anger at being made a fool of by that girl. His brother had assured him that she would never return. He slammed his fist into the tree. They should be making a move against Wren now. He was promised this would be his moment to shine. His eyes filled with hatred before he pulled out a slip of parchment and a small vial from his pocket. He eyed the vial with a cold smile. One arrow tipped with this will kill anyone. No healing can diminish its effects. His smile widened as he held up his hand and snapped his fingers. A raven suddenly appeared and landed on his arm. He attached the parchment to its leg and spoke a quick word in elven. The bird flew away in the direction of the cliffs to the south. He was tired of waiting on his brother and would remove the prince on his own.

***

Sara trailed behind Jake as they followed Rin and Wren toward the clearing. She watched Rin talking with her brother. A small smile crossed her face when she noticed that Rin still had a grip on his arm.

'They must be close,' she thought. 'It's nice that she is happy.'

Rin glanced back at her with a raised eyebrow, 'Have you been practicing the mind blocking spell?'

Sara heard Rin's voice in her head, and she grimaced. She peeked up at her and shrugged.

Rin frowned, 'Practice!'

Sara nodded and looked back at the ground in front of her. This was the Rin she was used to.

As they neared the edge of the clearing, Sara looked up when Rin suddenly fell silent. She watched as Rin fell a step behind her brother. She walked to his right and Jaeha came up to walk on the left. Sara was confused by the sudden change in their demeanor as they left the cover of the woods. When they entered the clearing, she could see tents sprawled out before her. Her brows furrowed when they did not look like any tents she had ever seen. They were hand sewn animal hides that had been dyed to a dark green and they were in the shape of a cube that tapered to a pyramid at the top.

Once they got closer to the tents, Sara could see elven warriors milling around. They all stood when Wren approached. She bit her lip and tried not to make eye contact as she walked through the troops. They were eyeing her, Jake, and Paige with wary looks. She turned her attention to the number of tents to try and distract herself, but she lost count at fifty when they reached a much larger tent near another edge of the clearing. This tent was twice the size of the others and had a thirty-foot clearance between it and anything else.

Wren entered the tent and most of the group followed. Raven and Hikaru stepped off to the side and did not go inside. They motioned for Paige and Sara to join them.

"We must remain outside," Raven said. "There are conversations where we are not allowed to be present."

Paige opened her mouth to protest when Jake stepped back out of the tent. He grabbed hold of Sara's hand and motioned for Paige to follow him.

"They go where I go," he said giving Raven a dirty look before he went back into the tent. Raven and Hikaru exchanged glances but did not try and stop them from entering without permission.

Sara let Jake pull her into the tent with him. They made their way to a large fur rug in the middle of the tent and sat down.

"I apologize for the unsuitable furnishings," Wren said with another frown. "I do not usually entertain guests here." He paused when Jake appeared to be having difficulties following what he said. "I am speaking too fast again?"

Jake shook his head, "No, I'm able to follow." He paused and sat up a little straighter. "There is no reason to apologize. I understand that frontline camps are not equipped with anything that is not needed for battle."

Wren's eyebrow rose in surprise before he nodded, "I appreciate your generous attitude toward the situation." He looked over at Rin. "Let us waste no more time. Tell me everything."

When Rin and Jake began to explain all the recent events to Wren, Sara looked around the tent. It was very spacious even though the furniture in it was sparse. There was a cot over in one corner. Sara could not help but wonder if it was soft. The layers of animal skins covering the logs gave it the appearance of a large fluffy comforter. Glancing down at the floor, she noticed that the tent did not have a real floor. The grass was covered by the large black rug. Sitting just on the edge of the rug, along the right wall was a small desk that had several paintings on it. One caught Sara's attention right away. It was one of Wren holding a small little girl with silver hair and green eyes. A smile crossed her face when she realized that had to be a small Rin. She appeared so happy in the painting that it made Sara's heart ache. It looked like a much calmer time.

With a sigh, she looked away from the painting and saw a small dagger laying on the desk right in front of the painting. Sara tilted her head as she looked at it and wondered if Rin might have made that for him. The blade was not straight and smooth, and the hilt was uneven and bumpy. She did not think it would even cut a piece of fruit. Another smile crossed her face when she decided Rin must have made it. Otherwise, why would he have kept a useless weapon? She scanned the rest of the desk and her eyes froze when they reached a painting on the other side of the desk. Her breathing started to increase as she stared at the elven couple. The woman was the one she saw in Rin's memories. She was the one who gave her the tiara. Sara shook her head and turned her attention away from the desk. That had to be her parents in that painting.

Looking at the far side of the tent, she saw a large table that appeared to have many little figures and flags all over the top. Her brows furrowed when she craned her neck trying to see more, but from her angle, she could not make out much more of the table's contents.

"Londar started all of this?" Wren's sharp voice interrupted her thoughts and Sara looked back over at him. He did not appear to be angry, but Sara heard an undertone to his voice.

"Yes," Rin replied, her voice quiet. "He somehow knew I would be in the cave and knew what incantation to use."

Wren's expression remained calm, but it darkened, "What business does his brother have in my ranks, I wonder?" He looked toward Jaeha. "Send someone to keep an eye on Hildvae. I did not trust his intentions before, but now I am certain he is not here to serve under me." Once Jaeha nodded and stuck his head out of the tent, he looked toward Jake. "Thank you for all you have done to assist in this strange situation. I am in your debt for looking after my sister."

"I didn't do any more than I'd hope someone would do for my sister if she were lost," Jake replied with a small shrug.

"There are not many who would step forward and assist," Wren said with a frown. "Keeping this in mind, I would normally present you with a gift of thanks, however, I am not in a position to do so at this time. Once we reach our capital, I shall see that it is done." He paused and tilted his head when Jake started shaking his head. "It is our custom."

Jake sighed, "I'll accept whatever you deem appropriate." He paused before he straightened his back again. "But, may I have some say in what it will be?"

Wren's expression became curious as he regarded Jake, "What do you request of me?"

"I'd like to request that you give me your word that you'll try to help us. The gift of help far exceeds anything else I can think of."

"You have my word that I shall do everything in my power to secure assistance for your home," Wren said, his voice serious. "Your actions warrant much more but if this is what you wish then I agree." He held out his hand and the two shook hands before he continued. "We shall discuss further details at a later time, for now, I wish to spend some time with my sister." He paused and looked toward Jaeha again. "Jaeha, there is an empty tent on the west side of camp. Would you show them to it?"

Jaeha tilted his head before an amused smile became fixed on his face. He gave Wren a slight head bow.

"Thank you," Wren said, his voice taking a sarcastic edge.

Jaeha's expression did not change as he looked down at everyone sitting on the floor. He pushed the flap of the tent open, "This way." Jake, Paige, and Sara got up and followed him out of the tent. Kaedin trailed behind them. He paused and glanced at Rin before he walked out of the tent with a heavy sigh.

Once everyone was gone Wren turned to face Rin, "I believe you have made a wise choice in the ambassador. He appears to have a good head on his shoulders."

"I am a good judge of character," she replied with a roll of her eyes. When her brother only nodded, she glanced over at his desk and her face grew embarrassed, "Why do you keep this?" She pointed at the dagger on his desk.

A fond smile crossed his face when he looked at what she was pointing to.

"It was a gift from my sister."

Rin rolled her eyes again, "It is terrible. You should get rid of it."

"No," Wren said with a shake of his head. "It is special because it is from you and I shall always treasure it." He paused and chuckled. "Besides, if I had thrown it out, you would have been quite angry with me."

"You are correct," she said with a grimace. "I would have been upset with you. However, I am now older and give you permission to get rid of it." Her eyes narrowed when her brother only laughed and shook his head. He was never going to give it up.

The two fell silent for a few minutes before Wren glanced back over at her.

"You have chosen Kaedin?" he asked. Rin looked up at him as surprise crossed her face. This is not what she was expecting him to ask her. "Do not look so surprised," he continued with a laugh. "Did you believe I would not notice the ring?"

Rin glanced down and saw that the ring Kaedin gave her was no longer concealed by her bracer. She tugged on it when she looked back up at her brother. "Do you not approve?"

"Would it matter if I did not?" Wren asked with a tilt of his head. She stared at him for a few moments before a smile appeared on her face.

"No."

"I figured not," Wren replied with a chuckle. "Did he ask for permission as is customary?"

Anger flashed across Rin's face, "Yes, and father told him never. He planned for me to be joined with Londar."

"What?" Wren gasped. "He attempted to force you into joining with him?" A dangerous edge slipped into his voice when he saw her nod. "I had no idea, or I would have protested on your behalf."

"It is all right," Rin said with a shrug. "I handled it on my own. I turned him down in front of the entire court. Fa..." She paused when she faltered on the word father. "The king was very angry."

"I am surprised they accepted your answer."

"They did not accept it. He tried to move forward with plans, but I refused to cooperate. He threatened to banish Kaedin if I did not do as he wished. I made my course of action quite clear if he followed through on his threat, and he backed off for now. I am certain that he still expects for me to do as he wishes at some point."

Wren folded his arms across his chest, "It appears that I have missed much by being away so frequently. I shall see to it that will never happen." He paused. "If it means anything coming only from me, Kaedin has my approval. I have always known the two of you were a match."

It appeared as if a large weight lifted off Rin's shoulders when she looked up at her brother with a relieved smile. "Thank you," she said as she gave him a hug. Having his approval was very important to her.

Wren returned her hug and the two stood silently for several minutes before he sighed. When he stepped back, he put both hands on her shoulders.

"I cannot stall any longer," he began. "I must know. I need to hear it from your lips before I believe the rumors." He paused and tightened his grip. "Is what I have heard about father from Ronin true?"

Rin's entire body went rigid, "Yes, it is what the well showed me." She could not bring herself to look up at him when he did not say anything right away. It seemed like an eternity before his grip on her shoulders loosened and she risked a peek at him. His face was devoid of all emotion and he appeared deep in thought. When he noticed her gaze, he looked back down at her.

"I had always wondered," he said. "The coincidence of your birth and the sudden murder of Lord Kanamae." He paused and let go of her. "Your silver hair should have been a complete giveaway."

Rin's gaze returned to the ground in front of her and her eyes grew troubled. "Does this change things for you?"

Wren stared at her for a moment before he understood what she was implying. He reached out and grabbed her chin. She startled but looked up at him.

"Never," he said, his voice firm. "You have been my sister since the moment mother first handed you to me. Nothing shall ever change that."

Rin tried to look away as her shoulders dropped, "I am only your half-sister." Her whispered voice quivered, and she glanced away from him.

He tightened his grip on her chin and her eye flicked back to his face. "I do not care. You are my little sister and I shall never give that up. I suggest that you make your peace with it." An amused half-smile crossed his face. "You are and will always be stuck with me."

Rin finally relaxed and cracked a small smile.

"That is better," Wren said as he released her chin. "However, I do believe it is time to head for home." He paused, and anger flashed across his face. "I believe I have some things that I would like to discuss with father. We shall leave for Nuenthras tomorrow at first light."

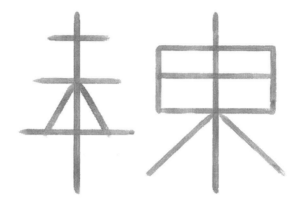

The sun was sinking behind the mountains to the west as the companions sat around a fire enjoying a freshly made stew. Rin watched while everyone relaxed and enjoyed the warm, quiet evening. She was grateful that they were having a quiet moment to unwind. After they left in the morning, she was not sure when they would have downtime like this again. She glanced over at Kaedin, who was sitting next to her, and noticed he was picking at his stew.

"What is troubling you?" she asked. He only shook his head and would not look at her. She gave him a knowing look which he saw out of the corner of his eye and he lowered the bowl of stew with a loud sigh.

"What does your brother say?" He asked, his voice hesitant.

Rin tilted her head in confusion when he still avoided eye contact. "What does my brother say about..." She trailed off with a look of realization. "Have you been worrying this entire time about whether my brother approved of you?"

He finally looked at her with an expectant, nervous stare.

"Of course, he does," she said with a smile.

"He does?" He asked seeming bewildered.

"He is not my fa--," she said with a frown. "He is not the king and has always cared for you." She paused again and looked up at him. "If you were concerned you should have asked. I did not think you would not already know the answer." She leaned over to kiss him on the cheek but jerked back and looked over at Sara. She was watching Jake walk over to clean off their bowls after they finished eating.

"Sara!" Sara jumped at the sharp tone of Rin's voice and looked over at her. "Are you practicing the mind blocking spell?"

Sara flushed and shrank a little, "No."

"Practice that spell," Rin said. "I do not wish to know what you think about Jacob." She shook her head with a small shudder as if to shake the memory out of her mind.

"Think what about me?" Jake asked as he sat back down next to Sara. Her face turned bright red and she refused to look at him. He glanced over at Rin.

"Absolutely not," she said, her voice short. "You shall have to ask her. I shall not repeat it."

Before Jake could ask her about it again, Sara leapt to her feet and hurried over to Paige. She tugged on her arm.

"We're going to bed," she said.

Paige stared at her in confusion before getting up with a sigh and following her into the tent. Rin watched them leave before glancing back at Jake. She chuckled at his puzzled expression.

A few hours later, only Rin, Raven, Hikaru, and Kaedin remained awake by the fire. Rin could not shake the feeling that something was off, and the others knew her instincts were usually correct.

"It is far too quiet," Rin said, her gaze going to the forest beside them. "The animal sounds are gone."

The others listened and noticed that she was right. Besides the crackling of the fire, the night was silent.

"Wake up Jacob," she said as she stood up. Her eyes did not leave the forest and the clearing.

Raven hurried over and shook Jake awake. Jake pushed his hand away and started to protest but Rin waved her hand and he remained silent. She crept toward the edge of the firelight and paused when a soft, low horn could be heard. A second later it was answered by several others all around them. She started to back up when she jumped to the side as a large black arrow flew right by her head.

"Orcs! We are under attack!" She yelled as she spun in place. "Raven, Hikaru remain with Jacob and the girls." Without waiting on a response, she dashed in the direction of her brother's tent. Kaedin was right behind her. The two disappeared around another tent when orcs came running into the camp with swords in hand.

Jake was rooted in place for a few seconds as he observed the strange creature in front of him. Its dark green skin and brown armor seemed to make it blend in with the forest while its deep orange eyes almost glowed in light of the fire.

"Jake!" Raven yelling his name startled him and he tore his eyes away from the orc. He jumped to his feet and ran over to the tent where Paige and Sara were still sleeping.

"Stay in there," he yelled as he jerked the cloth covering off his staff. With a gasp, he ducked under a blade before he spun the staff and blocked the next blow. He brought it around and ran the orc through with the large blade on his staff. Stepping to the side, he dodged another sword. He brought the staff around again and caught another orc in the stomach with the end, then with a quick spin, he stabbed it in the chest. Having a second to stop, he glanced around and noticed there were only a handful of orcs in this part of the camp. It only took Raven and Hikaru a matter of seconds to finish the ones that remained, and they appeared at Jake's side.

"We must move," Raven yelled over the battle sounds coming from the rest of the camp. "They may need our assistance elsewhere."

Jake nodded and stuck his head inside the tent. Paige and Sara were both awake now and they looked up at him. He motioned for them to follow, "Stay close." They followed Raven toward the other end of the camp. Hikaru took up position behind the girls and kept an eye on their back.

***

"We are under attack!" Rin yelled in elven as she raced through the camp. Any enemy that came within arm's reach of her dropped dead. "Clear out the camp then secure our perimeter!"

The battle-hardened elves were immediately at the ready and they formed into quick battle groups of five or six. They followed Rin's orders without question. She continued to cut through the enemy until she skidded to a halt by her brother's tent. Wren and Jaeha stood back to back with katanas drawn on the ruins of Wren's tent, surrounded by a large group of orcs and massive horse sized wolves with more pouring in from the forest. The wargs circled around the orcs with loud snarls as their riders directed them where to go.

Rin narrowed her eyes when she saw that her brother was already injured. His shoulder was covered in blood from what looked like a warg bite. She blew a slow, low whistle. Anyone not trained to listen for that sound would have overlooked it with all the other battle sounds, but Wren looked up as soon as he heard it. The two made eye contact and Rin raised her arm.

"No!" He yelled, but she ignored him.

"Pevanas!" A strong wind slammed into a group of orcs and sent ten of them sailing across the clearing. Without waiting for the rest of the surprised orcs to react, she began making a path through them. In a matter of seconds, bodies of orcs were strewn around her feet as she made her way forward. Kaedin moved with her, his katana in hand, as he killed any orc that came up behind her.

They fought their way through the orcs until they reached Jaeha and Wren. As soon as they reached them, Jaeha pushed Wren in front of him and they started to make their way back through the path Rin and Kaedin had created. They did not make it very far when they felt the ground begin to shake. Rin glanced over her shoulder and saw a troll bearing down on them. She spun and pushed her brother hard. He staggered to the side out of the way of the troll's club. Rin leapt back but got caught by the edge of the club. She yelped in pain when it sent her flying across the clearing. She landed twenty feet away and went down in a tangle of orcs. Grimacing, she fought her way free and got back to her feet. Her steps were unsteady when she had to jump to the side and the troll's club crashed into the ground causing it to shake. She prepared to dodge again when the troll raised its club again, but before it could swing at her it was pierced by multiple arrows. It howled in pain and turned its attention away from her.

Rin glanced behind her and saw that the rest of the elves were coming to help. They had secured their camp and could now focus on pushing the rest of the enemy back. When she found the elf leading the rest, she nodded to him. He pressed a fist to his chest in response before he turned his attention back to the troll.

Returning her attention to the battle, she scanned the area until she caught sight of her brother and Jaeha again. Kaedin was still with them helping to protect Wren. She started to move toward them when she saw a glimpse of something metal in the trees. Taking a closer look, she saw that Jyldar was in the tree with an arrow trained on Wren. She gasped and took off at a sprint across the clearing. Without warning a warg leapt into her path from the side. She dropped and slid underneath it. Thrusting her daggers up, she stabbed it in the stomach as she flew under. Pushing herself back up with her hands, she kept her forward momentum going.

"Ksáetras," she yelled when she saw Jyldar release the arrow. A force wall sprang to life between the arrow and her brother. She kept running toward Jyldar and watched as he waved his hand the second before the arrow hit the wall. It changed direction and flew right at her.

"Pevanas," she gasped and barely had time to get her hand up to cast the wind spell. It managed to turn the arrow but left a small scrape across the palm of her hand before it dropped to the ground. Her gaze flew back to the tree and her face clouded with anger when Jyldar was gone. Muttering under her breath, she spun and dropped several more orcs before they began to retreat into the trees. She watched them go until a sharp pain in her hand caused her to look down at it. Her brows furrowed when she saw several strange looking black lines across her palm and a sudden wave of dizziness washed over her. Shaking her head, she attempted to shake off the feeling as she reached down to pick up the arrow Jyldar shot at Wren. Before she could touch it, Jaeha grabbed her hand.

"Do not touch that," he said, his voice sharp. He reached down and picked it up before he smelled it. His expression grew angry as he slammed the tip into the ground. "It smells of everdark."

"What is everdark?" Jake's voice caused Rin to glance up. Raven, Hikaru, Paige, and Sara joined them as a large group of elven warriors busied themselves with picking off any remaining stragglers.

"It is a poison," Jaeha replied with a frown. "A quite lethal one."

Rin clamped her right hand closed as she made her way over to Wren. She put her left hand over his shoulder and closed her eyes to heal the wound. Wren's eyebrow rose when he noticed her using her nondominant hand to heal him.

"What does it do?" Jake asked. The doctor in him took over as he tried to gather as much information about the poison as possible. If he could have to deal with it, he needed to know about it.

"The effects to someone who is not bonded is too gruesome to describe," Jaeha said before he paused and glanced at Wren. "I do not understand why he would try and poison Wren with this. While there is no form of healing, anyone with a bonded would not die. He had to be aware of this."

"What would happen to them?"

"The poison would spread through their bodies turning every vein black. It shall fade but some could be permanent. They would be on death's doorstep and only their bonded's blood would keep them alive. It is quite painful and fast acting." Jaeha paused. "It could be seen as advantageous to some since the elf would then be immune to the effects in the future."

"If it kills an elf how would the blood of another elf keep them alive?" Jake asked, something about all of this seemed off to him. Jaeha only tilted his head before he looked over at Wren.

Rin was finished healing his shoulder, but she staggered when she stepped away from him and grabbed her right hand as another sharp pain lanced through it. Kaedin glanced at her when he sensed the pain and moved so that he was standing beside her.

Wren frowned as he watched Kaedin move closer to his sister. "Show me."

Rin's head snapped up and she grimaced when she realized that her brother already knew something was wrong. With a heavy sigh, she opened her right hand and showed him the palm of her hand. He grabbed her hand, so he could get a better look. She flinched but did not make a sound. The whole palm of her hand was already covered in black lines that were creeping up her wrist.

"We are not waiting until morning," Wren said, his voice serious. "We are leaving tonight and shall be flying. We must make it to the stronghold at Lyrin as soon as possible." He paused and looked around before he waved an elf over. "Captain Lielpe, you are to secure this camp in case of another attack. I am leaving now."

"Yes, my lord," the captain replied before he disappeared into the camp.

"All of you shall meet me over by your tent in about fifteen minutes," Wren said as he headed over to the remains of his tent with Jaeha. Raven and Hikaru disappeared with Jake and the girls in the direction of their tent.

Kaedin and Rin made their way that direction, but they moved slower. Rin ground her teeth together in frustration. She had not even been home a day and had already been wounded twice. It made her feel like she was a burden to her brother. Kaedin glanced at her when he sensed the change in her emotions. He put his arm around her shoulders and pulled her closer to him. She leaned into him and took comfort in his presence.

When they arrived back at the tent, they found Raven had the tent bag slung over his shoulder while they waited on Wren.

"Why aren't we going to port?" Jake asked now that they had a moment they were not moving.

Raven glanced over at him. "There are port blocks on all of the settlements and cities, plus large areas around military outposts. It is safer and easier to avoid detection if we fly."

Jake opened his mouth to ask another question, but Wren came striding up with a small bag on his back.

"Let us go," he said without pausing. They all headed into the open area beyond the tents. Jaeha, Hikaru, and Kaedin walked a short distance away from everyone and began to glow. Jake's mouth dropped open in shock when they changed into silver dragons. His head started to shake as he took in their appearance. The size between them varied a great deal, but they all had a ridge of spines that ran from the top of their head to the tip of their tail. Their silver color appeared an almost bluish silver in the light of the fires and the moon.

"They're dragons," Jake said, his voice flat. "That's what you were attempting to hide until now. A bonded is an elf and dragon pair that share blood. That's why their blood would keep the elf alive."

Wren tilted his head with a frown when he looked over at Jake, "I have attempted to conceal nothing from you."

"They have," Jake said looking over at the dragons. "I don't understand what they could gain from it."

A low growl from Jaeha caused Jake to look up at him. He had to take a few steps back when Jaeha moved closer to him or he could not see his face. The dragon was huge. He was noticeably the largest of the three and he looked much older in dragon form. Kaedin was the smallest and Jake could tell he was not as old.

"We did not wish to reveal our true nature until we were certain that we could trust all of you," Jaeha growled. "If your people were interested in experimenting on an elf could you imagine their interest in a dragon? We only exist in your legends."

Jake frowned but could not argue with him, "That's probably true, but I wouldn't be one of them."

Jaeha regarded Jake for a moment before he growled again and bowed his head to the side. "I apologize for keeping our secret for so long. You speak the truth when you say that you do not act as most of the others we witnessed in your world. Forgive me."

"It's fine," Jake said as he folded his arms over his chest. "I would appreciate no more secrets." When Jaeha nodded, he glanced over at Rin. She was making her way over to Kaedin.

"No," Wren said. "You will be flying with me. Kaedin shall take Jake and Sara."

Rin looked back over her shoulder. "What? You cannot possibly put them on a dragon alone. They have never flown before and should be paired with us."

"And when the poison affects you enough that you cannot stay on? Who shall keep Sara from falling then?"

"I am not as weak as you believe," Rin snapped at him. He only raised an eyebrow before he led Jake and Sara over to Kaedin.

"There is a break in the spines on his back," Wren said as he pointed up at a place between Kaedin's wings. "You shall sit there. Once you are on, you can hold the spines for balance if you must, but you should be all right. Kaedin will be gentle, I am certain." He glanced at Kaedin before he turned, grabbed Rin's arm, and headed over to Jaeha.

Jake watched him leave before he looked back at Kaedin. He could not conceal all of his apprehension and Kaedin growled under his breath.

"I don't like this any more than you do," Jake snapped before he picked Sara up by the waist. She could not reach to climb up and Kaedin was forced to lay down flat on the ground before she could get up. Once she was finally situated, Jake hesitated and looked at Kaedin again.

"Get it over with," he said with a loud growl.

Jake narrowed his eyes in irritation before he climbed up Kaedin's side and sat down behind Sara. When he was seated, he glanced around and saw that Paige was sitting behind Raven on Hikaru, and a very unhappy Rin was sitting in front of her brother on Jaeha.

"Let us go," Wren called when he was certain that everyone was ready. The dragons spread their wings and leapt into the air. They set a brisk pace as they flew away from the camp.

Several hours later the sun was rising, and Rin glanced toward Kaedin. They were still traveling fast, and she could sense that he was beginning to tire. A scowl crossed her face when she could not attempt to lessen his exhaustion with magic since she was stuck with Wren. She looked up at her brother to say something when Jaeha veered off to the side to put some distance between them and the others.

"The young one is struggling," he growled. "He is still small to be carrying two." He had noticed that Kaedin was starting to lag a little bit.

Wren looked over at Kaedin and sighed, "Find a place and we shall rest for an hour or two."

Jaeha drifted closer to Kaedin and Hikaru before he roared. The three dragons started to descend. A little while later Jaeha found a small shelter clearing for them to land in and they all dropped to the ground. The large dragon sank his claws into the forest floor and before he could close his wings Rin slid off his back. She turned and glowered at her brother.

"As you can see, I am just fine," she snapped. "I am half dragon besides having a bonded. I shall remain with Kaedin from now on." Without letting her brother respond, she spun on her heel and marched away.

Wren slid down Jaeha's side as he watched her walk away. A look of disapproval was fixed on his face when he could see all of her veins were already black.

"Our lady is a handful as always," Jaeha said with a low growl. "It is good to see that has not changed after her ordeal." He growled again when Wren did nothing other than glance at him.

Rin slowed to an unhurried walk once she was out of earshot. Her face contorted into a grimace of pain when she grabbed her hand. The point of the poison entry was causing her the most pain. She pushed her pain away when she got close to Kaedin. He was back in elven form and was laying on the ground with his arm over his face. She sense that he was exhausted and sat down beside him. Taking hold of the hand not over his face, she closed her eyes, "Āijabūeta."

He sighed as soon as the word was out of her mouth. Her magic flowed into him and relieved some of his fatigue.

"Thank you," he said, his voice quiet. He lifted his arm off his face and when he saw her his eyes opened wide.

"I look that poorly?" She asked with a forced smile.

His expression shifted to one of concern, "You are in pain."

She tilted her head with a sigh. It was not a question. She knew he could sense that she was hurting.

"It is not more than I can handle," she said.

Kaedin frowned before he motioned for her to lay down next to him. He knew she was in worse shape than she was letting on. After he extended his arm on the ground, she laid down beside him and rested her head on it. He draped his other arm over her and a few short minutes later they were both fast asleep.

Jake, Paige, and Sara were sitting with Raven and Hikaru a little way away from Rin and Kaedin. Hikaru was sprawled out on the grass next to Raven already asleep.

"Why is there such a size difference between the dragons?" Jake asked, breaking the silence.

Raven looked up at him, "Their age determines their size." When Jake gave him an expectant stare he sighed. "Jaeha is the oldest so he is the largest, but even he is not full grown yet."

Jake's eyes widened in surprise when he realized Jaeha would get larger. The massive dragon already stood fifty feet tall, and from the tip of his nose to tail was one hundred and ten feet long. His wings fully extended were a full one hundred and thirty-five feet.

"I'm afraid to ask this, but how old are all of you?" Jake asked, his eyes filling with curiosity. "I get the feeling that you are much older than we think you are."

Raven shifted, his discomfort visible, before he glanced at Paige with a frown.

"What?" She asked with a pout. He only shrugged before he sighed and looked back over at Jake.

"I supposed I shall start with the youngest," he said. "Lady Rin and Kaedin are both four hundred and nineteen. This is why Kaedin is so much smaller than Jaeha and Hikaru. He is still only a young adult dragon."

"The youngest?" Jake could not keep from interrupting.

Raven nodded slowly, and his expression grew wary before he continued, "Hikaru and I are next, we are both around eight hundred and fourteen. This makes Hikaru an adult dragon." He paused as if trying to gauge his reaction. "Lord Wren and Jaeha are the oldest of our group. They are both one thousand two hundred and nineteen, I believe. We do not keep close track of our ages." He paused to collect his thoughts before he continued, "Jaeha is an ancient dragon but he will not be considered fully grown until he reaches elder at fifteen hundred."

Jake could only stare at him in complete disbelief. The idea of living so long was such a foreign concept that he could not wrap his head around it.

"How do you live so long?" Sara's quiet voice caused Raven to look over at her. He hesitated before he frowned again.

"My people, as well as most races in my world, are immortal," he replied. "We only die if we are killed." Raven watched Paige, Jake, and Sara for a few minutes before he turned his attention away from them. They needed a moment to process everything he just told them.

"You're over eight hundred years old?" Paige asked. She had her hands on her hips when she looked over at Raven. When he only nodded, she scowled at him. "Why didn't you tell me?"

"I did not have much of an opportunity before now," he said with a tilt of his head. "Besides, I did not wish for you to react as you are now. It has made you uncomfortable."

Paige rolled her eyes, "It doesn't make me uncomfortable. It does make me wonder why in the world you'd pick me to date if you're so much older than me."

"You are special," he said with a smile. It slipped from his face a second later when he noticed the look of disapproval on Jake's face. "I believe we should discuss this later." Raven made a point not to look back at Jake.

They all fell silent for a while before Jake looked back over at Raven. He still did not understand something.

"If Rin is considered to be very young, why does she have so much responsibility?" he asked. "I have heard some of the elven warriors refer to her as a general and that is how she introduced herself to my father."

Raven looked up to reply but glanced behind Jake instead. Jake turned around and found Wren standing there looking down at him.

"Why do you wish to know about my sister?" His expression gave nothing away as he regarded Jake.

"Mostly curiosity, I guess," Jake replied. "I'm still trying to figure out how this world works, and something seems off with your sister somehow."

Wren tilted his head and his eyebrow rose before he sat down next to him. "You appear to be far more intuitive than I gave you credit for," he began. "You are correct in your observation that what involves Rin is not the norm." Jake nodded but did not say anything as he waited for Wren to continue. "You are also correct that she has far too much burden on her shoulders for one so young. Knowing what I do now, I believe our father placed this burden upon her out of spite. She would not become what he wanted her to be, so he would assign her impossible tasks. He attempted to cause her to fail." He paused with a grimace and looked over to make sure Kaedin and Rin were still asleep. "I have said too much. She does not know father tried to set her up to fail. Be certain that none of you speak of this." Once they all nodded, he stood up to leave.

"So, she really is a general?" Jake asked.

Wren frowned, "Yes, she is the general of the dragon riders and a commander of the ground troops." He paused, and his expression became serious. "She is quite skilled and performs as one far beyond her years due to my father's constant pressure. Now, no more about my sister. It is time for us to leave. Prepare yourselves." Without waiting on a response, he walked away.

Rin woke after what felt like only a few minutes to Kaedin gently shaking her by the shoulder. She rubbed her eyes trying to keep them open when she looked up at him. When she moved to sit up she gasped. Her whole body felt like it was being jabbed by tiny pins and needles. Looking down at her arm, she noticed that the veins were still getting darker. She opened and closed her hands while rotating her forearms. Everything still seemed to be working right. She did not want to have an issue when she was up on Kaedin and prove her brother right.

"He is watching," Kaedin whispered to her. "Are you certain that you will be all right? You appear worse."

She looked up at Kaedin and could see his face was drawn with worry. He glanced out of the corner of his eye in Wren's direction before he shifted enough that she was hidden from view. She grimaced as she fought to repress the pain running through her.

"I shall be fine," she replied, her voice determined as she stood up and looked over at her brother. He raised an eyebrow in response before turning to gather his things off the ground.

"How long do you estimate she has before she cannot handle it anymore?" Wren asked as he looked up at Jaeha.

"Hours at most," he replied with a low growl. "We shall have to remain close."

Wren was not pleased as he glanced beside him when he noticed movement. He watched as Jake walked up to him while Jake spun the staff in his hand.

"I guess I'm with you this time," Jake said, his voice giving away his discomfort.

"Get situated and I shall be up in a few minutes." Wren replied before he headed over to where Rin and Sara were climbing onto Kaedin. Rin was already in place when Wren reached them.

"Take my hand," Rin said as she reached down. Sara stood on her tiptoes while balancing on Kaedin's front leg and was just able to reach Rin's hand. Once Sara had a firm grip, Rin pulled her up in one smooth motion. Sara scrambled to get to the open spot in Kaedin's spines behind Rin.

"Are all of you prepared?" Wren asked when he stopped beside Kaedin.

"Yes," Rin said, her voice sharp. She gripped her hand while it sent sharp pains up her arm after helping Sara.

Wren noticed and sighed but chose not to argue with her. She would find out soon enough that she would not be able to stay alone on Kaedin. He walked back to Jaeha and once he was on his back all the dragons again rose into the sky.

"We should practice the mind blocking spell," Rin said after they were in the air for a while. "You must learn to use it as soon as possible."

Sara hesitated, "Are you sure you're okay for that?"

"Yes, I am fine," Rin's reply was short when she glanced back over her shoulder.

Sara looked down at Kaedin's back. "I can feel you shaking," she whispered.

"I am fin--."

"I can as well," Kaedin interrupted.

Rin sighed before she slid forward enough that she was no longer touching Sara. "Both of you shall quit worrying this instant," she said, her voice still short. "I am not foolish enough to continue when I cannot handle something. If it becomes too severe, I shall tell you. Now, not another word about it."

Kaedin let out a low growl but wisely did not say anything else. Rin frowned when she could sense he was unhappy with her.

"Okay," Sara said. "I will practice."

A little while later, Sara had made no progress in being able to use the spell on her own. She still needed Rin to push her magic out and was becoming frustrated. Rin finished helping her for the fifteenth time when Rin leaned forward suddenly. She rested her head on Kaedin's back for a few moments before she sat up, her breathing increasing.

"I need you to land," she gasped. "I am going to be sick."

Kaedin looked down and his face grew concerned, "I cannot land." They were flying over the southern end of an enormous lake and the closest shore was a couple miles away.

Rin looked around for a moment trying to figure out what to do before she slid to the right. She held onto the spines on his back to keep from falling off.

"Slide forward and hold on," she said between hard swallows. "I shall return in a moment." She climbed forward a little bit before she slid down Kaedin's front right leg. He opened his claw and caught her. She managed to pull herself forward enough to be hanging off the edge of his claw before she began to vomit. It was several minutes before she eased back into his claw. She laid there until her stomach stopped churning and her breathing returned to normal.

"Please help me back up," she said, her voice quiet.

Kaedin lifted his claw as high as he could, and Rin made the short jump back to his back. She grabbed at and almost missed the spines on his back. Sara gasped and clutched at her arm causing Rin to flinch with a gasp, but she allowed Sara to help her back into place. Once she was sitting again, she laid her head against his back.

"Thank you," she whispered.

Sara was concerned as she looked down at her. When she grabbed Rin's arm, she could feel that Rin was burning with fever and Sara wondered how she could keep going. Rin heard her thought and closed her eyes against the rising nausea.

'I do not wish to be a burden,' Rin thought.

"I don't think they'll think you're a burden if you let your brother help you," Sara said.

Rin sat up and turned so that she could see Sara, "I did not say that out loud." She flipped her left hand over and attempted a simple spell. Her eyes widened when it did not work. "I cannot do magic." She gasped as a wave of coughing shook her body and when she pulled her hand back there was a small streak of blood.

"I believe I have reached my limit," she muttered.

Kaedin growled but before he could respond he suddenly veered to the right as multiple black orc arrows streaked by barely missing them. Rin spun in place when she heard Sara scream. She was not holding on like she was supposed to and went flying off Kaedin's back. Kaedin tucked his wings and plummeted down while he spiraled around so that he could drop underneath her. He caught up to her in seconds and swooped under her. Attempting to slow down, he spread his wings with slow movements, so he did not slow too fast. Once they were fully extended, they drifted upward toward her.

Rin reached out to grab Sara's hand, but she was flailing around too much. "Take my hand!" She yelled as she reached for her again.

Kaedin struggled to remain level as he was forced to continue to drop as Rin tried to catch Sara. When they were not far above the water, he noticed they were too close to shore. He roared when the orcs started firing more arrows at him and they bounced off his side.

"Reach Sara!" Kaedin was distracted for a moment when Rin yelled at Sara again. He let out a small pained roar when he could not dodge the large rock, thrown by a troll, and it slammed into his wing. The main bone in the front of his wing cracked from the force of the impact.

"Come on, Sara!" Rin tried again to get hold of her, but her hand slipped through hers. She glanced away from Sara for a moment and paled when she saw the orcs reloading another volley. As they pulled back their bows, Jaeha appeared between them and the orcs. He breathed a massive cold breath attack as he flew by them. Rin finally managed to get hold of Sara and pulled her back onto Kaedin's back. As soon as Kaedin felt her back in place, he pulled up and began to climb. He was at such a steep angle both girls leaned forward to stay with him. Jaeha kept pace at his side until they were out of range. Kaedin was panting from the strain of carrying two and his injured wing. He floundered in the air for a second before Jaeha bumped his side with his nose to get him righted.

"Glide," Jaeha said while he flew beside him. Kaedin opened his wings as far as he could and started to regain his breath. He glanced back over his shoulder his face filled with worry. Rin, who was now past her point of endurance, was collapsed forward on his back beside the spines. She was exhausted.

"Hold steady," Wren called to the dragons as Jaeha and Hikaru glided up right next to Kaedin. Wren leapt off Jaeha and landed on Kaedin behind Sara. Kaedin growled when he floundered again with the sudden added weight.

Jaeha nudged him, "Easy."

Kaedin did not reply as he struggled to remain in the air while Wren grabbed Sara and leapt with her onto Hikaru. Raven helped Sara sit down in front of him. Once Wren was certain that she was safe, he jumped back to Kaedin.

"I cannot heal you in the air," he said as he picked up Rin off his back. "We shall take the added weight and divert course to a protected valley. Can you make another twenty miles?"

"Yes," Kaedin replied with a pained growl. His wing was sending sharp pains into his side. Wren leapt back over to Jaeha, leaving Kaedin with no passengers. He sat back down and put Rin in front of him. The dragons made a wide sweeping turn and headed to the south, toward the closer mountain peaks.

"There is a valley beside that mountain," Wren said as he pointed to a peak in the distance. "It is protected on all sides by steep cliffs and there is fresh water. We shall have to remain there a day or two until Rin and Kaedin recover. The stronghold is too far." He looked back at Jake and when he only nodded, he turned his attention back to Rin. He had laid her sideways across Jaeha's back so that he could see her face. She was resting back against the arm around her back.

"I told you to stay with me and not return to Kaedin," he said, his voice firm. "I have witnessed what this poison causes."

Rin gave him a dirty look before she sat up off his arm. "If I had then Kaedin would have had to catch Jake and Sara." She paused to take a couple breaths. "If Jaeha were to bank too sharp now, Jacob would fall. He is not holding on with his legs."

Wren glanced back and sighed when he saw that she was right. He raised an eyebrow and Jake shrugged with a slight grimace.

"Sorry," he mumbled.

Wren turned back around when he felt Rin collapse back against his arm. She was coughing again, and her breathing was becoming labored.

"Be at ease," he said, his voice gentle. "This is the worst part and by tomorrow it should start to lessen." She only nodded and closed her eyes.

A little less than an hour later they came upon the valley in the mountains that Wren mentioned. It was a beautiful haven locked in between snowcapped peaks. There was a small lake in the middle that was fed by a waterfall that ran down from the mountain above. There was a small clearing to the south of the lake and the rest of the valley was filled with trees.

The dragons made one large pass before they dropped to the ground in the clearing. Kaedin moved into the cover of the trees and plopped down. He left his injured wing stretched out. Hikaru just laid down where he landed. Even though he was much larger than Kaedin, carrying three was difficult for him. Raven reached up to help Paige and Sara down when Wren walked up to him.

"I know that you are already tired," he said glancing at Hikaru. "However, I must know what is in that orc party and whether it is safe to remain here. I need the two of you to scout them."

Once Paige and Sara were off his back, Hikaru stood back up. Raven jumped up onto his back, "We shall return as soon as we are able."

"Stay out of sight and be cautious," Wren said. Raven bowed his head before Hikaru eased off the ground. Paige and Sara raised their arms to cover their faces from the wind created by his wings. Once he was far enough off the ground Paige watched them fly away. Her face was worried when she looked back at Sara. She did not want him to go back.

Hikaru flew hard away from the valley and headed back the way they had come. They made the flight back to the lake in half the time now that Hikaru was not concerned about dropping Sara and Paige.

"Arāesya," Raven said when they approached the shore. They disappeared from view and Hikaru landed in an open portion of the beach a fair distance from where they were attacked by the orcs. Once on the ground, he crouched down and concealed himself under the cover of the trees. Raven slid off his back and disappeared into the forest without a word. He slipped through the dense underbrush without making a sound. After a few minutes, he heard the guttural sound of orc voices up ahead. He slowed and crept forward until the edge of a clearing came into view. Easing closer, he concealed himself in a bush as he watched the activity. There were several dozen orcs rushing around gathering and sharpening weapons. He watched for a few minutes before his eyebrows shot up in surprise. Several humans entered the clearing from the far side. They retrieved some of the weapons before returning the way they came.

Raven eased out of the bushes and skirted around the clearing. He caught up to them and followed as they led him to a second, much larger clearing. Pausing, he glanced all around before he slipped across the path unseen. He started to move through the underbrush again when something large, moving in the clearing, caught his eye. His breath caught in his throat when he saw a fully grown elder red dragon in the middle of the clearing. He hesitated for only a moment before he moved as close to the dragon as he dared.

"You are a fool," the dragon snapped.

Raven frowned when he could not see who it was speaking to and shifted to the side to try and get a glimpse. The dragon snapped its tail and Raven's eyes narrowed in anger when he saw Jyldar.

"My plan would have succeeded if the orcs were not useless creatures," Jyldar said as he folded his arms over his chest.

The dragon roared and whipped around to face him, "If you had waited on the rest of the dragons like you were told, the prince and that entire unit would be dead. Instead, he has now escaped due to your incompetence."

Jyldar flinched back from the dragon. It was so angry that small flames were beginning to spark from its mouth.

Raven took several cautious steps backwards so that he could head back to Hikaru. He had to get this information back to Wren. He only made it a few steps when the dragon whipped around and sniffed the air.

"It appears that you have an uninvited guest," it growled as it looked in Raven's direction. Raven froze in place until he noticed Jyldar look right at him. He glanced down and cursed when he realized his invisibility spell wore off. Without looking back up, he took off at a sprint into the trees.

"Stop him!" Jyldar yelled.

Dozens of orcs and humans chased after Raven, but he did not slow as he dodged around trees and leapt over clumps of bushes. When he reached the smaller clearing, he let out a high, shrill whistle as he continued to run. More orcs leapt to their feet and took up the chase. Arrows were whistling by all around him when he broke out of the tree cover. As soon as he was out in the open, Hikaru plucked him up off the ground and flew away at top speed. Raven scrambled up his leg and climbed onto his back.

"They have an elder red," he said as he sat down between the spines. Hikaru growled under his breath and pushed himself to fly faster. They did not make it far before they heard an ear-splitting roar from behind them. Raven rotated to look back and saw the red dragon rising up out of the trees. It headed straight toward them. Hikaru shifted their course and headed away from the valley. He continued to fly hard and managed to keep the larger dragon from catching them until they were back by the mountains. It breathed a large stream of fire in their direction causing Hikaru to go into a sharp dive to avoid it. Spinning to the side, Hikaru streaked into a tight corridor through several mountain peaks where he had the advantage. He was much more maneuverable than the massive red dragon. The larger dragon trailed behind him and waited for its moment to strike. As soon as the narrow pass ended the red dragon lunged at him. It slammed into his side and knocked him into the side of a cliff. Hikaru roared in pain but twisted enough that he could breathe an ice attack in its face. The red dragon backed off to shake off the ice. Hikaru took the opening and shot ahead of it. Howling in anger, the red dragon breathed a fireball at him which he only managed to dodge partway. It collided with the left side of his back. He roared in pain again but managed to duck behind a large outcrop, hiding them from view.

"Arāesya," Raven gasped, and they disappeared from view. Hikaru dropped to the ground and changed back to elven form. They dove behind several large rocks. Hikaru glanced at Raven when he could sense his pain. Raven clutched at his badly burned side as he fought to remain still.

"They have to be here," the red dragon growled as it circled above them. "They must be caught and disposed of, no one can know we are working together yet. All of the preparations are not yet finished."

"I shall handle it," Jyldar snapped from where he was perched on the dragon's back. "Allow me off here. They are injured so it should be an easy kill."

The red dragon growled again before it drifted away from their hiding spot to find a large enough place to land.

"Can you port us?" Hikaru asked in an urgent whisper.

Raven nodded and put his hand on Hikaru's arm. He closed his eyes in concentration and pictured the valley in his mind. "Ēlipor ntāera," he whispered, and they disappeared.

***

Wren watched Raven and Hikaru fly away before he turned back to the clearing. He tilted his head in thought before he headed over to the pieces of the tent Raven left on the ground. After picking them up, he dragged them into a small opening that was still under the cover of the trees. He could not shake the feeling that they needed to remain out of sight.

"Jake, Sara, Paige, and I shall see to the tent," Jaeha said as he walked up carrying Rin. He laid her on the ground in some soft underbrush. "You should see to Kaedin's wing."

Wren frowned when he noticed that Rin was unconscious. He glanced up at Jaeha and nodded before he watched Sara and Paige walk past him. Once they were working on setting up the tent, he headed back down to the edge of the tree line where Kaedin was asleep on the ground. He rested a hand on Kaedin's wing causing him to snap awake. Kaedin flinched away from him.

"Easy," Wren said, his voice quiet. "I shall heal the wing." As soon as Kaedin realized it was Wren who touched him, he relaxed, and Wren put his hand back on his wing, "Rujhāe." Wren's eyes were closed as he poured healing magic into the wound and it was several minutes before he opened his eyes with a sigh. "That is the best I can do. There could be some lasting pain because we did not get it healed quickly enough."

Kaedin only nodded as he allowed himself to glow and returned to elven form a few seconds later. A grimace crossed his face when the pain from the wing radiated through his back and part of his left arm.

"Thank you," he said when Wren reached down and helped him back to his feet. Once he was standing his attention shifted to the tent. He could sense that Rin was quite unwell, and his face clouded with worry.

"She will be fine in a day or two," Wren said when he noticed his expression. "Your blood will keep her alive." He motioned toward the tent and the two of them walked further under the cover of the trees. When they reached the tent, they noticed that the others were finished setting it up and were all sitting around the outside of the tent watching them approach.

"Until Raven and Hikaru return we must remain under cover," Wren said as he sat down. "Do not leave the shelter of the trees." He fell silent once Jake nodded and turned his gaze to the sky. His brows furrowed as he calculated the amount of time since the rider pair left. It was bordering on too long and he was growing concerned.

"How do you and Jaeha know so much about that poison?" Jake asked suddenly.

Wren regarded him for a moment before he nodded in approval, "It is as I suspected, you are quite observant and intuitive." He paused. "We know about everdark because I have already been through it many years ago." He pulled up the sleeve of his shirt to show Jake the mark the poison left. There was a large black circle where the back of the arm and shoulder meet. Several black lines branched out from the circle.

"Rin doesn't know?"

"Why would she?" Wren asked with a wry smile. "It happened several centuries before she was born."

Jake shook his head as disbelief crept across his face, "I still can't believe you guys are that old."

Wren only chuckled before he turned his attention back to the sky. When he saw no sign of Raven and Hikaru his expression darkened.

"He needs help!" Hikaru's voice broke through the silence when he yelled from the clearing. He had Raven's arm over his shoulder and was supporting most of his weight. Wren and Jake were both on their feet and across the clearing before they could move. They helped them get over to the tent.

Wren eased Raven to the ground, and he stifled a gasp when his burned side touched the grass. Wren reached down to heal him, but Raven grabbed his hand to stop him.

"There were dozens of orcs and humans, that I could see," he gasped. "They appeared to be preparing for an assault of some kind." He paused with a grimace when he moved too much. "There was an elder red dragon with them. He spoke of more coming and Jyldar was with them."

"Allow me to heal you and then we shall discuss this further," Wren said, his voice firm. He could see the pain on Raven's face. Once Raven relaxed back onto the ground, Wren closed his eyes and held his hands over the wound, "Rujhāe." It took several minutes before the burns were healed. When he opened his eyes, he sighed with a raised eyebrow. Raven was already asleep after the healing. Shaking his head, he stood and moved away from Raven and Paige took his place. She took hold of Raven's hand and held onto it while he slept.

While Wren was tending to Raven, Jake helped Hikaru over to the tent. His burns were minimal since he sustained them in dragon form. Jaeha was able to heal them and he, like Raven, was asleep on the ground. Wren glanced over and when he saw that Hikaru was taken care of he looked toward the lake. He stood unmoving for a while before he looked at Jaeha. The dragon tilted his head and the two appeared to have a silent conversation.

"I shall take care of it," Jaeha said. "They must be warned, and I should be able to make it back before you must move everyone."

"Be careful," Wren replied as the two clasped forearms. "May the winds blow in your favor."

Jaeha gave Wren a slight bow before he turned and left the valley. Wren stood until he could no longer see him before he walked deeper into the woods.

Sara watched Wren walk away and worry lines formed between her eyes. She knew he had to be worried about Jaeha going somewhere alone. While she did not know exactly what was going on, she figured out enough to know he had to be going to warn someone. She sighed before she glanced up at Jake, who was sitting next to her. He noticed her gaze right away and wrapped his arm around her shoulders. She leaned against him and rested her head on his shoulder.

"This place is pretty crazy," Jake said looking down at her. "I've been through combat before and it doesn't come close to this."

"It seems like a scary place," she whispered.

Jake watched her for a moment before he pulled her onto his lap and wrapped both arms around her. She flushed bright red and her entire body went rigid as she looked down at her hands.

"Yes, it is," he said, his voice soft. "Watching you fly off Kaedin and knowing I couldn't do a thing to help you was the scariest thing I've ever been through." He tightened his grip on her and she could not help but relax.

"Sorry," she mumbled before she put an arm around his back. He rested his cheek on her head and held her as the two fell silent.

It was nearing midnight when Sara rolled over with a sigh. Every time she tried to fall asleep, she woke up a short time later. After waking for the third time, she gave up and laid awake staring at the canvas roof. After a while she looked around the tent and her brows furrowed when she realized that Rin was gone. Sitting up, she peeked through the opening at the front and found Rin curled up next to the fire. She was watching the flames but looked up when Sara walked out of the tent. Sara hesitated and did not sit down with her until Rin tilted her head toward the fire. She sat down and the two turned their attention to the flames.

"Are you having difficulty sleeping?"

Sara looked up when Rin spoke to her. "Yeah, I keep dreaming of falling off Kaedin." Her face flushed, and she looked down at her hands.

"I can see how that could be frightening," Rin said with a shrug before looking back at the fire. Sara peeked at her a couple times before she took a deep breath.

"You can't sleep either?"

Rin glanced at her, "No."

"Why?" Sara swallowed hard when she noticed the disapproval on Rin's face when she asked the question. "Sorry," she mumbled and looked down at the ground.

"If I attempt to sleep, I shall wake Kaedin."

Sara glanced up at her, but Rin would say nothing more about it and the two fell silent until Sara plucked up her courage.

"Can I ask you a question?"

Rin raised an eyebrow, "If you wish."

"If they're dragons why do they stay in elven form? Wouldn't they rather be in their normal form?" Sara asked, her voice shaking. Her face was filled with discomfort until she saw a fond smile cross Rin's face.

"Do you wish to hear the tale?" Rin asked when she looked back at Sara. When Sara nodded, she leaned back and looked up at the sky. "It begins at the time of the forging of Asaetara and prior to the war that split the races. The gods and goddesses worked for countless years crafting and forming our world. They wished to make the homes for their people perfect. Once the world was created to their liking the gods and goddesses placed the first of the races into the world." She paused with a smile. "Amongst the first of the elves was a maiden by the name of Arlaeyna. She was the most fair, intelligent, and was desired by all. When none of them caught her eye, she became saddened and traveled across the newly formed world. Her travels took her far and wide before she happened upon a settlement of dragons."

"The king of the settlement was a strong dragon by the name of Takaeda. He welcomed Arlaeyna into their midst with open arms. She was hesitant to be among such large creatures, but his genuine kindness warmed her heart. He did not pester her with constant pressure to court and for the first time she was truly at ease."

"The two spent centuries becoming the closest of friends." Rin paused again and looked back into the fire. "Neither one was aware of the feelings that were developing for the other until orcs attacked the settlement. Takaeda fought to protect his home but nearly lost Arlaeyna when he was too large to follow her. He felt as if his heart would tear in two and for the first time realized that he cared for the fair elven maiden."

"After the fighting subsided, he confessed his feelings to her and was overjoyed when hers were the same as his, but it was not long before he fell into a deep depression. The great dragon began to fade when he knew the two could never be joined. Arlaeyna in a desperate attempt to save his life pleaded with Lord Ruehnaer, the guardian deity of the elves, but he had no answer for her and Takaeda grew weaker. Arlaeyna refused to leave his side and remained with him. Her devotion to him caught the attention of Lady Kikaeyo, the guardian deity of the dragons. It pained her to see one of her children in so much despair and she appeared before Takaeda. She gave him a choice. Remain in dragon form or give some of his magic in exchange for the ability to take elven form. Takaeda lifted his head for the first time in weeks and made his choice. Rin paused and reached toward Kaedin. She rested her hand on his arm. "Since that day all dragons have had the ability to take elven form."

Sara's eyes were wide when Rin was finished with the story. She was surprised that the dragon would be willing to give up so much until she her thoughts drifted to Jake. Her expression changed, and she understood. She would give up almost anything to make sure that he was okay.

"Does this answer your question?" Rin asked. Sara nodded, and Rin tilted her head toward the tent. "You should attempt to sleep it is quite late."

Sara hesitated before she stood up to head back inside. "Thank you," she whispered before disappearing back inside.

The next two days passed slowly while they recovered and waited on Jaeha to return. Rin was feeling better and back to normal by late the first day and was anxious to continue on to Nuenthras.

Jake and Paige exchanged yet another glance when Rin walked by them. The change to her appearance from the poison was drastic and made her look more intimidating. The everdark left her with permanent black lines on the arm and palm of her right hand and left her lips black. There were also black lines that circled her eyes around the lid and made her green eyes even more noticeable. Kaedin even seemed to be having a little trouble adjusting as he watched her walk by again.

"All of you must stop staring," Rin said, her voice short. She gave them all a dirty look.

"Sorry Rin," Paige said with a grin. "You really look different. I mean, I totally like it and think it's awesome, but it's a huge change. It's like you have permanent lipstick and eyeliner."

Rin rolled her eyes and went back to pacing. Sara watched her for a minutes before she shook her head with a grimace.

'Not cool,' she thought. 'Just freaky.'

"I heard that," Rin snapped.

'You must learn that spell,' she thought. Her frustration bleeding into her thoughts. Hearing Sara's thoughts all the time was beginning to annoy her.

"Why?" Sara asked. "I really can't do it."

Rin whipped around with an incredulous look. "How do you not know the reason?" She snapped. "It is most distracting to have someone else's thoughts in your head. If the distraction was to come at the wrong moment, it could be disastrous."

Sara glanced at her before looking back down at the ground. She still did not really understand how it could be such a big deal. What could her errant thoughts possibly do?

Rin started to pace around the tent again when a sudden roar caught her attention. She motioned for them all to go deeper into the cover of the trees. They all backed further from the tree line and a few seconds later Wren and Kaedin appeared beside Rin. She edged forward a little so that she had a clear view of the lake.

A few minutes passed before several young red dragons landed in the clearing of the valley. They stopped to drink from the small lake. As she watched from the bushes, another two landed after the first group. They appeared to be hauling what looked like a wagon between them.

"How much farther?" One of the dragons carrying the wagon growled. The biggest of them turned and roared.

"Not much farther," it snapped. "Quit complaining and let us go." The two carrying the wagon walked over to the water's edge and got a drink while the others began to take off again.

Rin caught her brother's attention with a small hand wave. When he looked at her, she tilted her head in the direction of the dragons. He shook his head no. She gave him a dirty look before looking back at the two carrying the wagon. Tilting her head, she studied it for a moment as they took off. She glanced at Wren and once she saw he was not looking at her. "Cūdāe."

Wren's gaze flew back to her and he watched as she disappeared. He shook his head in frustration and looked at Kaedin. The dragon's full attention was on the wagon getting father away from them.

"Where?" Wren hissed in his ear. Kaedin pointed at the wagon before he moved to follow her. "No, they will see you as soon as you transform." He grabbed Kaedin's arm to keep him from leaving cover.

"I cannot allow her to go alone," Kaedin said, his voice worried. He looked back up at the wagon and tried to get his arm free, but Wren tightened his grip.

"If you follow her now, you shall give away our position. She is on her own, but the gods help her when she returns. I have several words I wish to share." Wren's voice became hard, giving away the anger that was concealed below the surface.

Kaedin held his ground for a moment before he exhaled hard and nodded. Once he did, Wren let go of his arm. Kaedin frowned and folded his arms across his chest before he started pacing back and forth in their small hidden area.

***

Rin appeared in the wagon between the two red dragons. She laid down among the contents. The dragons seemed to notice the added weight but when they looked over at the wagon, they did not see her. She observed the contents as best she could without moving around. It was full of all kinds of weapons and armor. Her brows furrowed when she did not recognize the insignia on the armor. It was a black fist holding a silver hourglass. The sand appeared to be frozen in mid shift. While she contemplated the insignia, the dragons flew for a while before they began to descend.

Rin risked a quick glance over the edge of the wagon and saw that they were near the base of the mountains. The sun began to dip lower in the sky as it got closer to evening. She noticed a massive cave up ahead and figured that must be where they were headed. Ducking back down, she closed her eyes and pictured in her mind where she wanted to go.

"Cūdāe," she whispered and disappeared. She ported to a clump of bushes close to the entrance of the cave. When she arrived in the bushes, she did not move for several minutes before she eased forward enough to see out. There were orcs, humans, and small red dragons going in and out of the cave at a brisk pace. She frowned when she could see multiple runes along the cave opening. The ones closest to her, she recognized as anti-magic runes. She stared at them trying to figure out a way to slip into the cave unseen when movement caught her attention.

A massive, almost seven-foot-tall, orc came striding out of the cave. His thick, strong muscles could be seen through the dark brown leather armor that complimented his dark green skin. It made it, so he could blend in with the trees around him without any effort. There was a large two-handed ax strapped to his back as he observed the camp around him with dark orange eyes.

Rin flattened against the ground when she saw him and closed her eyes to cast a port spell.

'Oh Paige, can't you just be quiet for a minute or two?' One of Sara's thoughts broke through her concentration. She shook her head trying to regain her focus and did not notice the huge hand reach down and grab her shirt. The massive orc jerked her out of the bushes and tossed her onto the ground in front of the cave. Rin gasped when she hit the ground but rolled and was back on her feet in a split second, daggers in both hands.

"General Rilavaenu," the orc growled with a look of disgust. "I heard unpleasant rumors that you returned."

Rin glanced around. The orcs and humans stopped working and readied bows.

"Oragg," she said, her voice flat.

He grinned at her as he pulled the ax off his back, but instead of rushing at her, he nodded his head. Everyone around them unleashed their arrows at her. With movements almost too quick to see, she blocked every one. She stood breathing heavily after the first wave but did not take her eyes off Oragg. She knew she could not do this very long and waited for the opportunity to port. The orc knew this and made sure to stay close enough that she could not escape. He stepped to the side and the two circled each other before he nodded again. Another round of arrows streaked toward her. She blocked them all as she kept her distance from the orc.

"I see you have not lost your touch," he growled. "It would be boring to kill the general if you were weak." He leapt at her. She jumped to the side and brought up her daggers. The ax connected with them with arm numbing strength. He pushed hard against her while their weapons were in contact and shoved her several feet. She leapt to the side again to get away from him. He turned around and stalked toward her. Her eyes flew around the clearing looking for an opening and when she found none her full attention returned to Oragg. He paused and nodded again. Arrows streaked at her and she managed to block several before she heard a 'Paige, stop,' in her head. The split-second distraction was all it took and in an instant, she was shot with six arrows. She gasped and somehow managed to remain on her feet.

Oragg grinned at her when she stumbled. He spun his ax in his hand as he savored this moment. Removing the rider general would be the greatest thing he ever accomplished.

Rin knew it was now or never and clamped her eyes closed.

"No!" She heard Oragg's furious yell when he realized she was attempting to port.

"Ēlipor ntāera," she gasped. She disappeared a second before his ax could connect.

***

Kaedin leapt up from where he had been sitting beside Wren. He could sense the sudden, intense pain that Rin was in and he had to get to her. Wren got to his feet when he saw the concern on Kaedin's face.

"What is wro--?" Before he could finish the question, Kaedin was not standing next to him anymore. He sprinted out of the trees and into the clearing where Rin just reappeared. She stumbled as her clothes became more soaked with blood by the second. Reaching up, she grabbed the arrow closest to her heart and pulled it out. She cried out in pain as she sank to her knees. Kaedin was by her side when she reached up to pull out the second arrow stuck in her chest. He grabbed her hand to stop her.

"Hold her," Wren ordered as soon as he dropped to his knees beside his sister. Kaedin pulled Rin toward him without a word and held her while Wren worked. He removed the second arrow from her chest before he got the two out of her back. She cried out in pain with each one when it came out and struggled to remain as still as possible. When he pulled the one out of her leg, she did not make a sound. She was beginning to drift in and out from losing so much blood.

"Hold her tightly," Wren said, his voice hard. The last arrow was stuck in her stomach and was going to be the most painful to remove. Kaedin's face was clouded with worry as he tightened his grip on her. She screamed in pure agony when Wren pulled the arrow free. He flinched but closed his eyes as he dropped the arrow on the ground.

"Rujhāe," he said, and his hands began to glow. It took several long minutes before he stopped the flow of magic and opened his eyes. Once he was finished, Rin curled into a ball as she fought to deal with the pain that remained. Kaedin watched her as he held her. It took her a while before she pushed away from him and staggered to her feet. He stood with her and kept a firm grip on her to keep her from falling. She took a few unsteady steps before she caught sight of Sara. She and Jake came over when they saw the commotion.

Anger flashed across Rin's face and she took a step toward her. "You must learn to block your thoughts!"

Sara's face filled with guilt, "This is my fault?"

"Yes!" Rin yelled as she wrapped an arm around her stomach. "I told you a distraction at the wrong moment could be disastrous."

Sara shrank back at her harsh words. Jake was not pleased, and he moved so that he stood between them. Rin ignored him and stepped around him. He reached out to stop her but Kaedin grabbed his arm. The look on the dragon's face left no room for Jake to misinterpret what would happen if he touched her.

"You must decide now if you shall be a burden or an asset!" Rin continued. "This world is not like yours. We do not have time for burdens when enemies are beginning to surround us on all sides!" She took a deep breath and staggered sideways, the loss of blood catching up with her. She reached back for Kaedin to keep from falling. He was beside her in an instant and picked her up before he walked back under the cover of the trees.

Sara watched him walk away with a look of disbelief. She felt terrible that she had caused Rin to get injured. Jake moved closer to her and tried to put his arm around her shoulders, but she stepped away from him. She ran toward the trees in a direction away from Rin and Kaedin.

Jake reached out to stop her but pulled his hand back before he touched her. He did not want to force her to talk to him. His attention shifted to Rin and Kaedin and his face clouded with anger as he walked toward them.

"You were quite hard on her," Kaedin said, his voice soft. He sat beside Rin off to the side of the tent. She was hunched over with her arms around her stomach. He rubbed his hand across her back as he watched her. His concern was still visible on his face.

"She must learn," Rin whispered between clenched teeth. "I can forgive her this time but if something were to happen to you because of a distraction, I could never forgive her."

He sighed as he leaned forward and kissed her hair, "I know."

She bent over a little farther and rested her forehead on his chest. He shifted to move closer, so she did not have to lean so far, but she gasped when he moved.

"I am sorry," he said, his voice soft. She clamped her eyes closed and did not say anything as she took several slow deep breaths. Kaedin's attention remained on her until he noticed Jake walking up to them. His eyebrow rose, and his expression became hard.

"What's wrong with you?" Jake snapped when he was close to them.

Rin sighed again before she lifted her head and looked up at him. Her eyes were filled with irritation, "She had to hear it, Jacob."

"You didn't have to tell her like that! She feels terrible now and is upset!"

"Asaetara is not a gentle world. All of us cannot treat her like a fragile child, or she will not survive." Rin paused with a grimace. "It is my duty to tell her how things really are, and it is your duty to treat her with care."

Jake glared at her and took an unconscious step closer. Kaedin was on his feet in a second and took an obvious step forward so he was between them. The tension between the two continued to rise as they regarded each other.

"I believe that is quite enough." Wren's unpleased voice caused Kaedin to glance away from Jake. When he saw Wren standing beside them, he sat back down beside Rin but did not take his eyes off Jake. "Jaeha has returned," Wren continued with a frown. He could see there was still tension between Kaedin and Jake. "We shall be leaving as soon as it is dark."

Jake fought to keep his frustration off his face before he turned without a word and headed off to find Sara.

A couple hours later, the camp was broken down and they were almost ready to continue the rest of the journey to the capitol. Rin told her brother everything she saw, and he was just as worried as she was. They seemed to be gaining more enemies by the hour and needed to reach Nuenthras.

Rin stood next to Kaedin waiting on Sara to join her. She only had to wait a few minutes before Paige and Sara approached her. They were clinging to each other's hand. Raven trailed behind them but kept his distance. Rin watched them approach, her face an unreadable mask. Her arms were both around her middle.

Paige and Sara glanced at each other as Rin continued to regard them in silence. Rin caught a glimpse of movement behind them and noticed Jake standing about ten feet away. She did not acknowledge him as she looked back at the girls.

"I... I don't want to be a burden," Sara whispered as her grip on Paige's hand tightened.

"Neither do I," Paige said, her voice sure and confident.

Rin looked at each of them for a moment. They felt like she was looking for something before she glanced at Raven. He shifted under her gaze but did not look away.

"You shall train Paige to use a katana," she said.

Raven bowed his head in response to her words.

"No daggers?" Paige asked with a frown.

Rin gave her a long hard look, "No, your movements are too slow, and you are too tall. You shall be trained with a katana or nothing."

Paige grimaced before she nodded, even she could tell this was not something up for discussion.

"Learn your magic," Rin said when her attention shifted to Sara. Once Sara nodded, Rin walked around the far side of Kaedin. When she was out of sight, she leaned against him with a heavy sigh. Pain was etched on her face when she tightened her arms around herself.

"Wow, she really doesn't like us now," Paige said as she folded her arms across her chest.

Raven glanced at her with a frown, "Of course she does, or she would not have given her permission for me to train you."

Paige's skepticism could be seen on her face, "She was really cold just now."

"Yes, she was, however, that has nothing to do with you," Raven said, his voice becoming sharp. "She is in great deal of pain from the wounds. The healing shall not remove the pain until tomorrow at the earliest. My lady is attempting to block out all of the pain so that we may travel."

Paige's eyes widened and the anger she was feeling fled, "Oh, I didn't know." A sheepish smile appeared on her face when she shrugged. Raven did not appear impressed when he sighed and shook his head. He headed toward

Hikaru without another word. Paige hesitated with a frown before she hurried after him.

Sara watched them leave before she glanced at Kaedin. He tilted his head up, indicating that she should climb up. She fidgeted with her sleeve as she walked over and looked up at his back. With an uncomfortable sigh, she tried to climb up but had no idea where to put her feet. After a couple tries, she stepped back and looked at Kaedin again. He was too high off the ground for her to make it on her own. Even laying down flat, his back was still fifteen feet off the ground. His sigh came out as a low growl when he shifted his front leg back so that she could stand on it, but before Sara could try Rin came up behind her. She shook her head with a sigh when she realized Sara could not climb up on Kaedin. Rin moved around her and pulled herself up onto Kaedin's back before she reached a hand down to Sara. After climbing up onto Kaedin's leg, Sara reached up and grabbed Rin's hand. Rin pulled her up in one swift motion. As soon as she was up, she let go of Sara's hand with a grimace and put her arm back around her stomach.

"I'm sorry," Sara whispered as she got settled on Kaedin's back. She was careful not to bump Rin when she sat down.

"You are forgiven," Rin said after she forced the pain back down.

A few minutes later all the dragons were back in the air and they flew hard to the north. They traveled for two days straight with minimal breaks. It was just after sunrise the third day when they stopped for the last time. Wren informed them that they would reach the capital in the next few hours. Rin looked in the direction of her home. She was becoming more anxious the closer they got. What would be different? What would the king do? Her face clouded with worry when they flew off again. She knew her wait would be over soon.

It was nearing mid-afternoon when the great elven city of Nuenthras became visible on the horizon. The city was built upon the Ilvaerel Plateau that was nestled against the base of the Ilthaes Mountains. Only the single steep and winding road leading to the gate in the twenty-foot-high brilliant white walls could be seen from a distance. The rest of the city was below the walls and situated in the massive valley that encompassed the entire interior of the plateau. Buildings were tucked among the trees, concealing most of the city if you did not know it was there. Around the top edge of the plateau, the white walls continued with battlements evenly spaced. The two on either side of the gate had large blue flags, with a silver willow tree above a concave moon, blowing in the breeze.

As they neared the city the enormous force wall that covered it could be seen. Raven pulled out a horn from his pack and blew one long loud blast. An answering horn from the city was heard a few seconds later and the force wall disappeared. A massive elder silver dragon and his rider were perched above the main gate watching them approach. The dragon bowed his head as Wren and Jaeha passed over the gate and entered the city. He raised his head and leapt to his feet when he caught sight of Rin. His rider bowed his head as soon as he saw her and put a fist to his chest. As soon as she was passed, the dragon roared loud enough to cause the city walls to shake. His roar was answered immediately from multiple places all around the city. The riders now knew that their general was home.

Wren glanced back at his sister and saw a small smile on her face. Even though she was young, her men cared for her and it made him proud.

She worked hard to keep them safe in battle and never concealed the odds of a difficult situation. They knew they could trust her, and it showed in their complete confidence in her decisions.

Once Raven and Hikaru brought up the rear and passed the main gate the force wall appeared back in place. The dragons flew over the treetops and headed for the palace at the far north side of the city. The large building was tucked among giant trees and the thicker forest ran right up to the walls on two sides.

Rin sighed when she saw that the palace did not appear like it was different from the last time she was here. The walls and the force wall around the city were both strange and foreign to her. She frowned when she could not come up with a reason for why they built the walls. Something was not right about the whole thing.

The dragons made a pass over the palace before they circled back and made a smooth landing in a small clearing in front of the palace. Rin slid down and was relieved when the pain from her wounds was now gone. She reached up to help Sara when an elf dressed like Rin came sprinting up to her.

"My lady," he called as he grabbed her in a hug.

Rin stiffened and Kaedin let out a low warning growl causing the elf to release her at once. He stepped back as his face flushed a light pink.

"Forgive me, my lady," he said. "I am so relieved that you have come home safely that I forgot my place."

Rin shook her head in exasperation at her second in command. "It is good to see you as well, Commander Orbryn."

He gave her a hasty bow, "Do you have any orders for us?"

Rin glanced around before she stepped forward, so she was standing right next to him.

"Durlan, get my riders out of this city. All of them, by nightfall. I cannot explain right now. Have half report to the camp by the portal, and the other half split between Lyrin and Caradthrad," she said, her voice so quiet only he could hear her.

Orbryn's eyes widened in surprise but he did not question. He bowed again before he disappeared in the direction of the rider barracks. Once he was gone, Rin glanced back and found Kaedin back in elven form.

"Having them leave the city?" he asked.

"I believe you know me too well," she said with a small smile before she motioned for Sara to follow her. They walked over to where Wren stood waiting with Jaeha and Jake.

Once Raven, Paige, and Hikaru joined them, the small group headed toward the palace. Rin moved so that she was in her normal place just behind and to the right of her brother. When they neared the door, she took a deep breath and sighed. Wren glanced back at her and could tell she was nervous and uncomfortable, but the determination in her eyes caused his worry to fade. He knew she would be all right no matter what happened.

Wren turned his attention back to where he was going just as they walked through large, light brown, carved wooden doors. The shapes of vines with ornate leaves adorned both sides of them. They entered the entryway of the palace and Sara could not keep from glancing up at the vaulted ceiling. It rose fifteen feet above their heads and the roof was supported by thick light brown wooden beams. Looking back down, she saw the floors were pristine, brilliant white stone.

Wren did not pause in the entryway as he went straight ahead and walked through another set of doors. They entered a massive room with the same vaulted ceilings. There were at least forty of the elven nobility milling around in the throne room. They all parted and bowed as Wren made his way through them. He acknowledged the nobles as a group with a quick nod of his head. When he reached the other side of the room, a couple could be seen sitting on two thrones made of woven willow branches.

Rin looked up and her eyes started to tear when she saw her mother sitting at the front of the room. Her mother glanced at them as they approached, and her eyes widened before they rimmed with tears. She moved to get up, but the king put his hand on her arm. Giving him a fierce glare, she jerked her arm free and leapt out of the chair. She rushed down the stairs toward her daughter.

"Rilaeya," she cried when she grabbed her in a suffocating hug. Rin wrapped both arms around her mother and held on while they both cried. Wren watched them for a moment before he stepped closer and put his arms around them both. His mother looked up at him with tears in her eyes.

"Thank you for finding your sister," she whispered.

"Come, Luaera," Kilvari's irritated voice echoed through the large open room. "You are creating a scene. Return to your place."

Luaera ignored her husband and did not release her daughter. Wren looked up at him with a frown before he let go of them and shifted so he stood between them and his father.

"Why are you here?" Kilvari demanded. "Have you abandoned your post?"

Wren narrowed his eyes when several of the nobility around him chuckled. "I have abandoned nothing. I found my sister and it is my duty to see her home safely."

His father frowned, "I believe she is capable of finding her way home alone."

Rin glared up at him as she stepped away from her mother. Luaera glanced back and forth between her husband and children before she marched toward her seat with a scowl. "Thallawren has acted as he should," she said, her voice hard. "I would expect nothing less of him after finding his sister when we have searched for her for nearly twenty years." She sat down but the expression on her face did not change. Kilvari eyed her with disapproval before he turned his attention back to Rin. He appeared most unpleased to see her and his eyes narrowed the longer he looked at her.

A few moments later, his eyebrows raised in surprise when he noticed the betrothal ring on her hand. "Have you finally come to your senses and accepted the proposal?"

Rin stiffened, "I made it quite clear that I would not accept that proposal."

"There is no other that you could accept," he snapped as he came down the steps. "I have approved no other match for you." His gaze turned to Kaedin with a look of disdain.

"As I informed you before, you shall not choose for me."

Kilvari reached out to grab her arm, "You shall not make a fool of me any longer. You shall be joined with whom I deem appropriate."

Rin moved to step back, so he could not touch her, but a second later she found herself looking up at her brother's back.

"I do not approve of your choice for Rin," Wren said as he pushed her farther back with one arm. His father rounded on him.

"I did not realize that you had the authority to approve," he said, a dangerous edge to his voice. "Your opinions are only of value when it comes to matters of war."

Wren gave no ground as he stared at his father. The tension in the room continued to grow when neither backed down.

"Kilvari," Luaera called. Her calm voice seemed to soothe the entire room. "I do believe that you have an audience with Lady Hildvae soon, perhaps this is a matter that should be handled privately."

Kilvari and Wren both seemed to realize at the same time, that half of the elven court was watching them, and the king turned away. He headed back to his throne and sat back down.

"Who are these humans and why have you brought them into my presence?" Kilvari asked with a scowl. He glanced at Jake, Paige, and Sara who were standing behind his children.

Wren stood up fully, "Allow me to introduce to your majesties and the court, Ambassador Jacob Riverwood and his companions Miss Paige Riverwood and Miss Sara MacCoinnich."

Jake attempted to push down his nerves when he moved to stand beside Wren and bowed to the king and queen.

"Your majesty," he said without lifting his head as he waited to be acknowledged.

"Why are you here?" Kilvari asked, his tone short.

Jake looked back up at him and swallowed hard. Wren tried to prepare him for this, but he was still not sure how he was to behave. He once again fell back on his training and spoke to the king as he would a high-ranking officer.

"I have come to request an audience with your majesty," he said, his voice calm and confident.

Kilvari's eyes narrowed again. Humans were not this well-spoken, and he grew suspicious of where they came from. A sharp look from Luaera caused him to frown.

"I shall grant you a short audience tomorrow afternoon. Until that time feel free to venture into the city." He paused and looked at an attendant standing along the wall. "Tarsil, show them to the new guest suite." A smug grin crossed Kilvari's face. "Oh, and I shall assume since you brought them here that you shall look after them until their audience."

A short, round older looking elf stepped forward and motioned for them to follow him. Neither Wren nor Rin responded to Kilvari before they turned to follow Tarsil from the room. Several of the nobility chuckled as they walked across the room and by the time they made it through the doors Rin was furious. She clenched and unclenched her hands as they made several turns. Not paying attention to where they were going, she glanced up when Tarsil stopped in front of a large brown door. He opened the door and led them into a large room. She started to walk inside before she froze as a look of hurt flashed across her face. These were her rooms. Kilvari had turned her rooms into a guest suite and all of her things were gone. It appeared as if she had never been there.

Wren and Jaeha exchanged shocked glances. The last time they visited the city her rooms were still intact. Rin backed out of the room and moved to go back down the hallway when Kaedin grabbed her hand.

"Do not run," he whispered.

She glanced up at him then the hallway before she looked at everyone around them. Her entire body started to tremble, she could not stand the idea of being weak in front of them.

"Take me with you," Kaedin said, his voice cracking. Without stopping to think, she buried her face against his chest as his arms came around her. The two disappeared a second later.

Wren watched them disappear before he stormed into the room. He was so angry that he started pacing back and forth. A scowl crossed his face when he was forced to shorten his steps, so he did not run into the large dining room table.

"What is wrong?" Jake asked as he observed the guest suite. He could see three doors leading off from the main room. One contained several beds along the side walls with a large ornate mirror at the back and a large brown rug covering the white stone floor. The second room was a study with large windows covering the back wall and had several chairs and a large desk sitting on the red wood floors. The last door led into a decent size washroom.

"These are Rin's rooms," Wren said, his voice hard. "The last time I was home, about a year ago, nothing in here was changed. This was done recently but I do not know why. He does nothing without a gain, but I cannot fathom his reason for this or what it could possibly gain him."

Jake folded his arms with a frown. "I thought he would be happy to have his daughter back."

"She has not told you?" Wren stopped pacing and turned to face Jake. When he saw the confusion on his face he sighed. "The day my sister disappeared, she discovered that my father is not her real father. She accused him of murdering her real father in front of his sons." He paused with another sigh. "She speaks the truth."

Jake paled, "Then why are we here? We should have stayed miles from here."

"You are correct," Wren said with a nod. "That would have been the wisest course of action, however, I suspect that my father may be involved in something deeper, and we must know for sure. It appears as though our world is on the brink of war and knowing who our allies are is imperative."

"I should've left them at home," Jake said as he glanced at his sister and Sara. "I thought they'd be safer with me. I had no idea what we were getting into."

Wren sighed again and put his hand on Jake's shoulder. "I believe that you made the correct choice in bringing them with you. What you have told me makes me certain that they are safer with us. We shall keep a close eye on them and you." He released his shoulder and looked around the room. His gaze went to Raven when he noticed that Hikaru and Jaeha were both missing. Raven glanced up when he noticed his gaze.

"Rin," Raven said before he turned his attention back to assisting Paige with learning the proper way to hold a katana. Wren watched for a few moments before he headed toward the door.

"I shall return shortly," he said. "Remain in this room and do not leave until I return." He waited until Jake nodded before he left the room and closed the door behind him.

Sara let out a huge sigh as Wren shut the door. She was sitting beside the wall on the far side of the room trying to pull out her magic. She still could not get it to come out on her own.

Jake walked over and sat down next to her. "What's wrong?"

"I can't get this magic to cooperate," she said with another sigh. "I don't understand how to get it to come out." She paused with a look of apprehension. "I really am trying now."

Jake took one of her hands in his, "I'm sure you will get it. Try again."

She flushed at his touch and glanced up at him. He smiled and gave her a small nod of encouragement. She closed her eyes again and tried to pull the magic out, but it seemed like every time she tried to grab it, it would move away. Jake squeezed her hand when he heard her exhale hard. He could tell she was getting frustrated. Her brows furrowed when a sudden thought came to her. Rin said that she pushed her magic. This time Sara tried to push the magic instead of attempting to grab it. She envisioned the magic flowing from her hand to Jake.

"Look." Jake's quiet voice caused her to open her eyes. The hand in his was glowing a faint blue. She gasped in surprise and the glow vanished.

"I did it," she said in disbelief.

"I told you that you could do it," he replied with a gentle smile. He lifted her hand and kissed the back of it. Her face turned bright red as she bit her lip. He stared at her for a moment before he leaned over so his face was right next to her ear. "You're very cute when you do that."

She took a sharp breath and gazed up at him. When he leaned back and looked down at her, she could feel her heart rate accelerate so much she thought it would burst. Jake tilted his head before he lifted her hand again. He held it against his chest, and she could feel his heart was racing just as fast as hers.

"I may not show it," he whispered. "But you affect me too."

With a shy smile, she hesitated before she leaned over and hugged him. He appeared surprised for a split second before a smile spread across his face. This was the first time she initiated a hug. They stayed like this for several minutes until Raven cleared his throat. Sara jumped and pull back. She forgot Raven and Paige were still in the room. Her face was so bright red she looked like a lobster. Jake sighed as he looked away from her and up at Raven with a frown.

"Do you not think you should be training?" Raven asked with a knowing look.

Jake glanced at Sara again, "Yeah." His voice was unhappy when he stood up and went to get his staff. Sara watched him go before she tried to calm her racing heart enough that she could return her attention back to practicing her magic.

***

Rin and Kaedin appeared in a small clearing deep in the forest surrounding the palace. Kaedin knew this spot well. It was where Rin would disappear to when she was young and upset. He said nothing as he held her until she was ready to move.

"I do not know what I expected," she whispered. "I suppose it was foolish to believe that I would be welcomed home."

Kaedin tightened his grip. "Lord Kilvari is a fool. Forget what he thinks. Only remember the welcome of Lady Luaera, she was beside herself with joy."

Rin leaned back enough that she could see his face. "You are right. I shall only think of my mother." She paused with a frown. "I wonder if she knows about my rooms."

"I am certain that she does not. She would never have allowed him to do that to your things."

"I wonder if he found the hidden compartment," Rin said, worry creeping into her voice.

Kaedin tilted his head, "You had a hidden compartment in your room?"

"Of course, I kept all of my most important possessions hidden in it. The gifts from my mother, gifts and letters from Wren, and your letters to me."

"You kept them all?" He asked with a crooked smile.

"Yes, they are important to me." She paused, and her expression fell. "I shall be most unhappy if they are gone."

"I shall write you more," he whispered as he gazed down at her. She smiled in response and stood up on her toes and kissed his cheek. He reached up and rested his hand on her cheek as he started to lean down. Pausing with a loud exhale, he kissed her forehead and rested his head against hers.

"I want to kiss you," he said, his voice low and husky. Neither of them looked at the other.

"As do I." She took a shaking breath. "However, we should do things properly." A frown crossed her face when she heard him breathe a heavy sigh.

"I know," he said. "I shall always respect your wishes even if they may be difficult."

"Perhaps we should go elsewhere." She shifted when she could sense his desire. "I need to find a katana that I can modify for Paige."

He lifted his head and looked down at her, "That would be wise."

Shivering at the low tone of his voice, she took hold of his hand and the two turned away from each other. They headed through the trees as they walked toward the city. When they neared the edge of the clump of trees near the palace, Kaedin released her hand and fell into step just behind her. She glanced back at him before they stepped onto the path. As soon as they were visible Hikaru and Jaeha appeared beside them and they both fell into step behind her without a word.

Rin looked back with a raised eyebrow. She was not surprised to see Hikaru, since she knew he would find them, but she was not expecting her brother's bonded to be there also. "Is my brother that worried?" She asked when they turned onto the main road.

"Until we leave the city, Lord Wren wishes for me to remain with you," Jaeha said, his voice quiet so that none of the passing citizens could hear him.

Rin tilted her head with a look of disapproval. "I do not require anyone to look after me."

Jaeha bowed his head, "Forgive me, my lady but I must do as your brother has asked."

Rin's expression did not change as she turned her attention back to where they were walking. Once she noticed the people of her father's city around her the look vanished. The people greeted her with warmth and pleasure at seeing her again. She returned their greetings and thanked them for their kind words. No matter what was going on with her and the king, she did her duty for the people of Nuenthras. They were always kind and caring toward her.

It took them a while to weave their way through the people and buildings built among the massive trees of the valley. When they reached a small two-story building in a small open clearing, Rin stopped and looked up at it with a fond smile. Nothing here had changed. This building, while it matched the easy, naturally flowing design of the others, had a large free-standing chimney made of light tan stones off to the right side. At its base was the rest of the forge and a large silver colored anvil.

Rin peered into the windows that lined the front of the store and her smile widened when she saw the various weapons on display. She pulled the thick wooden door open and walked inside. Kaedin followed her while Jaeha and Hikaru remained outside.

"Great Darzak's beard you are finally back!" An elderly dwarf called as soon as he saw her walk into his shop. He hobbled around the counter and tried to brush off some of the soot on his thick leather apron. When he was within arm's reach, Rin grabbed him in a tight hug. He stiffened and cleared his throat while his face turned a brilliant red.

"It is wonderful to see you, Baldrim," Rin said with a smile. "I feared you would no longer be here."

The dwarf left out a deep throaty laugh, "I am not that old yet. I still have plenty of years left to keep you youngsters in line."

Rin's smile widened, and she looked back over her shoulder at Kaedin. He was just as happy to see the dwarf as she was. He was like family to both of them.

"How are those daggers I made for special for you?" Baldrim's question caused Rin to look back over at him. She flipped her wrists and the daggers appeared in her hands.

"They are fantastic as always."

He took them from her and looked them over before he frowned, "You have not been sharpening these as often as you should." His voice was gruff as he hobbled over to his workbench. After spending several minutes on the blades, he handed them back to her. "Well, out with it. I know you did not just come here to visit."

"You are correct," Rin said with an amused smile. "I must find a katana."

Baldrim rubbed his hands together with a pleased smile. "Male or female? Height?" As he threw questions at her, he made his way over to a display rack with several katanas that were already crafted.

"Female, about six inches taller than I am," Rin replied.

He looked over each blade before he selected two different ones and headed back to the counter. After he laid them down in front of her, Rin glanced back at Kaedin. He stepped forward and picked up each sword in turn. They were far too short and light for him, but he moved through several motions with each one. When he was finished, he handed the one that was a little bit longer with a dark brown leather hilt to Rin.

"Good eye," Baldrim said with a satisfied head nod. "You were paying attention."

Kaedin only smiled. It was the old dwarf who taught him what to look for in a good blade. He watched in silence while Baldrim and Rin finished the transaction for the katana. When she was done, she went back behind the counter and hugged Baldrim again. The dwarf cleared his throat, "Do not be such a stranger and for goodness sake, do not get lost again."

"I shall do my very best," she said with a smile as she stepped back from him. "We shall come to see you soon."

"All right, all right," he said, his voice gruff. "I have work to do." He waved them out of the shop before turning back to a shield.

Once she was back out on the street, Rin headed back toward the palace. The sun was sinking behind the edge of the walls and she knew Wren would be looking for her soon. They made it halfway back to the palace before a little elven girl dashed up to them.

"Excuse me, excuse me," she called as she ran up to Rin.

"Yes, child?" Rin asked when she stopped and looked down at her. The little girl peered up at her with big, hazel eyes. She pushed thick, brown curls out of her face.

"Are you really the princess?" When Rin nodded, she grinned. "Oh, good! I have made something for you. My mama told me that you got lost before I was born."

Rin chuckled and knelt in front of the little girl. "What have you made for me?"

The little girl held up a pink flower made out of parchment, "It even has a compass in the middle, so you will not get lost again." Rin took the flower and smiled when she saw the small hand drawn compass in the center of the flower.

"That is a wonderful idea," Rin said. "I thank you for such a thoughtful gift."

A proud smile crossed the little girl's face and a murmur ran through the couple of elves that paused to see what was going on.

"Will you wear it?"

"I would be honored. Will you put it in for me?"

The little girl was vibrating with excitement when she took the flower back from Rin. Her little fingers trembled when she stuck her tongue out a little bit in pure concentration. She put the flower into Rin's hair just above her right ear. When she was finished, she stepped back with a grin, "It is perfect." Her voice was filled with confidence.

"Thank yo..." Rin trailed off when an elven woman rushed up to them. She gave Rin a hasty bow before she pulled the little girl away from her.

"Forgive me, my lady," she said, her face flustered. "My daughter speaks out of turn." She gave the little girl a look of disapproval.

Rin got back to her feet. "There is nothing to forgive. The child has given me a lovely gift and I shall treasure it."

"Thank you, my lady," the woman said with a sigh of relief.

Rin nodded before she looked down at the little girl, "Thank you for the gift." She turned away from the woman and child and began to walk down the road again. The handful of people that gathered started to disperse as she passed through them. They were almost back to the palace when Rin paused as a group of city guards approached them.

"Lady Rin."

"Yes?" She asked, her voice wary.

The guardsman shifted, and his discomfort became visible when Kaedin and Jaeha moved to stand on either side of her.

"My lady, I have orders to bring you to your father's study."

Rin's eyebrow shot up. "You may inform my fa--, him that I shall come to his study later." She started to walk past the guards but one of the other guardsmen stepped forward to block her path. Rin stopped with a frown.

"My lady, his majesty said right now," the first guard continued. "Please come with us. I do not wish to resort to force."

"There are not enough of you to take me anywhere by force," she said with a laugh. "If he has an issue with me then he can come and find me. Now, stand aside and allow me to pass." She once again moved to walk forward and this time the guard put his spear in front of her. In one swift motion, she grabbed and twisted the spear, jerking it out of his hands in a split second before she dropped it on the ground at his feet. "Stand aside!"

The rest of the guards stepped back, and she walked past them. She headed into the palace and returned to the guest rooms. When they arrived back, Paige, Jake, Raven, and Sara were still training. Everyone, except Raven, appeared like they were getting tired.

Rin acknowledged them with a head nod before she walked into the room with the beds and closed the door. Kaedin watched her go before he walked over to Raven.

"This is for Paige," he said as he held out the katana. "Rin shall modify it for her later."

Paige took the katana before Raven could get it. Her face filled with excitement, "Sweet! My own sword." She started dancing in place and Jake glanced over at her. He grimaced and shook his head, his sister armed was not something he thought was a good idea.

Once she closed the door, Rin made her way over to a small stone in the wall beside the mirror. She pried it loose and breathed a sigh of relief when she saw the hole behind it was still full. Pulling everything out, plus the flower from the little girl, she wrapped it all in a piece of cloth. After it was wrapped, she secured the package with a piece of twine before she slipped it into a pocket on her vest. Without stopping to survey the room, she headed back toward the door when a sudden glow caught her attention. She glanced at the mirror and froze in place. After a few seconds, she stepped toward it with slow cautious steps and gasped when she was close enough to see an older version of herself looking back at her from the mirror.

"Touch the mirror," the older Rin said. "Hurry, he tries to stop me already."

Rin stared at the mirror and was unable to react.

"Touch the mirror! You must hurry and leave tonight."

Rin swallowed hard before she reached out and put her fingers on the surface of the glass. She gasped again when images appeared in her mind.

She could see inside her father's study. He was speaking to Londar, but she could not hear what they were saying before the vision shifted. She saw her old rooms. The entire group lay dead on the floor. It appeared as if they just finished their evening meal.

The vision stopped, and Rin staggered backwards with a small gasp. When she could shake off the disorienting effects of the vision, she looked back at the mirror. It was only her looking back. She stared at it, her face blank, for a few seconds before she bolted back into the room with the dining table.

"Stop!" She yelled and everyone in the room froze. "Has anyone eaten?" When they all shook their heads no, she breathed a small sigh of relief and walked closer to the table. She could only stare at the food for several moments before she took a deep breath and raised her hand. "Prāetan

Jhēkāer." She passed her hand over the nearest dish and it began to glow green. Her eyes widened in shock when she realized the vision was right.

"What is go--?" Jake started to ask when the door of the room opened, and Wren walked inside. He paused with his hand still on the doorknob when he noticed something was amiss.

"What?" He asked looking toward his sister. Rin did not look at him as she pointed to the glowing green dish of food on the table and his eyes narrowed. "He attempted to poison all of us?" His voice was laced with disbelief.

Rin still did not look up at him as she continued to stare at the food.

"Rin, what is it?"

"I saw this," she whispered, her eyes still on the table. "The mirror in the other room just now. I... it appeared like me, 1...like an older version of myself. She said we must leave tonight."

Wren raised an eyebrow as he listened to her. "I heard rumors that you might possess this type of power, but I never truly believed it was possible."

"What powers?" She asked, finally looking up at him, but he only shook his head.

"Now is not the time and Lord Ronin would be better suited to tell you then me. Right now, we must focus solely on fleeing the city. I never imagined things would be in such a sorry state."

"I cannot leave yet. I saw fa—him, speaking with Londar in his study. We must know what they are discussing."

Wren shook his head, "I shall not risk you to find out. We leave now."

Rin frowned as she regarded her brother. "She must have shown it to me for a reason. We must know what they are speaking about. Is this not the reason you came here in the first place?"

Wren shook his head again. He had made no mention to her about gathering information and yet she knew anyway.

"Have everyone leave the city and I shall meet up with you," she continued when he said nothing.

Wren put both hands on the table in front of him and dropped his head with a sigh. He appeared to be deep in thought and Rin tilted her head as she watched him. She could tell he hated the idea of allowing her to do this, but they needed the information.

"Very well," he said, his voice reluctant. "However, Jaeha and I are remaining behind to ensure that you make it out safely." Kaedin moved to take a step forward. "No Kaedin, if we were to fail, you must be outside the city, so you may go after her."

Kaedin was not pleased but he gave a begrudging nod after making eye contact with Rin. She agreed with her brother, but she also wanted him safely out of the city. Who knew what her father might attempt, and she would not risk him.

"Raven, Hikaru, get everyone out of the city unseen," Wren continued. "We shall meet at the ruins of Varalei. It is off the main road and there are no guard patrols."

Everyone gathered their things and after only a couple of minutes were ready to leave. Raven led the way while Hikaru brought up the rear as they left the room. Once they were gone, Wren looked over at Rin. "We shall be close," he said before he and Jaeha both disappeared through the door.

Rin watched them leave before she took several deep breaths. When she was calm, she headed toward her father's study. Once she reached the door she stopped. Her head tilted when she could hear voices through the door. She pressed an ear against the wood in hopes of being able to hear without entering the room, but the door was too thick. Moving back a step, she raised her hand and knocked. The voices inside stopped.

"Come in." She shivered when she heard her father's clip reply. It took her several long moments before she pushed the door open and moved to step inside. Her eyes widened when she knew right away that she was in trouble. Kilvari stood right beside the door and he grabbed her arm to jerk her further into the room. As soon as the door slammed shut, someone else grabbed her other arm and she felt a sharp prick on the side of her neck. Her entire body collapsed to the floor when her body could no longer move.

"That will only last a few minutes," Kilvari said as he walked back over to his desk.

"Miss me?" Londar asked as he secured a gag in her mouth. Rin's blood turned to ice when she heard the familiar voice in her ear. He was rough when he pulled her arms behind her back and secured them. When he finished tying her feet together, he stood back up.

"Do what you need to do, then get rid of her," Kilvari continued when he saw that she was secure.

Rin's eyes filled with hurt when she looked at him. She could see him from where Londar left her on the floor. Kilvari glared at her before he came over to stand right in front of her.

"Stop looking at me," he growled. "I cannot take it anymore. It is like looking at him every day." He pushed her over with his foot, so she could not see him anymore. "I should have taken care of you the day you were born. That would have prevented everything."

"I shall take care of it," Londar said, his voice cold.

"See that you do," Kilvari snapped. "I cannot have her getting in the way of our plans. Taking the offensive against our oldest allies shall not be easy, even without interference." He paused and looked at a piece of parchment on his desk. "Will the red and black dragons be ready soon?"

Londar had Rin slung over his shoulder when he looked back at Kilvari. "Priestess Kakehal confirmed that her people are prepared. The black dragons are almost ready. They only wait fo--." A sudden knock on the door caused him to back away from it. "Arãesya." He disappeared from view just before the door flew open and a guard rushed inside.

"My lord, all of the riders are gone."

"What?" Kilvari demanded. The guard blanched at his lord's anger and took several steps backwards.

"Th... they are just gone, my lord. The ambassador is missing as well."

"Find them," Kilvari bellowed as he pointed at the door. The guard bowed before he bolted out of the study. As soon as the door closed, Kilvari stormed around the end of his desk. Londar reappeared a few seconds later and pulled Rin off his shoulder. He held her up by the arms for her father. Kilvari grabbed a handful of her hair and yanked her head up

"You did this," he growled. All she could do was give him a defiant glare and his face became red. A few seconds later he slapped her hard across the face. "This is the last time you shall ever defy me. Get her out of my sight."

Londar slung her back over his shoulder and slipped from the room. Once he was in the hallway he looked around. "Arãesya." He disappeared from view and he made his way out of the palace. When he was outside, he hurried over to a wagon that was already waiting. A couple of humans jumped out of the wagon when he appeared beside it. One of them was holding a large burlap sack. Londar dropped Rin on the end of the wagon.

Rin waited a second for him to move before she kicked him hard in the face. He staggered backwards and fell from the force of her kick. She was able to get her feet free in one quick motion but stumbled when she tried to stand. All of her movement had not yet returned. Londar leapt back to his feet and punched her hard in the stomach.

"Vēijal," he snapped, and a small lightning bolt shot through her. She gasped and crumpled forward. He caught her and threw her into the back of the wagon. She let out a small muffled yelp when she landed on her arms and her head hit the side of the wagon. Londar jumped in the back and grabbed hold of her face.

"That hurt," he spat. "I cannot wait to get you back to the demon realm. I shall have such fun with you." The tone of his voice caused Rin to shiver and a smug smile crossed his face as he pricked her neck with the needle again. He could tell she was afraid of him and he enjoyed it.

Once she was unable to move again, Londar climbed out of the wagon while the humans put her inside a large burlap sack. They tied it closed and left her in the back of the wagon. Londar looked around again before he stepped out of the way.

"Take her to the rendezvous point."

"Yes, my lord."

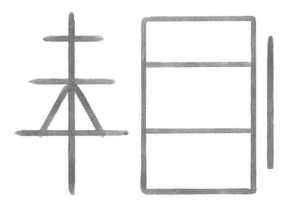

The human snapped the reins over the backs of the horses and the wagon started to move away from the palace. They traveled through the city in a slow, unhurried manner so they would draw no attention. It took them a while before they were through the city and out of the gate. A couple of miles down the side of the plateau Wren and Jaeha attacked. They killed the four humans in a matter of moments and Wren leapt into the back of the wagon. He reached down and ripped the sack open. His expression hardened when Rin looked up at him and he could see her eyes were rimmed with tears. Without a word, he freed her from the sack and bindings. She wrapped her arms around his neck and buried her face on his shoulder. He held onto her as he stood up and jumped out of the wagon with her. As soon as his feet were on the ground, Jaeha appeared beside him and they set off at a brisk pace down the road.

"There is nothing that you must tell me," Wren said in a hushed voice. "I heard and saw everything." He paused and tightened his grip. "They are both quite fortunate that I was not alone tonight. If Jaeha was not with me, I do not believe I would have been able to restrain myself." He glanced down at her when she nodded against his shoulder. She did not lift her head. "I apologize it took so long. We could not get to you without witnesses." He frowned when she again only nodded, and he fell silent. It was several miles before she finally looked up.

"I can walk," she whispered. He set her back on her feet and she fell into an easy pace beside him. They walked in silence for a while before he glanced over at her.

"Rin."

She looked up at him when he did not continue. He tilted his head when he noticed the vacant look in her eyes but was unsure what to say to her.

"I am sorry," she said when she noticed he was worried. "It is difficult knowing the elf I cared for as a father has hated me since the day I was born. I remind him of Lord Kanamae."

Wren stopped walking and grabbed her shoulder, "He has not always hated you. I was there when you were young. He cared for you and I believe he still does. His guilt causes his current course."

"Perhaps," she said as she shrugged his hand off and continued to walk. He sighed before he followed her. As much as he wished to, this was something he could not solve for her. She had to deal with it in her own time.

A short time later they approached the ruins of the outpost of Varalei. Wren slowed when the first of the collapsed stone buildings came into view. He looked around before he whistled a low, slow tone. The answering sound was immediate and came from a large building to their right. They walked into the ruined building and found the others waiting on them.

Rin headed straight to Kaedin as soon as she saw him. He put his arm around her shoulders as she leaned into him but when she still would not look up at him, his face clouded with more worry. He knew things had not gone to plan when he sensed her pain and emotions.

"We must keep moving," Wren said. "The silver dragon capital city of Caradthrad is the safest place for us to head. We shall be safe there for a while."

"How far is it?" Jake asked from where he stood with his sister and Sara.

Wren tilted his head, "I am uncertain of your units of measure. I can tell you in days of travel if that will suffice?" When Jake nodded, he continued, "By foot, it shall take us close to two weeks. We would normally be able to make the trip in closer to one, but I do not believe your companions would be able to keep pace."

"We aren't going to fly?"

"We cannot," Wren said with a shake of his head. "The dragons would be spotted as soon as they transformed. Porting is also out of the question due to the port block on the city as well as the steep dangerous terrain leading up to the gates." When Jake asked no more questions, he looked over at Jaeha. "Laethys?"

"It shall, more than likely, be watched but I can think of nowhere closer to gather supplies," Jaeha replied with a frown.

"Gather your things, we leave now," Wren said with a sigh.

The group slung their packs over their shoulders and waited. Wren looked at his sister and it took her a few moments to notice his gaze. Once she did, she looked up and found everyone waiting on her.

"We shall move fast," she said with a frown. "I am certain they will send horses after us soon and we must reach the edge of Rythilion Forest before they do." She turned and set out at a slow run.

The way forward was not an easy path. She was leading them through the tall grasses to keep them hidden from the road. As they traveled, she glanced up at the sky, using the stars and large moon to keep them on the right path. It was not long before she glanced back and noticed that Sara and Paige were already struggling to keep up. She stopped with a heavy sigh and walked back to them. She took the girl's packs and slung Sara's over her back. Handing Paige's to Raven, he took it and put it over his shoulder before she moved away from him.

"Can you carry her and keep up?" Rin asked Jake as she took everything he was carrying. She handed Kaedin the pack and medical bag while Hikaru took his weapon.

Jake glanced over at Sara before he looked back at Rin. "On flat terrain, yes, but I don't know on hills."

"Let her run as long as she is able then carry her," Rin said after she studied him for a moment. "We cannot slow down. If you tire too much my brother or Jaeha can assist in carrying her."

Jake nodded as he reached over and took hold of Sara's hand. Rin motioned them all forward again and they began jogging. They ran for almost an hour before Rin raised her hand and they all stopped. She dropped to a knee and they all followed suit. Jake exhaled hard when he let Sara off his back. He had carried her for the last half an hour. She gave him an apologetic look. He just shrugged and pulled her down beside him.

"Do you require a break?" Wren asked. "We have covered many miles."

Jake frowned when he glanced at Sara. "Yeah, that probably would be a good idea since I don't know how far we have to go."

"I shall take her this leg," Wren whispered. "Sh--." He stopped talking when Rin raised her hand into the air again. With her right hand, she signed the number three twice, a sideways two, then her thumb and pinky, and a quick point to the left.

"What does that mean?" Jake asked in a whisper.

Wren leaned over so that he was closer. "The first three were numbers. Ten, ten, and five. The fourth was the troop type, cavalry. The last was the direction they are in." When Jake did not appear surprised, Wren tilted his head. He found the reactions of Jake intriguing since the humans of Asaetara were so different and far less intelligent.

"Why does she take point?"

Wren's eyebrow shot up at the question and he gave Jake a long hard look before he replied. "This is what she does, the riders act as scouts for my ground troops. She is quite good and has always been able to hear much farther than I can."

Jake nodded before they both fell silent. Several minutes passed before Jake could hear the cavalry Rin said was there. They waited until the sound of hooves faded into the distance before she stood up and they started running again.

More than an hour passed before she held up her hand to stop them. Wren set Sara down as soon as he stopped.

"I apologize if I was rough with you at all," he whispered.

She shook her head no, that he had not been rough, and went back over to Jake. He grabbed her hand as soon as she was within reach.

Rin held up one finger and slipped into the grass. Jake watched her go but made no move to follow her. He figured she must want them to stay put since no one else moved. A few minutes passed before Rin reappeared. Her expression was grave as she maneuvered over to Wren without a sound. She glanced at Jake before looking back at her brother.

"The bridge up ahead is swarming with cavalry and city guards," she whispered. "We could go further upstream, but it will force us to swim across. It shall also add travel time."

Wren shook his head with a quiet sigh. He had anticipated this would happen but hoped their head start would have prevented it.

"Upstream is our only option. We cannot be caught." As soon as her brother made his decision, Rin turned and slipped back to the front of the group. She motioned everyone to follow her again and they moved forward at a slower pace. With so many troops nearby, they had to go slower to avoid detection.

Paige could not keep from sighing when they were only walking. She was starting to have trouble keeping up and did not want to have to be carried like Sara. Raven reached back and took hold of her hand. He pulled her with him as he kept pace with Rin.

Rin led them through the grass for what felt like an eternity to Sara before she stopped. Rin held up one finger again before she slipped forward. When she returned moments later, she motioned for them to gather around her.

"I see no one," she said. "We shall go in two small groups. Jake, Sara, Kaedin, and I will be one group. Raven, Hikaru, Jaeha, Wren, and Paige will be the other." She glanced at Jake and when he nodded, she led them out of the grass and to the edge of the river.

Sara's eyes widened with fear when she saw the water rushing past. The river was swollen from its usual banks due to recent rains and was now nearly a quarter of a mile across. Sara started shaking her head, there was no way she could swim that far.

"Cross here," Rin said pointing to a point in the river where it was the narrowest. She started into the river and the others trailed behind. They trudged through the deepening water almost a quarter of the way across before it was over all of their heads. Sara did the best she could to keep up with Jake as he swam beside her, but the currents were quite strong. He stayed on the downstream side, so she could not get washed away from him. They were nearing the halfway point when he noticed she was floundering. He wrapped an arm around her, just under the arms, and started pulling her with him.

"Sorry," she mumbled.

"It's fine," he said between heavy breaths. The exertion of pulling them both across the rushing river left him a little winded. When they were almost across, he glanced over at Rin and Kaedin and almost stopped swimming. His surprise was clear on his face when he saw Kaedin was pulling Rin with him.

"You can't swim?" Jake asked.

She gave him a dirty look, "Hush." It was obvious that she was bothered by the fact she had never been able to learn to swim.

Jake did his best to swallow his chuckle as he finished crossing the river. Once they reached the far shore and climbed out, Rin blew a quiet, low whistle. When the other group made their way out of the grass and began their trip across the river Rin looked back at Kaedin.

"Please take Jake and Sara into the grass and wait for me," she said, pointing at the tall grass about fifteen feet away from the river. Kaedin raised an eyebrow and she could see he was not pleased, but he did as she requested. Once they were out of sight, she turned her attention back to the river. The other group was over halfway across, and everything was going smoothly until Rin's head snapped up. She waved her hand and motioned that horses were coming. Wren, Jaeha, Raven, Paige, and Hikaru picked up the pace and climbed out of the river. They hurried into the tall grass. Rin was still on the edge of the grass trying to cover their entry point when several horses came into view. She dropped to the ground where she stood and did not move. Being just inside the grass, anyone who stopped too close would be able to see her.

The elves slowed their horses as they approached her hiding spot. The one in front looked around for a minutes before he stopped his horse.

"Why are we out this far?" He complained to one of the other elves. "No one would attempt to cross this far upstream."

"Our orders were to check," the second elf replied. "Everyone search this area so that we may head back."

While the elves dismounted, Rin glanced up at the sky when the light around them dimmed. The moon was covered by a thick cloud. Rin looked back at the elves before she tried to ease deeper into the grass. She only moved a little when she froze as a sword tip slid past her ear and pressed into the side of her throat. Without moving she glanced up at the guard out of the corner of her eye. The cloud covering the moon shifted allowing the light to illuminate her face. When the guard got a good look at her, his eyes widened, and the sword dropped.

"Did you find something?" The elf in charge called to him. The guard stepped to the side so that Rin was blocked from view.

"No sir," he replied. "I thought I did but it was just an animal."

The captain remounted his horse, "I do not see anything. Let us head back to the bridge."

The guard beside Rin did not move to get back on his horse. "Sir, I...uh... need a moment for uh.... some relief." His face flushed a brilliant red when he could not come up with a better excuse.

"All right," the captain said with a laugh. "Be quick and catch up to us."

"Yes, sir." The guard watched as the other elves rode off. Once they were out of sight, he sheathed his sword and turned to face Rin. "My apologies, my lady, I could not tell it was you until the light of the moon returned." He waited for Rin to stand before he continued. "They know you make for Caradthrad. All roads are being watched, as well as Lyrin and Laethys. Though if I am correct, Lord Wren's troops and your riders are in Lyrin. This may provide you with some support." He paused and glanced back over his shoulder. "Please go, my lady, I shall see to covering your tracks."

Rin reached out and put her hand on his shoulder. "Thank you for your assistance and be certain that you are cautious. I do not wish for you to be harmed for helping me."

He bowed his head and put his fist against his chest. She squeezed his shoulder before she let go and slipped into the grass. When she found the rest waiting on her, she motioned them all to follow her. She pushed them harder over the next several hours as they continued to run across the plains. They needed to get to the cover of the forest before the sun rose. By the time they reached the outskirts of the woods and Rin allowed them to stop, everyone was showing signs of fatigue. Wren and Kaedin were both breathing heavy when they dropped the extra packs on the ground. They had taken them when the others were struggling to keep up. Jaeha sighed when he set Paige back on the ground. She was unable to keep up and he was forced to carry her for the last hour.

Jake let Sara down, but he did not sit down with the rest right away. He paced for several minutes while he caught his breath and allowed his heart rate to come back down. He was not sure he could have gone much farther without a break.

"From here we shall travel slower," Rin said looking back at the group. "Rest for a little bit then we must keep moving." She paused and glanced at Raven. "Give them some of the water and I shall return in a few minutes." Once he nodded, she slipped into the underbrush.

When Rin was gone, Jake sat down and laid back on the ground. Sara sat down next to him and gripped his hand.

"Are you okay?" she asked. He only nodded as he covered his face with his other arm, and it was only a matter of moments before he was sound asleep. Sara watched him sleep for a little while before she reached over and brushed some dirt off his elbow. Her expression fell with a sigh, she felt terrible he had to carry her.

A snapping of a twig caused her to look up and see Rin was back. She was carrying a large cloth full of berries and was handing them out to everyone in small squares of cloth. When she reached Sara, she gave her two of them.

"He will need to be awake soon," Rin said with a frown when she saw Jake was asleep. She did not wait for a response before she moved past them to continue passing out the berries.

Sara opened one of the clothes and stared at the berries. They looked similar to raspberries, but they were a bright yellow color instead of red. She hesitated before picking one up and putting it in her mouth. As soon as she bit into it her eyes widened in surprise. They were very sweet and tasted almost like a candied apple. With a small smile, she ate several more before she dumped the rest of hers into the cloth for Jake. She figured he needed them more than she did. After waiting as long as she could, she was gentle when she shook him awake.

"Already?" He asked with a quiet groan.

"There are some berries Rin gathered," Sara said, her voice quiet. "You should eat before we have to move again."

Jake sat up with a large yawn and took the cloth from her. He opened it and tilted his head before he tried one. "Not bad," he said as he glanced back at her. "Did you eat?"

Sara nodded and showed him her empty cloth. He again tilted his head but did not say anything further. They sat in silence while he munched on the berries until Rin motioned for them all to get up. He put the last two into his mouth before he got up and held his hand out for Sara. She took hold of it and he pulled her to her feet. A shy smile crossed her face before they both picked up their packs.

Once everyone had their own gear back, Rin set out at a brisk walk. It was still fast but much slower than she was pushing them before. She led them without any hesitation deeper into the forest. As they continued on the mountains in front of them got larger. They traveled for several more hours before Paige and Sara were both exhausted. Raven was holding Paige's hand and helped her along. Sara was almost asleep on her feet as she stumbled along. She tripped over a rock in the dark and pitched forward. Jake caught her in time to keep her from falling.

"How much farther?" Jake asked with a frown. "The girls can't keep going without some rest."

Rin frowned and glanced up at the sky. The first hints of dawn could be seen in the lightening of the sky.

"A couple more miles," she replied. "There is not much time left before sunrise and we are too close to the road to remain in the open." She paused and looked at her brother. "A rider safe place is just to the south in the Prydaer Mountains. We should make for it if we plan to rest for more than an hour or two."

"I don't think they will make another mile or two," Jake said, irritation slipping into his voice. He was also exhausted, and it was beginning to show.

"We must make it to a protected place," Wren said, and Jake looked over at him. "If we must carry them then that is what we shall do. Rin would not push so hard without a reason."

Jake sighed, "I know." He slipped the pack off his back, and Rin took it from him. His eyebrow raised but he did not say anything while he got Sara on his back. By the time he was ready to go, Rin had four extra packs over her own shoulder and Paige was on Raven's back. Without another word, Rin picked up the pace and they covered the last four miles much quicker. When they reached a spot along the bottom of a steep cliff covered by a thicket she stopped and dropped the packs. She pushed her way through the thicket to reveal a small cave concealed behind it.

"Jhyōta," she said, and a small flame appeared in her hand. After checking to be certain that the cave was secure, she came back out and allowed them all to enter. The cave was nothing more than a large hole into the side of the cliff. It was just barely big enough for all of them to fit. In the far back corner, there was a small cache of supplies. There was dried meats, blankets, and canteens.

Once they were inside everyone laid out their blankets and got as comfortable as possible on the cold stone floor. Jake, Paige, Sara, and Raven were clumped together at the back of the cave. They were asleep as soon as they laid their heads down. Rin took the spot beside the cave entrance and Kaedin sat down right next to her. When she noticed that everyone was laying down, she put out the flame in her hand.

"How often have you used this cave?" Wren asked with a yawn from where he laid down on the opposite side of the entrance.

A slight smile crossed her face, "More times than I would like to count."

"Does anyone other than riders know of its location?"

"No," Rin said as her smile slipped. "We are the only ones who use it and we keep our safe places secret."

Wren chuckled at her tone as he rolled over with another large yawn. He was asleep a few minutes later. Rin watched everyone around her sleep for a while and by the time she laid down the sun was peeking over the tops of the mountains.

A few short hours later, Rin jerked awake and sat straight up with a gasp. She was almost panting and soaked in sweat. It took her several moments to collect herself enough that she remembered Kaedin. She looked down at him and was relieved to see he was still asleep. Her entire body started to tremble as she drew her knees to her chest and rested her head on them.

"Rin?" Her head snapped up when she heard Sara's whispered voice. She stared at her for a moment before wiping her face off with her hands.

"Should you not be sleeping?" Rin asked with a frown.

Sara fidgeted with her sleeve before she moved closer and sat down on the edge of Rin's blanket.

"I can't sleep," she said. "You're having nightmares."

Rin's eyebrow shot up before she dropped her head onto her fingertips. "You have not seen the memories before now?"

"No, this is the first time."

"It must be because we are in such close proximity," Rin said with another frown. "I cannot control my magic while I sleep."

Sara pulled on her shirt sleeve, "Have you had them for long?"

Rin lifted her head and gave her a look of disapproval before she sighed. "They began when I woke in your world."

"Do you want to talk about it?" Sara asked, her genuine concern visible. "They're..." She trailed off when she was not sure how to bring up the subjects of the nightmares.

"No, I do not." Rin's answer was sharp. "I apologize for waking you. Return to your bedroll and sleep, I shall remain awake."

"Don't you need to sleep too?"

"You need it much more than I," Rin said as she pointed at Sara's blanket.

Sara hesitated before she got up with a sigh. She could not help but wonder if what Rin said was true. If the nightmares began before they left she was the one in need of a good night's sleep. With another sigh, she climbed back under her blanket. There was no point arguing with her, she knew Rin would not budge. Sara closed her eyes and was asleep again within minutes.

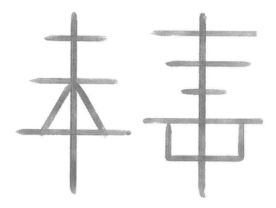

$\mathfrak{I}$t was late afternoon when everyone began to wake up one by one. Sara yawned as she sat up and glanced over at Rin. Her eyes filled with concern when she noticed she was still sitting in the same place.

'I hope she is okay,' Sara thought. 'She must be tired.'

Rin glanced over at her with a raised eyebrow, 'Stop fretting over me. I have been far more tired than this in the past.' Rin tilted her head with a frown. 'Have you been practicing your mind blocking spell?'

'Yes,' Sara thought. 'But you're more tired than you think. I can hear more of your thoughts than normal.'

Surprise flashed across Rin's face before her eyes narrowed. 'Keep practicing and drop it.' She gave Sara a final hard look before turning her attention back to Kaedin.

Sara's shoulders dropped, and she sighed. She did not notice that Jake looked back and forth between her and Rin. It did not take him long to figure out that the two were talking. His brows furrowed but he decided not to ask her about it. Whatever Rin had to say she apparently did not want all of them to hear.

Once everyone gathered their things, Rin led them along the base of the mountains. They were moving slower than the previous day and it appeared as if Rin was proceeding with more caution. After only a little while Rin raised her hand to stop them.

"We must cross the main road," she whispered. "Allow me to go first and once I am across, I shall signal when you may follow."

"Take Raven with you," Wren said when he realized she meant to go alone.

Rin glanced up at him with a frown before she shook her head with a sigh. She gave him a reluctant nod as she and Raven disappeared into the underbrush. The others stood in silence until they heard a short, high pitched whistle. Wren motioned them all forward and they stepped out onto the road. He waited in the middle of it until they were all across, then he brought up the rear. Once they were all across Rin turned and continued to lead them along the mountain line.

Sara tried her best to keep her mind focused on the where they were going but it was not long before she was wringing her hands as she walked. She was so preoccupied with Rin's nightmares that she tripped over a large root. Jake got an arm around her just in time to keep her face from hitting the nearest tree.

"What's up?" he asked. "You're really distracted."

"I can't tell you," she said, the tone of her voice rising. "She... she doesn't want anyone to know so I can't say anything. I don't even think Kaedin knows and I..." She trailed off as she glanced at Rin.

"Does it affect all of us?" His voice became sharp and she peeked back up at him. She shifted when she could see that he was not pleased.

"Please don't put me in the middle," she whispered as her gaze fell to the ground. "I would tell you if I could."

Jake put his arm around her shoulders. "I'm sorry, that was not my intention. I'm just worried about keeping you and Paige safe." He pulled her closer to him when she nodded. The two fell silent as they continued to walk.

Several hours passed before the thick underbrush started to thin out. The trees were shifting from less of the leafy deciduous tree to more pine trees. Rin called for a short rest in a small clearing between large trees. They all sat crowded together while they shared the dried meats they took from the rider's cave. Rin paced by where Sara was sitting while she looked up at mountain range above them.

'Where do we cross? Closer to the road or closer to the coast? Would they expect me to lead them the easiest path? Or would they know I would take them deeper into the woods? Which route do I take?'

Sara's eyes widened when she heard so many of Rin's thoughts. She never heard them unless Rin wanted her to hear them.

'I can hear you,' Sara thought as she watched Rin. Rin froze in place when she heard Sara's thought and glanced at her out of the corner of her eye.

'You can hear me?' When Sara only nodded in response to her thought, she exhaled hard and walked further away from her. "Jhyōta." She flipped her palm over and cast a small weak flame. Her brows furrowed before she put it out.

'I must be more tired than I believed.'

Sara did not respond to that thought. She knew that was not meant for her to hear. When Rin glanced back at her, she grimaced and gave her a small shrug. That was all Rin needed to see to know she heard her thought.

'Not a word!' Rin turned away from Sara, "Let us go." Her voice was irritated as she snatched her pack off the ground. Everyone got back to their feet and headed off again. Rin did not allow them anymore breaks and lead them until it was almost dawn. She stopped in a small spot where there was a dense thicket. They pushed their way into the center where there was a small opening and set up a camp.

"We can only remain here for a couple of hours," Rin said. "It is far too open, but I know that some of you need a rest. There is another cave a couple of hours from here. We shall take a longer rest once we reach it." She paused and looked over at Jake, Paige, and Sara. "Rest while you can."

Everyone but Wren, Jaeha, and Kaedin laid down and were all asleep within minutes. Wren laid down but watched the sunrise through the tree branches above him.

"I shall keep watch," Kaedin said.

Rin shook her head, "No, you should sleep. I shall handle the watch." She looked away from him when she saw the disapproval flashed across his face. She knew he could sense that she was tired. He watched her for a moment before he decided not to push the point and laid down. Rin sighed and rested her head on her knees once she was the only one awake. Her hands started to tremble when it was quiet. The memories that plagued her dreams were far worse since she was poisoned with everdark. She fought off sleep as long as she could before her eyes would no longer stay open and she drifted to sleep.

Sara woke with a startled gasp an hour after she fell asleep. She was horrified by what she saw in her dreams and her gaze flew to Rin. When she saw that she was not awake yet, she got to her feet and hurried over to her. She could see that Rin was jerking in her sleep with a look of fear on her face. Sara was so focused on waking up Rin that she tripped over Kaedin. He woke in an instant, his hand going for his katana before he paused. Confusion crossed his face when he realized it was Sara who fell on him.

"Wha--?"

"Terrible nightmares," Sara blurted. "She can't block me out when she sleeps, and I've seen them. They're like flashbacks or something. She said I couldn't tell anyone."

Kaedin sat up and glanced at Rin before he looked back at Sara. "It is all right." His voice was quiet and calm. He could see that Sara was upset. "Go and try to rest. I shall take care of it." He pointed back at her bedroll.

Sara stared at Rin for a moment before she finally nodded and headed back to her blanket. Kaedin watched her walk back before he noticed that

Wren was also awake. He looked over at him and Wren only tilted his head before he laid back down. He knew Kaedin would take care of his sister. Once Wren was no longer paying attention to him, Kaedin slid so he was right next to Rin.

"I am here," he whispered. The response was immediate, and she calmed at the sound of his voice. He lifted her onto his lap and leaned back against the tree trunk behind him while he rested her head against his chest and wrapped both arms around her. When she started to jerk again, he whispered into her ear again and she would calm.

Sara watched them for a little while before she could relax enough that she could sleep. When she started to drift off, she wondered if he had done this for Rin before, he seemed to know just how to handle it.

It was an hour before sunset when Rin woke up. Kaedin looked down at her when he felt her stir and watched her eyes open. They filled with confusion when she lifted her head and looked around. She found the others all awake and huddled at the other end of the camp. They were whispering to each other and eating more of the dried meat.

"Why did you allow me to sleep so long?" Rin asked when she noticed it was almost sunset. She tried to sit up, but he did not let go of her.

"You needed it," he said before he paused with a frown. "Why did you not tell me?"

She appeared confused for a moment before closing her eyes with a sigh. "I did not wish to worry you. She was not to tell anyone."

"It worries me when I can sense something is wrong and you will not tell me." He paused and tightened his grip. "Depend on me."

"I am sorry," she whispered when she looked up at him. "I shall attempt to refrain from carrying all the burden myself." She paused and laid her head back on his chest. "I do not wish for you to believe I do not depend on you. I need you far more than you realize."

"As do I," he whispered.

She leaned back and kissed him on the cheek before she moved to get up. This time he let her go when she tried to stand.

"We must get moving," she said looking at the others. Paige and Sara shared unhappy glances before they shoved their blankets back into their packs. It did not take long before they were all prepared and were again on the move. Rin continued to lead them along the line of the mountains. They traveled for a little while before Rin motioned for her brother to join her.

"What do you have in mind?" He asked as soon as he joined her at the front. She glanced up at the mountains before she looked up at him.

"I recommend that we head for the cave I mentioned earlier," she began. "It will be a safe place to remain while I make for Myrabelle's home. She will be able to assist us with supplies to make Caradthrad." She paused and looked over at the mountain beside them. "I believe we will have to fly at night under invisibility to cross the mountains. Sara and Paige would not be able to make the climb without leaving us exposed during daylight hours."

"You will not go alone to Laethys," Wren said. "You shall take someone with you."

Rin rolled her eyes in frustration, "It would be much simpler for one to slip in rather than two. You know this. I am going to fight no one. We need food unless you would rather hunt, but that shall slow us down even further."

"Raven will go with you," Wren said, his voice becoming hard. "He is light and quick on his feet and would be able to keep up with you." Rin opened her mouth to protest but a sharp look from her brother caused her to clamp her mouth closed. "Need I remind you what just transpired when you went in alone?"

Rin gave him a dirty look, but she could tell by his tone that he would hear no refusal from her. She pressed her lips together before she nodded. He seemed satisfied and he fell back to walk with the others.

Several hours later they arrived at the cave and slipped through the thicket covering the entrance. Rin stood near the front watching while the others set up their camp. As soon as she noticed that her brother and Kaedin were occupied she slipped out the front. Without looking back, she took off at a run in the direction of the village. She pushed down the apprehension beginning to rise in her. Her brother would be quite angry when he realized she did not do what he asked. She shook her head and returned her focus on where she was going. It would be far easier to slip in alone.

Wren glanced up from his bedroll when Kaedin approached him. He saw the expression on his face and looked around the cave. When he saw that Rin was gone, he cursed under his breath, "How long?"

"Not long but she is moving fast."

Wren looked over at Raven. He was listening to the conversation and started shaking his head as soon as he noticed Wren's gaze. "I cannot catch her. I could track her, but she is too fast for me."

"No," Wren said after a few minutes. "Remain here, with so many attempting to find us it would be unwise to send you after her." He paused as his expression became hard. "I am not pleased that neither you nor Hikaru noticed she was gone. Be certain that this does not happen again."

Raven's face paled, "Yes, my lord." His gaze fell to the ground in front of him and he did not look back up.

***

Rin flew through the forest now that she was not hindered by the group. She covered the ten-mile distance between the cave and Laethys in a little under an hour. When she reached the outskirts of the village she slowed and approached a small house. It stood alone among large pine trees off the main road. It had a more rustic feel than the large city of Nuenthras. The home was constructed on a base of large stones with enormous logs stacked to create the walls. The roof was covered in sod and a small chimney ran up the right side.

Crouching down beside a large pine tree, Rin scanned the area around her before she made her way to the backdoor of the home. When she reached it, she knocked with a light touch, twice, pause, once, twice, pause, three times. She did not wait long before the door flew open and an elven woman, about her mother's age, jerked her inside.

"What in the name of the gods are you doing here?" The woman asked as she dashed around the house closing all the curtains. "Do you not know they are looking for you?"

Rin stayed crouched by the backdoor. "Yes, I know Myrabelle, but we needed assistance. This was the only place I could think of to get supplies so that we could make it to Caradthrad."

Myrabelle sighed before a sudden knock on the door caused her to jump. "Hide," she hissed. "This place is crawling with the city guard." She rushed over to Rin and shoved her under the table. It was covered with a long green tablecloth that went all the way to the floor and hid Rin from view.

"Arāesya," Rin whispered, and she disappeared from view as Myrabelle went over and opened the door.

"What took so long?" The guard snapped. He entered the home uninvited.

Myrabelle folded her arms over her chest and gave him a dirty look. "Well, I am not about to go rushing to the door. I have more important tasks to see to than to keep letting you interrupt me." She scowled when several more guards entered her home.

"You are aware that we have the authority to search any house at any time," the first guard said.

"So, I have been informed."

The guards made their way through her home opening all the cabinets and looking under the bed. They made a mess of the place before they turned to leave. The guard in charge pulled up the tablecloth as he walked by. When he did not see anything, he dropped it and it fell back into place.

"You are clear," he said, his voice short as he pulled the front door open.

"I could have told you that," she snapped. "Are you going to clean up the mess you just made?" They ignored her as they exited the home and closed the door. "I thought I got away from all this nonsense when I left the army." She peeked through the curtain. "Goodness knows I care for your brother but that father of yours. I cannot stand him." After locking the door, she turned back to the room. "Come on now, come out where I can see you." Rin appeared beside her causing her to start. "Good grief, are you trying to give me a heart attack?"

Rin grinned with a small shrug, "Apologies."

Myrabelle looked her over for a moment before she grabbed her in a fierce hug. "It is good to see you, girl. I heard from your mother that you were missing. She was most worried about you." She released her and stepped back. "Now, what in the world is going on? Why is everyone after you and your brother?"

"I cannot explain it all now," Rin said with a sigh. "There is war coming and we must reach Caradthrad to warn them." She paused and tilted her head. "You should join us. We could use your skills."

"Oh, you do not need me," Myrabelle said with a laugh.

Rin's expression turned serious. "We need everyone we can get. My f-- the king, has turned traitor and plans to attack Caradthrad."

"Well of all the foolish things I have ever heard that has to top the list," Myrabelle said as her eyes widened. "I will help. Take all the food you can find here in the kitchen and I shall make for Caradthrad in a couple of days."

Rin followed her into the kitchen. Myrabelle started pulling out all the fresh fruits, vegetables, bread, cheese, and dried meat she had and put it into large burlap sacks.

"What about you?" Rin asked when she realized Myrabelle gave her everything.

"Oh, hush, I can get more in the village in the morning." She handed her another large sack full of potatoes and a small bag filled with glass bottles. "Take this too but only use those potions if you must." When Rin nodded, she ushered her toward the backdoor. "You must go now. I have nothing else I can give you and those guards could come back at any time." She gave Rin another hug before she pulled the back door open. Rin stepped outside and leaned up against the house as Myrabelle closed the door. She remained there until her eyes had time to adjust to the dark. Once they did, she crept back to the pine tree. When she got there, she set all the bags down. A grimace crossed her face when she realized she could have used the help. It was going to be a struggle to get all the food back the ten miles to the cave. After putting the strap of the bag with the potions over her head, she picked up the sacks and slipped back into the forest. She only made it a few miles when she heard voices up ahead. Without a sound, she set the bags down on the ground before she tiptoed toward the voices. When she got close, she ducked behind a tree before peering around it. She saw several humans with large dogs. They watched as the dogs sniffed along the ground. It appeared as if they were searching for something. She observed for a few minutes and started to creep back to the bags when a voice caused her to freeze.

"Those animals are useless," Londar snapped. "We must find her now! Get them moving."

Rin's breathing accelerated as she scrambled backwards. She dashed back to the supplies and snatched them off the ground before she ran in the direction of the cave. She was careful to give the area where Londar was a wide berth when she ran past. After a couple of miles, she was breathing heavy from all the extra weight and was forced to stop. She crouched beside a large tree to catch her breath when she heard the sudden howl of a dog not far behind her. A shiver ran through her when she realized they must have picked up her scent. She jumped up and grabbed the bags but did not move. Her entire body was trembling, and she looked all around in a panic. She had no idea what to do, her rising fear was clouding her judgement.

Making a split-second decision she clamped her eyes and tightened her grip on the bags. "Ēlipor ntāera raitama." The supplies disappeared as soon as the words were out of her mouth. As soon as they were gone, she climbed the nearest tree and jumped through the treetops as she ran. She prayed this would confuse the dogs, but she still headed away from the cave until she was sure. Dashing across the branches, she leapt into another tree and stopped on one of its large branches that could conceal her. She laid down on her stomach and waited. Only a handful of minutes passed before the men and dogs came into view with Londar following them. She risked a peek over the side and terror flashed through her eyes when she saw him directly under the branch she was hidden on. Holding her breath, she did not move so that she was as quiet as possible.

"Well?" Londar snapped making Rin jump. She began to tremble worse and wished she had listened to her brother.

"They have lost the scent," one of the men replied.

Londar spun and kicked the nearest dog. It yelped and scurried away from him. "Like I said, useless!" He paused and looked around. "She must still be close. I felt the hint of magic earlier. Keep looking!" He did not move away from the tree while the humans followed the dogs as they searched.

Rin struggled to remain as still as possible. She knew even a slight movement could give her away. Again, she was frozen in fear. It was preventing her from making a rational decision and she knew it. She started to feel light headed from hyperventilating when an idea came to her. If she could talk to Sara maybe her brother could help her. She clamped her eyes closed and focused on reaching Sara.

***

Sara was sitting at the back of the cave practicing her magic while Jake trained with Paige and Raven. She glanced up when she saw Kaedin leap to his feet. His head tilted like he was listening to something before he headed for the cave entrance.

"What is wrong?" Wren asked as he stepped into his path.

Kaedin frowned but looked at him. "She is afraid, something must have happened. I must go to her."

"No, you cannot. We do not know what is going on and we cannot jeopardize our position. She knew what she was getting into when she left alone."

Kaedin opened his mouth to argue when bags of food appeared in the middle of the cave. Wren and Kaedin both looked over at them, their surprise visible.

"She risked a port spell," Kaedin said as he tilted his head again. "She is moving farther away from the cave." His gaze turned back to the entrance and he started to leave but Wren grabbed his arm.

Sara was watching them when she heard Rin's voice in her head.

'Sara! Sara!'

Her brows furrowed, 'Rin?'

'My brother.... or.... or Kaedin...I...I do not know what to do. L...Londar is here."

Sara's eyes widened when she could tell that Rin was frantic from her disjointed, racing thoughts. She got up and hurried over to Wren and Kaedin. They were arguing about whether Kaedin could leave the cave.

"Wren, Kaedin," Sara said. Neither one of them heard her the first time.

'Sara, hurry please!'

"Wren, Kaedin," she repeated, louder the second time. They both stopped talking and looked down at her when she raised her voice to be heard over them.

"I can speak with you later," Wren said as his eyebrow rose. "I apologize but I cann--."

"Londar is here," Sara interrupted. "Rin doesn't know what to do."

"Where?" Wren's mannerisms changed in an instant and his hand strayed to the katana strapped at his waist. Sara looked down at the ground for a few moments before she looked back up.

"She said they are tracking her with dogs four or five miles from here. Londar is right under the tree she's hiding in."

Wren tightened his grip on Kaedin's arm to keep him from leaving. "Tell her to port. We shall risk the exposure of the magic. Let him come here."

Sara closed her eyes this time and her brows furrowed as she tried to understand what was going on.

"Well?" Wren asked, his voice sharp when she did not look back up right away.

"She said he would know as soon as she tried to port," Sara said, her voice filled with concern. "She didn't think she could get the spell off before something. She didn't finish."

"Tell her to get back here now, or I shall come out there after her." A hint of Wren's anger and frustration began to slip through his calm exterior. Sara closed her eyes again but when she looked back up at Wren, she shook her head. There was no response.

Rin realized almost too late that communicating with Sara used a slight amount of magic. She broke off communication and held her breath.

"There it is again," Londar said. "She is very close. Find her!"

The men began searching in earnest. They wanted out of this forest. Londar started to pace at the base of the tree before he looked up.

"One of you check up there."

Rin's eyes widened in panic and she realized the only choice she had now was to port. She closed her eyes and tried to concentrate but the sound of someone climbing the tree threatened to cause her to lose focus. She kept expecting Londar to appear on the branch.

"My lord, I found her," the human gasped in surprise. Her eyes flew open and she saw he was on the branch with her. She clamped her eyes closed again.

"Ēlipor ntāera." She cried once she was able to picture the cave in her mind. The human dove at her but she disappeared just before he could touch her. When she appeared in the cave, Kaedin was by her side in an instant and he grabbed her by the shoulders.

"Stop leaving without me," he said, his voice poorly controlled.

She looked up at him, her eyes filled with fear as she grabbed his face with both hands. "Do you not understand? He almost killed you. I thought he had, I cannot ris—." She could not continue when her emotions cut her off. He pulled her to him and held her head against his chest.

"I understand but I cannot protect you if I am not with you." He tightened his grip when he could feel her trembling in his arms. "Do not be afraid, I am here." He did not loosen his grip until he could feel her start to calm.

"Rin." She turned her head enough that she could look up at her brother. He was standing beside them and she could tell by his tone that he was not happy. She moved to step back and felt Kaedin tense before he let go of her. After taking a step back, she looked up at Wren.

"Do not ever go somewhere alone again," Wren continued. "Not until he is dead. Do you understand?" She nodded, and his hand unconsciously clenched into a fist. "No, say it. Say that you understand. I shall not lose my sister to that elf."

Her gaze fell to the floor at his feet, "I understand."

He stood silent for several moments before he seized her in a tight hug. "Do not do this again," he said, his voice softer. "I fear for you now that I know what he is capable of doing. Do not leave Kaedin's side even for a moment."

"I am sorry," she mumbled.

He let go of her with a loud sigh before he looked at the others in the cave. "Gather your things, we must leave."

It only took a matter of minutes before everything was gathered and they waited by the cave entrance. Wren scanned the area in front of the cave before they headed outside. Hikaru moved away from the group first and transformed back to true form. Raven and Paige climbed up and got situated.

"Arāesya," Raven said as Hikaru leapt into the air and they were invisible when he rose above the trees and hovered.

Rin looked over at Wren and he shook his head no. He would go last. She nodded and Kaedin moved away from her. Sara and Rin hurried to get onto his back once he changed. They were just getting seated when they all heard the howl of dogs. Rin looked over at her brother and he was already moving away from Jaeha.

"Arāesya." Rin whispered and Kaedin eased off the ground as soon as they were invisible. He got above the trees and waited on Jaeha with Hikaru. Rin looked down and watched her brother jump onto Jaeha while Jake scrambled to climb up.

"Arāesya." Wren managed to get the invisibility spell cast just as the first dog came into view. He reached down and pulled Jake up when Jaeha spread his wings. They were rising off the ground when Londar ran into view. Londar looked up with a curse when he felt the wind created by Jaeha's wings.

"Āega bulāe," he yelled. A large fireball shot from his hand in the direction he guessed the dragon was in.

"Ksāetras," Wren said as he threw up his hand causing them to become visible. A force wall appeared in front of them and the fireball exploded when it slammed into it. Londar glared at them and he began the spell casting movements for a large spell. Jaeha twisted in the air and breathed a huge cone of ice. Londar dove to the side to avoid it and by the time he was back on his feet Jaeha had them out of spell range.

"Āega bulāe," Londar yelled and another fireball flew toward them, but Jaeha dodged it with no trouble.

"Arāesya," Wren said, his voice hard. They disappeared from view and all three dragons flew hard. "If I had no one else with me this would have ended tonight." He glanced back at the tiny figures on the ground.

Jake glanced back but did not say anything. His attention was on Sara. He did not want her to get caught up in something because of Rin.

"Rin would allow nothing to happen to her," Wren said when he caught Jake's expression.

Jake pressed his lips into a firm line. "I'm not so sure. It would be an accident, but she can't control everything. We've already seen that."

"Do not doubt my sister. She would sacrifice herself without a second thought to keep someone else from suffering for her."

Jake leaned back from Wren with a grimace. He had not intended to make him angry. Wren's eyes narrowed when Jake said nothing further and he returned his attention to where they were going.

The dragons all flew as fast as Kaedin could manage. They only had a couple of hours before sunrise and they needed to get across the mountains. Rin looked back again. She felt foolish for allowing Londar to get so close to them. Her hand clenched into a fist when she swore that she would be more careful. They had to make it to Caradthrad in one piece. When she turned back to face the mountains, she prayed they would be able to shake off any pursuit. She shook her head, somehow, she did not think it would be that easy.

The dragons flew hard over the next several hours to get them over the mountains before the sun rose. When they landed on the far side even Jaeha was showing signs of fatigue. The almost sixty-mile flight took them near the coast. Wren made the choice to fly the longer distance because it gave them more of a chance to travel undetected since they would be farther from any major roads.

Rin had her hand on Kaedin's back when he returned to elven form. He staggered, and she grabbed him with both hands to keep him from falling over.

"Apologies," he mumbled as he straightened back up. He was exhausted from the long flight even with the assistance of Rin's spells

"We need a place to rest," Wren said when he stopped beside his sister.

Rin's eyes were worried when she glanced up at him, "I know of nothing that is not hours from here."

Wren frowned as he observed the group. Kaedin appeared almost asleep on his feet while Hikaru was laying on the ground flat on his back. Jaeha looked up at him from where he was sitting with his back against a tree trunk.

"We shall do what we must," Jaeha said, his voice firm. "If we must continue to travel then we shall do so." He glanced at Hikaru and Kaedin as he spoke. The two younger dragons both nodded.

"I will be fine," Kaedin whispered to Rin. "Do what you must."

Rin's expression did not change before she looked to her brother for his decision.

"Get us to a safe place," Wren said. "Everyone is in need of a decent rest before we attempt to traverse the marshes." He reached down and picked up Jaeha's pack before he could get to it. "Divide the load so they are free from the added weight."

The dragons tried to protest, but neither Wren nor Rin would listen, and they quickly divided their things among them. Once they were finished, Rin led them away from the mountains. She weaved her way through the enormous deciduous trees that grew on this side. Their leaves of crimson and silver had a subtle sheen from the early morning sun.

Traveling on this side of the mountains was much easier due to the lessened underbrush but after only a couple of hours, Rin dropped back to walk beside Kaedin. She rested her hand on his back as they walked. Not long after Raven moved so that he was closer to Hikaru and kept a close eye on him as they walked.

Wren and Jaeha exchanged worried glances. They knew that the younger two dragons were struggling to remain on their feet. The almost sixty-mile flight in a handful of hours left them exhausted.

"How much farther?" Wren asked as he moved to walk with Rin.

She glanced around to verify their location, "Two hours if we can maintain this pace." She glanced at Kaedin and he made so sign of response. He just kept walking. Her brows furrowed with worry when she could sense his fatigue. She wished she could do something to help him, but she had already used all of the spells she could, and they were not helping anymore. Glancing down, she stopped when she saw the bag of Myrabelle's potions. The others all came to a stop and looked at her confused. She did not acknowledge them as she rummaged through the bag of glass bottles and pulled out one that had a bluish liquid in it.

"I believe we need to use some of Myrabelle's potions if we are going to make it," she said as she held up the bottle. "This will take away their fatigue for a short time, but it will come back, and it shall worsen when it wears off." She looked to Wren again for his decision.

Wren glanced over and saw Hikaru leaning on Raven to remain on his feet. "Use it."

Rin hurried over to Hikaru and handed him the bottle. "Drink one small sip," she said. He did as she asked and made a face after he swallowed it. A look of understanding flashed across Rin's face. She had had to use a potion or two in the past and knew they tasted terrible.

When Hikaru was finished she took the bottle and went back to Kaedin. He took a small sip but made no response to the taste. His face was blank when he handed it back to her. She put the stopper back in the top and slipped it back into the bag while they waited. Only a few minutes passed before the effects of the potion were noticeable. Hikaru was no longer leaning on Raven and appeared much more alert. Kaedin took his bag back from Rin and she could sense he was no longer so exhausted.

They started moving again, this time faster than before, she knew they had to reach the safe place before the potion wore off. A little less than two hours passed when Rin led them up to the trunk of a massive willow tree. She waved her hand in front of it and a door appeared in the side of the trunk. Grabbing what looked like a small lever, she pulled it, and the door opened to reveal a narrow set of stairs leading up into the tree. She looked back over her shoulder.

"Be very cautious," she said. "The way is quite narrow and there are no handholds." She turned back and started up the stairs. When she reached the top, she stopped and waited for the others on the small five-foot square platform thirty feet above the forest floor. She waited until they were all present before she took several steps onto a shaky, unsteady walkway that connected to another much larger platform.

"I would recommend that Paige and Sara should sit to cross," she said. "It shall move so you must cross one at a time." She crossed the rest of the way with no issue.

Kaedin followed her, then Hikaru and Raven, but when Sara approached the walkway, she froze at the edge of the platform. Her eyes were wide as she stared at what she was supposed to somehow cross. The tiny, rope bridge was only about a foot wide with no sides, and it swayed and shook just from the light breeze.

"There's no other way across?" Jake asked when he got a good look at the bridge. He knew Sara was not the most coordinated and did not think she was going to make it across.

"No," Rin answered from the other side.

Jake sighed before he turned to Sara. "I'll go first. Do like she said and sit down. You'll be fine, and I'll do what I can to help from the other side."

She nodded but started to fidget with the bottom of her shirt. Jake watched her for a second before he turned his attention back to the walkway. He stepped out onto it and a frown crossed his face when he realized it was quite unstable. Putting both arms out to the side for balance, he focused on the tree ahead of him and crossed it. When he reached the other side, he motioned for Sara to follow him. She sat down on the edge of the platform and slid onto the walkway. Her legs hung off either side and she could only use her arms to try and scoot forward. After only making a third of the way across Sara was stuck. She did not have the upper body strength to keep moving.

Rin shook her head with an exasperated sigh. She had never met someone who was so physically inept. Rin was forced to walk back out onto the walkway and help her. She stepped over Sara and put her arms under hers before she lifted and helped push forward while Sara slid. They only managed to move little bits at a time and Rin's expression grew more unpleased by the second. Lifting a hundred pounds was not easy for her, but she had the best balance of all of them.

When they only had about a quarter of the path left Rin's grip on Sara slipped. She sat back down hard on the walkway causing it to tilt. Rin lost her balance and slipped off the edge. She twisted in the air and managed to catch hold of Sara's legs. Sara gasped and leaned forward as she clung to the platform with both arms to keep from sliding off.

"Do not move," Rin said as she reached up with one hand to catch hold of the bridge. Once she got hold of it, she released Sara's legs and pulled herself back up. She sat on the walkway for a minute before getting to her feet.

"Can you reach her?" She asked, her voice irritated, as she glanced at Jake who was watching them from the platform. His face was drawn with worry.

"I'll try," he replied without a moment of hesitation. He laid down on the platform and slid partway onto the walkway. He reached his right hand out to Sara. "Reach for me." His eyes did not leave Sara when she let go with one hand and reached out for him. Their fingertips brushed but Jake could not get a grip on her. He eased out a little bit further until he could grab her hand and pulled her toward him. Rin crouched on the walkway when it started to wobble.

Jake had to stop twice while he pulled Sara across the bridge so that he could slide himself backward off the walkway, but he never let go of her hand. After what felt like an eternity to Sara, Jake had her off the bridge and safely on the platform. She gave him an apologetic frown before she glanced toward Rin. Now that the way was no longer blocked, Rin walked off without a word.

When everyone was across, they started setting up their blankets so that they could sleep on the square twenty-foot sized platform. There were no walls but there was a roof built of tree branches. It blended in and appeared like a natural part of the tree. Rin had Jake and the girls put their blankets closest to the trunk of the tree. She did not want them falling off in their sleep.

Once everyone was settled, Rin made her way to the edge of the platform. She sat down and let her feet hang off the edge. She had her eyes closed listening to the sounds of the forest when Wren walked up and sat down beside her. They just sat in silence for a while before Wren spoke.

"What do you think?" he asked. "How do you think we should proceed from here? I cannot think of a route that does not run the risk of confrontation."

Rin opened her eyes and looked up at her brother. She hesitated, "I do not believe you shall approve but I know of a hidden way into Caradthrad."

"I have never heard of there being a hidden way into the city," he said with a frown. His brows rose as suspicion clouded his face.

"That is because you have never used it," she said with a grin. "Did you not ever wonder how Ronin and I always escaped from you? You would attempt to keep us in the city when we would visit and yet we got out no matter what you did."

He gave his sister a long look of disapproval before he sighed, "I suppose this should not surprise me. The two of you were always inventive and clever."

"I believe this is our best and only option if we wish to make it undetected," Rin said before her voice became serious. "I only worry about the condition of the path. It has been many years since anyone has used it and there are a few treacherous spots." She paused and when Wren only nodded, she continued, "We must travel by day from now on. I will not be able to navigate the marshes in the dark, but I am uncertain we should remain here that long. A full twenty-four hours in one spot is not wise with so many searching for us."

Wren tilted his head, "I believe this is as good a place as any to wait for the sun. If you cannot navigate in the dark, we have no choice."

"Will that not give him too much time to track us?" Her voice was filled with apprehension when she unconsciously wrapped her arms around herself. Wren noticed the change in her demeanor and frowned.

"Rin do not fear him," he said, his voice soft. "I understand why you would be afraid but do not give him that power over you. You are stronger than he is, and he knows it. Why else would he resort to such methods?" He paused and looked down at her. "What have I always told you?"

"Be calm," she whispered. "Nothing can be accomplished if you are not calm.

"Correct," he replied. "If you are focused on remaining calm there is no room in your mind for fear. You were not calm tonight and it could have ended poorly." Rin shrank at his words. She did not wish to fail her brother. "Do not think you have failed," he continued with a knowing look. "You have accomplished much and done great things for one so young. I do not wish for this one elf to ruin anything for you."

"I shall do better," she whispered.

He reached up and ruffled her hair," I am certain that you shall be fine." She gave him a dirty look and pushed his hand away. "Why do you not try and get some sleep? I shall keep watch."

Her expression fell, and she looked down at her hands, "I wish to wait for Kaedin to wake."

"Are they truly that bad?" He asked with a frown. It was rare to see her bothered by something and it worried him. When she did not reply he put a hand on her shoulder. "Rin?"

She kept her eyes locked on her hands, "Yes, I... I keep seeing him almost take Kaedin from me. O...or being trapped in the circle." She glanced up when she felt his grip on her shoulder tighten. His face was clouded with concern and it caused her to look back down with an embarrassed shrug.

"Wait for Kaedin," he said, his voice gentle. "He seems to be able to assist you." He let go of her shoulder and got up. "I shall sleep."

She watched him walk down the platform and lay down on his blanket before she sighed. Drawing up her knees, she rested her chin on them while she stared at the mountains. She found comfort in the sounds of the forest around her while she mulled over everything her brother had said. She knew he was right but was not sure how to keep calm around Londar. He truly scared her, and she hated it. She balled her hands before she stood up with a frown. He would not control her.

Turning her attention to something else, she looked up at the sky and saw that it was late morning. She made her way across the platform to a small fire pit. If they kept it small they should be able to have a fire. This would allow her to make a stew out of a large portion of the fresh vegetables. They would be able to eat it tonight and it would keep for in the morning. Stepping around the fire pit, she moved to the far end of the platform where the supplies were kept. A frown crossed her face when she realized the wood supply was empty. Her riders knew better than to leave nothing in their safe places.

With a loud sigh, she peeked over the edge of the platform. If they were going to have a fire she had to get kindling and logs. Her gaze drifted over to her brother and Kaedin while she struggled with the decision of whether to go alone or not. She knew they would not wish for her to go alone. At the thought of recent events, a shiver ran through her. She took a deep breath and moved over to where Raven was sleeping. As much as she did not wish to wake anyone, she knew she could not go down alone. She put her hand on his arm and shook him awake.

"Time already?" He asked while he rubbed an eye with his hand.

"I apologize," she said. "I require your help for a little while." He sat up right away. "I need to start a stew but there is no wood in the supply cache. I should not go down alone to retrieve what we need."

Raven did not hesitate as he pushed his blanket aside and stood up. "Of course, you should not, my lady. I shall go with you."

Rin nodded with another frown before the two made their way to the base of the tree. It did not take them long to gather enough firewood to keep a small fire going for a day. Once they returned to the platform they placed all the wood near the fire pit.

"Thank you," Rin said. "You may go back to sleep if you wish."

Raven nodded with a large yawn before he headed back over to his blanket. He was asleep again in a matter of minutes. Rin shook her head. She felt like it had been a waste to wake him up.

A few hours later, Rin had a stew boiling in a large pot on a tripod she built with sticks. She added another log to the fire when she saw Jake move out of the corner of her eye. Looking over at him, she saw he was sitting up rubbing his face with his hands. His hands trembled enough that she could see from a distance.

"Jacob, are you all right?" Her quiet question caused him to jump and his gaze flew to her. He did not realize anyone was awake. When he only stared at her, Rin tilted her head as her eyebrow rose. She could see that something was bothering him.

"Does...Does having to take a life ever get easier?" His voice was so quiet she almost missed the question. She walked over to him and sat down.

"I can only speak for myself," she began. "The act of taking a life itself is not difficult, but the guilt of taking it lingers. For me, that has never lessened. I shall carry with me for life everyone whose lives I have ended." She paused until Jake looked over at her. "I do take some comfort in knowing the lives I have taken are evil beings, but it does not change the fact that they are dead. I am uncertain if this assists you at all. Were the orcs the first time you took a life?"

Jake nodded, "I work to save lives not take them." His gaze fell to the staff that was laying on top of his gear.

"I am sorry to say that only you can find a way to deal with taking a life," she said, her voice sad. "I would be more than willing to listen if you need to talk, and I am certain my brother or Kaedin would also be willing."

"Right..." Jake said before he could stop himself.

She shook her head with a sigh. "I know that the two of you do not always get along, which I cannot say I do not understand. You both wish to protect what is most important to you and this often puts you at odds." She paused, and a fond smile crossed her face as she looked at Kaedin. "He is most kind and would be willing. We have all been through what you struggle with now."

Jake could not conceal his skepticism when he glanced at Kaedin. He was not sure he would be as generous as she said. When he looked back up and noticed the look of disapproval on her face he shifted.

"Thank you," he mumbled.

"It is no trouble," she said as she stood up and returned to the fire. She tended the stew until the others began to wake near sunset. After putting out the fire Rin handed everyone bowls of stew before she took Kaedin's and walked over to where he was sleeping. She sat down beside him and put her hand on his chest to wake him but stopped when she felt the large scar through his shirt. Her expression darkened when she ran her fingers along it. It was an inch thick and extended from right below the right shoulder joint, all the way across his chest at a slant that ended at the bottom of his ribcage on the left side. She balled her hand into a fist and almost could not keep tears from welling in her eyes.

"I am so sorry," she whispered. "This is my f…" She trailed off with a startled gasp when Kaedin put his hand over hers. She thought he was still asleep.

"No, it is not," he said. "I will not hear you say it. As you said to me, it was beyond our control. If you wish for me to believe it then so must you." He sat up when she dropped her head and he wrapped an arm around her. She leaned into him and put her head on his arm.

"I shall try," she whispered after a few moments. He kissed her cheek before he took the bowl of stew out of her hand.

"Have you slept?"

Rin shook her head and would not look up at him. "I was waiting on you."

He said nothing as he moved off the blanket and motioned for her to lay down. She peeked up at him before she laid down and he slid closer to her, so his leg was against her back. She could not hold back the relieved sigh and her eyes closed on their own.

"Rest easy," he said in a gentle voice. "I shall not leave your side."

She did not have a chance to even nod in response before she was sound asleep.

While Rin slept, everyone else finished their meal and they hurried to clean up before it became too dark in the tree to see. Once the sun sank below the horizon the only light they had was from the moon and stars, but most of this was blocked by the branches of the roof. Paige was the only one that was really bothered by this. She could not find anything to occupy herself and she laid on her back staring up at the roof. She already complained several times about being bored. In frustration, Wren told her to try and sleep or it would be a very long night.

Kaedin remained beside Rin as he told her he would. He looked out the side of the platform toward the mountains deep in thought until a sudden glow caught his attention. Looking down, he saw a light coming from one of Rin's vest pockets. His eyebrow rose as he pulled what was glowing from her pocket. It was no larger than an inch across and looked like a small black stone. The light emanating from it was an eerie red that illuminated tiny runes along the top and bottom. A look of realization flashed across his face.

"Lord Wren," he said looking up. "He is tracking her with this." He paused and tossed the stone to him. "He must have slipped this into her pocket before you and Jaeha freed her."

Wren snatched the stone out of the air and only looked at it for a second. His face grew angry when he recognized it as a tracking stone. He stood up as he weighed their options, but the sudden sound of dogs, just audible in the distance caused his head to snap up. He cursed under his breath before he closed his eyes in concentration.

"Ēlipor ntāera raitama," he said, and the stone disappeared from his hand. As soon as it was gone, he opened his eyes and surveyed the group before he shook his head. "We have too many innocents with us. He would use that against us if we engaged him now." He paused and glanced toward the sound of the dogs. "Raven, Hikaru, attempt to lead them away from here."

Kaedin grabbed Rin's bag that was next to him and pulled out the only extra shirt she had. He tossed it to Raven, who caught it and disappeared off the platform with Hikaru on his heels.

"Everyone must be silent," Wren whispered. "We cannot afford a confrontation now."

Sara shifted closer to Jake and he put his arm around her. Her nerves were beginning to show now that she knew Londar was close to them again. She glanced over at Paige and noticed she was staring at where Raven had disappeared. It was obvious by the look on her face that she was not pleased he left.

They only had to wait a few minutes before Raven and Hikaru reappeared on the platform. Raven rushed over to Wren as soon as he saw him.

"That will not work for long," he said. "He is prepared this time. There are dark elves with him."

Surprise crossed Wren's face, "How many?"

"I counted at least fifty that I could see." Raven glanced up at Hikaru who nodded in agreement to the figure.

"Did you see in which direction the marches lie?" Wren asked, to which Raven shook his head no and again glanced at Hikaru.

"They lie to the southwest, but I could only see what I believe is the edge since the moon reflects off the water," Hikaru said.

Wren fell silent for several minutes before he looked up. "We must leave. There is no point in remaining here waiting to be discovered. We make for the marshes and if luck is on our side we shall have time to wait for the light. Everyone gather your things." He did not wait for a response before he headed over to Rin and Kaedin. "How long has she been asleep?"

"An hour, two at the most," Kaedin whispered.

Wren stared at his sister for a moment before he shook his head with a small grimace. "She shall be most angry when she wakes up, but we need her to rest so she may guide us effectively." Kaedin tilted his head confused. "I am about to cast a sleep spell on her. That is unless, you would prefer to wake her, and inform her we must carry her, so she may rest and not leave a scent trail."

Kaedin thought long and hard as he watched Rin sleep. "Will a sleep spell even work?"

"If she were awake no, but since she is asleep already perhaps," Wren said with a small shrug as he knelt beside them. He put his hand on Rin's forehead. "Ungāeh." As soon as the word was out of his mouth Rin glowed a pale yellow for a few seconds before it faded. They both almost held their breath waiting to see if she woke up. When she did not, Wren breathed a small sigh of relief before he stood up. Kaedin wasted no time and wrapped the blanket around her so her arms would not fall while she slept. He scooped her up and waited for the others to be ready. They were dividing up the gear. Jake and Hikaru took most of it, leaving Wren and Jaeha unburdened in case of battle.

"Raven you will take point," Wren ordered. "Let us go."

Raven moved closer and, once he was certain everyone was touching, he closed his eyes. "Cūdāe." They risked the short port spell to get them out of the tree since they could not wait for Paige and Sara to traverse the walkway. Once they were back on the ground, Raven led them at a jog away from the tree. They traveled quick and it was not long before Sara started to fall behind.

Jake dropped back to run with her. "Grab hold of my shirt," he whispered. She did as he asked, and he picked up the pace, so that they were keeping up with the group. "You can do it. Just breathe."

Sara grimaced and did her best, but she never enjoyed physical activity and usually stayed inside. She managed to keep up for another mile before she could not run anymore. Raven noticed the trouble she was having and dropped back to run beside Wren. He did not say anything when he glanced up at Wren. His lord looked back at Sara and Paige before he shook his head with a sigh. After getting a nod of approval from Wren, Raven moved back to point and slowed to a brisk walk. He led them for a couple of hours before he raised his hand and they came to a stop. While the others rested, he slipped back to Wren.

"We do not have much cover left," he whispered. "The forest ends once we approach the marshes and there are still several hours until dawn." He paused and glanced down at Rin. "I cannot navigate the marshes. I can only get us as far as the small wooden dock that marks the safe entry point. We could wait at the edge of cover for light or I could skirt around the marsh and take us around the northern banks of Lake Kiyoyaema."

Wren glanced up at the sky before he made his decision. "Take us to the entrance and we shall wake Rin there. Perhaps Lord Ruehnaur shall allow luck to be on our side."

After he heard Wren's orders, Raven moved back to point and motioned for everyone to start moving again. He led them on a different course as he headed for the marsh entrance. They hurried for several miles before Paige and Sara were both lagging behind. Wren and Jaeha noticed and dropped back. They each took one of them by the hand without a word and pulled them along with them. The girls shared uncomfortable glances.

"Why don't we carry them like before?" Jake whispered when he walked up to Wren.

"We cannot afford for those of us who can fight to be fatigued before a battle even begins. They must keep up on their own."

Jake frowned as he glanced at the girls. He could see they were both unhappy, but he knew Wren was right. It was a risk they could not take. He looked at Sara and gave her an apologetic shrug, there was nothing he could do. A strained smile flashed across her face. She was very uncomfortable with Wren holding her hand.

A short while later they reached the edge of the forest. Raven was skirting along the edge when he dropped into a sudden crouch. The others followed suit and waited. A few seconds passed before a group of four dark elves walked by where they were hiding. Raven watched them pass before he slipped silently out of the bushes behind them. His daggers appeared in his hands and he killed all four of them before they had a chance to reach for their weapons. Without pausing he dragged their bodies into the bushes to hide them. Once they were out of sight, he returned to the group. He moved to motion them forward when he noticed the unsettled, shocked look on Paige's face. She had seen him kill orcs before, but not with the same precision and deadly accuracy he just used. It only took him seconds with nothing but his daggers, his katana was still strapped to his back. He tilted his head before sadness crossed his face. Without a word, he turned and led them out of the forest.

They crept across the open flat land between the forest and the marsh edge as quick as Sara and Paige could manage. When they finally reached the entrance the first rays of the sun were beginning to peek over the mountains. They got onto the platform and crouched down so they were less visible from a distance.

Wren moved over to Kaedin and put his hand on his sister's forehead to dispel the sleep spell. He closed his eyes, "Dūkāerav." Before he could pull his hand back, she jerked awake. Her eyes were filled with confusion when she looked up at him.

"What...?" She trailed off when she realized she was mummified with a blanket. She glanced toward Kaedin, annoyance visible on her face. He set her on her feet, and she shrugged out of the blanket. "What is going on?"

"Londar slipped a tracking stone in your pocket. Kaedin found it,"

Wren said. "They track us now."

Rin shivered when her brother said Londar's name and forced herself to look around. She got her bearings while her brother filled her in on the rest of what happened.

"I am pleased to hear it was not my carelessness that allowed him to find us," she said, her voice angry when her brother finished. "Why did you not wake me before now?"

"You were in need of rest," Wren said.

Rin narrowed her eyes and glanced at Kaedin. He was keeping his attention away from her when he could sense she was not pleased. She pressed her lips together with a frown before she turned back to their surroundings. It only took her a few minutes to come up with a plan to slow the pursuit of Londar and the dark elves.

"If I set runes along the platform and the marsh edge, I can cause the waters to rise. It would conceal the path and they would be trapped until the waters receded."

Wren glanced up when he heard a distant howl of a dog. "How long?"

"With Raven's assistance, ten minutes." She watched her brother while he appeared to be determining the best course of action.

"Do it," he said. "However, you must be quick."

Rin turned to walk off the platform and Raven followed until Paige's loud voice caused them all to flinch.

"Why does he have to go?" She asked, her eyes not leaving Rin. When no one answered her, she folded her arms with a scowl. "Why?"

Raven drifted toward her. "This is the job that I perform with the riders." His face was confused as he tried to figure out what was wrong.

"No one else can do it? You've already done two crazy things. It's dangerous." She put her hands on her hips when she had to look up to see his face. His eyebrows rose when he realized what the real issue was, and he glanced at Rin.

"Quickly," she said, her voice flat before she disappeared off the platform. She started to set runes while he turned back to Paige.

"This is nothing," he said with a smile. "We are all enjoying ourselves. Nothing dangerous has been done yet."

Paige's mouth dropped open until she saw the grin on his face. She punched him on the arm when she realized he was messing with her. "That's not funny."

He chuckled, "I shall be fine." Another grin crossed his face and Paige could not help but roll her eyes. He had a special knack for making her feel better. When he saw that her mood had improved, he leaned down and kissed her forehead.

"Be careful," she whispered. He gave her a confident smile before he hurried after Rin. Paige just shook her head and walked back over to Jake and Sara. She ignored the less than pleased look on her brother's face while they waited.

They did not wait long before Rin and Raven returned. As soon as they did, Rin led them off the platform and into the marshes. The path forward was treacherous. Large pools of water surrounded them, and any false step could cause you to sink, in an instant, neck deep in thick mud. Rin chose the path forward without any hesitation or missteps. They managed to traverse several miles before a sudden commotion caused them all to look back. A large group of dark elves were sprinting across the plains. The flat terrain made it possible to see for many miles in every direction.

"Keep moving," Rin said, her voice calm. "If they do not know the correct path, they shall never make it through." She continued forward at the same steady pace. They traveled for several hours with the dark elves in pursuit. The runes only delayed them by an hour or so. Rin slowed the pace again when they came upon the beginning of the delta system for the river that was fed by Lake Kiyoyaema. She surveyed the area before picking the correct path. This was the most complicated portion of the journey. The river and its branches made the way forward even more difficult to traverse.

She led them to the edge of the first offshoot from the main river when she stopped. A low rumbling sound drew her attention in the direction of the lake. Her face paled when she saw the thick, dark storm clouds on the horizon above the lake. The rumbling sound grew louder by the second and she looked down at her feet. The water was rising, and her breath caught in her throat. Her gaze flew back upstream, and she saw the river rising in a flash flood.

"Flood," she yelled as she spun around. She watched as Wren and Raven got a firm grip on Paige and Sara since they were closest to them. Rin looked away from them and her eyes met with Kaedin's. He was near the middle of the group, but he made a quick leap in her direction. She reached her hand out to him just as the flood waters slammed into them. Their fingers brushed before she disappeared as the waters dragged them all downstream.

Jake was knocked off his feet when the flood waters crashed into him. He struggled to get back to the surface and was forced to let go of all the bags he was carrying. They were dragging him down. While the water tossed him around, he got the backpack off his back and swam hard for the surface. As soon as his head broke the surface, he took several deep, gasping breaths to catch his breath. He fought with the current while he scanned the waters. Before he got washed downstream, he saw that Kaedin had been unable to get to Rin before the waters hit. He remembered that she could not swim.

A sudden flash of a hand above the water caused him to look over and he caught a glimpse of Rin not far from him. She struggled to get back to the surface but could not make it on her own. Without hesitating, he swam hard in her direction and managed to get a grip on the back of her vest before she could sink further. He pulled hard and got her head above the surface. She started gasping and coughing as soon as her face was out of the water, but she only managed to get small gasps of air. Jake hooked his arm under hers and returned his attention to keeping them afloat in the rough water. They were washed miles off their original course before the flood waters began to subside.

"Are you okay?" Jake asked when they came to stop on a rocky beach. She only nodded while she continued to cough. He let go of her as he searched the beach for the others. Relief coursed through him when he saw Wren and Sara walking onto the beach, the waters had washed them into the ocean. Raven and Paige were also heading in their direction as well as Hikaru and Jaeha. Raven left his arm around Paige while they walked.

Now that Jake knew Paige and Sara were both safe, he looked back at Rin and jumped when Kaedin was just there. He had not notice him join them.

"Thank you," Kaedin said, his voice serious while he rubbed Rin's back.

Jake shrugged, "No problem." He glanced up when Sara sat down next to him. Reaching over, he pulled her toward him and wrapped his arms around her. "Thank you for helping them." He said as he looked up at Raven and Wren.

Wren bowed his head to the side in acknowledgment, "You have my gratitude for assisting my sister."

"It's no trouble," Jake said as he again shrugged. It really was no big deal to him. Saving people was what he did.

Wren tilted his head before he looked at the group. "Is everyone all right?" When they all nodded, he continued, "Let us hope that has bought us some time. Hopefully, they did not fare as well as we have." He paused, and a frown appeared on his face. "Were any of you able to keep your packs?"

"I had to let them go," Jake said. "They were weighing me down too much." He shifted, and his feelings of guilt appeared on his face. The majority of the supplies had been with him.

"It is not your doing," Wren replied. "If they had been divided more adequately then perhaps, we would be in better shape, but there is no point worrying about that now. Let us search the beach before we leave."

Everyone but Rin and Kaedin got up and searched the beach. When they were finished, they sat clustered in a small circle. They only managed to find two blankets, some ruined dried meats, one canteen, and Jake's staff. The potions were still in their possession because they had been hooked to Rin.

"This could be problematic," Wren said with a heavy sigh. "We are still more than a week from Caradthrad." He looked over at Rin and frowned when he took in her appearance. Kaedin was sitting behind her so that she could lean back on him. She was still breathing a little too fast and just looked unwell.

"I am fine," she snapped when she saw the concern on his face. "I just swallowed too much water."

Wren's frown deepened but he did not argue with her. "Do you know where we are?"

"I am uncertain of our exact location. I believe we shall have to follow the coast until we make it passed the marshes. The paths would be unrecognizable after the flood."

"We should get moving," Wren said as he stood up. "We only give our pursuit a chance to catch us by remaining here."

Everyone was reluctant to get up and start moving. Even the elves and dragons were tired and in need of rest. When they were all back on their feet they looked to Rin to lead them. She glanced at them before she shook her head.

"Raven will take point."

Raven's eyes widened in surprise and he hesitated before he bowed his head. "Yes, my lady." He turned and led them across the beach closer to the ocean. The trudging through the sandy, rocky terrain was difficult, but it was safer than getting too close to the marsh's edge.

Rin folded her arms across her chest while she walked. Kaedin glanced over at her when she moved and could see that she was shivering. It was a chilly morning. He moved closer and put his arm around her shoulders.

"I have nothing dry to give you," he whispered when he pulled her against his side.

She sighed before she glanced up at the sky. The bright sun that had been shining moments before was being covered by clouds moving in from the south. "I pray these storm clouds do not make it worse."

He glanced up when she mentioned the clouds and a frown became fixed on his face. The wind was picking up and the dark, menacing clouds were growing closer.

"It shall be a miserable day," he mumbled as he tightened his arm around her shoulders. She did not say anything as they continued to walk. It was not long before the temperature began to drop as the storm drew closer. The faint smell of rain came when the winds blew harder.

Jake looked up when he heard the sound of approaching rain on the ground. A grimace crossed his face when he realized they were going to get rained on. He glanced over at Sara and noticed she was shivering from the winds. Stepping closer to her, he put an arm around her and drew her closer so that he could block some of the wind.

"We need to find shelter," Jake said. "The girls are going to get hypothermic if we don't get them warm soon."

Wren frowned when Jake used the unfamiliar word, but the rains caught up with them before he could ask what it meant. The water flowed down his face causing his frown to deepen as he glanced at Jake. "There is nothing," he said, his voice short. "All we can do for now is keep moving." Without another word, he spun and started moving again. Jake gave him a dirty look before he shook his head. This was miserable.

It was nearing midday when Raven called a stop and they all huddled together as they took a short break. Wren observed them one by one before he sighed.

"If I am correct we should be nearing the Yakutori Plains," he began as he wiped water off his face. "I believe we must make for Saelyris. We have been knocked so far off course that the detour should not add much time." He paused and glanced at his sister and Sara. "It would be unwise to keep them outside in the rains overnight. The temperature shall only drop further."

"How far is it from here?" Jake asked, his arm still around Sara while he rubbed her arm with his other hand, trying to warm her up.

"Another half a day if we maintain the same pace," Raven said when Wren looked to him for the estimate. Jake only nodded before he looked at Sara and Paige. He could tell they were both exhausted.

"Is it safe to go to a city if people are searching for you?" Jake asked looking back at Wren. The elf regarded him for several moments before he sighed again.

"No, it is not, but I do not see what choice we have in our current situation." Wren stood up and motioned for them all to get up. "We do not have time to delay."

Raven took the led again and varied their course. They traveled the rest of the day in the cold, pouring rains before the lights of Saelyris could be seen. The small port town was the only place that ships could make berth. Its two huge docks stretched almost half a mile out to sea and there were massive ships tethered along both sides. The town itself was built on several platforms fifteen feet above the surface of the ground. It was supported by massive evenly spaced logs.

Raven stopped when they reached a section of the grass that was unusually tall. He knelt down so that they would be concealed from curious eyes. Everyone looked to Rin and Wren for their plan. Wren straightened fully so that he could see the town in the distance. He could just make out the two city guards in front of the main gates.

"We cannot approach. They would recognize us at once," he said with a frown. "Our best course of action is to send Jacob into the city to procure a room an--."

"He knows nothing of our currency or customs," Rin interrupted. "They shall be suspicious of him as soon as they hear him speak."

Wren's face darkened with disapproval. "I am aware, but this is our only option and we must get you and Sara out of the rains. You are both freezing."

Rin gave him a dirty look but fell silent. She knew her brother was correct.

"What do I need to do?" Jake asked drawing their attention to him.

"You shall go into the city and procure a room in the cities' tavern or inn, whichever has space available. Once you do, you will need to signal us so that we may sneak into the city and hide in the room. In order for us to remain out of sight, we need your assistance."

Jake peeked at Saelyris through the blades of grass. "Which building is the inn and tavern?"

Wren gave him a layout of the main road of the town before he pulled a few coins from his pocket. He sighed when he looked them over. "This is not much, but it should suffice."

"Those are qlaesdin coins," Rin interrupted again. "Humans use pliqini. It would draw attention to him as soon as he tried to use the coins. Humans do not carry elven currency." She grimaced when she saw the look of irritation on her brother's face. "Though, I suppose if that is all we have he must use it."

"As I was saying," Wren said, his voice short. "This should suffice for a room for one night. Once we finish determining a plan, I shall explain the coins before you head for the city." He paused and looked up at the sky. The rains were coming down harder than before and it was causing him to become more irritated. "When you enter the inn, or the tavern, be cautious, and you must be mindful of what you say. They will expect you to be foolish and slow. Do your best to appear less intelligent and more subservient. It shall draw attention if you do not." Wren paused and looked over at Sara. He tilted his head before he continued, "I believe it would be wise if you took Sara with you. Even though her hair will draw attention, it is uncommon for humans to travel alone and I do not think sending your sister would be the best choice."

Jake nodded in agreement. He knew Paige would never be able to play along and if someone insulted her, she would react to it without thinking. After getting Jake's approval, Wren handed him the coins and explained what each one was worth. Jake stared at them when he was finished and tried to commit everything Wren told him to memory. Each of the coins had the same symbol stamped into the surface. He recognized it as the willow tree symbol he had seen on the flags in Nuenthras. Turning them over in his hand, he looked at each one closer. The only difference between them was the size.

"Do you have any questions?" Wren asked bringing his attention back to him. Jake slipped the coins into his pants pocket before he shook his head. "Very well. Be cautious and use the signal when you are ready."

Jake and Sara got up and headed toward the port town. He took hold of her hand when they got closer to the torches lighting the walls. She peeked up at him and he squeezed her hand when he could feel her trembling.

"We'll be fine," he whispered before they approached the gates. The two guards watched them walk inside the city before they exchanged glances. One of them slipped into the city behind them. Jake glanced back over his shoulder when the guard moved. His brows furrowed with concern, but he forced his attention back to the buildings lining the main road. He had to make sure they went into the correct one or they would appear even more suspicious. They passed several merchant shops before he paused. The inn was further down the street in a quieter section of the town and the tavern was right beside them. He glanced up at it and decided the noisy, crowded tavern was the best place to try first. If things got out of hand hopefully, they could disappear in the confusion.

Jake tightened his grip on Sara's hand before he pulled her up the front steps and into the tavern. They both stopped just inside the door to allow their eyes to adjust to the bright light. Swallowing hard, Jake regretted his choice almost immediately when silence fell over the entire place. He scanned the room and noticed it was filled with races he was not familiar with. There were dwarves, large and burly humans, silver dragons, elves, and what he assumed were elves, but their skin was a light grey and they had brilliant pink eyes. After a couple of tense moments, the conversation started again, and Jake sighed, but did not lower his guard. The large humans and several of the elves were still watching them. He tried to keep from glancing at them as he crossed the large open room and approached the bar.

"What ye be wantin'?"

Jake looked over when an elven woman with the light grey skin spoke to him. She had a tray in her hands and was dressed in a revealing dress. Her pink eyes filled with irritation when he did not respond right away. "Ye humans all be the same. I needin' to be speakin' slower?"

Jake fought to keep his annoyance off his face. "We need room." He almost grimaced when he tried to make himself sound unintelligent.

"Aye, we be havin' a couple," she replied. "Ye be speakin' with the owner. He be tendin' the other end of the bar." She pointed at an elven man who was serving drinks to a couple of city guards. They appeared as if they had just come off duty. Jake bobbed his head in understanding before he did his best to lumber toward the man. The owner looked up when he noticed them, and his eyes narrowed. He seemed to be appraising them and Sara tightened her grip on Jake. Something about the way the owner and the city guards looked at them made her more nervous. It felt like they recognized them. She peeked over her shoulder and her face grew more fearful when she noticed the city guard from the gate had followed them inside.

"Jake," she whispered as she tugged on his arm and brought them to a stop. He kept his eyes on the owner and city guard, but he leaned closer to her. "I think they know us. That guard from the gate followed us in here." Her voice was quiet and panicked when she whispered into his ear. Jake lifted his head and looked back toward the door and watched as several more guards walked into the tavern. He scanned the room, searching for another exit.

"Can I help you with something?" Jake's eyes flew back to the owner when he asked them a question. He shook his head no and eased away from the bar toward the large double doors that led into the kitchen. The elven woman who spoke to him earlier emerged carrying a tray with food and drinks.

"Wait just a moment, I wish to have a word with you," the owner said, his voice suspicious as he walked around the end of the bar.

"What is the trouble, Thoridan?" One of the city guards sitting at the bar asked before he stood up from his bar stool. Thoridan did not reply to the guard as he continued to move closer to Jake and Sara.

"Where do you hail from? You do not seem to be from around here," Thoridan continued and Jake only shook his head no.

"Want room," Jake said while he pushed Sara backwards and stepped back. Thoridan tilted his head before his gaze turned to Sara and he stopped moving. He stared at her for a moment before realization flashed in his eyes.

"It is 30 pliqini for a night," he said looking back at Jake.

Jake regarded him for a few moments before he shrugged his shoulders, "Too much. We leave." He knew if he pulled out the elven currency it would seal their fate. The city guards were moving closer the longer they talked.

"Surely you have that much," the owner said as he glanced at a guard and nodded. "If you are with our lord and lady, I am certain you have plenty."

The entire room froze for a split second before Jake dove for the kitchen doors. He rammed them open with his shoulder and they slammed into the barmaid. The new tray of food she was carrying flew from her hands when the doors knocked her backwards. Jake sprinted through the kitchen while he pulled Sara with him. He did not bother to look back when he heard the loud commotion behind them and ran straight for the backdoor. After he threw it open, they dashed back out into the rain and turned to run when more city guards appeared from around the end of the building. Jake weighed their options in a few seconds, and he jumped at the guard not in the bunch. He caught him by surprise and knocked him out of the way. Jake shoved Sara through the opening, "Run!" He spun to face the other guards moving in and managed to incapacitate two before the others got hold of him. One of them hit him hard in the back of the head causing him to crumple to the ground unconscious.

"Jake," Sara cried while she tried to get free of the guard holding onto her. She had not been able to get away when Jake told her to run.

"Be still," the guard snapped at her. He dragged her with him while two of the others picked Jake up off the ground. They took them to the small two cell prison in the center of the city. After tossing them inside and locking the door all the guards but one left. He stood watching as Sara rushed to Jake and tried to wake him. Her eyes were panicked when she felt the large knot on the back of his head.

"Why'd you hurt him? We didn't do anything wrong." Tears of anger and fear gathered in her eyes while she grabbed a handful of Jake's shirt.

The guard tilted his head as curiosity crossed his face, "You are more intelligent than the normal humans. That is quite intriguing. Where are you from?" He paused before he frowned when Sara would not answer him. "A pity. You shall be taken back to Nuenthras since his majesty has an interest in you." The guard paused again. "Where are Lord Wren and Lady Rin? You were both with them."

Sara's gaze flew back to the ground in front of her. She refused to say anything further and eventually the guard moved away from the door.

"Be prepared," he said before he was out of earshot. "His majesty will not be so kind if you fail to answer his questions. You shall leave in the morning." He walked through the door of the prison and slammed it closed behind him.

Sara started to tremble at the mention of Kilvari. She knew he was not going to be kind to them if they were taken back to Nuenthras. After a few minutes, she shook her head and turned her attention back to Jake. He was still unconscious. She ran her fingers over the knot on his head before a look of determination crossed her face. Clamping her eyes closed, she held her hand over the injury. "Rujhāe." The hand over Jake's wound started to glow a faint blue. Her brows furrowed as she fought to use her magic. Several long minutes later she gasped and lost control of the spell, but the knot on his head was half the size. She was taking slow deep breaths so that she could try to heal Jake again when he groaned. He reached for his head when his eyes opened a little bit.

"Jake?"

He glanced around until he saw her sitting beside him. His head was resting on her legs.

"What happen...?" He trailed off with a grimace when his head started pounding from trying to talk. Sara's face filled with more worry when she could see the pain on his face. Once the pain started to subside, he looked back up at her. His expression darkened when he saw the look on her face, and he grabbed her hand.

"I'm okay," he whispered. "Tell me what happened." He fought to keep from grimacing again so that Sara would talk to him. She hesitated before she told him what happened. Once she was done Jake, with a slight shake of his head, sighed. He should have been more careful and left as soon as he thought they were in trouble.

"I'm sorry," he mumbled.

"It's not your fault." He only squeezed her hand in response. The more fully awake he became the more pain was beginning to register. He flinched when he touched the spot on the back of his head.

'Sara!' Sara jumped when she heard Rin's voice in her head and Jake gasped from the sudden movement. She looked down at him and saw his eyes were clamped closed against the pain throbbing in his head.

'What is going on?' Rin's thought almost made her jump again before her eyes filled with hope.

261

'We need help,' Sara thought in a panic. 'They recognized us, and Jake is hurt. I healed it a little bit but he ne--.'

'Slow down! Tell me everything.'

Sara took several deep breaths to calm back down before she told Rin everything that happened since they left for the city. When she was finished, she waited in nervous silence for a response.

***

Wren was pacing through the grass now that the sun had set, and they were hidden from view by the darkness. The thick storm clouds kept the moon's light from breaking through them.

"It has been too long," he said turning to face Raven and Hikaru. "One of you must slip into the city and find out what is amiss." He paused, and his head dropped. "I should never have sent them in there. If they are harmed it is my doing."

"I shall try and speak to Sara," Rin said as she moved to stand beside her brother. She rested her hand on his arm. His face darkened further when he noticed that she was still shivering. He closed his eyes with a frustrated sigh before he nodded. Rin looked away from him and focused on allowing Sara to hear her thoughts. It was several minutes before she glanced back up at her brother and he could tell something was wrong.

"They were recognized," she said, her voice barely audible over the rains. "The city guard put them in the prison and Jacob has been injured."

Wren whipped around so that he could see the small town. His face was calm and collected even if he was not. "Tell her we are coming." He looked over at Jaeha and the dragon tilted his head. "Get them out and meet us on the other side of the town."

"Are you certain? They will pursue us," Jaeha said, unable to conceal his surprise.

"I am not worried about pursuit," Wren said, his voice sharp. "If they wish to challenge me then I welcome it. I have been chased from my home and while I do not wish to harm my people, I will not tolerate being hunted."

Jaeha bowed his head, "I shall free them and meet you. Do I have full permission to act?"

"Yes." Once Wren gave his permission, Jaeha moved away from the group. He glanced back before he allowed himself to glow and in seconds he was back in true form and rising into the sky. He streaked toward the city and roared so loud that it shook the buildings when he descended on the prison. City guards poured into the streets but only a handful raised any kind of weapon to him. They recognized him at once.

Jaeha ignored the handful of arrows coming his direction as he tore the roof off the prison with a swipe of his front claw. He roared again as he plucked a shocked and terrified Sara off the ground with one claw before grabbing Jake with another. Snapping his tail in irritation, he caught a couple of guards and sent them flying across the main street. A low angry growl caused the remaining guards to back away from him. He rose higher into the sky before he streaked for the far side of the town. As soon as he was no longer over the city Wren appeared on his back and Hikaru and Kaedin flew up next to him. Without a word, the three dragons flew hard through the pouring rains.

Wren glanced back and watched as some of the city guards were mobilizing to attempt to follow them. He stood up on Jaeha's back and moved up to his shoulder before he slid down his leg. Catching hold of his claw, he put a foot on one of his toes so that he could see Jake and Sara. His eyes filled with concern when he saw Jake laying against Jaeha's claw with his hand on his head. Without a word, Wren put his hand on Jake's arm causing him to start in surprise. He watched the grimace flash across his face before Wren closed his eyes, "Rujhāe." It took Wren a couple minutes to finish healing the wound before he opened his eyes.

"Thanks," Jake mumbled as his eyes started to close on their own. Now that the throbbing had lessened, the pain was not keeping him awake. Wren observed him for a moment more before he climbed back up to Jaeha's back. He got seated again before he looked behind them. In the distance, he spotted the light of multiple torches and his eyes narrowed.

"Are you all right carrying both of them?"

"We shall get farther if I keep them, rather than burdening the young ones," Jaeha replied with a low growl.

"Then get us as far as possible before we must take a rest."

Jaeha did not respond other than to pick up the pace as they headed straight for the large mountain range, that was just visible in the distance.

The dragons flew hard for almost a full twenty-four hours before Jaeha finally slowed and descended toward the base of the Naraeshiki Mountains. He laid Jake and Sara down before he dropped to the ground over them. Wren leapt off his back and hurried over to them while Jaeha changed back.

"Are you both all right?" He asked as he reached out and assisted Jake to his feet.

"Yeah, we're okay," Jake said with a frown. "I should've been more careful. I didn't think they'd be able to recognize us."

Wren shook his head, "It is not your fault. I should have anticipated the complication." He paused and glanced over at the others. His eyes narrowed when he noticed that Rin was still shivering. "We shall take a rest here and get everyone warm. Find a secure place where we can build a fire."

Jake started to move away to help gather wood for a fire when Wren grabbed his arm. He glanced back at him.

"Remain here with Jaeha," Wren said. "Sara is cold as well and you need to rest." Jake frowned before he sighed and nodded. He moved over to Sara and the two of them sat down with their backs against the rocky cliffs behind them.

In a short time, the group managed to find a small cave a few hundred feet above the forest floor. It was just large enough that they could all lay down and still have a small area for a fire pit. Raven made quick work of building a roaring fire in the small pit he created out of the stones. Once the fire was going, they covered most of the entrance with thick pine branches to conceal the glow given off by the fire. It was not long before the entire cave was quite warm, and they were all comfortable for the first time in days.

"Everyone get some sleep," Wren said when he noticed that Rin was no longer shaking. "We have traveled quite far and should reach the city in another day, but the road is not easy." No one argued with him and they all laid down on the warmed stones. It was not long before they were all asleep.

Early the next morning, Rin crouched by the entrance and peered through the tree branches as she listened to the conversation below them.

"Have you found anything?" An elf asked as he looked over at his companion.

"No, it is as if they vanished. All roads to Caradthrad are being watched, there is no way that they can slip through."

"Do not underestimate our lord and lady," the first one said. "They shall not be easy to capture and take back to his majesty."

The second elf cleared his throat, "I do not wish to detain either of them. Something does not seem right about all of this."

"Shhh," the first one hissed. "Do not allow the captain to hear you say such things. He shall have you flogged."

The second elf shuddered at the thought of being flogged before they both fell silent and disappeared into the trees. Rin eased back once they were gone. This was the third patrol she had seen pass by the cave since sunrise. A look of concern crossed her face before she slipped across the cave and shook her brother awake by the shoulder. He was groggy for a few moments as he rubbed his eyes.

"What is it?" He asked when he saw it was Rin who woke him. She glanced at the others, who were still asleep, before looking back at her brother and telling him what she had seen. When she was finished, he just shook his head.

"This certainly complicates matters," he said. "Can you still get us to the hidden entrance?"

"Yes, but we shall have to climb up from here," she replied. "I fear if we make for the easier climbing spot we shall be seen." She paused and looked over at Sara. "Though, I am uncertain that they can all make the climb."

Wren followed her gaze before he sighed. "How far is it?"

"The narrow ledge that we must traverse to reach the path is hundreds of feet above us. I worry that even Jacob will be unsuccessful in this instance."

"I can carry Miss Sara if required." Both Wren and Rin looked at Jaeha when he spoke. Neither had realized that he was awake. "I believe Hikaru would be more than capable of doing the same for Paige."

Wren seemed to consider the idea for a moment before he nodded, "That sounds plausible. Do we have anything that we can use to create a harness or strap, so they do not have to hold on during the climb?"

"The blankets we were able to salvage from the flood should suffice," Rin said. "If we cut them into strips, we can create slings with them."

"And for Jacob?" Wren mused aloud as he surveyed the group. "Perhaps, if we have enough material from the blankets we can create ties. He would be able to tie off with one of us in case he has an issue." He paused and glanced back at Rin. "I believe Kaedin would be the best choice if Jaeha and Hikaru are both burdened with one of the girls."

Rin hesitated before an uncomfortable grimace crossed her face. She could not imagine that Kaedin would be too pleased having to assist Jake. "I am uncertain that would be wise, perhaps, he should assist Paige in..." Her voice trailed off when she realized Jake would not like that idea either.

"They shall do what is required of them," Wren said, his voice sharp. "We do not have the luxury for personality differences. The two will work together if it is of benefit for the group." When Rin shrugged with another small grimace, he turned his attention toward the front of the cave. It was nearing mid-morning and he frowned. "We shall wait for nightfall before we attempt the climb. Make the needed preparations."

Over the rest of the day, they worked on cutting the blankets into long strips. Raven and Hikaru used these and braided them together to create strong, thick lines. Most of these were then woven into a sling that would support Paige and Sara's weight. Once they were finished, Wren had them gather around so that he could explain the plan to them. When he was finished, he could see the concern on Jake's face.

"Do not worry," he said. "We shall get all of you to the path."

"Why can't you just port us up there?" Paige asked with her arms folded over her chest. "Or let the dragons fly? I mean that would be so much faster."

Wren shook his head, "Caradthrad's port block extends this far and if we attempted to fly we would be spotted at once." He paused with a frown.

"I do not wish to harm my people to protect us."

Paige rolled her eyes before she moved closer to Raven. All this hard-physical activity was beginning to annoy her. Wren tilted his head with a look of disapproval at her reaction before he just shook his head. "It is time to go," he said, and he motioned for Jaeha and Sara to go first.

Sara tightened her grip on Jake's hand for a moment before she made herself let go and walked over to Jaeha. She looked up at him when she reached him.

"If you would, Miss Sara," he said holding the sling away from his body. She stared at it and hesitated. The sling was over Jaeha's left shoulder before it ran across his back and chest. An open end hung on his right side. She peeked up at him but still did not move. Her face started to flush when she realized everyone was watching her.

"It's okay," Jake said as he walked over to her. "You just need to get into the sling and sit down on it." Sara bit her lip when she noticed she was going to be right up against Jaeha. "You have to be close so that he can carry you. If it's too loose you could slip out."

She glanced up at Jake before she moved closer and slipped the sling over her head. Jake helped her pull it down until she was able to sit on it. Once she was secure, he stepped back and looked up at Jaeha. The dragon bowed his head a little before he turned his attention toward the cave entrance. He moved closer to the edge and scanned the woods at the base of the cliff. When he saw no signs of torchlight, he got a firm grip on the stones.

"Hold on to me and try to remain as still as possible," Jaeha said glancing at Sara. She swallowed hard before she nodded and wrapped her arms around him. He waited until she had a good grip before he started the long climb up the cliff face.

As soon as he was above the cave entrance Rin followed behind them so that she could help in case they needed it. Behind her, Hikaru started up with Paige clinging to him. He made it several feet before he had her adjust her grip so that he could move easier. Raven remained close to them as they climbed.

Wren watched until Raven cleared the entrance before he glanced at Kaedin and Jake. Neither one appeared pleased that they would be working together, and he frowned.

"It is your turn," Wren said with a tilt of his head. "Kaedin shall start and Jake will follow close enough to keep the lines taunt. I shall be behind you."

Kaedin raised an eyebrow but said nothing as he started to climb. Jake frowned before he trailed behind him. They climbed at a slow and steady pace for a couple hundred feet before Jake paused with a loud exhale. He just pulled himself up to another foothold and his arms were beginning to shake. Looking above them, his face went blank when he could not see how much farther they had to climb. His gaze went to his hands. They were shaking even though most of his weight was on his legs.

"It is not much farther," Kaedin called from where he was stopped a couple feet above him with the ties taunt. He could see that Jake was beginning to struggle.

Jake glanced up at him before he nodded and continued to climb. He made it almost another hundred feet before he reached for a grip and his hand slipped off. His face paled with a gasp and he tried again. This time he was able to get a weak grip, but he could feel his hand slipping. He breathed a small sigh of relief when he spotted Sara and realized that the ledge was only twenty more feet above him. Grinding his teeth together, he forced his exhausted body to keep moving and managed to cover the last twenty feet on his own. He reached up to grab the top of the ledge, but his hand started to slip back off. His grip was gone.

Kaedin was still close after making the ledge. He glanced back at the edge and when he saw Jake slipping, he dove across the stones. Wincing when his side scrapped across the rocks, he caught Jake's forearm to stop his fall. He tightened his grip on Jake's arm before Jaeha rushed over and assisted him. Between them, they were able to haul Jake up onto the ledge.

"Thanks," Jake said once he was sitting on the stones.

Kaedin gave him a small head nod in acknowledgement before he moved to stand beside Rin.

After a short rest, Rin got them on their feet, and they made their way along the narrow ledge. It was jagged and rocky as it wound its way along the mountain's edge. There were sections that were less than a foot wide. When they reached the first section, Jake got a tight grip on Sara's hand. Even though he was still spent from the climb, he did not want to risk her falling off.

Sara had her back pressed against the sheer rock face behind her. Her eyes were wide as she tried to keep from looking down. Only the reassuring presence of Jake beside her kept her moving forward. She peeked up at him, but he did not look back at her. His entire focus was on keeping them safe.

Rin led them for what felt like an eternity before she stopped on a section of the ledge that widened. The others came to a halt and waited while she searched for something along the cliff. She ran her hand across the stones until she found a small one that was shaped like a half moon. Pushing on it, a thick stone door swung into the mountain revealing a small pathway.

"This is a dwarven door," Wren said, his voice wary.

Rin shrugged before she grinned at him, "Baldrim created it for us."

Wren's eyebrows shot up. "How did you convince Baldrim to craft this for you?"

"Ronin can be quite persuasive when he wishes to be. Plus, Baldrim has always liked us."

Wren just shook his head in exasperation. He could not fathom the time and secrecy that it must have taken to build this so no one knew of its existence.

Rin watched him for a minute as her smile widened. Thwarting her brother was something she enjoyed. After a few seconds, she turned and headed through the doorway and down the path. She followed it until it opened into a large cavern. The roof had several large holes in the stones and the moon shone through dimly illuminating the room. There was a large waterfall at the far side of the room and a small river running along the back edge of the cavern before it disappeared back into the stones. The path hugged the left side and climbed up at a steep angle.

"Watch your step," Rin said. "This is always quite wet and shall be slippery." She continued along the path with unfaltering steps on the steep slope. The others trailed along behind her as best they could. The path was soaked making the stones treacherous.

Once they reached the top, the path veered to the left away from the river. They traveled for a while before it opened into another large cavern. Before they could walk into it Rin stopped and held up her hand when something on the other side of the room caught her attention. The others quit walking and watched as she slipped forward alone.

She crossed the cavern at a slow jog and followed the path to the entrance of a third and much larger cavern. Crouching beside the entrance, she turned her attention to the footprints she had noticed moments ago. Her face clouded with worry when she realized they were what she feared. She started to ease back when her gaze turned to the cavern in front of her and she froze. There were at least a hundred dark elf males, armed for battle and waiting in the cavern. Rin scrambled backwards until a sudden movement to her right drew her attention. A dark elf was making its way in her direction. Her eyes narrowed when its dark grey skin and black leather armor made it almost impossible to see them in the dark of the cave.

Without pausing to think, her daggers appeared in her hands and she leapt at him. She stabbed the dark elf through the throat in one quick motion. He collapsed to the ground with a gasping gurgle before she stabbed him again. She paused long enough to make certain that he was gone before she spun and sprinted back the way she came.

When she dashed back into the cavern where the others were waiting, Wren's hand drifted to the hilt of his katana. He knew something was wrong before she had time to say anything.

"There are dark elves," she gasped as she skidded to a halt. "At least a hundred. They must be going to attempt to breach the city. We must warn Caradthrad."

A sudden commotion on the other side of the room caused them all to look up. Dark elves were streaming into the cavern with weapons in hand.

"Stay together," Wren said as he drew his katana. "We cannot run and must fight our way through them."

Weapons appeared in the hands of everyone but Paige and Sara. Raven pushed them behind him and Hikaru before they prepared as a group to face the flood of dark elves. They were surrounded and within seconds there were bodies strewn across the ground at their feet.

"Keep moving," Wren yelled over the battle. "We cannot get pinned down. Push forward!"

As a group, they pushed through the elves and made some progress toward the other side of the cavern. Rin spun in place and dropped two more dark elves before a figure moving through the horde caught her attention. The elf making her way through the others was the only female on the battlefield. She wore all black robes with a red feathered snake biting its own tail embroidered on the front.

Rin watched her approach. She knew this was a priestess of Lady Avdotyae. The guardian deity of the dark elves who enjoyed causing chaos within her own people. Rin tilted her head to try and make out the insignia on the sleeve of the robes but could not see it. She frowned when she was unable to determine which temple this priestess called home.

"There is a priestess," Rin said moving closer to her brother. "I cannot see the temple insignia so watch for others. She will not have come alone."

Wren glanced up and followed her gaze. He fought to keep his expression blank. This was not a complication they needed when they were already hopelessly outnumbered. Before he could reply, the dark elf priestess stopped in the middle of the cavern and moved her hands in a large circular motion. Rin leapt in front of the group and she just managed to plant her feet as the priestess shot a huge flame stream from her hands.

"Nahdāema," Rin said. She brought her hands up as if she was catching the spell. It pushed her back several feet, but with a twist of her hands, she redirected the spell into the cavern wall. It crashed into the stones and caused a huge chunk of the wall to split off and come crashing to the floor. The entire room shook from the force.

The priestess eyed Rin with narrowed eyes. It was obvious that she was unaccustomed to having someone stop her spells. Rin moved closer so that there was more distance between her and the group. The other dark elves stopped fighting and watched their priestess. They were certain that she would be victorious.

"General Rilavaenu," the priestess said, her voice dripping with disgust. "I heard rumors that you were capable with the arcane arts." When Rin said nothing, a look of anger flashed across the priestess' face. Her daggers appeared in her hands and she leapt toward Rin.

Wren kept a close eye on his sister while he led the others around the edge of the cavern. While the rest of the dark elves were distracted, they had to keep moving. They made it more than halfway across when he paused. The priestess had launched at Rin again and Rin leapt to the side as she brought her daggers around. The priestess blocked them and slashed at Rin with her own. Rin blocked them before the two began exchanging blows with movements too fast to see. Their deadly dance continued until the priestess spun and her dagger connected with Rin's shoulder leaving a deep stab wound. Rin did not acknowledge the wound as she twisted to the right and plunged a dagger into the priestess' side while she caught her across the face with the other.

With a howl of rage, the priestess leapt out of Rin's reach and the daggers disappeared from her hands.

"Phanumura," she shrieked. An ice bolt flew from her hands and Rin was forced to jump out of the way. "Phanumura!" Another bolt of ice shot from the priestess' hands and Rin spun in place as she brought up her hands.

"Ksāetras," Rin said, her voice still calm. A force wall appeared in front of her and blocked the ice bolt.

The priestess continued to throw spells at Rin, and it appeared Rin was on the defensive while she dodged or blocked each spell. She remained calm as she waited for an opening.

"Āega bulāe," the priestess yelled. A fireball shot from her hands and flew toward Rin. Instead of blocking it, Rin leapt to the side.

"Phanumura," Rin said, and ice streamed from her hands.

The priestess was just able to jump out of the way with a furious glare. She once again planted her feet and moved her hands in a large circle. Rin frowned and got into a grounded stance. She could see the spell would be large this time. Raising her hands like before, she waited for the priestess to act.

"Jhyōta!" The flames that were created were so large that they were almost twenty feet across.

"Nahdāema," Rin said as she brought her hands out to the side. She pushed them back together causing the flames to condense into one spot before she caught them. Pouring her own magic into the flames to strengthen them, Rin fought to keep them under control before she twisted her hands and redirected the flames back at the priestess. The priestess was so shocked that Rin redirected the flames that she did not have time to move. She was incinerated in seconds and there was nothing left when the flames subsided. Rin sank to a knee breathing heavily. The last redirect had almost been too much for her.

The dark elves around her were frozen in shock before a furious howl ran through them. They leapt toward Rin with unconcealed hatred. Kaedin managed to reach her first and jerked her back to her feet. He stepped in front of her and began to engage the first dark elves that reached them. Rin glanced toward the exit of the cavern as she backed up until she stood back to back with Kaedin. She saw her brother and the others start attacking the dark elves from the other side in hopes of drawing some of them away from her and Kaedin.

Returning her attention back to the battle, she and Kaedin moved together with movements that meshed seamlessly. They soon had several dark elves lying dead around their feet.

"We must move," Rin yelled over the battle. She was beginning to tire and could sense that Kaedin was as well. Kaedin reacted to her without saying anything and started to move toward the others. They made it almost halfway before they could go no further. The dark elves were pressing in on them from all sides and Rin knew if they did not get a break soon they would be in trouble.

"Āega bulāe," she said as she raised her hand. A large fireball dropped all around them and killed several more dark elves. Rin paused to catch her breath and noticed there were still many dark elves left in the cavern but the flow into the room had slowed. She glanced over her shoulder and Kaedin tilted his head toward her brother. They started moving again without a word.

***

Jake had the girls backed up against the wall behind him when he stepped forward to meet the rush of dark elves coming their way. He spun the staff in his hand before he brought it up to block a blow from the first dark elf. With a quick sidestep, he spun it back the other direction to bring the blade around and stabbed it into the elf's side causing the elf to stagger backwards and fall. Jake managed to take out several more before he found himself surrounded. Spinning the staff in a wide arc, he forced several of them to step back and he used the opportunity to drop two more of them. He glanced back over his shoulder for a second and his face paled. Several dark elves were behind him and moving toward Paige and Sara. He cursed under his breath and tried to make his way back over to them. The momentary distraction was all the closest dark elf needed and it lunged at him. It brought its katana around and caught Jake in the side. He gasped and staggered to the side when it left a long, deep gash. Twisting around, he swung the staff over his head before bringing it down and stabbing the large blade into the elf's shoulder. The dark elf cried out in pain but before he could move, Jake brought the staff around again and killed him.

Spinning in place, Jake looked toward Paige and Sara and saw that Sara had somehow managed to get a weak forcefield around them. He could tell she could not hold it long as it started to flicker under the barrage of attacks from the dark elves' blades. He again tried to get back over to them but before he could move he was surrounded.

"Dūkāerav!" Jake glanced back again when he heard a dark elf say a spell word. His eyes filled with fear when he saw that Sara's force wall was gone.

"No!" He cried when they swung a katana at his sister and Sara. A sudden clashing of the blades caused Jake to freeze for a moment. Raven was in front of Paige and Sara with his katana raised. He had managed to get between them and the dark elf before the blade could connect. Remaining close to the girls, Raven dropped dark elves all around him before one managed to get close. It stabbed at him with a dagger and sliced him across the back. He gasped as he twisted and ran the elf through with his katana. Taking an unsteady step, he dropped to one knee. Seeing him at a momentary disadvantage another dark elf rushed him and brought his sword down for a killing blow, but another sword blocked it. Raven glanced up in surprise and saw that Paige had her blade between him and the dark elf. She was shaking with fear but held her ground. She twisted the blade like Raven taught her and she stabbed the elf in the stomach. A look of shock was frozen on the dark elf's face as he stumbled backwards. His face contorted with anger when he saw that she was human. He jabbed his katana forward and managed to stab her in the chest before she could get out of the way. Paige gasped before she crumpled to the ground.

"Paige!" Raven cried as he scrambled back to his feet. He killed any dark elf that was close before he dropped to his knees beside her. He held his hands over the wound and closed his eyes. "Rujhāe, Rujhāe," he repeated before his eyes flew open. The healing spell was not working. "Lady Rin, I cannot heal her!" His voice was panicked as he scanned the cavern looking for Rin. When he saw her sprinting toward them, he moved a little bit so that Rin had room. She knelt beside Paige and held her hands over the wound in her chest, but she paused before she cast the healing spell.

Her face grew sad, "She is gone."

Pure disbelief froze on Raven's face. "No, no, I was right here," he gasped. Rin tried to put a hand on his shoulder, but he jerked away. He did not acknowledge her as he reached down and brushed Paige's hair out of her face.

Rin glanced up and saw Jake running toward them. When he reached them, he dropped to his knees beside his sister. Rin's eyes clouded with more sadness and she moved to stand up when she saw an older version of herself standing beside them.

"Ryvāind," older Rin said. "Say it now! He is attempting to alter the past. I only have a few moments. We cannot lose her yet." Rin just stared at her. "Now! Touch her and say it!" Older Rin reached down and touched Rin on the shoulder. Rin hesitated before she put her hand on Paige's arm.

"Ryvāind?" As soon as the word was out of her mouth, Rin felt an enormous amount of power being forced out of her. Her whole body began to glow with a bright white light and her insides felt like they were on fire. She let out a small cry of pain as the power continued to increase. Glancing down at Paige, her eyes widened in shock when it appeared as if time was rewinding on just her. Rin collapsed to the side when older Rin stopped forcing power out of her. She could not comprehend how time had rewound two minutes and Paige was alive again. Raven gasped in shock, but he had his hands over her wound in seconds.

"Rujhāe," he said as his voice cracked. When he was finished healing the wound his eyes flew open and he grabbed Paige's face with both hands. "Are you all right?" The words sounded choked.

She was visibly disoriented, and it took her several moments before she nodded. He pulled her onto his lap and clung to her. His eyes were filled with tears, but he wiped at them before they could fall.

Jake had a firm grip on Paige's hand when Sara came up and wrapped both arms around him. She could see that he was distraught over the fact that he had nearly lost his sister. Her own tears soaked into his shirt when she rested her head on his shoulder. She could not imagine life without her best friend.

When Rin sat up with Kaedin's help Jake glanced over at her. "How?" he asked.

"I do not know," she replied, her voice weak. Her entire body still felt like it was burning, and blood dripped from her fingers because of the wound in her shoulder. She frowned when she could not heal the wound. All her magic was gone after the battle with the priestess and the time magic.

"We must get inside Caradthrad," Wren said when he, Jaeha, and Hikaru joined them. They were all exhausted. "We shall discuss what happened later." He paused but when no one moved he frowned. "Now, we must move. There are still too many of them."

Raven stood with Paige in his arms, ignoring that his back was wet with blood from the large wound. Hikaru hurried over so that he was closer to them. Jake released Paige's hand and stood with Sara's help. He leaned on her while he held a hand against the wound in his side.

"Which way?" Wren asked once Rin was back on her feet. She started forward while she leaned on Kaedin for support. They hurried as fast as they could manage. Wren stayed close to his sister and handled any dark elf that got too close to them while Jaeha dropped back and brought up the rear.

They made their way into another large cavern and headed toward a path leading off to the right. Halfway across, an ice bolt suddenly appeared and flew straight at Rin. Kaedin pulled her back and stepped forward to cover her. The ice slammed into his back causing him to flinch when it connected but he made no other reaction. Being a silver dragon, he was immune to the effects of cold. Once the bolt disappeared, he turned to face where it came from while keeping Rin behind him. Another priestess stalked forward and came into full view.

"I challenge her!" Her angry voice echoed off the stones. "She has murdered our high priestess and I shall have satisfaction!"

Before Rin could respond, Wren stepped forward. "If you wish for an opponent it shall be me."

"If you wish to die sooner than the rest, I accept," she hissed at him. "You shall all die here! Phanumura!" A large bolt of ice shot from her hands in Wren's direction.

"Ksāetras," he said with a frown. He had no choice but to block it or it would have hit someone behind him. "Get them out of here!" He ordered glancing at Jaeha before he dashed forward to close the distance between himself and the priestess.

Jaeha tried to lead them further along the path but Rin refused to leave her brother. "You must lead them out of here," he said, his voice urgent. "I shall not leave my bonded behind."

"I was not left behind, and I shall not leave him. We will remain together," she snapped, her voice defiant.

Jaeha sighed and shook his head in frustration. He glanced at the others and could tell that none of them intended to leave either.

The priestess sent more ice in Wren's direction which he dodged as he continued forward. When he was within range, he brought his katana down at a sharp angle. The priestess leapt off to the side and brought her hands up for another spell. Wren spun and brought the katana down again, catching her arm with the blade.

"Pevanas," she gasped. A second later a strong wind pushed her backwards. Wren slid back several feet from the wind, but as soon as he stopped, he sprinted back toward the priestess. He knew he had to stay close so that she could not cast any large spells.

"Ksāetras," she said when she saw him getting close. A force wall cast in front of her, but Wren did not slow and raised his hand.

"Dūkāerav," he said, and the force wall disappeared with a quick twist of his wrist. The priestess' face paled and she started to back up.

"Jhyōta," she yelped, and flames shot out of her hand. Wren leapt to the side and the flames passed him leaving him unscathed. He once again brought his katana down and she scrambled to get out of the way. "Pevanas," she gasped. The wind pushed her away from Wren and put space between them again. Her face grew concerned. She knew that she could not compete with him in hand to hand combat and had to rely on her spells, but she needed distance to cast.

Wren kept the pressure on as he continued to press forward. She used more ice bolts and another wind spell. They seemed to be at a momentary stalemate as the pattern repeated several times. She cast another ice spell and Wren moved as if he would come forward but paused. This time he waited for the wind spell. As soon as she cast it, he sprinted in the direction she was going. He was fast enough that he would beat her.

"Phanumura!" She yelled, her voice frantic when she realized her mistake. Dozens of ice bolts flew at him and he managed to dodge most of them before one caught him in the leg. He stumbled and went down to one knee. The priestess landed and took the opening to begin to cast a large spell. Wren saw her start casting and forced himself up on his injured leg. He ran toward her and brought his katana down. His blade connected with her just before she could cast the spell and she crumpled to the ground dead. Wren stumbled backward with a hand on his thigh and jumped in surprise when Jaeha grabbed his arm.

"I told you to go," Wren said as Jaeha put Wren's arm over his own shoulder. The dragon helped him walk toward the others.

"Your sister refused to leave," Jaeha said with a frown.

Wren shook his head in exasperation. "We must get out of here. If there is another priestess we are finished. There is no one left in any condition to fight one."

Jaeha tilted his head before he nodded, he knew only Hikaru, Kaedin, Sara, and himself were uninjured. As soon as they joined the others, they continued along the path while Hikaru moved around them keeping any of the straggling dark elves that approached them away. When they reached the other side of the cavern, they took the path that led to the right. They hurried until they reached another cavern. This one was smaller than the others and on the far side, they could see a crafted stone wall. Hurrying as best they could they crossed the room while Hikaru fell back and brought up the rear.

Rin moved to the wall and felt along a row of stones near the middle. She found the small carving she was looking for and pressed on it causing a large stone door to swing open. They all rushed through the door and Hikaru pulled it closed behind him with a loud thud.

ℜonin stretched as he stood up from behind a large black solid wood desk. He ran a hand through his silver and red hair while he headed toward a balcony off his study. The study was a large room that had numerous books lining most of the walls. The far wall was open to the outside. It had great white pillars evenly spaced across the opening. The grey stone floors were covered with hand-woven dark brown and red rugs. There were several finely made chairs that were upholstered with black and gold fabrics.

When Ronin reached the edge of the balcony he sighed and rested his hands on the white stone railing. He looked down over the front of the city of Caradthrad. The great city was cut deep into the mountain below his feet. Caradthrad was situated thousands of feet above the surrounding forest in the front of Mt. Carad. It had been built millenniums ago and had never been taken in war. The part of the city that could be seen from the front was a large stone archway carved into the mountain above the massive stone gates. The gates were several feet thick and stood thirty feet tall. They were very similar to the gates on a dwarven city since they had assisted in their construction.

A large fully-grown silver dragon poised to strike was intricately carved into each side of the gate. The open area above the gates was large enough that a fully-grown dragon could fly through without being forced to transform. Just in front of the gate was a large landing where the steep narrow road leading up to the city ended. It ran up the mountain at a steep angle and could barely be seen when you looked at the front of the mountain. The balcony where Ronin stood was cleverly concealed in the face of the mountain, so unless you knew it was there it was nearly invisible. The rest of the city was buried deep inside the mountain. It ran for many miles with multiple levels.

Ronin turned and headed back into his study when he heard a loud knock on the door. "You may enter," he called.

A soldier opened the door and hurried into the room. He was dressed in dark brown leather armor and had a katana strapped at his waist. "Your majesty, another fifty thousand of Lord Wren's troops and another hundred riders have just arrived."

Ronin kept the surprise off his face when he faced the soldier, "See to it that they are housed."

The soldier bowed and left just as quickly as he arrived. Ronin watched him leave before his brows furrowed in thought. He still did not know what was causing Wren to send his troops to his city, but he knew something was amiss. It was almost six months ago when Wren asked if he could house some of his troops but did not explain why. Ronin agreed without question. He had known Wren his entire life and he was like an older brother to him. There was no reason not to trust him.

With a heavy sigh, Ronin was about to sit back down at his desk when a loud commotion on the other side of the room caused him to spin around. His hand went for his katana until he saw it was Hikaru that slammed the wall of his study closed. He stared at the group who had just appeared in his room in confusion until he caught sight of Wren. Jaeha was helping him into the closest chair. Ronin hurried to his study door and jerked it open.

"I need a healer at once," he ordered. One of the guards beside the door ran down the hall and Ronin stepped back into the room. He walked over to Wren.

"What has happened?" He asked when he noticed Wren was pressing both hands down hard on a large wound in his thigh.

"Dark elves," Wren said with a grimace. "They are in the tunnel behind us. I am uncertain how many are left."

Ronin's eyes widened before he looked over his shoulder at the other guards who were now standing in his study.

"Get our men into that tunnel and clear out the dark elves," he ordered. "Once you are finished, seal it closed."

Two of the guards dashed out of the room and sprinted down the hallway to get reinforcements before heading into the tunnel.

While Wren spoke with Ronin, the others in the group made their way further into the room. Raven sat down on the floor and laid Paige next to him. She reached up and pressed her hand against the wound on his back. Her hand only covered a small portion of it, but she wanted to help him. It was still bleeding, and he flinched when she touched it, but did not make a sound.

Jake and Sara tried to move toward a couch, but Jake fell forward. Hikaru grabbed him and helped ease him to the floor. He was pale and sweating from the freely bleeding wound in his side. Hikaru pushed both hands down hard on the gash causing Jake to gasp in pain.

"I am sorry," Hikaru said with a frown. "I have no spells left."

Jake only nodded in response as he closed his eyes. The room was trying to spin, and he did not wish to vomit. Sara took hold of his hand and bit her lip while she watched him.

It was not long before a healer rushed into the room. As soon as Wren saw her, he indicated that Jake and Raven needed to be tended first. She nodded and made her way over to Jake.

"I do not know how they would have known about that tunnel," Ronin said breaking the silence. "Only Rin, Riku, Baldrim, and I knew of its existence."

"Rest assured I told no one," Rin said. She and Kaedin had moved closer to her brother and Ronin in an attempt to get out of the healer's way.

Ronin spun in place his face filled with disbelief. "You have returned," he gasped after a moment. She gave him a weak smile and he stepped toward her. Grabbing her, he jerked her toward him and enveloped her in a crushing hug. She took a sharp breath at the sudden pain and he glanced down at her. His brows furrowed when he could see the pain on her face, and he loosened his grip. He frowned when he moved one of his hands and saw it was covered in blood.

"You are injured as well?" he asked. She gave him a half-hearted shrug and his frown deepened. "Rujhāe," he said while he held his hand over the wound. It took longer to heal than if one of the elves had cast the spell, but he was able to heal it. "It is rare that you are injured. What managed to harm you?"

Rin stepped back, and Ronin released her to Kaedin. "A high priestess of Lady Avdotyae was with the troops."

Ronin's expression changed in an instant. "A high priestess was with them?" His voice was shocked. "They do not venture from their temples unless it is a matter of great importance." He paused and glanced toward the hidden door into his study. "I owe all of you much, if they had breached the city here, I would be dead." His attention shifted for a moment to a chair near where they were speaking. He watched as Hikaru helped Jake into that chair before looking back at Rin.

Jake grimaced as he leaned back in the chair and looked over at Ronin and Rin while they continued to talk. An incredulous look crossed his face as he observed them. How could anyone not realize that they were related? Ronin was much taller than Rin but they both shared the same silver and red hair, and their eyes were the same shade of brilliant green. They even shared similar facial features, though Rin's were much more delicate.

"How in the world didn't you figure out that they were related?" He blurted before he could stop himself. Rin, Ronin, and Wren all looked in his direction and he shifted in the chair. He had not intended to say that out loud. Rin gave him a dirty look but did not say anything. Her gaze lifted so that she was looking up at Ronin and her shoulders dropped, dejected. She could see the turmoil on his face.

"It is all true?" He asked, his voice quiet.

She looked down at the floor before she nodded. Feelings of guilt and sadness coursed through her. It was her fault that Ronin and Riku lost their father.

Ronin noticed the change in her demeanor, and he pulled her into another embrace. "It is not your doing," he whispered to her. "Neither of us shall ever blame you for the actions of others." He paused until she peeked up at him. "Welcome home, sister." Her eyes widened in disbelief and a sad smile crossed his face. "Do not think on it too much. You have always been like a sister to me, so nothing has changed." Rin tightened her grip on him, and he held onto her until he noticed the healer was standing close to them. He helped Rin back over to Kaedin before he turned to face her. "Are you finished?"

"Yes, your majesty."

"See to it that rooms are prepared for everyone."

The healer bowed as she turned and then hurried from the room. Ronin watched her leave before he looked over everyone. His eyes widened when his gaze fell on Paige. He tilted his head and appeared to be confused and curious all at the same time. It took several moments before he could pull his attention away from her. He continued to observe the others and started to shake his head with a small amused smile.

"You all look terrible," he said as he looked at Wren. "It is truly a shock that the two generals of the elven nation would fair so poorly when my dragons faired this well."

A look of disapproval flashed across Wren's face, "It has been a long road."

Ronin nodded, he knew there was much to discuss but it would have to wait until they had a chance to recover. He was about to say as much when a loud knock on the study door caused him to look over. His expression darkened when it opened without his permission and one of his generals rushed into the room.

"Forgive me, your majesty," he said. "A rider has just arrived and insists that he must speak with you at once."

Ronin frowned, "Very well, Yosheido, show him in." Yosheido stepped to the side and assisted an injured rider into the room. Rin's eyes widened with concern when she saw him.

"Orbryn?" she asked. The elf froze when he heard her voice and it took him several moments before he staggered across the room and dropped to his knees in front of her.

"Forgive me, my lady," he gasped as he dropped his head. "I have failed you."

"What has happened?"

"I tried to stop her," he said, his voice panicked. "She would not listen."

Rin was becoming confused and even more concerned. She had never seen her second in command so shaken. "Who?" She asked but he still would not look up at her.

"Your mother," he whispered.

Rin felt as if her blood turned to ice as she moved enough that she could grab his shoulder. His eyes flicked to her face. "What about my mother?" Her voice was laced with fear and she squeezed his arm so tight it was painful, but he made no response to it.

"I... I was prepared to leave," he began, his voice distraught. "All the other riders were safely out of the city, but I noticed your mother. She appeared quite angry and I asked her what troubled her. She told me something about your father turning your rooms into a guest suite and she intended to speak with him." He paused and took a deep breath. "I could not shake the unease I felt, and I tried to convince her not to go. She refused and would not allow me to accompany her either. I attempted to tail her but got caught up with some city guards. They were demanding to know where you and the riders were. By the time I was able to get away from them and arrived at your father's study, I could hear raised voices. I tried to get into the room, but he had some kind of barrier over the door. He told her that if she was not on his side then she was also his enemy. I fought to get the barrier down as fast as I could, but it was too late. She was... was already gone. He..." Orbryn trailed off when he could not continue. The room was enveloped in a death like stillness while everyone sat in disbelieving silence.

"No," Rin gasped breaking the silence with great heaving sobs. Kaedin wrapped both arms around her and picked her up. She clung to him while he looked for somewhere to give her privacy. He saw Ronin tilt his head toward a door leading to his private rooms and he hurried through it.

"For...forgive me," Orbryn muttered. Ronin stepped forward and put his hand on the elf's shoulder.

"I am certain there is nothing to forgive," Ronin said, his voice soft. "We know that you did everything that you could." He looked over at Yosheido. "See that he is cared for and you are sworn to secrecy." He helped the injured elf back to his feet and ushered him to his general. Yosheido got a firm grip on his arm and assisted the rider commander out of the room. Once they were gone, Ronin looked back at Wren and found that he was watching him.

"He is no longer the elf that we once knew," Wren said, his voice cracking. "Please, allow me tonight and I shall be prepared to speak with you in the morning."

"Anything that you need is yours," Ronin replied.

"Thank you," Wren whispered before he headed for the door of the study. He pulled it open and disappeared down the hallway.

Ronin watched him leave as he unconsciously rested a hand on his chest. A sudden ache at the memory of losing his own father returned when he thought of what his close friends were now enduring. He grimaced; the pain never really goes away.

With a shake of his head, he glanced at one of the guards still inside the room. "Take them to the rooms that have been prepared and be certain that they need for nothing."

The guard bowed and stepped out of the room. He waited until everyone was on their feet and following him before he led them away from the study. They walked a short way down the hall. At the end, they took a large set of stone stairs down a floor. On the new floor, they passed several doors before the guard stopped in front of two large, dark brown doors. He knocked on the first of the two and it was opened by the healer who had tended them earlier.

"I shall take it from here," she said with a friendly smile. He acknowledged her with a head bow before he left to return to his post.

Sara peeked up at the elven woman standing in front of them. Her hair was a light brown and she was dressed in dark navy robes that were lined with silver. There were delicate runes along the bottom in a light sea blue that was the same shade as her eyes.

"I am Lyra," she said. "You shall be staying in these two rooms. The first is for the young ladies and the gentleman shall stay next door." She indicated a large black door a short distance down the hallway. Her eyebrows rose when she noticed the look of disapproval on Raven and Jake's face. "There is nothing to fear within the city. You are all safe here." She paused and folded her arms across her chest with a stern look. "It is not appropriate for you to share a room with the young ladies."

Sara looked up at Jake when she felt his grip on her hand tighten. Her face clouded with worry when she saw he was leaning on the wall beside him to remain on his feet.

"My lady," Jaeha said with a frown. "I understand that rules of propriety state that they must be housed separately, however, they have been through much, and the humans do not hold to the same rules."

Lyra shook her head, "I do not wish to insult their customs, but they must respect ours while they stay in our homes." She reached toward Sara and beckoned for her to come closer. Sara did not move, and Lyra sighed. "I shall not harm you, but I must be certain that you are both tended properly, and there is a bath and fresh clothing for both of you in the room."

Sara glanced up at Paige at the word bath. A grin appeared on both of their faces. Sara squeezed Jake's hand before she let go. He did not appear pleased, but he nodded with a sigh. If she wanted to clean up, he was not going to keep her from doing it. She gave him a shy smile before she headed into the room. Paige watched her go before she pointed down. Raven started to shake his head but a pout from Paige caused him to sigh and he set her on her feet. She clung to the wall and moved toward the room. Lyra hurried to her and helped to steady her so that they could walk through the door. Once they were inside, Lyra closed it behind them. The four left in the hallway stared at the door.

"I believe our room is next door," Jaeha said tilting his head down the hall. Raven and Jake both remained staring at the door until Jaeha cleared his throat. They both looked over at him and he again tilted his head toward the door. Jake frowned with a heavy sigh before he started to move down the hall with Hikaru's help. They all entered their room and closed the door once they were inside.

Paige and Sara sat on their bed once they were cleaned up. They were given noble attire and they both stared at the clothing. Sara had on a deep emerald green gown that came down to her feet. It was lined with silver lining and had a matching chain belt. Paige was dressed in a similar fashion, but her gown was a sunflower yellow. After a few minutes they both looked up and when they realized they were both staring at the clothes they giggled. It felt great to sit and relax together.

"Well, what about you?" Paige asked, breaking the silence. "I feel like exploring." A grin flashed across her face.

Sara was unable to conceal her surprise. "Are you sure? You... I mean... you were..." She looked down at the floor when she could not bring herself to say the word dead.

"I'm fine," Paige said with a frown. "I'd like to forget all about that. I mean, yeah, I still hurt but it's not that bad."

Sara nodded but was not convinced. She knew it was very painful after watching the elves deal with injuries, and they were stronger than Paige.

"Where do you want to go?" Sara asked with a heavy sigh a few moments later. "Are we taking someone with us?"

A mischievous grin flashed across Paige's face. "I have no idea, but that's half the fun and no way are we taking anyone. I don't want or need looked after."

Sara sighed again but nodded. She knew this was Paige's way of dealing with what happened to her. "Let's go." She said with a small shudder.

She was not looking forward to Jake and Raven's reaction when they got back. Paige did not notice and headed for the door with slow, heavy steps. She pulled it open just enough to peer into the hallway. When she saw no one, she pushed it open the rest of the way and after hooking her arm with Sara's, she headed for the stairs.

"Up or down?" Sara asked when they paused.

"Down," Paige replied without any hesitation. "We already kind of know what's up. We need to see if we can find the actual city and shops."

Sara smiled at her friend's enthusiasm as they headed down the stairs. They went down one level and paused to look around. It appeared to be more rooms like the floor above, so they continued down another set. The next several floors were all the same and they continued down. When they reached the bottom of the staircase it opened up into an enormous cavern. Their mouths both dropped open when they saw all the shops carved into the walls of the cavern with more vendors set up in aisles in between.

Paige's face lit up when she saw all the merchandise. She and Sara meandered their way through the shops and vendor stands. There was anything anyone could wish to find. Clothing, weapons, potions, magic items, herbs, and many different types of food.

"Dang, I sure wish we had some money," Paige groaned as she picked up a black leather, handcrafted backpack with multiple storage compartments. She sighed when she set it back on the table. Sara gave her an apologetic shrug before they continued walking. They made it through a few more shops when Paige started to tire, and they headed over to a large fountain in the center of the cavern. They sat down on the stone half wall around it.

"I sure hope things are going to calm down now," Sara said as she watched the people walk past them. There were folks from all over Asaetara in the city. Dwarves, dragons, elves, and a human or two could be seen from where she was sitting. Her brows furrowed as she observed the humans. They were Viking like and barbaric. It made her uncomfortable to be anywhere near them.

"I doubt that's going to happen," Paige said, pulling her attention back to her. "I mean especially with them just losing their mom."

Sara sighed, and her gaze fell to the floor. "I can hear a lot of her thoughts," she whispered.

"How bad is it?" Paige asked as she looked over at her.

"She is a mess. It sounded like she was blaming herself, but her thoughts stopped a few minutes ago. I hope she is asleep or something."

"Or Kaedin knocked her out," Paige said with a giggle. Sara just stared at her and Paige laughed harder. "I'm just kidding. He'd never do anything to hurt her." Paige paused, and her expression darkened. "I really hope she doesn't blame herself. I mean, I know what that's like and it's really painful." Sara only nodded and the two fell silent. She watched the fountain for a while before she saw Paige put her hand on her chest.

"We should go back," Sara said, her voice concerned. "You don't look that good anymore."

Paige sighed, but nodded without any argument. She was very tired, and the pain of the wound was becoming more noticeable now that her excitement was wearing off. Sara stood up and held her arm out for Paige to hold on to when she paused. Her eyes widened as she scanned the room.

"Do you remember which way?" She asked, her voice taking on a panicked edge. Paige glanced looked around before she grimaced. She did not remember the direction either.

"Let's just head back to the edge of the cavern and work our way around," Paige said as she pointed at the wall. "The stairs were on the outside somewhere."

Some of the panic fled from Sara's face when Paige was still calm. She helped Paige get up before they made their way to the side of the cavern. It took them quite a while and by the time they found the stairs Paige was struggling to keep moving. They only made it up half a flight before Paige leaned against the wall.

"Lean on me," Sara said, her voice concerned. "We need to get you back to the room soon." Paige frowned, but put her arm over Sara's shoulder. The two climbed a couple of flights before Paige had to sit down. She rested her head against the wall and closed her eyes. Sara started wringing her hands while she waited. She was afraid she was not going to be able to get her back to the room.

After Paige rested for a few minutes, she decided to try to get moving again. Sara helped her back up, but they only made it a handful of stairs before Paige sat down again.

"I'm sorry," she muttered, her voice weak. "I just can't go any further."

Sara glanced back and forth between the stairs and Paige. She did not want to leave Paige on the steps alone to go and find help.

"What do we do?" Sara asked as she sat down next to her.

Paige cracked an eye and looked over at her. "I don't know. Get Jake I guess." She grimaced when she said her brother's name. He was not going to be happy with them.

"Will you be alright waiting here alone?" Sara asked as she stood up. Paige leaned against the wall and closed her eyes again when her face grew pale.

"Yeah," she mumbled.

"Are you ladies in need of assistance?"

Sara spun around when a young male voice interrupted their conversation. She found a young man standing a few steps below them. His fine clothes of black with emerald trim caught Sara's attention. It was a stark contrast to his silver and blue hair, and pale, light blue eyes. He tilted his head when she did not answer and after a moment cleared his throat.

Sara's gaze dropped to the floor in embarrassment. "Yes," she whispered as her face flushed.

The young man approached them. "May I have your names and how may I be of assistance?"

"My name is Sara," she said, her eyes still glued to the floor. "This is Paige. She was injured and is still healing. I can't get her back to our room alone." She took a couple deep breaths before she plucked up the courage to peek up at him.

He knelt in front of Paige. "I can carry you if you will allow it," he said, his voice quiet and gentle. After Paige nodded, he picked her up off the step and started up the stairs. "Where is the room you are trying to return to?"

Um… I'm not sure. We…um…are on the floor right below Ronin's study. I mean…Lord Ronin," Sara stammered. She was not sure what she was supposed to call him.

The young man glanced at her out of the corner of his eye. It was filled with suspicion. "You know his majesty?" His voice was full of doubt.

"No," Sara said shaking her head. "I don't know him. We are here with Wren and Rin. They are the ones who know him."

"Rin is here?" The young man asked as he stopped dead. "When did you arrive?"

"Several hours ago, I think."

He gave her a long hard look before he turned and took the stairs two at a time. When they reached their floor, he moved to leave the stairwell and almost collided with Raven.

"Lord Riku, please excuse me," Raven said as he stepped aside to get out of his way. He glanced down, and his eyes widened when he saw Paige. "Paige?"

"I take it these two are with you?" Riku asked with an amused smile.

Raven nodded, "Yes, my lord. They were supposed to remain in their room and rest. I apologize if they caused you any trouble, and I can take her." Riku handed Paige to Raven before he smiled again.

"It was no trouble," he said. "And, it was a pleasure to meet you both. I am certain that I shall be seeing more of you." He paused, and a slight frown appeared on his face. "I would recommend that you be more cautious. There are some in the city that are not fond of humans."

Sara nodded in understanding. "Thank you," she said, her voice quiet.

"It was my pleasure," Riku said before he headed up the stairs toward

Ronin's study. Sara watched him leave before she looked over at Raven. "Who was that?"

"That is Lord Ronin's younger brother," Raven said as he looked down at her.

Sara's eyes widened. She was surprised someone so important would have helped them. Glancing back over her shoulder, she saw that Riku was already out of sight. When she looked back, she had to hurry to catch back up with Raven. He pushed the door open to their room and she followed him inside. Her gaze flew to the floor when she noticed Jake sitting in a chair near the door. He sighed in relief when he saw them before disapproval dominated his features.

"As I said they are both all right," Jaeha said from where he was standing along the back wall.

A frown appeared on Raven's face, "Only because Lord Riku found them. He was escorting them back to the room when I located them." He paused and glanced down at Paige. The frown slipped when she did not argue with him and he could see the exhaustion on her face.

"You must rest," he said, his voice soft. He moved over to the large double bed and laid her on one side. She was asleep before he could cover her with the blankets. He watched her for several minutes before he turned and faced the room. "I am not leaving."

Jaeha frowned before he glanced at Jake. "I assume that you feel the same?" Jake only nodded and Jaeha shook his head. "I wish you luck if Lyra finds you in here and I shall bid you goodnight." He shook his head again before he disappeared through the door and closed it behind him.

Once he was gone, Jake stood up from the chair and had to grab the arm to keep from falling over. He was still quite unsteady from the blood loss. Sara hurried to his side and put his arm over her shoulder. She helped him cross the room, but he stopped before they reached the double bed. He glanced around and when he realized there was only one single bed and a couch in the room besides the large double bed, he frowned.

"I'll take the couch," he said. "You should share the large bed with Paige."

"No," Sara said, her voice quiet. "I can sleep on the couch. You were injured and need the rest more than I do. You'll be much more comfortable on the bed."

Jake looked down at her before he sighed. He could tell by her expression that she was serious. "All right," he mumbled. He allowed Sara to help him the rest of the way to the bed before he wrapped his arms around her in a tight hug. The two held onto each other for several minutes until Jake leaned down and kissed the top of her head. He released her and sat down on the edge of the bed. She gave him a small shy smile and took an extra blanket folded at the end of the bed before she headed over to the couch. After moving several of the decorative pillows, she spread out the blanket and laid down. Once she was settled, she glanced over at the others and noticed they were all asleep. With a heavy sigh, she stared up at the ceiling for a while. Her racing thoughts were keeping her awake. She wondered what was going to happen to them now and whether Rin and Wren were doing okay. Her worry was threatening to overwhelm her when her eyes finally started to grow heavy. She drifted to sleep with those thoughts running through her mind.

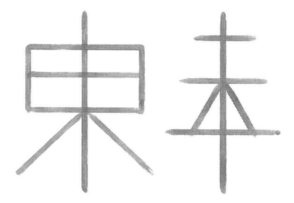

Ronin yawned as he entered his study the next morning just after sunrise. He paused partway through the door when he noticed that Wren was already waiting for him. The elf was sitting in a chair and looked out over the balcony. He was watching the sunrise and so deep in thought he did not notice Ronin had joined him.

"Did you get any rest?" Ronin asked.

Wren jumped, and his gaze turned to Ronin. It took him a few moments to collect his thoughts before he spoke. "A little." His attention returned to the sunrise and the two fell silent until Wren sighed. "How is Rin?"

"I am not certain," Ronin said, his voice sad. "When I looked in on them last night she was asleep. Kaedin took her to another room shortly after so that I could retire."

Wren nodded, he did not appear surprised that Kaedin was still with his sister. "He shall take care of her." His gaze did not leave the sky.

"He has always been good for her," Ronin said with a faint smile when a sudden thought occurred to him. "They were inseparable from the moment they met."

A nostalgic smile crossed Wren's face. "I remember that day quite well. They left no room for any other when the young dragons were brought. There was no dragon she would allow near her but Kaedin without screaming."

"Do you remember when he bit your father?"

"Oh, yes," Wren said with a chuckle. "He was quite cross with the whole situation. Kaedin should never have been brought and he found the

289

fact a noble dragon was not a match for her unacceptable."

"Rin and Kaedin gave him no choice. She would scream if they took him away and he would bite anyone who attempted to touch her."

"Only my mother and I could touch her," Wren said before his expression darkened. "He would not allow father to take her from the crib. Perhaps, he has always known what we did not. He never trusted my father even as a hatchling."

Ronin hesitated before he took a deep breath. "What is going on, Wren?"

Wren tore his eyes away from the sunrise and looked back up at Ronin. He regarded him as he slowly pieced together his thoughts before he exhaled hard. "My father intends to attack Caradthrad."

"What?" Ronin gasped. "Why would he do such a thing? We have been allies for millenniums."

"I believe he has been driven mad by his guilt, though, that is only my own speculation. I do not know for certain the reasons; all I know is that he in league with several of our enemies and we must stand together." He paused, and his expression grew serious. "If we do not, we shall all perish."

"I must know everything that you know so that I may protect my people."

Wren nodded, "I shall tell you everything that I know, however, Riku, Rin, and the humans that accompanied me must be present. They will all be needed to determine how best to handle this threat." He paused and looked back up at Ronin. "I need to know anything that you know about Rin's magic."

Ronin hesitated, and his eyebrow rose. "I am afraid that I know very little, but I shall reveal everything that is known."

Wren did not appear pleased, but he nodded. Once he did, Ronin moved to the door of his study. He pulled it open and one of his men appeared beside him. Ronin sent him to gather the others before he headed over to his desk. After sitting down, he looked back at Wren.

"There is breakfast on the table if you wish to eat," he said. "The others should be arriving shortly." Wren only glanced at him before he looked back out over the balcony. The two fell silent while they waited.

***

Rin woke just after dawn. She laid staring up at the ceiling for a while before she dragged her body out of bed. Wrapping her arms around herself, she headed out onto the balcony with downtrodden steps. Both of her eyes were red and puffy with large dark circles under them. The night had been long for her.

When she reached the balcony railing, she rested her hands on it as she looked out over the merchant area of the city. Her eyes followed the scarce movement within the city. It was still too early for most of the merchants to be preparing their shops for the day. After observing for a few minutes, she breathed a long, sad sigh as she closed her eyes and her head bowed. She could not believe that her mother was gone. Pain threatened to overwhelm her again and she struggled to push those thoughts out of her mind. She wrapped her arms around her body again when unbidden tears started to well in her eyes.

A sudden scraping sound behind her caused her eyes to open, but before she could turn an arm grabbed her from behind. It locked around her, pinning her arms down. She tried to kick at her attacker when he lifted her off her feet as if she weighed nothing.

"Kae--!" Another hand clamped down over her mouth and nose with a cloth covered in a strong-smelling potion. Rin held her breath and tried to wiggle free. She knew that whatever was on that cloth was going to knock her out if she breathed it in. After only a few moments she could feel her head starting to spin and her vision blurred. She tried again to call for Kaedin, but the cloth muffled her cries. Kicking as hard as she could, she managed to hit the man in the shin. He grunted at the blow but did not loosen his grip and she lost consciousness.

The man kept the cloth over her face for another few seconds to be certain that she was really out before he put it back in his pocket. He tossed her over his shoulder and moved toward the edge of the balcony. After only a couple of steps, he gasped in shock before he dropped to the floor dead.

Kaedin pulled his katana free and moved to check on Rin when he staggered backwards to avoid the blade of a great sword. He regained his footing and found that he was surrounded by seven more humans. They were all huge like the one dead on the floor. Their great swords were in their hands as they rushed him. Kaedin dove to the side and managed to get out of the middle before he rotated in an attempt to get them in each other's way. It was difficult to maneuver in such tight quarters and Kaedin was forced to jump back to avoid a blade. After dodging it, Kaedin slipped forward causing two of them to stab each other. He slipped under both blades and brought his katana up to block another. Risking a split-second glance, his face paled when he saw one of the humans trying to climb over the balcony edge with Rin. Cursing under his breath, he tried to make his way toward Rin but two of the humans launched at him. He was able to block one of the blades, but the other caught his arm. Twisting to his right, he stepped back to keep the blade from going deeper into his arm while bringing his katana around. He sliced the closest human across the chest, dropping him to the ground.

A sudden cry from the edge of the balcony caused Kaedin to look toward the sound. A momentary sense of relief washed over him when he saw that Hikaru had joined him, but it was short lived. The human carrying Rin fell backwards with Hikaru's blade through his chest. He lost his grip on her and she fell onto the railing before tumbling over the edge. Kaedin's heart felt like it stopped for a split second before Hikaru leapt off the balcony after her. Kaedin turned his attention back to the remaining three humans. He knew Hikaru was going to need his help to get Rin back up safely.

The remaining humans were being much more cautious as they tried to edge around and surround him. He shifted and mirrored their steps so that one of them was between him and the others. Taking a quick step to the right, he swung his katana at the nearest human. The human brought up his great sword and blocked the blow before he tried to swing it to the side. As soon as he was open, Kaedin stabbed his blade into his chest and the human crumpled to the ground. Kaedin pulled his katana back and barely managed to block a blow from one of the men left. He stepped to the side and just kept from being ran through by the third man's sword, but it caught him across the stomach, leaving a long, deep gash. Twisting to the left, he brought his katana around and killed the man who had just injured him. He staggered and dropped to a knee. The last man rushed in and raised his sword over his head to deliver a killing blow. Kaedin forced himself to leap toward him and he stabbed his katana into the man's stomach. The man stumbled backwards and Kaedin pushed him with his shoulder. Unable to stop his backwards momentum, the man tripped and tumbled over the balcony railing. Once the man was gone, Kaedin ran to the rope that was attached to the railing and peered over the side.

Hikaru jumped over the edge of the balcony when he saw the human drop Rin. He fell a short distance before he was able to get a grip on her. As soon as he did, he grabbed the rope beside him to stop their fall. He grimaced as it shredded the skin on his palm, but he did not let go of it. When he finally got them to come to a stop his grip on Rin slipped. Glancing up, his face grew concerned when he realized he could not move. His grip on Rin was not good enough for him to put her over his shoulder and he could not climb with one arm. Cursing under his breath, he tightened his grip on the rope and kept a close eye on everything around them. By the time he saw Kaedin stick his head over the balcony edge, his entire body was beginning to shake.

"Hurry," he called. "She is slipping."

Kaedin did not hesitate and grabbed the rope. He started pulling them up but frowned when he was struggling to keep a good grip on it. Ignoring his injuries, he looped the rope around his waist and started walked backwards. Now that it was anchored around him, he could pull them up. It was still difficult to lift both, but it only took him a few minutes to get Hikaru level with the balcony.

Hikaru glanced at Kaedin before he grimaced. He lifted Rin over the edge and was forced to drop her unceremoniously on the balcony before he pulled himself up the rest of the way. Sitting down with a loud thud, he glanced at his hand while he tried to catch his breath. It would not have been long before his grip gave out. After taking only a moment, he got back to his feet and picked Rin up off the ground.

"We must get out of here," Hikaru said. "There may be more, and you do not appear to be in any condition to continue fighting."

Kaedin grabbed his and Rin's armor and weapons off the floor and the cloth out of the dead human's pocket before he followed Hikaru to the door.

"Lord Wren and the others should be in Lord Ronin's study. We should head there," Kaedin said with a grimace.

Hikaru nodded in agreement and they headed down the hallway toward the stairs. Kaedin was winded by the time they reached the correct floor and he had to pause at the top of the stairs to catch his breath before they could continue. When they entered Ronin's study, they found the rest of the group was already assembled. Kaedin half fell through the door and dropped their gear on the floor. Wren leapt out of his chair and grabbed Kaedin by the arm as he stumbled toward the nearest chair. His shirt was soaked with blood.

"What happened?" Wren asked once he was sitting.

Kaedin pressed both hands against the large wound across his stomach. "Humans attacked us in our room." He moved one hand long enough to give the cloth to Wren. "They used this on Rin."

Wren looked at the cloth before he held it closer to his face to smell it. He jerked his face away from it and coughed a couple times before he glanced at Ronin. "I cannot tell what this is, but it is quite strong." He moved to hand the cloth to Ronin when Hikaru's raised voice interrupted.

"Where were you? We needed you!"

Raven looked up at him from where he was sitting beside Paige. "I was wit--."

"I know you were with her," Hikaru snapped. "There are duties that you should be seeing to and she is not one of them."

"He was injured," Paige said giving Hikaru a dirty look.

"Unless he is dead, he has a duty to protect Lady Rin," Hikaru's voice was hard. "A duty that he has ignored since we returned home. We nearly lost our lady this morning because he was not where he should be." Hikaru paused, his gaze returning to Raven. "I, for one, do not wish to lose my position as her guard. We have been by her side since she was born. Will you ruin this because of her?" His eyes flicked to Paige.

Raven looked back and forth between the two. "I do not wish to give up my position nor do I wish to give up Paige."

"I do not believe that you shall have that option," Hikaru said with an irritated sigh. "You may be forced to choose and if you do, who will you choose Raven?"

Raven did not answer as he stared back at Hikaru. He glanced over when he noticed movement and the color drained from his face. Wren was standing beside Hikaru.

"Is what Hikaru says true?"

Fear flashed across his face as he bowed his head, "Yes, my lord."

"How was Raven's assistance needed?" Wren's voice was hard and stern as he observed the rider pair in front of him. Hikaru looked up at him before he told him everything that took place. When he was finished, Wren's face was filled with severe disapproval.

"I am quite certain that I have already given you a warning about neglecting your duties," Wren said. He paused when Raven glanced up at him and he could see the concern on his face. "This is your last chance. I should replace you now, but I know that my sister cares for both of you. If anything like this happens again, you and Hikaru shall be replaced. Do you understand?"

"Yes, my lord," Raven said as his gaze returned to the floor in front of him. Wren was not satisfied with the answer but the door of the study opening drew his attention. He watched Lyra hurry into the room and make her way over to Kaedin. When she finished healing him and Hikaru's hand, he handed her the cloth.

"They used this on Rin," he said. "Do you know what it is?"

Lyra lifted it but before she got it anywhere near her face, she jerked it back. "That is quite strong. She could be out for days without the antidote." She paused with a frown. "I am not certain that I can get it. The ingredients for the antidote are difficult to find."

"What is it called?" Wren asked. His brows furrowed when he could see the frustration on her face as she thought.

"I cannot remember the common name but the substance on the cloth is derived from a night lily. It is a highly poisonous flower. The antidote is a mixture of several herbs but predominantly makae tree bark, which is quite rare."

Wren opened his mouth to reply but paused when they heard a draw open. He looked over and saw Ronin rummaging through a small drawer in his desk. When he found a tiny bottle that appeared like it was centuries old, he held it out to Lyra.

"I believe this is made from makae bark," he said. "This was my father's."

Lyra walked over and took the bottle from his hand. She pulled the stopper from the top and smelled the contents.

"This will do to wake her," she said with a satisfied nod. "I shall have to give her the additional herbs once she is awake." Moving over to Wren, she held the bottle out to him. His eyebrow raised in confusion. "Waking up after a night lily potion can be confusing. It would be best for someone close to her to wake her." She paused and glanced at Kaedin. "I do not believe it would be wise for Kaedin to attempt it since he was just injured. She might accidentally harm him."

Wren took the bottle and sat down beside Rin on the couch. "What do I need to do?" He asked as looked back over his shoulder.

"Hold the bottle in front of her face," Lyra replied. "She will attempt to get her face away so be prepared."

Wren frowned again before he got a gentle, yet firm grip on his sister's face before he put the bottle close to her nose and waited. After a couple of minutes, he looked back up at Lyra.

"She is really out," she said, her voice concerned. "Stay with it, she shall wake eventually."

Several more minutes passed before Rin began to cough and tried to get her face away from the bottle. Wren kept her head still but the longer it continued Rin started to breathe in wheezing gasps between coughs.

"Do not stop," Lyra said. "She should wake any moment."

Wren's eyes were filled with worry, but he did what Lyra instructed. Another couple minutes passed and Rin's breathing eased before she finally opened her eyes. She pushed at the hand holding onto her face. Wren let go but he could see that she was disoriented and agitated.

"Rin."

She tried to look up at him but could not focus. Her vision was still too affected by the potion. "Wren?" She asked, her voice slurred.

"She is fine," Lyra said when Wren looked back up at her. "I will give her the additional herbs, but it shall take hours if not a day or two for it to be out of her system. She will be groggy, disoriented, and her vision will be affected. I would not recommend leaving her alone."

"K.. Kae…din?" Rin's slurred voice interrupted.

Wren stood up when Kaedin appeared beside the couch and he took his place. "I am here." He took hold of her hand as soon as she tried to reach out to him. She became less agitated as soon as he touched her.

"Do not allow her to sleep for several hours or you will have to use the potion again to wake her," Lyra said, pulling Wren's attention back to her. "She shall need plenty of fluids and…" She trailed off when Wren raised an eyebrow. "If you wish, I could remain and keep an eye on her."

"Yes, please do so," Wren said, his voice grateful.

Lyra nodded with a small smile before she moved over to where Rin and Kaedin were still on the couch. Wren watched her for a moment before he looked to his side and found Ronin was waiting on him.

"The city has been sealed," Ronin said once he had his attention. "Any remaining humans, other than your guests, are being removed."

"Is there somewhere we can stay where we are all together? I do not wish to split up until we are certain that the city is secured."

295

Ronin thought for a moment. "Yes, though it is rarely used and may need to be cleaned up. The floor above us has a large common area with several smaller rooms attached to it. There are no balconies so the only way onto the floor is one staircase."

"That will do," Wren said with a heavy sigh. "I apologize for all the difficulties we are causing you."

Ronin could not help but chuckle. "I suppose I shall consider it payback for the years of trouble I caused for you."

"With my sister's help of course," Wren said with a half-smile and Ronin grinned in response. "I believe that we shall head up there now. The meeting shall have to wait until Rin is recovered."

"I figured as much," Ronin said as the smile slipped off his face. "I shall send someone up to fetch anything that you need."

Wren nodded and held out his arm to Ronin. The two grasped forearms. "Thank you."

Ronin shook his head. "No thanks are necessary. You and Rin are family to Riku and I, so make this as much like home as you wish."

Wren released his arm with a small head bow before he looked over at Kaedin. He watched the grimace flash across his face when he picked Rin up off the couch. Wren started to ask him if he wished for someone else to carry Rin but stopped. He just shook his head and turned his attention to the others.

"Follow me," he said before he headed out of Ronin's study. They all filed out of the room and followed him down the hallway.

It was nearing midnight when Sara woke up. She laid awake for a while before it became apparent that she was not going to be able to fall back asleep. Sitting up with a heavy sigh, she decided to return to the common room and read by the fire. After putting on a pair of silver flats she pushed the door to her room open. She paused and looked around the room as she tried to remember where the bookcases were located.

The large room she scanned had several large, thick black rugs that covered the floors while the walls were all bare stone. There were numerous chairs all around the edges of the room and a large table running down the center. Four smaller rooms were off the main hall and contained three single beds in each. On the wall space between the doors to the rooms, a large fireplace was on the far back wall and bookcases lined the other spaces.

Sara crossed the room and headed for the bookcase closest to the fireplace. There was still a large fire burning and it gave off enough light that it illuminated the books. She was so focused on the bookcase that she did not notice the faint light coming from the room just on the other side of the fireplace. When she heard the sound of hushed voices, she jumped in surprise and could not help but peek into the room. Her eyes widened when she saw Wren sitting on the edge of a single bed with Lyra beside him. He held one of her hands in his. Sara bit her lip and tried to turn her attention to the books, so she could find one before they noticed her near the doorway.

"Are you all right?" Lyra's quiet voice could just be heard from where Sara was standing. "I have been so worried since I learned of your mother."

"I am as well as can be expected," he said, his voice cracking. "I never could have imagined that he would do something like this."

Lyra slipped her hand out of his and wrapped both arms around him. He stiffened for a moment before he leaned enough that his head rested against her.

"I apologize that I could not come to you sooner," she whispered. "I knew this would be difficult."

Wren sighed before he sat back, and her arms slipped off. "Lyra I--."

"I know," she said. "However, that does not change the fact that I am your match and I shall support you as I see fit."

"You should find someone who can make you happy. I fear that I never will," he whispered.

Lyra folded her arms across her chest. "I already have. I shall follow my heart and that has always been you. Have your feelings changed?"

"No, my heart is still and always will be yours," he said, his voice soft. "I... I just cannot make you a promise. I spend far too much time on the front lines. I cannot join with you only to leave you alone. I do not wish for you to suffer over me."

Lyra reached up and took his face in both of her hands. "Do you not realize that I shall suffer the same whether we are joined or not? If I were to lose you the pain will not lessen because I am not your ayen."

He reached up and pulled her hands off his face. "I am sorry."

"I know," she said as pain filled her eyes. "I shall wait for you as always."

"Forgive me," he whispered. When she did not say anything else, Wren pulled her toward him and wrapped both arms around her. She rested her head against his chest and closed her eyes with a sigh. The steady beating of his heart soothed the pain coursing through her. He just did not understand, and she did not know how long it would be before he did.

Guilt appeared on Wren's face when he heard her sigh and he tightened his grip. He rested his cheek on her head before a slight movement caused him to glance out the door. When he caught sight of Sara holding a couple books his head snapped up. His eyes narrowed, and she spun and bolted. She did not stop running until she was back inside her room. Sara scrambled back into bed and covered her entire body with the blankets. She held her breath in the silence and it was several minutes before she relaxed a little bit. Tears started to rim her eyes when she realized she had heard something she was not supposed to and felt terrible about it. Those feelings soon started to turn to panic and she prayed that Wren would not be angry with her.

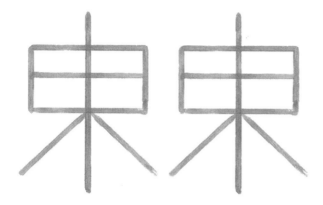

*E*arly the next morning, Rin woke with a pained groan. Her head was pounding, and the room was trying to spin. She opened her eyes and glanced around. She found that if she did not try to turn her head too fast the dizziness was tolerable until she tried to sit up. When she attempted to sit, her head spun causing her stomach to lurch. She snatched the bucket, sitting beside her bed, off the floor and started vomiting into it. Once she was finished, she noticed a soft hand on her shoulder pushing her back down.

"Be still," Lyra said as she took the bucket from her. "You are not ready to be up yet. I am surprised that you are awake already, though, I suppose that is because you are accustomed to pushing yourself far too hard." She paused and set the bucket on the floor. "You must remain in this bed for a few more hours and rest."

Rin swallowed hard a few times trying to keep from vomiting. "What happened?" She asked when she could safely speak.

"There shall be plenty of time for explanations later. For now, just rest." When Rin tried to give her a dirty look but could not manage and Lyra's eyes filled with concern. "Do you have a headache?"

Rin did not answer the question. "Where is Kaedin?"

Lyra pressed her lips together in irritation as she looked down at her. "He is fine and sleeping. Do you have a headache?" When Rin still did not answer Lyra folded her arms across her chest. "As stubborn as your brother. Lady Rilaeya, do you have a headache?"

Rin's eyes widened in surprise. No one other than her mother ever used her given name. While it was proper for Lyra to use it since she was almost as old as her brother, it caused a pang of pain to run through her chest. "Yes," she mumbled after a few moments.

"How bad?"

"It is pounding and makes me sick," Rin said with a frown.

"Remain in that bed and I shall return in a moment," Lyra said, her voice firm, as she stood up and hurried to the door. Her concern was no longer concealed once she was outside the room and searched for Wren. She needed that cloth again.

"What is it?" Wren asked warily when he saw her approach, he knew something was amiss by the look on her face. She stopped walking when she stood beside him, but she did not say anything right away. Her gaze turned to the others around the table. "They have my trust."

"I need that cloth again," She said once she received his approval. "I am afraid that I may have missed something."

"Why? What is wrong?"

"She is still having vision issues and has a bad headache. A night lily potion does not cause a headache and her vision should have returned to normal by now."

Wren's face clouded with worry, "I do not have the cloth. Ronin and I did not think it would be needed and it was destroyed." He paused with a frown. "Could it just be that it is due to it being so strong?"

"That is possible," Lyra said with a sigh. "I suppose I shall have to treat the symptoms and I pray that will be enough." She started to drift toward the stairs. "I must return to the healing ward and collect some supplies. Please see to it that she remains in bed. She has already attempted to sit up and caused herself to be sick.."

"I shall see to it," Wren said as he stood up from his chair. Once Lyra disappeared down the stairs he headed toward his sister's room.

Sara sighed out loud with relief when Wren left the table. She was so uncomfortable around him.

"What is wrong?" Jake asked. She glanced up at him but did not say anything. "Did something happen?" His voice grew wary when he watched her start wringing her hands with nervous energy. She opened her mouth several times to say something, but nothing came out. She knew Wren would not want her to say anything, but she did not want to keep secrets from Jake.

"I... I saw something I shouldn't have," she blurted after several moments.

Jake tilted his head and narrowed his eyes, but before he could reply someone clearing his throat caught their attention. They both looked up and found Wren standing beside the table again. He had forgotten the book he was reading before heading to Rin's room.

Sara turned bright red and her gaze dropped to the table. Wren tilted his head with a raised eyebrow before he sighed.

"Miss Sara, come with me," he said.

She cringed and started to fidget with her sleeve as she stood up. Jake opened his mouth to protest.

"Jacob, this does not concern you. It shall only take a moment," Wren said. He looked back at Sara and gestured toward her and Paige's room. She dropped her head and shuffled her feet as she followed him. Once inside, he closed the door.

"I'm so sorry," Sara mumbled. "I didn't mean to see anything. I couldn't sleep and was just trying to find a book."

"Stop," Wren said, and she fell silent. "I am not angry with you." Her eyes were filled with disbelief when she peeked up at him and he sighed. "Sara, I am a very private person and I do not wish for my private life to be known by everyone. If you must tell Jacob then so be it, but you must stop being so nervous around me. I could tell the moment I saw you this morning." He paused with a frown. "Everyone is going to notice something is amiss." She looked back at the floor to hide her embarrassment. "Is this agreeable to you?" He kept his voice as soft as possible. Knowing she was painfully shy, he did not wish to press her too hard.

"Yes," she whispered, but still did not look back up at him.

"Good," he replied, his voice relieved. "Now, I believe that you should rejoin Jacob. I am certain that he is most unpleased with me." His amused smile when he mentioned Jake caused Sara to relax. A small smile crossed her face when she knew he was right about Jake. Wren opened the door for her, and she headed back over to the table. She sat back down beside Jake just as Wren disappeared back into his sister's room. Jake watched her sit back down and waited for her to say something. She leaned closer to him.

"He just wanted to say he wasn't mad at me," she whispered. "I accidentally saw him with Lyra when I was trying to find a book." She paused and peeked up at him. "He said I could tell you, but I have to stop being so nervous when he is around." She shrugged when she was finished and started to fidget with the sleeve on her gown. Jake took hold of her hand to get her to stop.

"The healer, huh?" He whispered, and her eyes grew wide with concern. "I won't say anything, I promise." When he felt her relax, he leaned over and kissed her on the cheek. Her cheeks flushed as soon as he touched her, and he could not help but smile.

"Where is Lord Wren?" A sudden stern, angry voice filled the room, causing Jake and Sara to look up. They found a regal looking woman standing at the top of the stairs. Her arms were folded across the beautiful, bluish silver gown she wore. The lining inside the sleeves was white as well as the knotwork along the hemline. Her long silver and light brown hair was braided in an ornate fashion and tied with a white ribbon. Her light blue eyes were ice cold as she regarded them.

"I shall fetch him, my lady," Hikaru said as he jumped up from the table and headed toward Rin's room, but he only made it part way across the room when the door opened. Wren stepped out and looked over at the woman.

"Lady Shiokae," he said with a slight bow. "To what do I owe the pleasure?" The words he spoke were polite, but those who knew him well could hear the undertone of displeasure. Hikaru and Raven exchanged concerned glances.

"I have heard vicious rumors that you brought that child here," Shiokae snapped. "If that is the truth, I want her out of this city. She is not welcome here."

Wren jerked the door closed with a loud thud. "Forgive me, my lady, I do not believe that you have that authority. Only his majesty can make that sort of decision."

"Do not dare disrespect me in my own city," she said, her voice rising. "I have authority enough to banish one that is not welcome in my home."

Wren glanced back at the door behind him. He did not wish for Rin to hear any of this. She had far too much to deal with right now. "I mean no disrespect; however, I shall honor no such requests unless I hear them directly from his majesty."

As if on cue, Ronin hurried into the room. He took a moment to catch his breath when he stopped beside Wren.

"Mother, what are you doing?" He asked, his voice unhappy. Shiokae turned to face her son.

"I wish for that bastard child to be removed from this city at once," she said, her voice ice cold. "She is not welcome here."

"Absolutely not," Ronin said, his voice taking on a sharp tone. "She is my sister and shall be treated as such."

His mother was so furious that she balled her hands into tight fists. "I shall hear none of this nonsense about you having a sister. You do not have a sister. I would know."

Ronin narrowed his eyes, "Mother, if you do not wish to or cannot acknowledge the truth then I can do nothing for you. Riku and I have a sister, and it would be well that you make your peace with it and accept it." He paused with a frown. "I do not wish to be at odds." He stood up fully and gave no ground when his mother took a step toward him.

"My, that boy has quite a good head on his shoulder." Everyone looked toward the stairs and watched Myrabelle walk into the room. "What is all this nonsense I heard on my way up here?"

"This does not concern you," Shiokae snapped, with a look of disdain.

"Shiokae, if you intend to try and banish that child then you better believe that it involves me. I care for that child like a daughter and she does not deserve your ire. She had nothing to do with the choices of the adults who brought her into this world and has only suffered because of them. Now, act like an adult and not a spoiled child."

Ronin balked at Myrabelle's words as his gaze returned to his mother and he found her frozen in shock. Her mouth hung open for a few moments before she snapped it closed and her eyes narrowed.

"I do not believe anyone has ever dared to speak to me in such a disrespectable manner and it would be wise for you never to do so again."

Myrabelle crossed her arms over her chest and chuckled. "I shall speak to you however I see fit, especially if you are being a fool." She chuckled again when Shiokae's expression turned murderous. "Do not think that you can intimidate me. I have been around just as long as you have."

Shiokae's hands clenched into fists before she spun and stormed out of the room without another word. Ronin watched her leave before he sighed and glanced over at Wren.

"I apologize, I did not make it in time to stop her," he said.

"I did not believe that your mother was such a fool," Myrabelle said as she grabbed Ronin in a hug. "How are you boy?" She looked up at him and was unfazed by the look of surprise on his face. After a few seconds, he shook his head with a light chuckle and returned her hug. No one just grabbed him for a hug anymore.

"I am well," he said.

She stepped back and looked him over before she released him. "I suppose, though you look too thin."

Ronin was grateful when her attention turned away from him. She looked toward the stairs when she heard a noise and found Lyra hurrying up them, her arms loaded with several potion bottles and herbs. She stopped in surprise before a huge grin spread across her face when she saw Myrabelle.

"What in the world do you need all that for?" Myrabelle asked as she stepped forward and took some of the potions from her.

"Lady Rin," Lyra replied.

"Well, what happened?" Myrabelle demanded when Lyra did not continue. Lyra flushed a light pink before she hurried to tell the older woman what had happened. When she was finished and looked up at Myrabelle, she could see that she as deep in thought. After a few minutes, Myrabelle looked over at her.

"Have you checked for discoloration of the nail beds or eyes?"

Lyra shook her head no. "I was uncertain what else to check for."

"I guess we had better go and have a look," Myrabelle said with a sigh. "Make sure that you pay attention this time. I shall not be around forever." The two disappeared into Rin's room as Ronin and Wren shared an amused glance. They were both relieved they were not on the receiving end of one of Myrabelle's lectures this time.

Several hours passed before Myrabelle took her leave to go and settle into her own room. Lyra was still sitting with Rin when Wren walked back into the room. Kaedin glanced up from the book he was reading but when he saw it was Wren his attention went back to the book.

"How is she?" Wren asked, keeping his voice quiet. He could see that his sister was asleep and did not wish to wake her.

"She is doing much better now thanks to Myrabelle," Lyra replied with a frustrated sigh. "I missed the fire lace flower, but she has now had the appropriate herbs to counteract it and should be back to normal by morning."

"Thank you for tending her."

Lyra peeked up at him before she shrugged. "It is my job." When Wren raised an eyebrow, she sighed again. "You are most welcome." She looked away from him and returned her attention to Rin.

"I am surprised that she is asleep," Wren mused aloud a few minutes later.

Lyra chuckled, "It was not by choice. Myrabelle forced her to drink the sleeping draught. I am quite sure she will be most cross when she wakes."

Wren glanced up at Kaedin, who gave him a serious nod and he laughed. He could only imagine what his sister was going to say when she woke up. "Myrabelle does know what is best, hopefully, she will remember that in the morning." Lyra chuckled with a nod and the two fell silent. Wren watched his sister for a few more minutes before he headed back into the common room.

When he entered, he noticed Paige talking to Raven on the other side of the room. She was attempting to talk him into going for a walk, being cooped up in one room was driving her crazy. Raven glanced up and saw Wren. His shoulders dropped before he looked back at Paige, and once again shook his head no. Hurt flashed across her face before she stormed across the room and down the stairs alone. Raven watched her go with a conflicted look on his face before he sighed and looked down at the floor in front of him.

Wren glanced at Jaeha who was near the stairs. Jaeha bowed his head a little before he headed down the stairs after Paige. It did not take him long to catch up with her.

"Where are you headed?" He asked as he fell into stride next to her.

Paige started in surprise, but when she realized it was Jaeha she relaxed. "I don't know."

"You cannot just wander the city alone," Jaeha said with a sigh. "What would happen if one of the guards mistook you for one of the humans they have removed from the city?"

"I didn't think about that," she said as she slowed. "I did try to get someone to go with me." She folded her arms across her chest.

"Come over here and sit down." He indicated a bench in front of a large window overlooking the city. She hesitated before she followed him and they both sat down on the bench.

"Do you care for Raven?" Jaeha asked after several minutes of silence passed between them.

"Of course, I do," Paige replied without a moment of hesitation.

Jaeha's expression grew serious and Paige shifted when he started to make her nervous. "If you care for him, then you must allow him to perform his duties without fearing he will lose you."

Her eyebrows furrowed in confusion, "I don't understand."

"Paige, think about it," he said, his tone becoming softer. "Raven has known nothing other than protecting Lady Rin for the last four hundred years. Now, he meets you and it is obvious that he cares for you, but he has neglected his duties." He paused and took a moment to formulate his words. "You must allow him to do his duties or you must let him go."

Paige looked up at him with a scowl. "Why are you saying all of this? Do you want me to let him go?" Her voice was filled with anger and a hint of fear. The idea of breaking things off with Raven caused her eyes to start to tear.

"No, I do not wish to see that happen," Jaeha said with a sad smile. "I only tell you this so that you know what is at stake and how you may assist him. After Wren's threat, he must be quite confused about what path to take." Paige's expression grew more angry at the mention of Wren. Jaeha noticed and chuckled. "Do not be cross with Wren. It would not be an easy decision for him to replace Hikaru and Raven. They are quite close to Lady Rin."

"Why would he have to replace them both?" Paige asked as she folded her arms across her chest again. "It's not like Hikaru couldn't do it on his own."

Jaeha tilted his head. "They are a rider pair. Did you not realize this?" When Paige shrugged Jaeha's brows furrowed. "They are bonded the same as Wren and me. If Raven is replaced, then Hikaru must be also. A new rider pair would take their place."

Paige's face flushed with embarrassment. She had not realized they were a rider pair and felt very foolish. "That would explain why Hikaru was so mad," she mumbled.

"Yes, it certainly does," Jaeha said with a nod. "I am uncertain if you have noticed, but Hikaru is quite laid back. He has a very calm personality which makes him a good bonded for Raven's more spontaneous nature. They work well together and Hikaru rarely gets angry. It takes quite a lot to break his calm exterior."

Paige let out a large sigh as she stood back up. "I guess I have some talking to do." She did not wait for Jaeha and started back for the common room. He got up and hurried after her. When they arrived back in the common room, Raven sighed in relief when he saw that Paige had returned. He did not move toward her and watched as she walked up to him.

"Can we talk a minute?" she asked. His expression grew wary, but he nodded. The two went into Paige's room and closed the door.

The rest of the day was quiet and uneventful and by evening everyone was getting a little stir crazy from being forced to remain in the common room for two days. After noticing their discomfort, Wren agreed to show them around the city. He took Jake, Paige, Sara, and Jaeha with him and headed to the marketplace. It was crowded, and many suspicious looks were thrown their direction. Everyone in the city knew about the eviction of the humans.

Sara interlaced her fingers with Jake's and edged closer to him when all the suspicion directed at them was making her uncomfortable. He glanced down before he squeezed her hand and pulled her closer to him. They followed Wren while he introduced them to several vendors that outfitted his men before he stopped for a while at the fountain. He spoke with several rider pairs who came up when they saw him. Once he was finished, they headed back toward the common room. They were part way back to their floor when a soldier came sprinting up the stairs.

"Lord Wren," he called as he approached them. Wren stopped and looked back. The soldier handed him a slip of parchment. Wren broke the seal, opened it, and started to read. His expression darkened the more of the letter's contents he read.

"Tell them to move here now and evacuate the civilians as they go," Wren ordered. The soldier bowed and sprinted back down the stairs. Wren turned and hurried back to the common room. He walked straight to Rin's room and opened the door.

"How long until the sleeping draught wears off?" He asked Lyra as soon as he was inside.

"It will not wear off until morning at the earliest." She paused with a frown. "What is wrong?"

Kaedin watched when Wren looked down at Rin. The book was now resting in his lap. He could tell by Wren's demeanor that something was wrong.

"I need her awake now," Wren said, his voice short. "Can you do it?"

"I am sure that I can," Lyra said, her voice hesitant. "However, I am not certain how coherent she shall be, and she will have to sleep longer afterward to compensate for being woke early."

Wren just stared at his sister before he sighed in frustration. "Do it." He did not wait for a response before he went back into the common room. "I shall return shortly. Be prepared for a long meeting as soon as I have." He again did not wait for an answer as he disappeared down the stairs.

***

An hour later everyone was assembled around the table in the common room. Ronin and Wren sat on either end, so they could see everyone. Rin was present but was struggling to stay awake. She had her head resting on the table in front of her. It had taken Lyra almost the entire hour to wake her.

"The elven outpost at Vaerylis has been completely destroyed," Wren began, bringing everyone's attention to him. "As of now, the only known survivor is the elven child that made it to Lyrin with the news of the attack."

Rin sat straight up and looked at her brother after hearing the news. "That is quite close to Lyrin." Her concern for her men stationed there was visible.

"My troops and the riders are on their way here as we speak," Wren continued. "The riders should arrive by tomorrow while it shall take my men close to a week with them evacuating any civilians as they make the journey."

"Do we know what attacked the outpost?" Ronin asked.

Wren nodded, and his face grew grave. "The report I received said red and black dragons, orcs, humans, dark elves, and demons."

Ronin froze as his mouth dropped open. He glanced at Riku and his brother's reaction was the same. "They have combined forces?"

"It would seem so," Wren said. "We know that Oragg is involved plus my father, Londar, and Londar's brother, Jyldar. I am not certain yet as to the parts that they play but they are all involved. Londar's brother has been seen in league with an elder red and he already made an attempt on my life. His everdark tipped arrow got Rin instead."

Ronin's eyes widened as he glanced at Rin. He had wondered what had happened to change her appearance so drastically but had not had a chance to ask. His gaze drifted to the table in front of him as he leaned forward. He rested his elbows on the table and put his chin on his thumbs.

"We cannot possibly stand alone against so many," he said after a few minutes. "With your troops and mine, we are strong, but not enough for this. We need assistance."

"There is more than just us that must be considered," Wren said with a frown. "The portal that is allowing the black dragons and demons into Asaetara is connected to another world as well." He paused and held his hand up toward Jake. "The humans who have accompanied me are from this other world. I believe it is called Earth." When Jake nodded, he looked back at Ronin. "Rin knows more than I about their situation and I shall allow her to explain." He glanced at his sister and she propped up her head with her hand before she turned her attention to Ronin.

"Allow me to begin with formal introductions," Rin said. "This is

Ambassador Jacob Riverwood, his sister Paige, and his match, Sara MacCoinnich." She paused when Ronin got out of his chair and walked toward Jake. He extended his hand which Jake accepted after standing as well.

"Well met and forgive me," Ronin said as he released his hand. "I was unaware of your status or would have attempted to garner more suitable housing arrangements."

"The accommodations are more than adequate," Jake replied. "Thank you for allowing us to remain in your city."

Ronin bowed his head in acknowledgment before he returned to his seat. Once he and Jake were both seated, Ronin looked back at Rin and waited for her to continue.

"Jacob accompanied me to bring help back for his world," Rin said. "I was on Earth for many years though I was only aware for the last several months. From what I observed their world is unprepared to handle the enemies that will come through the portal. Before I left I gave them a small amount of our silver that they could use in their weapons." Rin paused, and her brows furrowed. "Their silver is a different compound from ours, which I do not entirely understand how that is possible, but it is useless. At this moment, I am uncertain if the silver I gave them will be effective in their weapons or not."

"What help are you proposing that we give them?" Ronin asked.

"I would like to send them weapons. Their weapons are strange to me and they are quite ineffective against the demons and I am certain they will be quite useless against the dragon's scales." She paused and appeared to ponder something before she continued, "If Caradthrad can spare them, I would like to send a couple thousand katanas along with two hundred of my riders. They will train the humans to use the weapons we send. I fear this is all we can do." She glanced at Jake and he only nodded. He did not know the exact odds, but he could tell that they were outnumbered.

"I believe that we can provide a thousand weapons, but beyond that, we do not have much. Our forges have not been running to full capacity for years," Ronin said as he looked to Riku for verification.

"That is correct. We only have a little more than a thousand weapons in reserve," Riku said. "He is also correct that our forges are not running fully. We lack quite a few raw resources and it has been quite some time since we have prepared for a war. In recent years, the riders and your troops Wren have been all that was required." He gave Wren an apologetic shrug.

"I suspected as much," Wren said with a frown.

"I would recommend those forges be brought to full capacity as soon as possible," Rin said, her face mirrored her brother's.

"Of course," Ronin said, his voice sharp. "But, how did you end up in their world?"

Rin shivered and glanced down when Kaedin reached under the table and took hold of her hand. "That is a long story."

"I must know everything if I am to make the best decision for my people," Ronin said as he leaned back in his chair.

Rin looked to her brother and once he nodded in agreement, she told Ronin what happened to her. When she was finished, he was staring at her with an incredulous look on his face. His gaze fell to the table again and he sat in silence for several minutes before his head snapped up.

"Londar was here a couple of weeks ago," he said as he clenched his hand into a fist. "He did not seek an audience and since I have never cared for him, I did not ask the purpose of his visit."

Wren closed his eyes with a frustrated sigh. "We must check everything. The defenses, gates, forges, almost anything, whatever his purpose it will be to our detriment if we do not find it."

Riku leapt out of his chair and walked over to an aide that was standing just at the top of the stairs. He gave him several orders before the aide dashed down the stairs. Riku returned to the table and a thick silence hung in the air while everyone was deep in thought.

"Jacob," Wren said, finally breaking the silence. "Is the aid that we can offer you acceptable?"

Jake regarded him with a long, hard look. "It'd be totally out of line for me to refuse any type of aid you can offer us." He paused, and a frown crossed his face. "But and I mean no disrespect, how are a few riders and swords going to really help us? No one in my world knows how to use them and even if we train, we'll be like little kids trying to fight."

Rin bristled at her riders being discounted so quickly and she opened her mouth to retort, but Wren raised his hand to cut her off.

"I understand your hesitation," Wren said with a heavy sigh. "If I was in your position, I would feel the same, but what you must realize is that we are proposing sending you some of our most elite men. We desperately need them here if they are not acceptable to you." He paused when Jake shook his head.

"I'm not saying that," Jake said. "I'm concerned that we won't be able to learn, and they'll have to take the burden of the fighting. I understand that they're elite troops but even elite troops tire or get hurt. We don't have healers like yours on Earth."

Wren and Rin exchanged glances. It was obvious that they had not thought about the lack of healers on earth.

"Most of the riders should be able to heal themselves," Rin said. "However, a healer may be a necessity we must send along as well. Sara would be able to get them back through the portal if they need more supplies."

Sara looked up at the mention of her name. She glanced over at Jake and he just shrugged. He did not know what Rin meant either.

"How can the child open the portal?" Ronin asked before Jake had the chance.

"Sara retained a small piece of my magic. The portal recognizes it and will allow her to direct the destination. Since it is not fully active, she and Jacob will have to be the go between for their world and ours."

Sara avoided Rin's gaze when everyone's attention shifted to her. She was not sure she had enough magic to do what Rin expected of her.

"Who is in charge in Jacob's world?" Wren asked drawing their attention back to him.

"Jacob's father, General Riverwood, is in command of the troops that are located around the portal," Rin said with a frown. "However, I intend to put Captain Iliwenys and Jacob in direct control of my riders."

Jake's eyes widened in shock and Wren tilted his head. "Do you have any combat experience?" he asked.

"I have some," Jake replied. "I'm a captain, so I have controlled troops in the past, but I'm a doctor and combat medic. I spend most of my time tending to the wounded."

Wren raised an eyebrow; he had been unaware that Jake was a military officer and a healer. After a moment he shook his head and looked back at his sister. "Why do you not wish for his father to control the riders?"

"I do not trust him," she replied without a moment of hesitation. "He seemed arrogant and overconfident the time that I met with him. I want someone who shall care about the men he risks." She looked over at Jake. He sighed but gave her a small nod. While he was worried she was putting too much faith in him, he would do his very best. He glanced down when he felt Sara squeeze his hand. She gave him a reassuring nod and he relaxed a little bit before a loud knock caused him to look back up.

"Come," Ronin called, and a guard came up the stairs two at a time.

"Pardon the intrusion, your majesty," he said. "There is an old dwarf requesting an audience. He asked for you by name, sir."

"Bring him up," Ronin replied.

A few minutes later the guard returned with two dwarves. The older of the two was leaning on a cane as he hobbled across the room. Ronin stood up when he entered.

"Baldrim," he said with a smile. "What brings you here so late?"

The old dwarf sat down in the nearest chair. "I have heard all sorts of terrible things and I figured you all would need my help." His voice grew gruff. "Cannot leave so much trouble to children."

"Who is with you?" Ronin asked.

Baldrim motioned the younger dwarf to come closer. "This is my nephew Bheldrom. I figured you all would need someone to break the ice if you want dwarven help." He paused as a scowl appeared on his face. "That father of yours was a fool when he insulted the patriarch. They will not be too keen to see an elf." Baldrim noticed Wren's expression darken at the mention of his father. "Speaking of your father, have either of you heard that he is blaming your mother's death on the two of you? He claims that you murdered her."

"What!" Wren and Rin exclaimed together.

"Now, calm down," Baldrim said looking back and forth between the two. "You both know that no one believes a word of it. The people are a little wiser than that." He watched for a moment as the two struggled to get their emotions back under control before he stood up. "We can discuss my nephew heading for Khor Daeruk in the morning. This old dwarf needs some sleep. It was a long walk."

Ronin walked them to the stairs. "Thank you for the assistance. If you are up for it, I would like to discuss getting our forges running fully."

"Of course, my boy," he said with a large grin. "I would be more than happy to assist with that. It has been a long time since I have used such a large, well-crafted forge." He hobbled down the stairs before Ronin could reply. Shaking his head, Ronin turned to return to the table when he heard a sudden thud. He looked over and saw Rin rubbing her forehead. She almost fell asleep and hit her head on the table. Lyra hurried over and handed her a small potion bottle. She drank a small swallow with a slight grimace.

"I told you it was a strong sleeping draught," Lyra said glancing at Wren. "That is the last of that potion I can give her. Once it wears off, she must sleep."

He nodded before he returned his attention to Ronin. "We must know about Rin's magic."

"All I really know are the legends," Ronin began. "They state that one born of silver dragon royalty and elven royalty has the chance to inherit great power. The ability to control elemental magic and time manipulation is what is told." He paused with a tilt of his head. "From what I can remember, the time magic can only affect short periods of time. Minutes at most. I believe that somehow the combination of the elemental and time magic gives the ability to open portals between different times and worlds."

Rin just listened in stunned silence. She still did not believe she really possessed the amount of magic they thought.

"You can see some time magic, correct?" Wren asked.

"Yes," Ronin replied with a nod. "Any silver dragon royalty can see things that are affected by time, but we cannot change anything." He paused and looked over at Paige. "I could tell the child was affected by time magic the first time I met her." She shrugged when everyone looked at her.

"Rin rewound time on her and saved her life," Wren said.

Ronin's eyebrows shot up, "You have already used the magic?"

"I do not know how," Rin whispered. "An older version of myself appeared and she did it somehow through me."

"I fear that you must learn to use these powers," Ronin said. "I believe this is the only way to close the portal."

Wren nodded. "I suspected as much but how does she learn? There is no one who can teach her. Are there any texts on the subject?"

"We lost most of our ancient texts when our uncle was banished to the demon realm," Ronin said with a heavy sigh. "The only way for her to view them would be to travel there and make her way into my uncle's castle."

The entire room went silent before Jake could not keep quiet. "How's your uncle in the demon realm? Isn't he a silver dragon?"

Ronin's expression grew solemn. "My uncle was once a silver dragon but when his family was lost to him, he sought revenge. He used dark magic and fell into darkness. His fate was to change into a black dragon. He is now a powerful king of the entire nation of black dragons." He paused. "I fear that he is the one behind all of this. I believe he intends to use the portal to break into this world so that he may reclaim his ancestral home."

"I believe that you are correct," Wren said, his voice quiet. "I also suspect that since they have not started the invasion and keep attempting to take Rin, the portal must not be fully active. The demons and dragons that have made the crossing are all small and weak."

Rin looked up at the mention of the portal again. She stuck her hand into her pocket and pulled out the small black book with the willow tree on the cover. "Do either of you recognize these letters?" She showed them the drawing of the letters she had copied down from memory.

Ronin looked at them before he shook his head. "No, I cannot say that I do. Where did you see this?"

"In the cave, where Londar started all of this," Rin whispered, and Ronin frowned at the mention of Londar.

"How do you two not recognize this?" Riku asked. Ronin glanced back over his shoulder and found his brother standing behind him. "That is the language we made up as children."

Rin's eyes widened as her gaze flew back to the lettering. "I cannot remember it anymore. It has been far too long. Can you still read it?"

Riku reached over and picked up the book. He tilted his head as he studied it for several minutes. "Memories fade," he said. "One will appear to open the way. Two worlds descend into chaos. Fate decided by blood. Good or evil reigns. Two worlds fall or rise by one."

"The other one?" Rin asked, her voice a barely audible whisper.

Riku turned the page and saw the shorter transcription of another inscription. "The path is open. Beware! Death awaits the unprepared." He handed the book back to Rin before she fell into deep thought. The messages were warnings to give them a head start about what was coming and her failure to be able to read it could have ruined the advantage.

Everyone around the table sat in silence while they let the words Riku read to them sink in. It was not long before Sara tried to stifle a huge yawn. She was getting tired. Jake leaned closer to her so that she could rest her head against his shoulder. She covered another large yawn with her hand before she leaned on him.

Rin glanced at the two before she sighed. "We must decide who is undertaking which tasks," she said. "I believe that Raven, Hikaru, and Paige should be the ones to seek assistance from the gold dragons.

"Why?" Wren asked, his voice sharp. "Should they not be with you? And, I believe that Paige should return home with her brother."

"Where I must go, I shall not take them," Rin said as she fought to keep her own concern hidden. "As for Paige, the gold dragons are difficult to get involved with the issues of the world. I believe that they will need her if they are to be successful."

"No," Jake said as he shook his head. "She has been through enough and is going back home."

"Do you really think I could make a difference?" Paige asked, ignoring the dirty look from her brother.

Rin held her gaze for several long moments. "Yes, I believe it shall depend mostly on you."

Paige stared at her for a few seconds before she glanced at Raven. She could see the concern on his face. "Then I will stay."

"Paig--."

"No Jake, they're helping us and if there's something I can do to help them, I'm going to do it." Her eyes filled with determination when she looked up at her brother. He stared back at her before his eyes narrowed in frustration. She was not going to back down and he decided to speak with her about it in private later.

Wren watched in silence before a frown became fixed on his face. He realized he was about to have the same issue with his own sister.

"Rin."

"No," she said. "I must do this if we are to have a chance to close the portal. You know this."

"I will not allow you to go," he said as he folded his arms across his chest.

"How will you keep me in? You could not do it when I was a child, and I have a few more tricks now than I did then."

"I do not know, but I shall," Wren said, his voice raising. "I am not about to allow you to go where Londar has been attempting to take you. You shall be giving them what they need. Do you not see this?"

"Of course I do, but what else can I do? How do we close the portal otherwise?" He gave her a hard look but did not answer. "How Wren?" Her voice raised.

Worry crept across his features and he sighed again. "I do not know."

"Then I shall go," she said, her voice dropping to a whisper.

The worry did not lessen on Wren's face as he glanced at Kaedin behind her. The dragon nodded as soon as he noticed his gaze.

"I go wherever she does," he said, answering Wren's unspoken question.

"I wish this time that you would not follow me," she whispered looking back at him.

"Not a chance," he said without a hint of hesitation.

She stared at him before she sighed. She already knew this would be his answer even though she only wished for him to remain safe in Caradthrad. After a few minutes, she looked back at Ronin. "Who shall accompany Bheldrom? We need someone to represent us to ask for dwarven aid."

"I shall go," Riku said before his brother could reply. "My brother and the generals shall be otherwise occupied."

Ronin looked at his brother and his concern was not concealed. He never liked sending his brother on any mission that could put him in danger. "Are you certain? It could be dangerous."

An amused smile crossed Riku's face. "I am certain I can handle it. If the ladies can fulfill their jobs, I can do this."

"Very well," Ronin said with a frown. "However, you must be the one to inform mother that you intend to leave the city."

Riku grimaced at the mention of his mother. He already dreaded the conversation.

"All that is left is to find a healer willing to accompany my rider's to Jacob's world," Rin said.

"There is no need," Lyra interrupted. "I shall accompany them." She looked over at Ronin, ignoring the blindsided look on Wren's face.

Ronin could not help but glance at Wren. "Lyra, there are plenty of other healers that could accompany them."

"No, there are not many fully trained healers," Lyra said. "Now that Myrabelle has returned that frees me from my duties and I may join them. I shall not send one of the junior healers when they are not prepared."

"Lyra," Ronin started again but she cut him off.

"Are you forbidding me to go, your majesty?" She folded her arms across her chest with a dirty look.

"Of course not," Ronin said, his voice hesitant as he avoided eye contact with Wren. "The healers are always free to come and go as they wish."

"No," Wren said.

Lyra ignored him and looked over at Jake. "You have seen my skills. Will you accept me as the healer to accompany you home?"

Jake glanced back and forth between Rin and Ronin for help. He did not want to make Wren angry with him.

"Absolutely not," Wren said, his voice rising involuntarily.

"Jacob? Is this acceptable?" Lyra repeated as she ignored Wren again.

Jake looked down at the table. "As I said before, I'm not in a position to deny aid that is offered to me."

Lyra nodded in satisfaction. "Very well, then I shall accompany you."

"Lyra!" Wren said.

She again ignored him as she stood and headed toward the stairs. "Please excuse me, if I am to be prepared to leave in the morning, I must go prepare my herbs." She disappeared down the stairs without looking back.

Jake glanced over at Wren and for the first time, he could see that he was upset. It took every ounce of willpower Wren had not to jump up and follow Lyra out of the room. Jake looked away before Wren could look back at him. He did not want to be on the receiving end when Wren said what was on his mind.

Rin covered her smile with her hand so that her brother did not see. She already knew how her brother felt about Lyra, even though he never told her. Her smile widened when she watched Lyra leave the room. Her brother needed someone that could stand up to him. Most of the women who fawned over him at court would have just done what he wanted. Rin knew he needed someone who would challenge him, which is why he gravitated to Lyra.

As she chuckled at her brother's discomfort, she suddenly felt her eyelids beginning to get heavy. She tried to reach for Kaedin when she realized the potion was wearing off but was asleep before she could. Kaedin was paying attention this time, and he caught her before she hit the table. Wren glanced over at the sudden movement.

"It appears as if we are concluded for the night," he said, his voice controlled as he fought to keep his emotions under control.

"That does seem to be the case," Ronin said. "However, there is one more piece of small business. It is not possible to have the weaponry ready to go at first light since it is nearly dawn now. We shall need a day to gather it."

"Very well, we shall leave at first light tomorrow." Wren only waited for Ronin to nod in agreement before he stood, strode across the room, and disappeared down the stairs. The others watched him leave before they all retired to their various room for a few hours of sleep.

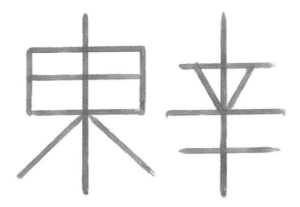

Lyra paused with a heavy sigh when she reached the bottom of the stairs. She glanced back over her shoulder before she headed down the hallway. Her apprehension started to show the longer she walked. She knew Wren was going to be upset with her, but she could not stand the idea of just waiting on him again. Her resolve continued to harden when she turned down a hall that led away from the healing wing. She was determined that she would remain busy and help.

After a fifteen-minute walk, she entered a large open area deep in the mountain. The large park was situated almost a mile from the front entrance. She paused and looked around before she followed the white stone path that branched in many different directions. A faint smile appeared on her face when she reached the ornately carved stone bridge that crossed the large creek. It ran through the whole park before disappearing into the mountain on the south side. She crossed the bridge and headed toward the massive white cherry tree in the center. Staring up at it, she moved around to the far side, that was hidden from the path before she sat down with her back against it. She leaned back and looked up. There was a small carved hole in the ceiling to allow the tree to have sunlight during the day.

She sighed as she allowed her body to relax as she stared up at the sky. A few stars were still visible in the faint early light of dawn. Wrapping her arms around her body to stay warm, she watched the sky as it lightened with the coming of the sun. Her eyes started to grow heavy when the strain of the last two days caught up with her and before she knew it, she drifted off.

Lyra had no idea how much time had passed when she woke with a small yawn. She started to move but frowned when she realized she was quite warm. After she woke up a little more, a small smile crossed her face when she noticed she was wrapped in strong arms. She knew without having to look up that it was Wren.

"You should not sleep alone in the park," he said, his voice soft. He had heard her yawn and knew she was awake.

"I did not intend to sleep," she said.

"Why did you not go to the healing wing as you said?" He asked as his arms tightened around her. "I was worried when I could not find you."

She sighed and tried to sit up, but he would not let go of her. "I knew you would be searching for me and I needed a little time alone."

"Lyra, yo—."

"I have decided that I shall help," she said as she tried to sit up again. He appeared reluctant, but he let her go. "I cannot stand the idea of remaining here and only waiting for you again. I must..." She trailed off when she noticed the many emotions flash across his face.

He reached up and took hold of her face with both hands. "I cannot lose you." His voice held a hint of fear she had never heard him use when he spoke to her.

"Do you enjoy how that fear feels?" She asked, her voice growing hard as she pulled his hands off her face. His brows furrowed before he shook his head no. "Do you realize this is how I feel every time that you leave?" She reached up and brushed her fingers across his cheek. "And, once you return, I must hold back for the sake of propriety. I cannot be at your side fully because you deny me." Her voice cracked, and she turned away from him. His gaze drifted to the creek and he remained silent for quite some time before he took both of her hands in his, causing her to look up at him.

"Forgive me," he whispered. "I have been such a fool." He paused and tightened his grip. "Why? Why have you not told me this before now?"

A sad smile appeared on her face. "Would you have understood before this moment?"

His gaze fell to their hands before he shook his head. "No, I would not have understood, not really," he said. "I always believed that I was doing the right thing." He paused, and his gaze returned to the creek. "When I was young, I witnessed a scout passing away from his injuries. When we journeyed to inform his ayen I was not prepared for the consequences." He tightened his grip on her hands again. "His ayen was so devastated by the loss that she chose eternal sleep over living without him. She did not even stop to consider that she left two small children in her grief. I never wished for anyone to suffer over me like that if I lost my life in battle." He paused again, and his gaze returned to her. "But I understand what you meant. I cannot imagine that I would be more afraid for you if we were joined. If... if you were my ayen these feelings would remain the same."

Lyra could only stare at him. He had never told her the reason he resisted being joined, and only hinted at it over the many long years. When she did not say anything, Wren's shoulders dropped. "Can you forgive me? I know I have caused so much pain for you."

She seemed to snap out of her thoughts when she could hear the pain and guilt in his voice. Leaning closer to him, she kissed him on the cheek. "Of course I forgive you, but you should have told me before, I would have understood." She tilted her head. "What do you plan to do now?" Her voice grew quiet when she asked the question.

"I intend to pledge my life to you for the rest of our days," he said. "I have been a fool for far too long and wish to waste no more time." He lifted a hand off hers and placed it on her cheek. "If you will consent, I shall find Ronin and I will be joined with you tonight."

A smile slowly spread across her face and her eyes rimmed with tears. "Of course," she gasped as she threw her arms around his neck. He wrapped both arms around her in a tight embrace and held her until she sat back. "It took you far too long."

"I know," he said with a heavy sigh. "I shall do anything that is required to make it up to you."

Lyra shook her head. "There is nothing that I require, being by your side is all I have ever desired."

He leaned closer to her and lightly kissed her hair before he pulled a leather cord out of his shirt. It was tied around his neck and had a charm and ring attached to it.

"Is that the charm that I gave you?" she asked.

He nodded, "It has never left me."

"I did not believe that you would keep it with you all the time," she said as she ran her fingers over the small willow tree made of silver.

"I believe it has brought me luck," he said while he retied the cord around his neck after removing the ring.

"I pray that it shall bring you much more luck and will keep you safe so that you always return to me."

He lifted her hand and kissed her fingertips before he stood and pulled her to her feet. "Come with me." He led her out of the park by the hand but walked so fast that she almost had to run to keep up.

"Wren," she gasped after a few moments of struggling to match his long strides.

He slowed and looked down at her before a boyish grin crossed his face. "I apologize, but I did say I wished to waste no more time."

She laughed but was grateful that he slowed his pace so that she could keep up with ease. They traversed the hallways until they reached Ronin's study. Wren knocked on the door before they stood waiting. A couple of minutes passed before Ronin pulled the door open. He just stared at them for a moment before he stepped back and let them in. He appeared to still be half asleep and was in his night clothes.

"What?" He asked through a large yawn.

"I must ask a favor," Wren said. "Would you be willing to join us?"

Ronin's eyes opened wide in surprise before a large grin spread across his face. "It is about time," he said with a laugh.

Confusion appeared on Wren's face. "How do you know about us?"

Ronin laughed again and fought to keep from rolling his eyes. "Who does not know that she is your match?" Another large grin crossed his face when Wren's eyes narrowed.

"I was unaware it was well known."

Once Ronin could stop laughing, he looked back at them. "Would you not rather have a priest join you?"

"I would prefer to have my friend join us," Wren said before he paused and looked down at Lyra. "Of course, if that is acceptable to you."

"Yes, it is acceptable," she said with a smile. "Do not think for a moment that I would give you a chance to change your mind?"

"I would not," Wren said with a frown which made Lyra's smile widen. She did not care who joined them as long as she was finally able to be joined with Wren after so very, very long.

Ronin motioned for them to follow him and they walked further into his study before he paused. A frown crossed his face and he moved back to the door. He opened it and waved a guard to come into the room. They needed a witness. Once the guard was in the study, Ronin performed a quick ceremony where Wren and Lyra exchanged their vows. When it was finished, Wren took the ring and put it onto the middle finger of Lyra's left hand. It was a braid of gold and silver stands that were folded into the shape of a delicate flower. The ring once belonged to Wren's grandmother.

After he put the ring on her finger, Wren pulled her to him and hesitated for a brief moment before he kissed her on the lips. She leaned into him while they shared the first kiss either had ever experienced. They had both held to the strict rules of propriety that was expected in the elven culture.

Ronin glanced away for a few seconds before he shook his head and cleared his throat. Wren lifted his head with a sigh and glanced over at him, "Thank you."

"You are most welcome," Ronin said with a smile. "Now, get out of my study."

Wren chuckled and gave him an exaggerated head bow before he scooped Lyra up into his arms and headed out the door. Ronin watched them disappear down the hall with a smile before he headed back to his room to sleep.

***

Early the following afternoon, Jake, Paige, and Sara were sitting at the table in the common room. Jake was regarding his sister and it was obvious to anyone in the room that he was not happy.

"Home is the best place for you. You shouldn't stay here and risk your life," he said.

Paige rolled her eyes at him. "I've already decided that I'm going to help. Besides it's not like I'll be alone."

"He was there last time and you remember how well that almost ended," Jake said, his voice hardening. "Rin won't be there to save you this time."

"That's not fair, Jake," she snapped as she glared at her brother.

"Yes, it is." They both looked up when Raven's voice cut into their conversation. He stood behind Paige, but his attention was on Jake. "I made a mistake in the cavern, but I swear to you that I shall die before I allow anything to happen to her again."

Jake's expression did not change as he held his gaze. "I'm going to hold you to that since she is too stubborn to do what she should." He paused, and his voice dropped. "If anything happens to my sister…" He trailed off and Raven only nodded. There was no need for Jake to finish the sentence.

Paige looked back and forth between them before she rolled her eyes again. "Good grief you two, everyone needs to chill out. All this stress is going to give you all grey hair." When her brother gave her an exasperated look, she shook her head. "I mean seriously Jake you worry way too much. Wren didn't give Rin nearly as hard of a time as you're giving me and she's going somewhere way more dangerous."

"We have no idea what he's saying to her in private," Jake said with a shake of his head. "And you're not Rin, you're an eighteen-year-old human girl with no fighting skills, not an elven general with magic and wicked fighting skills."

Paige gave him a dirty look. "I'm learning to fight."

Raven grimaced from behind her. He knew her skills were not that great even though she practiced every day.

"Yeah learning, not completely proficient like Rin."

"What about me?" Rin asked from where she was standing in the doorway to her room. Everyone looked over at her.

"I'm trying to get my hardhead sister to go home and explaining why your brother isn't giving you a hard time," he said, his voice unhappy. He was still angry with Rin for encouraging Paige to go.

"My brother shall have a few words for me, I am certain," Rin said with a chuckle. "I have only avoided them for now since I have been asleep."

Paige rolled her eyes. "Yeah, but he doesn't actually expect you to do what he says."

Rin laughed, "Of course, he does, but I am just as stubborn as he, though older brothers are often wiser and smarter than we like to give them credit for. I have on more than one occasion wished I had taken his advice. Be certain to remember what they tell you is because they care for you and do not wish to see you harmed." She paused before she gave Paige a conspiratorial glance. "Do not ever repeat what I have told you. I can never admit any of this to my brother it would cause his head to become far too large."

"Sounds like all older brothers are the same," Paige laughed.

Rin nodded before her attention shifted to Raven and all the playful nature she just displayed disappeared in an instant. "Are you prepared to leave tomorrow?" Her disapproval showed on her face when he shook his head no.

"We shall be prepared, my lady," Raven said.

She frowned but said nothing further before she headed for the stairs. Kaedin appeared beside her as she disappeared down the stairs. She walked through the hallways until she reached Ronin's study and knocked on the door. Once she received permission, she opened the door and walked inside.

"I wondered when you would come," Ronin said as he closed the book he was reading and laid it on his desk. He got up and moved to stand in front of the desk. "Are you certain about this path? It shall be quite dangerous, and you will be beyond our assistance once you are there."

"I do not see that I have any other choice if we are to close the portal. I must have the information that is there."

Ronin could not conceal his concern as he shook his head. He reached behind him and picked up a small brown leather-bound book.

"These are the only maps that I have of the demon realm." He said. "I am uncertain if they will be of use and I do not know if they are out of date." He paused and handed the book to her. "I have a contact by the name of Taeli who may be of assistance. There is a town called Zeixahl near the Zei river. You need to go to the Driest Bone Tavern and tell the bartender, silver bones crumble to pieces of time. He will be able to get in contact with her."

Rin listened intently while he spoke. She had to commit all the information to memory so that she did not endanger the contact.

"I am afraid that is all the assistance that I can provide," Ronin continued with a frown. "Be certain that you both disguise yourselves. I am certain that I do not need to tell you what shall happen if anyone recognizes you."

Rin shivered, "Yes, I know that I have many enemies that would relish in seeing me die in a painful way."

Ronin stepped closer to her and put his hands on her shoulders. "I may not have always known that you were my sister, but I have always cared for you as one. If I do not say this now, I will feel as if I am negligent in my duty to you. Do not go to the demon realm. It is far too dangerous with little chance of success. Remain here and we will find another way."

"I must," she whispered. "We have no way of knowing if there is another way to close the portal and it could take far too long to find out. I will not risk everything and everyone I care for being harmed before we could find the answer."

"You take far too much of the burden upon yourself," he said as he shook his head. "It is a dangerous trait that you share in common with your brother."

"In his case, yes, but I only do what I must."

Ronin raised an eyebrow and again shook his head. "Only what you must? You realize that his answer would be the same as yours."

"Yes, it would," she said with a faint smile. The two fell silent for a few moments before Ronin sighed.

"Look over what I have given you and ask any questions you may have tonight. I shall bid you farewell in the morning." He pulled her into a hug before he stepped back and released her. His gaze turned to Kaedin. "Be certain that she returns to us."

Kaedin bowed his head to him before he followed Rin out of the study. Ronin watched them go and stared at the door once they were gone. It was several long minutes before he looked away. He wanted nothing more than to keep those important to him inside the city where he could keep them safe. Shaking his head again, he returned to his desk and picked up his book.

Rin and Kaedin made their way back to the common room. When they walked up the stairs, Rin paused and scanned the room. Her eyebrow rose before she looked up at Kaedin.

"Have you seen my brother today?" she asked. Once he shook his head no, she looked toward Jaeha, who was sitting in a corner with an open book. He glanced up when he heard her speak. "Jaeha, where is Wren?"

He hesitated before he closed the book in his hand. "I have not seen him this morning." Shifting his gaze away from her, he tried to keep his face as blank as possible.

Rin's eyes narrowed as she watched him. "I must speak with him about plans for tomorrow."

"My lady, I believe he is occupied," Jaeha replied before a small smile slipped across his face and Rin's eyebrow shot up.

"What do you know that I do not?" she asked.

Jaeha could not help but smile. "I really am not at liberty to say, my lady." He paused and his smile widened. "Besides, I do not wish to be on the receiving end of your ire."

Her eyebrow rose again before she spun around and headed for the stairs. Jaeha jumped out of his chair and grabbed her arm.

"Where are you going, my lady?"

She looked up at him with a sweet smile and he grimaced. "I am going to find my brother, or you could tell me what you know."

Jaeha started shaking his head no. "My lad--."

"Tell me."

He swallowed hard before he sighed. "Your brother was joined with Lady Lyra this morning. He is with her."

Rin's mouth dropped open in disbelief before her expression changed to one of indignation. "He joined to Lyra without me?" When Jaeha nodded, she turned and tried to walk away but he still had hold of her arm.

"My lad--."

"Release my arm," she snapped.

He stared at her for a second before he let go of her arm and she stormed down the stairs. Kaedin and Jaeha exchanged worried glances before they hurried after her. She was already almost out of sight when they made it down the stairs. Without acknowledging either of them when they caught up to her, Rin headed straight for Lyra's rooms. When she reached them, she knocked on the door hard several times making it rattle on the hinges.

"Wren!" she yelled. She waited for a minute and when she got no answer her eyes narrowed in irritation. "I know you are in there! Do not make me break the door. You know that I can, and you must speak with me now!" She kicked the door to add emphasis to her words and only had to wait a few moments before the door flew open. Her annoyed brother stood in the doorway.

"What in the world are you doing?"

She folded her arms across her chest. "You were joined without telling me?"

"How di--?"

"It does not matter how I know," she snapped at him. "What matters is that you were joined without telling me. I have known for years that Lyra was your match and I never said a word. How? How could you do this? I have now missed a very important event in my brother's life!"

Wren just stared at her while she yelled at him. He seemed to be having trouble fathoming why she was so upset with him. "I did not think you would care so much," he mumbled.

Her mouth again dropped open in disbelief. "What? How could I not care?" She paused, and her eyes narrowed. "Does this mean that if Kaedin and I are joined without you then that is fine?"

"No, of course, that would not be acceptable."

"Then why would it be acceptable for you?" She demanded as she glared up at him. Wren was again just staring back at her, he was at a momentary loss for words. Jaeha covered his mouth while he tried to contain his laughter. He still found it amusing that this tiny little girl could make her older brother squirm.

"Lady Rin, we will be having a full ceremony later," Lyra's voice interjected into their conversation. Wren's eyes widened in surprise as he looked down at her.

"Do not try and rescue my brother," Rin said, her voice sharp. "He does not deserve it."

"I am not attempting to rescue him," Lyra said with a chuckle. "I do believe that your ire is well placed."

"Lyra?" Wren said in exasperation and she laughed.

"However, what I said before is the truth," she continued. "I just have not yet discussed it with him." She smiled up at him and he shook his head.

Rin glared at him before she stomped her foot on the ground in anger. "I suppose that will be better than nothing, but you are in no way forgiven!"

Wren raised both eyebrows, "You have not stomped your foot since you were a child."

"That is because you have not made me so angry since then," Rin snapped before she turned on her heel and stormed down the hallway. Kaedin glanced at Wren before he ran after her.

Wren watched her for a minute before he shook his head and glanced over at Jaeha. His eyes narrowed, "This was your fault, was it not?"

"Perhaps," Jaeha replied with a noncommittal shrug.

"Why did you tell her?"

"She did not entirely leave me any choice," Jaeha said with a half-smile. "She is far too observant for her own good."

Wren gave him a look of disapproval before glancing down at Lyra. "And you, are you not supposed to be on my side?"

"I am," she laughed. "However, I must also know when it is a lost cause and I am sorry to say when it comes to your sister yours is a lost cause."

He shook his head. "The women in my life shall be the death of me," he muttered under his breath. Jaeha chuckled and nodded before he headed back up the hallway. Lyra looked up at Wren once he was gone.

"You should go speak with her," she said. "This must be patched up before she goes…" She trailed off, unwilling to say the demon realm.

Wren's expression darkened. "I had almost managed to forget where she was intending to go. The joy of today had overshadowed all of my worries." He paused with a heavy sigh. "Unfortunately, it appears that reality has returned." He leaned down and kissed Lyra when she looked up at him.

"I shall go and speak with her. Will you wait for me here?"

"I would like nothing more, but I must prepare all of my herbs for tomorrow." She frowned when she saw the worry on Wren's face.

"Will you grant me one request?"

"That depends what you are requesting," she replied, her voice growing wary.

"Allow me to assign a rider pair to you."

Lyra tilted her head while she studied his face. "Will that make you more at ease?"

"Yes."

"I shall not like it," she said with another frown. "But, for you, I will allow it."

When she agreed, Wren sighed in relief and he leaned over and kissed her again. "I shall find you later." Once she nodded, he turned and walked down the hall. Lyra watched him until he was out of sight before she headed in the opposite direction. She had to prepare her herbs and potions for the next day.

Wren walked down the hallway deep in thought. His brows furrowed while he reasoned out where his sister would go. If they were home, she would go somewhere outside when she was upset. He headed for the park when he realized that would be as close as she could get inside the city. When he entered from the northern entrance he paused and scanned the part that he could see. He walked toward the tree in the center when he realized that his assumption was correct. Rin was sparing with Kaedin in the large open area around the tree.

"Rin," he said when he got within earshot.

She did not acknowledge that he said anything, even though Kaedin paused in the sparring. Turning her back to him, she started to walk away when Kaedin would not resume. Wren shook his head and tried to grab her arm. She spun and smacked his hand away with a scowl.

"I do not wish to speak with you." She again turned her back to him and started to walk away. He took several large steps and slid in front of her, so she had to pause to keep from running into him. Without looking up, she stepped to the side and tried to walk passed.

"Rin," he said as he reached out again. This time she pushed his hand away with more force, but he caught her sleeve. "Talk to me."

She jerked her arm backwards and the material slipped out of his hand. "I have nothing to say." She still would not look at him and his eyes narrowed. Before she could step away from him, he reached to stop her and this time she swung at him. He leaned back in time to keep her from punching him. "Leave me be." Her voice rose, and he could see the beginning of tears in her eyes.

His eyebrow rose, and he sighed. He shook his head when he realized he was going to have to push her to spar with him or they would not talk before she left the city. It had been years since he had to force her to speak with him. He moved so that he was in her path again and acted like he was going to reach for her. When she threw another punch at him, he blocked it and returned with one of his own. She ducked under it with a scowl.

"I do not wish to spar with you." She tried to push him away from her, but he did not budge, and she kicked at his shin in frustration. He stepped back and kept her from hitting him before he put his hand on her shoulder. She spun and brought her elbow up and caught him across the face. He stepped back with a frown before he reached up and touched his lip. When he pulled his hand back his frown deepened. She broke his lip open and it was bleeding. He took several quick steps forward and grabbed her shoulder again. She jerked his hand off and tried to twist his arm behind his back. He jerked it forward and grabbed the back of her shirt with his other hand. Dropping so that she was dead weight, her shirt slipped out of his hand. When she was on the ground, she rolled and got a few steps away from him before she got back to her feet.

"Return to Lyra," she snapped at him. "You care for her while you consider the feelings of no one else." Her eyes started to rim with unbidden tears, and she turned to bolt. Wren knew she despised crying in front of anyone and was already moving when she tried to run from him. He snatched her up around the waist with one arm and brought the other around her pinning down her arms.

"Let me go," she yelled as she kicked at him, but he did not loosen his grip. "Wren!" Her voice cracked, and tears began to run down her face.

"What troubles you?" He asked, his voice gentle. "Speak to me as you did when you were young. I have not lost your trust?"

Rin struggled for several more minutes to get free of her brother, but he was far too strong for her to break his grip. "I am afraid," she gasped, and she stopped fighting. "I cannot lose anyone else. Mother…" She trailed off and Wren's eyes widened in surprise for a split second. He had not heard her admit to being afraid since she was very small. When he felt her start shaking, he remained quiet. "It is my doing that mother is gone. She would still be here if I… And how do I fix it all? I know nothing about these powers! How am I to learn what I need and not be torn to pieces by those who hate us?" She paused and took several deep breaths before more came pouring out of her. "What do I do if Londar finds me? You will not be there to help me. You… you… and you join without me. Do I not matter to you? Father hates me, but I thought…"

"Rin do not for a second doubt that I care for you," Wren said, his voice sharp.

She started shaking her head, "I know, forgive me, I speak like a foolish child. These are things I should not be concerned with."

Wren frowned when he realized she was attempting to repress everything. "No, they are not. You must deal with them and not repress them. It shall only cause them to hold control over you."

"I know," she whispered. "Let me down."

He did not let go of her until he felt her relax. Once she did, he set her on her feet and let go. She stayed where he put her and did not look up at him. "I am most sorry," he said. "I should have considered your feelings about not being present when I joined with Lyra. I do not always understand what those important to me feel. Can you forgive me?"

"I must, because I care for my brother." Without looking up at him, she turned and grabbed him in a tight hug.

"I care for you a great deal." He said as he returned the hug and held onto her. "Do not be afraid while you are on your mission. You must be cautious and always thoughtful of your actions but never afraid. Fear will cause you to make poor choices." He paused and stepped back from her. "Promise me that you will not fear him. Kaedin shall be with you, there is no need to fear."

She finally looked up at him and it took her several moments before she nodded. "I promise."

Wren held her gaze for a few moments more before he turned and the two walked toward the entrance of the park. They were almost there when Rin peeked up at him.

"I am sorry about your lip," she said with a frown.

He glanced at her and shrugged with an amused half smile. "It has been a long time since I have had to push you to speak with me."

"Sorry," she mumbled as her gaze fell to the ground. He chuckled and tousled her hair. She looked back up and shoved his hand away with a dirty look, but the mood between them lightened. When they reached the entrance, they found Kaedin waiting for them. Rin walked over to him and he put an around her shoulders when she stepped next to him.

"Will you return to the common room?" Wren asked and they both nodded. "If you need me I shall be with Lyra." He ignored the grin that appeared on his sister's face before he turned and headed off down the hall.

Just before dawn the next morning Wren returned to the common room to check that everyone was preparing to leave. He took several minutes to be certain that they had all the gear that they needed. Paige and Sara were both wearing a set of rider gear instead of the dresses. Jake had his usual BDU pants and t-shirt with the black leather armor chest piece he was given. The rest of the group was dressed as usual while Lyra had her healing robes and satchel thrown over her shoulder. Everyone had a backpack filled with extra clothes and various supplies.

When Wren was satisfied that they had everything, they left the common room and made their way to the entrance of the city. In the entryway, they were met by Ronin, who was waiting on them. He bid each of them farewell in turn until he reached Rin. When he got to her, he paused before he jerked her into a tight hug.

"Be careful, sister," he whispered into her ear. She nodded as he released her. He looked up at the guards on top of the massive stone gates. "Open the gates." After several minutes they were pulled open with a loud clang.

Hikaru, Raven, and Paige were the first to leave. Paige waved goodbye to Jake and Sara from where she was sitting behind Raven when Hikaru flew out of the city gates. As soon as he was clear, he banked to the left and headed north toward the port city of Saelyris. Jake watched them until they were out of sight.

Riku and Bheldrom were next to leave with the two rider pairs that were accompanying them. Bheldrom clung to the spines on Riku's back as he flew out of the city gates. Riku made a slow, sweeping turn to the right before he headed east toward the dwarven capital, Khor Daeruk.

Once they were gone, Wren and Rin led the rest of the group out of the city. They headed down the steep, rocky road toward the portal. The two hundred rider pairs going to Earth followed behind with the wagons full of katanas. It was slow going and took them several hours to arrive at the camp beside the portal.

"We shall go through first," Rin said looking back at the riders. "Once we meet with the leaders, I shall direct the portal so that you may come through. Only ten pairs with one wagon shall accompany us now."

"Yes, my lady," Commander Orbryn said. He would be in charge of the riders remaining in Asaetara.

Rin spent several more minutes ensuring that her riders were prepared before she headed into the cave. She paused in front of the portal. "Join hands." She reached back and got a firm grip on Kaedin's hand while Jake took hold of Sara's. Sara held onto Lyra's with her other hand. The riders behind them did the same and two of them took hold of the horses' reins. Rin checked to make sure that they were all connected before she looked back at the portal. Taking a deep breath, she stepped into the spinning vortex. The others followed one by one until they all disappeared.

Thank you for reading Whispers of Time. Gaining exposure as an independent author relies mostly on word-of-mouth, so if you have the time and inclination, please consider leaving a short review on Amazon.

Or send me an email with your feedback!
gwen@gwenilimaris.com

Thank you again and please enjoy the following preview of Knowledge of Time, Book 2 in the Chronicles of Asaetara Series.

Preview:

Chronicles of Asaetara

Book 2

Knowledge of Time

Gwendolyn Ilimaris

Coming 2020

Rin stepped carefully out of the portal and into the cave on Earth. Knowing what to expect this time, she was able to keep them all from landing in a tangled heap on the ground. She scanned the cave and when she found it was the same as when she left, she moved forward enough that there would be room for everyone. Once the wagon and horses made it through, she stopped and looked to make sure everyone was all right. Her brows furrowed as she struggled to see around the wagons and horses from where she stood with her back pressed against the wall.

Jake and Sara were leaning against the rocks next to them taking slow deep breaths to try and calm their stomachs, while the elves and dragons seemed unaffected by the trip through the portal. When Rin was satisfied that they were all fine after the trip, she slid passed the wagon and headed toward the front of the cave. The others followed behind her until she paused when the faint glimmer of light from the outside was visible. She glanced back over her shoulder and motioned for Jake to join her in the front.

"I believe that it would be best for you to go first," she said once he stood next to her. "I am certain that the way shall be guarded, and they do not know me."

Jake only nodded before they headed for the entrance. When they reached the threshold, Jake stopped dead and his mouth dropped open. The dense pine forest that had blanketed the steep slope when they left for Asaetara was gone for more than a mile in every direction. All of the trees had been cut down to make room for large tan canvas tents, military vehicles, various forms of weaponry, and ammunition storage.

Jake made a disapproving sound in the back of his throat the longer he observed the scene in front of him. This was his uncle's land that now looked like nothing more than a muddied open field. After a few moments more, he shook his head with a frown and started walking again. They did not make it far before they found themselves surrounded by armed soldiers with guns pointed at them. Jake raised his hands and held them in front of him as he waited for one of them to speak.

"On the ground now!" A soldier near the middle demanded.

"I'm Captain Jacob Riverwood," Jake said without moving to comply with the order. "Who's addressing me?"

The soldier who spoke appeared to hesitate before he glanced at one of the other men. He tilted his head up the slope and the man dashed up the hill toward the cabin.

"I'm sorry, sir," the soldier said looking back at Jake. "But I have orders that anything coming out of that cave is either shot or arrested. On the ground please, sir."

Jake still did not move and glanced at the soldier's uniform looking for rank. "Sergeant," he said with a frown. "Stand down, you are insulting the people who have come to offer their assistance."

"I can't sir, these orders come from a higher-ranking officer."

"From who? General Riverwood?" Jake asked with a frown, his eyes narrowing.

The sergeant shifted, "Yes, sir."

"So, these orders came from my father?" Jake asked, his voice hardening. "Sergeant, you had better stand down before word gets back to him." He frowned as he waited on the sergeant's reply. His dislike at having to use his father to attempt to remedy the situation was like a bad taste in his mouth.

The sergeant seemed to flounder as he looked toward the cabin several times. Jake watched in silence and could not keep from glancing beside him when he noticed a subtle movement. He found Wren had moved closer to him during the confrontation. The elf was now right beside Jake with Jaeha just behind him. Wren only raised an eyebrow when the two made eye contact and Jake returned his attention to the sergeant. He did not need Wren to tell him that the elf was growing concerned about the outcome of this conversation.

"Stand down!" A firm voice yelled from up the slope. Jake looked passed the soldiers and saw his father walking toward them at a brisk pace. By the time he reached them, all of the soldiers had lowered their weapons and stood waiting for further orders.

"What's going on here?" General Riverwood snapped, "I'm quite sure I gave orders to let me know the minute the captain returned, so why do I find him surrounded by soldiers with weapons aimed at him?"

Preview

"I'm sorry, sir," the sergeant mumbled.

Riverwood glared at the sergeant before he spun in place and looked up at Jake. "Where have you been? It's been almost three weeks since you left."

"It was not a short journey," Jake replied.

His father scowled at him before he glanced at everyone standing behind his son. The scowled shifted to a look of intense dislike when he saw Rin, the memory of her porting him came to mind. "You can explain it all later," he snapped looking back at Jake. "Come up to the cabin." He turned to walk back up to the cabin when a large ball of light streaked out of the cave.

Rin spun and watched it land thirty feet away in a large open meadow that was beyond the human's tents. She saw the light crash into the ground and as it began to fade, ten lesser and one great demon appeared. The black, fire covered greater demon stood up and stretched out its fire rimmed wings with a low growl. It towered over the military vehicles and supplies around it when it stood to its full thirty-foot height. With another growl, it reached up and rubbed a flame covered hand over its large black horns that were on the top of its head. It appeared to be confused until it finally noticed the elves. As soon as its blazing red eyes locked on Rin, it let out a ferocious roar and pulled a massive sword out of a charred scabbard on its hip.

"We'll handle it," Riverwood snapped when Rin started to move forward.

She paused and looked back at him with a raised eyebrow before she held her hand up toward the demon. "Be my guest."

The general glowered at her before he turned his attention back to his soldiers and began issuing orders. They opened fire on the demons, but it became apparent quickly that their bullets were doing almost nothing, even the lesser demons appeared unbothered by the projectiles.

Rin observed the situation and raised her hand to block the demon's spells causing it to growl at her. It raised both hands and a huge stream of fire flew in their direction. Rin leapt out in front of the group and threw both hands into the air, "Ksāetras!" A force wall appeared in front of her just in time to block the large flames. Spinning in place, she looked back at her riders and pointed two fingers toward the demon. Without waiting on a response, she ran toward it with two rider pairs and Kaedin on her heels. As soon as they were in front of the line of soldiers, she threw her hand up again. "Ksāetras!" Another force wall sprang to life behind her to protect everyone near the cave. She glanced at Jake when the dragons started to glow.

"Don't fire," Jake yelled as he watched the dragons change back to true form. He scanned the soldiers to be certain that they were not going to attack the dragons. When he saw that most of them were too stunned to move, he returned his attention back to the dragons and demons. The two dragons standing next to Kaedin both towered over him and their riders were on their backs waiting for Rin.

She started to issue orders in elven and the riders and Kaedin's response was immediate. They all leapt into the sky and circled around the greater demon while it swung its sword. Splitting up, they came around the demon from three different sides as they breathed large streams of ice before banking hard to come around again.

While they were attacking the large demon, Rin unsheathed her daggers and began attacking the lesser demons on the ground. She seemed to dance through them as they stood no chance and soon laid dead in a pile at her feet. When she was finished, she let out a high shrill whistle while she sheathed her daggers. Kaedin veered from his original course as soon as he heard it, he streaked down low and plucked her up off the ground. He climbed back into the sky while Rin got situated on his back. As Kaedin approached the demon again, it stabbed its sword at them causing Kaedin to dive out of the way.

"Phanumura," Rin said. A large ice spike flew from Rin's hand and crashed into the demon causing it to stumble backwards. "Iliwenys, now."

An elf with sandy blonde hair glanced her direction before his dragon banked hard to come back around at the demon. As soon as they were close, "Phanumura." A large cone of ice shards streamed from Iliwenys' hands while his dragon breathed another large breath attack. The demon roared in pain and fell with a crash that shook the ground around it. Sitting up, it roared furiously and threw its hand into the air causing a massive wave of flames to streak toward the dragons. All the dragons scattered as they dodged out of the way and circled back around.

Rin whistled again, this time in a lower tone, and both elves looked over at her while the dragons kept an eye on the demon. She held up both hands with two fingers held up as she pointed to each side of the demon before twisting her hands in a circle. The elves said one word to their dragons and they split apart. One headed for the left, another for the right, while Kaedin headed straight down the center. As soon as they were within range, all three dragons breathed their large ice attacks at the demon.

"Phanumura!" Rin and both elves cast enormous ice spikes and slammed them into the greater demon. It roared, sending frantic flames in every direction, before it started to flounder under the assault. With another ferocious roar it swung its sword at Kaedin causing him to roll onto his side, but he did not let up on the breath attack. A sickening growl came from the demon before it collapsed back on the ground and started to glow.

"Back!" Rin yelled in elven and all three dragons feathered away in time to escape from the large explosion of flames from the demon. As the flames died down, Rin dropped the force wall and the dragons landed in front of the group of soldiers. The two large elder dragons returned to elven form as soon as they were on the ground. During the battle more soldiers joined the ones already around the cave and they did not wish to accidently step on someone.

Rin watched until the flames were gone before she turned and walked back toward the general. Kaedin trailed behind her, being mindful of his steps, since he did not change back yet. He growled low in the back of his throat when his distrust of the soldiers around him caused his eyes to narrow.

"Stop them!" Ravencraft yelled when he appeared from out of nowhere. "They're here to invade!"

Several of the soldiers moved toward Rin but a loud warning growl from Kaedin brought them all to a halt. He leapt toward Rin and was standing over her when a couple of the soldiers raised their weapons toward him.

"What are you waiting for?" Ravencraft yelled.

Kaedin shifted and his claws dug into the ground as he crouched lower in preparation of a leap. A low growl was coming from him when a larger dragon appeared over top of him. He glanced up and found Jaeha standing over both him and Rin.

"We are not here to fight you," Jaeha said with a low growl. The soldiers glanced back and forth between him and Ravencraft.

"Stand down!" Jake yelled as he ran in between the dragons and soldiers. "They're here to help us!"

"He's not your superior officer," Ravencraft snapped giving Jake a fierce glare. "I am, now follow your orders!"

The soldiers still hesitated as they looked up at the massive dragon looking down at them. When none of them moved, Ravencraft snatched one of the rifles out of a soldier's hand and pointed it in Rin's direction. She had managed to crawl her way out from underneath Kaedin and was standing by one of his front legs. Her head tilted when she noticed Ravencraft and she raised her hand into the air.

"That is enough!" General Riverwood ordered. "Everyone will stand down this instant!" He watched as all the soldiers lowered their weapons, relief evident on their features. Ravencraft hesitated while he glared at Rin before he lowered the gun with a scowl. The general narrowed his eyes as he observed the colonel.

"No one is to raise a weapon to these people again," Riverwood continued. "And, yes, colonel that is an order."

"Yes, sir," Ravencraft growled, his voice dripping with contempt as he handed the rifle back to the soldier he had taken it from. He turned on his heel and stalked away without another word.

Riverwood watched him leave before he looked back at Jake. "Come with me." He headed up the hill toward the cabin. Jake hurried over and grabbed Sara's hand before he followed his father. The others, after casting wary glances at the soldiers, fell into line behind Jake while Jaeha brought up the rear still in dragon form. When they reached the cabin, Kaedin transformed back to elven form and followed Rin into the cabin with Jake. The other riders remained outside with the wagon. Jaeha glanced at Wren as he laid down in between the riders and the rest of the camp. When he got a slight head nod from Wren, he turned his attention to the human camp sprawling across the slope below him.

Jake followed his father up the stairs and into what used to be the living room. His eyes narrowed in irritation when he realized that all of the furniture was gone and had been replaced with a large table and chairs.

"Where are all of Uncle Steve's things?" Jake asked, his voice hard, as he looked over at his father.

The general motioned toward the chairs. "It has been stored," he replied as he pulled a chair away from the table in the middle and sat down. He paid no attention while the others moved to take a seat.

Rin glanced at her brother with a raised eyebrow when he moved to sit on one end of the table and not in the center. He noticed her expression and leaned closer to her. "I wish to observe," he whispered to her in elven. She turned her head away from him with a subtle nod and sat down in the chair facing the general.

"Bring the other senior officers here now," Riverwood snapped at the aid who was standing in the room. He scurried from the room before the general returned his attention to Rin.

"Now, what's the story?" Riverwood demanded.

Rin raised an eyebrow, "What story is it that you wish to know? I am certain that I know several, but they are generally for children." Her voice grew hard by the time she finished, and she folded her arms across her chest.

"Why were you gone with my son for so long?"

"As your son informed you, it was a long journey."

The general was about to retort when the aid reappeared in the room with several more officers. They crossed the room and sat down in the open chairs around the table. When Rin noticed that Ravencraft was among them she frowned.

"Forgive me," Rin said, looking back at Riverwood. "I have no desire to have any further dealings with the colonel."

Riverwood glanced between her and Ravencraft. "He's part of the senior staff and must be present at any type of war council."

Rin tilted her head. "General, in our world honor, respect, and trust are highly regarded," she said choosing her words carefully. "I find him untrustworthy and with little honor. If you wish for us to deal with him further than you must vouch from him. Any discretions he commits will be considered yours." She paused and locked eyes with Riverwood. "Will you vouch for him?"

Riverwood narrowed his eyes as he regarded her. It appeared like he was trying to decide whether she was serious. "No, I will not," he replied finally.

"Then he must leave, or we cannot proceed."

The general frowned before he looked over at Ravencraft and pointed toward the door. The colonel's face started to flush a deep crimson.

"Do you seriously intend to let this little girl dictate how these proceedings will be handled?"

Rin bristled at being called a little girl but managed to keep her reaction hidden. She glanced over at Wren and saw that he was not concealing his disapproval so well.

"Out colonel." Riverwood's short tone brought her attention back to him.

"Is that an order, sir?" Ravencraft hissed causing anger to flash through the general's eyes.

"Yes."

Ravencraft slammed his hand down on the table causing Sara to jump where she was sitting. Jake glanced at her before he reached under the table and took hold of her hand. Her gaze flicked to his face when he touched her, and he gave her a small smile before returning his attention to his father.

"I have done as you requested," Riverwood said, his voice short. "Now, why did you bring weapons in those wagons and not silver? How does that help us at all?"

"It is not practical for us to attempt to supply you with enough silver for your projectiles," Rin said with a frown. "The katanas may be used more than once."

Riverwood was already shaking his head, "What's impractical is trying to train all of our men to fight with a new weapon. Did you even think of that young lady?"

Rin's eyebrow shot up, "The rider pairs that I intend to send to assist you shall be in c--."

"Rider pairs?" Another officer cut her off. "You can't mean the twenty men that you brought with you. That's nowhere near enough men."

"Besides they all look like they're kids," the general chimed in. "How much experience could they really have?"

"The men that I intend to send to you are highly trained with many years of combat experience. The--."

"Young lady...," the general trailed off when Wren suddenly stood up from his chair. Rin leapt to her feet and moved so that her brother could take her seat.

"I believe that I have heard enough," Wren said, his disapproval visible on his face. "Is it your custom general to disrespect those who have made a long journey to offer you assistance?"

Riverwood gave Wren a hard look, "Who are you?"

Rin scowled at the general. "You would be addressing my older brother, Prince Thallawren," she said, her voice sharp.

The general shifted in his seat when he realized that he had just insulted royalty. A second later his expression hardened, and his arrogant exterior returned.

"I find it quite unpleasant to watch you disrespect my sister. If it were not for her and your son, I would not be inclined to offer you much assistance after seeing how you treat your guests." Wren paused and made eye contact with the other officers around the table. They all shifted under his gaze. "We seem to have a matter that must be settled before we may continue. It is apparent that you are judging us by our appearance. What do you know of elves, general?"

"I don't know anything about elves," Riverwood replied, his voice dripping with sarcasm. "They're just a made-up story."

Jake grimaced when he saw the flash of anger in Wren's eyes as the elf regarded his father. He could not imagine what his father was thinking.

"I shall once again ignore your insulting comment so that I may enlighten you," Wren said, his voice becoming sharp. "We do not age the same as you. While you see us as quite young, I can assure you that we are not." His eyes narrowed. "My sister, who you are fond of insulting for her age, is in fact over four hundred years old. I am over twelve hundred. Every single one of the elves and dragons that are with us and may be sent to you, are lifetimes older than every one of you."

Riverwood could not keep his eyes from widening in surprise, "That's impossible."

"As are the dragons and demons that are on your doorstep."

The general stared back at Wren for a few moments before he glanced over at Jake with a frown.

"Everything he tells you is the truth," Jake said, answering the unspoken question. "It would be best if you actually listen to them." He did not break eye contact when his father seemed to be considering his words.

"We might have gotten off on the wrong foot," Riverwood said as he looked back at Wren. "I suppose we should find out how we should be addressing you."

Wren raised an eyebrow at the once again sarcastic tone. His eyes narrowed when he realized his sister was right, this man was arrogant. He wondered for a moment how Jake had turned out so much different than his father before he returned his attention to the general.

"I am customarily referred to as Lord Wren while my sister is Lady Rin." He paused and tilted his head. "Or you may use our rank if you prefer, we are both generals. The choice is yours, as long as it is respectful, I am not overly concerned with titles."

Riverwood nodded with a heavy sigh before he looked up at Rin who was still standing behind her brother. "Continue," he said.

Preview

Rin glanced down at Wren and waited until he gave her a slight nod. "As I was saying," she began. "The riders that I intend to send to you shall be in charge of training the soldiers with the katanas. They will more than likely take on most of the fighting responsibilities until Captain Iliwenys deems that your men are prepared."

"There's no way that a group of troops are that good."

Rin narrowed her eyes, "They are equivalent to what I believe you call special forces." She glanced at Jake when she was uncertain, she had used the right word.

Jake nodded before he looked over at his father. "They are like special forces on steroids. What you saw today was only three pairs."

Riverwood frowned, it was obvious that he still did not believe everything that they were telling him. "How many are you sending?"

"I shall bring two hundred pairs of *my* riders to assist you," Rin said. "However, there shall be some stipulations on their use." The officers in the room started murmuring amongst themselves causing Riverwood to look over at them.

"Sir, do we really want that many of them here?" One of the other colonels asked. "What if Ravencraft has a point?"

The general looked back up at Rin with an expectant stare, but it was Wren who answered. "Gentlemen, if it was our intention to invade it would already be finished," he said, his mannerisms becoming serious. "You have multiple issues with the layout of this camp, and we would have accomplished it with just the few we have present now."

"That's impossible," Riverwood scoffed. "We could easil--."

"Rin could take out most of this camp on her own with one spell," Jake interjected with a frustrated sigh. "I've seen her take out many enemies alone and you just watched her kill ten demons on her own without magic. They mean what they are telling you."

"Prove it," Riverwood snapped.

Rin appeared taken aback for a moment before she tilted her head with a frown. "You wish for me to destroy your camp?"

"No," Riverwood said with a shake of his head. "I want to see a spell that could take out our camp. There is no way you are capable of that."

Rin's expression did not change as she looked down at Wren. He was observing the general with a look of disapproval. It took him several long minutes before a frown became firmly fixed on his face.

"Very well," Wren said, his voice short. "This is the only time I shall allow such a thing. Our magic is not for your entertainment and once we show you, there will be no more doubts." Once the general nodded Wren continued, "If any of your soldiers raise a weapon to my sister when she casts this spell then negotiations are over. You shall be on your own."

"Fine," Riverwood snapped as he stood. Only the general, one other officer, Wren, Kaedin, Jake and Rin stepped outside the cabin. Riverwood pointed to a large clearing beyond the tents that was twice the size of the camp.

Rin followed his gaze before she glanced up at Wren, he gave her another slight head nod and she looked back at the clearing with a sigh. She took several steps forward and put the palm of both hands together. She closed her eyes and began twisting her hands in a circular motion, "Āega bulāe." Pulling her palms apart she began twisting them around an invisible ball that she made larger. When she opened her eyes again, she pushed both hands toward the clearing and a fireball shot from her. It was the same size as the clearing, and it exploded just above the ground. An intense wave of heat washed over everyone a few seconds after the explosion.

Riverwood stood staring at the clearing in stunned silence for several long minutes. He had not expected them to be telling the truth and now that he realized they could destroy his entire camp in seconds, he was now wary of these strange people.

"Alright," Riverwood said. "I've seen it with my own eyes, and it appears that I might need to more open minded." He headed back inside the cabin without another word and the others followed him. Once they were all seated again, Riverwood continued, "What are these stipulations you mention earlier?"

Jake glanced up and almost rolled his eyes when he heard the polite tone his father was using now. He had not realized just how arrogant his father was until this meeting. The man was only polite if he knew you could kill him.

"My riders shall not report to you nor will they be under your control," Rin said. "They shall report directly to Captain Iliwenys and your son."

"I don't want troops in my camp that I can't control," Riverwood snapped with a frown. "Why are you allowing my son to control them?"

"As I told you before, I find him trustworthy and capable," she said before she looked over at Jake. He met her gaze, but nothing showed on his face. "I know that he will not risk their lives needlessly."

Riverwood still did not appear pleased as he regarded her for a few moments. "Fine," he said finally. "I guess we'll have to live with that. What else do we need to know?"

Rin looked to Wren. "From here forward you shall be dealing with me for any future need of aid," Wren said, his voice hard. "Our world is on the brink of war and communication will be vital for us to be able to provide you with assistance. Jacob and Miss Sara shall be your go between. Miss Sara has the ability to activate the portal and shall be given strict instructions on when to do so. She is never to come through without Jacob for any reason, it will be far too dangerous. If the attempt is ever made, I shall bring my men home."

Preview

"You're telling me we have to babysit?" Riverwood's tone became condescending as he looked over at Sara.

"She'll be with me," Jake replied with a sharp glare. "There'll be no need for anyone else to look after her."

Riverwood's eyes narrowed with disapproval at his son's reaction. His gaze shifted to Sara and his expression darkened when he realized this girl meant something to his son.

"One last thing," Wren said, bring Riverwood's attention back to him. "One of our healers shall be present to assist with the healing of training wounds. I expect that you shall show her the utmost respect or Jacob will bring her home." He gestured toward Lyra as he spoke, and she gave the general a stern look when he glanced up at her.

"We'll see what we can do."

Wren fought to keep his rising anger off his face at the general's less than acceptable response. "Do you have any further inquiries for us?" He asked, only the slight shake of his voice giving away his anger.

"When are these men supposed to arrive?" One of the other officers asked.

"They shall arrive tomorrow morning once we open the portal again. When they are all safely through my sister and I shall be leaving."

Riverwood nodded before he turned to the aid standing along the wall. "Take them to an empty tent and make sure they have enough beds. Then figure out a place for these girls to stay after tonight."

"Yes sir," the aid replied before he looked at Rin and Wren. "Please follow me." He gestured toward the stairs. Rin and Wren exchanged quick glances before they both stood up and followed the aid. The others hurried to follow them out of the cabin. When they headed into the camp Jaeha, still in dragon form, and the other riders fell into step behind them. Jaeha struggled to make his way through the tightly packed tents without stepping on anything. Once they reached the far side of the camp the aid stopped in front of a tent.

"These two are empty," he said pointing to two tents on the very edge of camp. He only waited long enough for Wren to nod to him before he turned and jogged back toward the cabin. Once he was out of earshot Wren looked down at Rin.

"I am not pleased by this situation at all," he snapped. "We need to speak about several things, right now."

Rin sighed before she nodded. "We shall speak but allow me to assist the riders in finding a suitable location for their camp first."

Wren frowned before he breathed a heavy sigh and nodded. He knew how important it was to her to see that her men were taken care of before anything else. "Be careful," he said, his expression darkening. "I trust none that I have met."

Preview

"I shall," she replied before she motioned for the riders to follow her. They walked until they reached the far side of the large clearing. Tall slender pine trees still grew all along the edge of the open meadow, Rin stopped and scanned the forest and meadow before she turned around. The human camp was almost half a mile away.

"I believe this shall be suitable and large enough for everyone when they arrive," she said looking up at a rider pair that was standing next to her.

"Yes, my lady, this will do," the elf replied.

The two stood in silence for a few minutes while the other rider pairs worked to erect their tents. Rin looked back up at the elf, "Be wary Captain Iliwenys, only trust Jacob. The others do not seem honorable and I wish to see all of you return home."

Iliwenys looked down at her, his dark grey eyes serious. "I shall do my best, my lady."

"The dragons should remain in true form as much as possible. They are more protected that way and I am certain that the human's projectiles cannot get through their scales."

"Do you believe that they will attack us?" He asked with a frown.

Rin nodded, "I believe some may try. Colonel Ravencraft is not to be trusted. I know Jacob will try to prevent any hostilities, but in this case, he is outranked." She paused and looked back up at Iliwenys. "If you need assistance get a message to my brother or Commander Orbryn."

"Yes, my lady."

"One last thing, make certain that no harm comes to my new sister. I wish for Ventoris and Kenshin to be assigned to her."

"It shall be done."

She nodded before she extended her arm toward him. The two grasped forearms before she turned to walk away.

"Be safe, my lady," Iliwenys said, his voice quiet. "We already await your return."

Rin acknowledged him with a slight head bow before she headed away from the riders' camp. She followed the edge of the clearing and checked the terrain as she went. There used to be a stream that ran down this slope and she wanted to be certain that it would not affect her riders' camp. She made it almost back to the first set of human tents when a faint popping sound caused her to pause. A split second later, she felt a sudden sharp pain in her back between her shoulder blades. She gasped from the impact of what hit her before she staggered forward a step as she raised her hands to her chest. It felt like there was a crushing weight on her chest and she could not take a deep breath. She dropped to a knee as she struggled to deal with the strange sensations. This was like no wound she had ever experienced.

"Damn," a low voice growled from behind her. "That should have been a kill shot."

Preview

Before she could turn to see who was there, she was hit hard in the face. She collapsed to the ground and only caught a glimpse of booted feet before everything faded to black.

Pronunciation Guide

Characters:
Arlaeyna – Are-lay-nuh
Baldrim – Ball-drim
Bheldrom – Bell-drom
Durlan Orbryn – D-er-lan / Or-br-in
Hikaru – Hee-kah-roo
Jaeha – Jay-ha
Jyldar Hildvae – Jill-dar / Hill-d-vay
Kaedin – Kay-d-in
Kanamae Silvarin – Con-uh-may / Sill-v-air-in
Kilvari – Kill-v-are-ee
Londar Hildvae – Lon-d-are / Hill-d-vay
Luaera – Loo-air-uh
Lyra – Leer-uh
Myrabelle – Meer-uh-bell
Oragg – Or-rag
Raven Raloren – Ray-ven / Ruh-l-or-in
Riku Silvaerin – Ree-koo / Sill-v-air-in
Rilaeya (Rin) Rilavaenu– Rye-lay-uh / Rill-uh-vay-noo
Ronin Silvaerin – Row-n-in / Sill-v-air-in
Saeldre – Say-ld-ray
Shiokae – Shee-o-kay
Taeli – Tay-lee
Takaeda – Tuh-kay-duh
Thallawren (Wren) Rilavaenu - Th-all-ah-wren / Rill-uh-vay-noo
Thoridan – Thor-i-dane
Yosheido – Yo-shay-dough

Places:
Asaetara – A-suh-ter -uh
Caradthrad – Care-ad-th-rad
Khor Daeruk – Core / De-rook
Laethys – Lay-th-is
Lake Kiyoyaema – Key-yo-yay-muh
Lyrin – Leer-in

Appendix

Naraeshiki Mountains – N-are-e-she-kee
Nuenthras – Noo-en-thr-ah-s
Okukumo Forest – Oh-coo-coo-mo
Saelyris – Say-leer-iss
Vaerylis – Vay-rye-liss
Varalei – Var-uh-lie
Yakutori Plains – Y-ah-koo-tori
Zei River - Zi
Zeixhal - Zi-x-hall

Guardian Deities:
Lady Avdotyae – Ah-v-o-tie-yay
Lady Kikaeyo – K-i(like ick)-kay-oh
Lord Ruehnaer – Rue-h-nar
Darzak – Dar-zak

Miscellaneous:
Ayen – Aye-yen
Aywin – Aye-win
Makae Trees – M-ah-kay Trees
Pliqini – Pl-i-kini
Qinaros – K-in-ah-rose
Qlaesdin – K-lay-s-din

Fig. 1

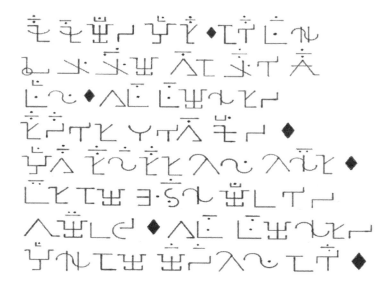

Fig. 2

About the Author

Gwen lives in a quaint little cottage that is nestled among the large pine trees of the Okukumo Forest. Within a short walking distance, the coast of the Khindell Ocean offers hours of places to explore with her beloved dragon....

Okay, okay, not really but a girl can dream right?

Gwen really lives in a quiet, midwestern town with her husband and three rambunctious boys. She has an associate of arts degree in creative writing with a bachelor of arts in English still in progress. Her love of storytelling is what keeps her motivated to keep writing every day.

If you would like to know more about the author, you can follow her on Facebook or her website. The links are listed below.

www.facebook.com/gwenilimaris.com

or

www.gwenilimaris.com

Made in the
USA
Lexington, KY